# LORDS OF VALOUR

'THE GOBLINS SHRIEKED their shrill war cries and charged, only to be met head-on by the vengeful dwarfs. In the confines of the tunnel, the grobi's weight of numbers counted for little. As they turned and fled, Grimli was all for going after them, but Dammaz laid a hand on his shoulder.

'"Our way lies down a different path," the Slayer said.' – *from* **Ancestral Honour** *by Gav Thorpe*

'MOLLENS SNARLED WITH surprise. The hulking Reiklander advanced towards him, his own glistening blade held downwards. With a speed and grace which belied his hefty frame, the Reiklander leapt with a savage howl. Mollens twisted and struck. For one terrible moment the two men gazed helplessly into each other's eyes, then the Reiklander collapsed into the cold mud.' – *from* **The Judas Goat** *by Robert Earl*

IN THE GRIM world of Warhammer, the bloodthirsty followers of the Ruinous Powers ravage the land. But the human realms have their own shining defenders: noble warriors, sworn to fight to the death for those under their protection. LORDS OF VALOUR is a storming collection of all-action fantasy short stories from *Inferno!* magazine, that follow the never-ending war between the champions of darkness and light.

WARHAMMER FANTASY STORIES

# LORDS OF VALOUR

### edited by Marc Gascoigne & Christian Dunn

A BLACK LIBRARY PUBLICATION

Games Workshop Publishing
Willow Road, Lenton,
Nottingham, NG7 2WS, UK

First US edition, June 2001

10 9 8 7 6 5 4 3 2 1

Distributed by Simon & Schuster
1230 Avenue of the Americas
New York, NY 10020

Cover illustration by Martin Hanford

ISBN 0-7434-1166-8

Set in ITC Giovanni

Printed and bound in Great Britain by
Omnia Books Ltd, Glasgow, UK

See the Black Library on the Internet at
**www.blacklibrary.co.uk**

Find out more about Games Workshop
and the world of Warhammer at
**www.games-workshop.com**

# CONTENTS

# FAITH
## by Robert Earl

'WHAT ABOUT THIS one?' Claude the retainer asked with poorly disguised irritation, holding up the bloody prize.

'As I've already told you,' his master replied sharply, 'that is not good enough. I want something... more.'

Claude shrugged and dropped the blood-spattered head back into the dust. The orc's rictus grin leered up at him insolently, but he resisted the urge to give it a kick. Knights had funny ideas about things like that. But then, knights had funny ideas about a lot of things.

With a grunt of disgust Claude turned his back on the grisly trophy and stalked off to collect the evening's firewood. As he reached the tree-line he heard the sibilant hiss of whetstone against steel. It was the first of the evening's hundred sweeps, the ritual that kept the knight's sword sharper than any tooth or fang in this wilderness.

In spite of himself, Claude felt the sound cutting through his ill humour. This de Moreaux, Gilles, the third of his line to rely upon the old retainer's good offices, was the first to have taken care of his own weapons. And when Claude's rheumatism had bitten deep, curling and crippling his hands, Sir Gilles himself had ordered the older man to rest whilst he foraged and rooted for the herbs needed for a cure. Not many knights would have lowered themselves so far as to serve a servant.

On the other hand, not many knights would still be traipsing around the Massif Orcal at this time of year for any reason, let alone an apparently never-ending quest for a trophy large and impressive enough to return with.

Claude, stooping to lift a dry twist of wood from the debris that littered the forest, grimaced at the thought. True, the sun was still warm on the leathered skin at the nape of his neck, and even this mild exercise of bundling firewood was beginning to dampen his brow. But despite the comfortable heat the leaves on the trees of this valley were already beginning to redden with an autumnal fire. A thousand traceries of red and gold raced and tumbled through the green sweeps of their boughs, a final explosion of colour before the skeletal days to come. He knew that in a fortnight, a month at the most, those leaves would be gone, mulch beneath the ice and rain of winter.

He also knew that in a fortnight, a month at the most, the rheumatism would be back. Claude's fingers twitched at the thought. If he were still out here when the ice came there would be no escape from the pain. It would eat into his bones with a fervour beyond the powers of any poultice to soothe. Every movement would become an agony, every joint would ache like shattered glass. It was too much.

Still muttering to himself, the old man claimed a length of splintered branch to complete his load then turned back towards their makeshift camp. He found Sir Gilles sitting cross-legged by the edge of the clearing. Apart from the repetitive whisper of the sharpening stone along the blade of his sword, the young knight remained as upright and as silent as one of the Lady's stained glass saints.

Claude surreptitiously watched the blank mask of his master's face as he built their fire. Not the slightest hint or ripple of emotion stirred the even symmetry of his dark Bretonnian features, yet still the old man knew what lay behind the shuttered windows of the youngster's eyes. He knew, and in knowing despaired of a return to their demesne before winter's misery began.

It was all the fault of Gilles's brother, Leon. Leon the brave. Leon the fair. Leon who, after a scant two weeks of questing, had returned with a massive troll's head the size of a cart-wheel and the blessing of the Lady.

If only Sir Gilles had found a prize to match that, Claude thought unhappily, we'd be home by now.

He struck a shower of sparks into the tinder heart of the fire and stooped to blow them into life, his sigh lost in the operation. A few tiny flames leapt up and Claude tended them, fed them, watched them grow. After a few moments the kindling was a fist of fire, bright even in the light of the setting sun. He imprisoned the blaze within a latticework of thicker sticks and swung the pot containing the evening's stew into the heat. Only then did he realise that the sound of the whetstone had ceased. He glanced up at his master. The knight had sheathed his sword and slipped into that deep breathless trance that seemed to be the mark of his kind.

*Knights!* Claude shook his head resignedly. Thirty-four years as an equerry and his masters still remained a mystery to him. Perhaps it was because the Lady asked so much of them. Perhaps it was because they truly were a different breed. Who knew?

Claude shrugged and turned his attention back to the pot. As he stirred the glutinous soup, a sudden gust of wind sprinted down the valley, rustling through the falling leaves with a thousand chill fingers. One more harbinger of winter. Silently cursing the fate that seemed set to keep him here, the old man pulled up his collar and waited for the stew to boil.

'THE LADY IS beauteous indeed,' breathed Sir Gilles.

The quiet intensity of the statement twisted Claude around in his saddle to follow the knight's gaze. But a quick glance around was enough to still the sudden, startling burst of hope that had flared within his chest. The Lady had not appeared. All that could be seen from the eyrie of this valley pass was the usual panorama of the Massif Orcal. Claude pulled the tattered blanket that now served him as a cloak around his scrawny shoulders and studied the scene.

Beyond the distant heights, the slopes were shot through with a thousand shades of wintry dawn sunlight, the colours a sharp contrast to the depths of the valley floor, now a grey sea of morning mist. Claude pulled his threadbare blanket tighter around his shoulders and yawned.

'If you don't mind me saying so, sire–' he began.

'We should make the most of the fine weather remaining to us,' Sir Gilles completed for him. The look of rapture faded from his face and he turned to regard his old retainer. 'You are correct, of course, Claude. First, though, I will sit a while in this place. I feel her presence here, I'm sure of it. Why don't you wait for me over the slope, and perhaps brew some of that filthy Empire tea of which you are so fond?'

This last was with a smile, the first crack in the knight's iron mask for days. The expression was as fleeting as the rise of a trout, yet in that brief moment Claude had read the lines of frustration and exhaustion that his master's composure had so well concealed. For a moment the old man felt his own worries swamped in a swell of sympathy.

'I'll wait as you say, sire,' he assented, turning to lead their horses over the crest of the ridge. Behind him Sir Gilles sank to his knees, hands clasped together in silent prayer before the upright hilt of his sword. As he set to beside the fire once more, Claude snatched a quick glance at the tableaux. He felt a sudden burst of affection and shook his head.

'You're getting sentimental in your old age,' he scolded himself in a mutter as he split the kindling sticks needed to boil his water. 'Too sentimental by half.'

The ripe globe of the autumnal sun climbed into the cloud streaked depths of the sky. Claude sat and drank his tea. When he had done that, he lay back and let the warmth of it sink into him.

Sharp-edged shadows stalked across distant slopes and valleys as the sun began to rise higher. The light was bright but unnatural, thin and brittle like before a storm. Claude was watching a hawk spiral overhead on the first of the day's thermals when a furtive movement from below snatched his attention. He lowered his gaze to where a grove of stunted bushes below rustled and moved jerkily against the wind.

Claude froze and watched the undergrowth for any further sign. Perhaps it was just a trapped deer, or some sort of mountain hare. He didn't want to disturb his master for such a–

With a sudden snap the bushes burst apart and a ragged creature sprang out.

'Sire!' the old man bellowed, leaping to his feet with adrenaline-fuelled agility. He fumbled at his belt for his dagger, struggling to unsheathe it in time, and snatched a glance at the tattered form that even now approached him. Only then did he realise that beneath the layers of dirt and bracken it was human, a man. He found himself fumbling for words of greeting or warning but, before he could find either weapon or challenge, Sir Gilles arrived.

His appearance was silent, marked only by a sudden rush of displaced air. Gone was the man, the youngster Claude had known since his swaddling days. Gone was the tiredness, the yearning. Gone was the humanity. All that remained of Sir Gilles now was the knight, the steel-clad killing machine. The dark stormcloud of his cloak whipped around him, driven either by the wind or by the corona of terrible energy that radiated from him. Claude, without even noticing that he was doing so, flinched away from his own master.

Despite the layers of metal which encased his form, Sir Gilles bounded forward with all the grace and poise of a big cat. With the hiss of steel slicing through air, his sword was in his hand as he leapt towards the newcomer.

'Thank the gods!' the man said, his features wild with a confusion of fear and happiness. After a moment's hesitation he threw himself to his knees. 'Our prayers have been answered.'

The knight hefted the length of his sword, flicking it upwards in an effortless arc that sent a wink of sunlight flashing along the edge. And for a moment, just one moment, Claude was certain that the blade was about to guillotine down across the newcomer's shoulders. But of course it did not. The Lady, bless and protect her, would not have allowed it.

Yet how would it be, the old retainer suddenly found himself wondering, if the knights of Bretonnia should lose their respect for the Lady?

Claude shuddered, suddenly cold, and switched his attention to the stranger who still knelt before Sir Gilles.

'...prayed for you to come for weeks. It's become too much, far too much,' the man continued to babble, tears glinting unashamedly in the corners of his eyes. 'None of us can sleep at night, none of us can work. Where are they going, where? One more and we're leaving, I swear it.'

The man's voice was beginning to edge upwards into the realms of hysteria. Seeming to realise it, he paused and took a deep breath. Then turned his red-rimmed eyes back to the knight.

'You will help us, sire, won't you?'

Sir Gilles, who until now had remained poised for combat, suddenly relaxed. He sheathed the wicked length of his sword and raised his visor to reveal a hungry, wolfish smile.

'Have no fear. I am sworn to help men such as yourself,' he reassured the peasant, whose grubby features split open into a wide grin of relief. 'How far is this village of yours?'

'In the next valley, sire. If you have horses it will take a few hours at the most.'

'Yes, we have horses. Perhaps you can help Claude here saddle up... ah, how are you called?'

'Jacques, sire, Jacques de Celliers. And thank you.'

Sir Gilles waved away the man's gratitude and turned to face the bright rays of the mid morning sun. Claude led the newcomer to the horses. It took them a few minutes to saddle the beasts and lead them back to where the knight still stood.

Somehow Claude was not surprised to find his master's head bowed and his lips moving in a silent prayer of gratitude.

THE INN WAS PACKED.

Even with the trestle tables pushed back into the shadows there hardly seemed room to breathe. Claude had even considered slipping back outside, away from the choke of this room, but somehow the tension of hope and fear that sawed through the smoke-filled air kept him still. That and the presence of Sir Gilles, of course.

The knight sat comfortably within an almost tangible sphere of personal aura that none seemed willing to invade. He looked as calm and serene as always as he chatted to those around him about their crops, their children, the first signs of change in the season.

Claude saw the awe that washed across the features of those being spoken to, watched it being reflected on the faces of their neighbours. In a gesture that he would have denied even under torture he straightened his back and smiled with pride. Sir Gilles was, after all, his knight.

Not until François, the village elder, made his entrance did the meeting come to some sort of order. The inn door was thrown open by a burst of cold, eastern wind and the old man stalked into the warmth of the room. He had hooked one claw-like hand onto the shoulder of his nephew for support or perhaps guidance through the chill darkness that now laid siege to the building. Favouring Sir Gilles with what could just about have been taken for a half-bow, he then studied the depths of his guest's face with yellowing eyes as puffy as poached eggs. For several long moments the two men regarded each other until, with a grunt of satisfaction, François lowered himself onto one knee. Claude could almost hear his bones creaking.

'Please,' Sir Gilles said earnestly, 'there is no need to kneel, especially for one as steeped in the grey hairs of wisdom as yourself.'

'Thank you, lord,' François said curtly. His nephew helped him back to his feet and led him to the cutaway oak barrel that served as the old man's seat of office. Knight and elder faced each other across the few feet of swept earth which lay between them and, in place of any common currency of small talk, smiled.

'I thank you for coming to our aid,' François began. 'I only wish I could tell you what we need that aid against.'

The knight shifted in his chair, eyes beginning to sparkle with a quickening interest.

'Your man Jacques here told me something of your dilemma,' he said, gesturing towards the peasant. Jacques, who had become something of a local hero since his return this afternoon, puffed himself up with pride at the mention.

'Perhaps, though, you could tell me the full history of these, ah, events.'

François nodded and sighed. Staring past the knight's head into some invisible point beyond the inn wall he began to speak, the years seeming to weigh down on him as he did so.

'It began after the first of the year's harvests, just after the festival of the summer corn,' he started, his voice dull and hopeless. 'This year we took a goodly crop, thanks to the brightness of the sun and the depths of the rains. In fact, after we had filled the granaries we had a surplus. We felt rich so, for the first time in years, we stopped the river trader and exchanged a few bushels for gold. At first I thought – we all thought – that was what had led to Pierre's disappearance.'

'How so?' the knight demanded. He leant forward eagerly, elbow rested on one knee and eyes locked on the elder's tragic countenance. His right hand, seemingly of its own accord, had stolen down to brush against the hilt of his sword. Claude regarded his master with a wry smile. Now that action beckoned he looked more warrior than gentleman, and more wolf than either.

François, though, seemed oblivious to this change in his guest's character. His attention had wandered far beyond the present murky depths of this world and into the past. He sighed and, with an obvious effort, dragged himself back to the here and now.

'How so? Well, because when a man has gold in his pocket and the sun is warming the stone of the high passes it's only natural for him to consider straying. Especially when…'

François eyes flickered upwards with a sudden guilty start and he broke off in consternation. Claude wondered what had caused his host's evident discomfiture until, from behind him, a woman's voice rang out.

'Especially when he's married to such a shrew. Isn't that what you were going to say, François de Tarn?'

Claude turned to regard the speaker. She was, he thought charitably, a solidly built woman. The black cloth of her smock looked hard-pressed to contain the bulk of her hips and chest. Despite her impressive girth, though, her face look pinched, sharp and hard even in the dull glow of the rush lights.

Shrew-like indeed, thought Claude sadly, and felt pity welling up inside of him. He could guess how it must have been for this woman when she tried to tell her neighbours of her husband's disappearance. How they must have frowned and talked of search parties in public whilst privately wishing the runaway all good speed.

'No, Celine, I wasn't going to say that,' the elder rallied, cutting through the thread of Claude's speculation. 'I was going to say that when a husband and wife have problems... well, you know.'

'Yes, I know,' the widow sighed, suddenly deflated. François shrugged uncomfortably and ploughed on.

'Anyway, about a week after Pierre was taken we lost Charles. Then Alain the smith. Then Bastien. Then Fredric and Sullier right afterwards. And then... then the children, Sophie and Louise...' His voice trailed off into nothingness and he swallowed painfully.

As the old man had recited the terrible litany of the lost it had been punctuated by choked sobs or low, miserable moans from the assembled villagers. Claude shifted uncomfortably. The air felt greasy with the grief and fear that was tearing this small community apart. The tension, almost unbearable, crushed down on his chest.

But if the weight of their misery had made any impression on Sir Gilles he wasn't showing it. The only emotion visible on the knight's face was a terrible hunger, an eagerness that reminded Claude of boar hounds straining at the leash. For the second time in as many days the old retainer faced the gulf that lay between them and shivered.

'So,' the knight said, his tones crisp and oblivious to the pain around him. 'What sort of intervals are we talking about between disappearances?'

'It varies.' François shrugged his shoulders. 'Between Pierre and Charles ten days. Between Sophie and Louise only three.'

'The children. Not as much meat on them, I suppose,' Sir Gilles mused aloud.

Behind him Claude heard a stifled cry and a rush of feet to the door.

'And you found no sign of a struggle? No smashed doors, no cries in the night?'

'No.' The elder paused for a moment, his eyes flickering over the assembly before he continued. 'Charles was taken from his very bed whilst his wife lay sleeping beside him.'

Sir Gilles nodded. One moment crawled slowly into the next, the time marked only by the rise and fall of the wind outside and the spluttering hiss of the rush lights within. When the knight finally spoke it was with a cry that sent those nearest to him lurching backwards.

'Of course! Where do you bury your dead?'

'In the crypt behind the shrine,' the elder replied, puzzlement adding a fresh tide of wrinkles to his brow. 'Why do you ask, lord?'

'And tell me, do you have a store of garlic here?' the knight continued uninterrupted.

'Of course, my lord. What kitchen doesn't?'

Claude shared the old man's confusion until, with a sudden flash of inspiration, he remembered a tale from one of the castle grimoires. A tale of nocturnal vanishings and blood black in the light of the moon. A tale of strange weapons, garlic and water and…

'The only other things you'll need are sharpened staves.' Sir Gilles rubbed his hands together and sighed with satisfaction. He looked, thought Claude with a touch of awe, like a man contemplating a feast or a day's hunting.

'Well,' the knight prompted his host after a moment or two, 'could you find such staves of which I speak?'

François, the bafflement which marked his liver-spotted features reflected in the faces of the rest of the assembly, nodded slowly.

'We can certainly make some, and that within the hour. But, my lord, Charles and Pierre were woodsman, with woodsman's axes. If their weapons failed them, what use will sticks be to us?'

Claude watched a touch of irritation flicker across the brown depths of the knight's eyes before he answered.

'Using steel against the thing which now preys upon you is like trying to drown a fish. No, don't ask me why. Only the Lady knows how these things gain their terrible strengths. All I know is that against the vampire the peasant's only weapon is wood, his only shield garlic.'

'The… vampire?' François asked, eyes widening in horror. A chorus of whimpers and low curses rushed through his fellows, the sound as soft and insistent as the chill wind that even now tried the locks and hinges of the inn.

Claude felt the hairs raise themselves one by one along the back of his neck as he moved unthinkingly with the press of bodies that huddled closer to the knight. As the crowd around him shifted with the restrained panic of a herd of cattle before a storm, he noticed the furtive glances they cast towards the shadowy corners of the inn and the rattling shutters of the windows.

*Vampire!* It was a name to chill the hardest of hearts, a name to conjure up a thousand half-remembered terrors from the darkest nights of childhood. Claude was suddenly very grateful for the claustrophobic mass of warm bodies that were packed so tightly around him.

'Am I right in thinking, my lord,' François began with all the caution of a man taking the first step out onto a tightrope, 'that you intend to lead us against this beast?'

'No, I don't think so,' Sir Gilles replied. There was a sudden, angry murmur of protest from the crowd and, for the first time, the knight seemed to notice them. He looked up and the granite wall of his gaze cut off their protests with a guillotine's speed.

'I won't be leading you good people anywhere,' he continued, turning back to François as if there had been no interruption. 'I will go now to await this monstrosity in the crypt you mentioned. Such things are usually tied to their burial grounds, making a mockery of these resting places with their filthy presence. Meanwhile, you'll bring everyone back here tonight and arm yourselves against the creature's attack.'

A thoughtful silence descended upon the villagers. Claude could almost taste their relief.

'Any further questions?' the knight asked.

'I don't think so, sire.' François shook his head. 'But is there naught we can do for you?'

Sir Gilles looked into the old man's eyes and smiled, the expression cold and humourless. 'Yes. Make sure that nobody goes anywhere on their own until this is finished.'

'Even to the latrines?'

A ripple of nervous laughter spread through the confines of the room at this. Sir Gilles was pleased to hear it. Better foolish catcalls than blind terror.

'Even to the latrines,' he replied presently. 'Now, who will show us to this sepulchre?'

IT WAS DARK and, despite the bulk of Claude's borrowed blankets, cold. He could smell the thin, metallic scent of rain on the wind and feel the choking weight of cloud that blocked out even the scant light of moon and stars. Only the guttering red fire of their rush lights gave the two figures any trace of light by which to keep their lonely vigil.

They sat like mismatched bookends on either side of the burial pit, these two, their very presence defying the hungry shadows of the sepulchre's maw. Claude glanced across at his master, a little awed as always by the man's inexhaustible capacity for stillness.

Only the silvery glitter of the knight's hooded eyes gave any indication that he was awake, or even alive. That same glitter was reflected in the straight-edged length of steel which lay across his begreaved knees. Sir Gilles had been strapped into his full armour as he had given the villagers their last instructions.

'Stay together. Even if it breaks in, don't panic. Stand shoulder to shoulder and call for me. But don't pursue it. Remember, stay together.'

Claude, remembering the earnestness of the young knight's expression and the terrified eyes of the villagers, smiled. Had Sir Gilles really believed any of that frightened herd would have charged a vampire, a drinker of souls?

The old retainer's grin faded as he studied the reassuring lines of his master's face. The steel dome of his helmet was gone, a concession against the near-blinding darkness that enveloped them, and even in the flickering half-light of their peasant torches Claude could see the look of peace which had fallen across Sir Gilles's trail-hardened features. The expression reminded him of the knight's father. He had had the same look about him on the night before the Battle of Ducroix. It was only at times like these, whilst sat in the very eye of the storm, that the Lady's chosen warriors seemed to find true peace.

A sudden burst of wind whistled around his ears and the old man shrank down further into his blankets. It had started to warm up within this little cocoon. Claude yawned and stretched, luxuriating in the rare feeling of comfort. Gradually, little by little, his thoughts melted away into dreams.

He jerked back into wakefulness with a guilty start, eyes springing open like traps. It was too late. Sir Gilles was regarding him with the tolerant composure that the older man found so irritating. Claude opened his mouth, fumbling for an apology, but the knight silenced him with a gesture.

'Try to sleep, Claude. I will need your wits about me in the morning.'

'Sire, I said I would share your watch and I will.'

'And I said there was no need. Sleep. If I have need of you I will wake you, have no fear of that.'

'Well…' Claude begin, then stopped and shrugged. The heavy droop of his eyelids weighed more than any arguments. And, at his age, what did he have left to prove?

'Thank you, sire.'

Sir Gilles nodded, the gesture almost imperceptible amongst the wind-chased shadows of the night, and returned to his silent meditation.

A few moments later Claude began to snore. The wind, as if in response to the old man's guttural breathing, blew harder. It screeched through the draughty eaves of the burial pit, groping with icy fingers at the chinks and hinges of the knight's armour and setting the forest-lined slopes of the valley aroar. The distant trees rushed and splintered as though some mighty beast had been set loose amongst them.

Sir Gilles, unmoved by the rising tumult, sat and waited. Soon even the rise and fall of his servant's breath was drowned beneath the howls of the wind, but this hardly concerned him. And when the rush lights started to die, one by one, he merely smiled at the memory of how darkness had frightened him as a child. That fear was gone now. It had gone the way of all other fears during his training as a knight.

All other fears but one, of course, the last and the greatest. And with the Lady's help that final fear would be vanquished tonight.

The last of the torches died, its flame strangled by a sudden gust. In the blinding depths of the darkness that remained, Sir Gilles sat and awaited his destiny, a murmur of thanks on his lips.

If he survived this night's trial he knew that he would be blessed indeed. If he survived this night all would know that the blood of his line ran true in his veins and that his faith in the Lady was true. Yes, all would know it. Even himself.

He just hoped that the vampire, when it came, would be the equal of its reputation.

CLAUDE AWOKE TO dew-soaked blankets and tingling joints. His knuckles felt hot and swollen, blistered from within. There was no real pain, not yet, but in the vulnerability of the single unguarded moment that separates sleep from wakefulness he made a mistake. He thought about what might be going on beneath his reddening skin.

He imagined the gristle in his fingers swelling, choking off the blood. He imagined the nerve endings rasping and sawing against granite-edged bone, fraying like lengths of twine. He imagined a colony of rat-headed creatures eating into the very stuff of him, their burrows growing deeper and more painful by the minute.

With a low moan he clenched his fists, damning the first sparks of pain the movement ignited. The cold, he knew, would fan those first few sparks, tend them and feed them until they twisted his hands into crippled, burning claws.

Well, to the hells with it. If he had need of his hands the Lady would unclench them. And if the pain became unbearable the Lady would take it away. In one way or another, She would take it away.

The old man sighed and opened his eyes. The dawn sky above him was as sombre and cheerless as a shroud, lacking even a smear of cumulus to cut through its grey monotonous weight. Claude shrugged indifferently and climbed to his feet. At least it wasn't raining. He wrapped his blankets around his thin shoulders and yawned. Time to start on breakfast. Now where had he left those damn horses?

He coughed, more out of habit than anything else, and swept the camp with his gaze. It wasn't until he noticed the dark bulk of the sepulchre that remembrance hit him with an impact as dizzying as vertigo.

This was no trail camp, no woodland clearing or rocky overhang. There would be no quiet breakfast routine here, no wistful meditations. This was Celliers, the village where Sir Gilles had finally found a monster worth killing.

But Sir Gilles was nowhere to be seen.

'Sire?' Claude called, his voice cracked with sleep and uncertainty.

'Sire?' he called again, louder this time against the dumbing curtain of fine mist that had begun to dampen the air.

There was no reply. Claude wrapped the roll of blankets tighter around the frail stalk of his neck and studied the ground. A deep depression still marked the spot where the knight must have kept his vigil last night, although some of the crumpled blades of grass had already sprung defiantly back. The old man shook his head and hissed. His master must have been gone a fair while.

'Sire?'

No reply.

He looked further and studied the semi-circle of burnt out torches that surrounded the spot. Their black stumps jutted out of the damp earth like a jaw full of bad teeth. None of them, it seemed, had been disturbed.

'Si–?' Claude began, and then froze. He listened, straining his ears against the blanket of drizzle that had begun to fall. For a while there was nothing more than the muffled sounds of a damp and dreary morning and the distant croak of pheasant. One minute crawled towards the next, then the next. Finally the old man began to relax. His ears must have been playing tricks on him, he decided.

Then he heard it again.

The low moan drifted as softly as a dandelion seed on the morning's breeze. Claude listened cautiously as the cry faded back into nothingness and shivered suddenly as it ceased.

His fingers, arthritis forgotten, clenched tightly around the heft of his stake.

Surely that weak and inhuman keening couldn't be from a man, he told himself, let alone a knight.

Yet where was Sir Gilles?

Once more the cry came floating through the haze, raising the wiry hairs on the back of Claude's neck. He waited until the fell voice began to wane and then, with a blasphemous combination of curses and prayers, the old retainer lurched forwards towards the sound.

He left the burial pit behind him and stomped past the dripping grey bulk of the village shrine and the first of the houses. The village seemed as desolate and empty as any ghost town. There were no scurrying children or scolding women or singing artisans. All that moved here was the drizzle, its silent rain weighing down on an atmosphere already leaden with dread.

The moan came again, louder this time. Louder and closer. In fact, Claude decided as he shivered the weight of blankets off his shoulders, whatever was making the noise seemed to be around the next corner.

A ghostly reflection of his master's wolverine smile played around the old man's lips, a nervous reaction as he plucked the dagger from his belt with his free hand. Then, with a last murmured prayer to the Lady, he stepped around the corner.

And froze.

Sir Gilles was there, the centrepiece of the huddled mob of peasants. The sight of his broad armoured shoulders shook a delighted bark of laughter from Claude, who allowed the wavering point of his stave to drop.

'Sire! You're all right?'

'Yes, of course,' the knight replied, a pair of puzzled lines marking his brow as he turned. 'Why shouldn't I be?'

Claude shrugged, still smiling with relief. Then the plaintive wail that had brought him here rang out again and for the first time he noticed the girl.

She squatted in the cold and damp of the earth, supported on either side by two solidly built village women. They flanked her protectively, like two mother hens with a single chick, but she obviously drew scant comfort from their presence. The girl herself was pitifully thin, the bundled rags she wore incapable of hiding the frailty of her frame. Every shuddering breath she took seemed to rattle down the knuckles of her vertebrae, every choking sob seemed ripe to burst the tight cage of her chest.

Claude felt obscurely glad that her face was turned away from him. He had heard such misery before, of course. From battlefields and deathbeds and scaffolds he had become familiar with the sound of the human heart torn and bleeding. Yet had he ever heard such horror mixed in with the grief?

Without giving himself time to think the old man pushed forward into the mass of cringing villagers who encircled the girl. He looked over her shoulder to the… the shape that lay upon the crimson turf.

Just think of it as meat, he told himself. It's not human. Not now.

But the signs of the thing's humanity were still horribly plain to see. Almost half of its face had been left, the exposed tendons and drained flesh conspiring to lock the man's face into a final eternal scream. Some of its fingers also remained. They were as rigid and gnawed as the branches of autumnal trees and even more dead. Claude studied the savaged expanses of the man's forearms, shoulders and neck. The frenzy of half-moon bite marks somehow reminded him of a head of corn.

Biting back a sudden rush of bile, the old man looked away and studied the faces of the villagers whilst composing himself. He read the disgust and frightened rage he had expected, the emotions as clear as any sculpture could ever make them. But there was something else there too, something that skulked guiltily behind their horror like rats behind a skirting board.

It took Claude a moment to recognise it as relief. The realisation snared his revulsion, gave it a target. Selfish swines! Relieved for their own worthless skins even with this child choking her heart out over the corpse of her father. His lips drawn back in a silent snarl, he turned to François, the village elder.

'I thought you were told not to let anybody go out on their own,' he spat.

But if François heard the anger in Claude's voice he gave no sign of it. 'We didn't let anyone go out on their own. Jules here, Lady guide and protect him, went out with Jacques. Jacques whose absence from the village stopped the killings. And whose return brought them back.'

Claude stepped back and dug thumbs into his forehead in an effort to stop the turmoil of his thoughts.

'Look at the wounds on Jules,' François added. 'What beast leaves marks like that?'

Claude gazed steely eyed at the carcass. It was the same as a hundred others he had witnessed. His career had led him through many valleys a lot more death-illed than this one. He had seen savaged bodies abandoned by all manner of wild beasts. Aye, he thought grimly, and ones trained to it too. Yet something about this one was different.

'Of course!' he finally cried out, voice thick with horrid realisation. 'The teeth. The bite marks. They're like mine. I mean like any human's,' he added hurriedly – even this far from the border, Sigmar's hungry witch hunters had ears – and daggers. 'So Jacques was the vampire?'

'No, he's no vampire,' Sir Gilles cut in with a sigh. 'He only has human teeth. He's just a man. A sick man.'

'Sick?'

'Yes, sick of mind. Or Chaos-tainted perhaps. It matters not. My cousin told us of it the last time he returned from the Empire. There they call it the madness of Morrslieb, the contagion that flows from the Blood Moon when it's at its zenith. That is when your problems began, isn't it?'

This last was addressed to François. The old man shrugged vaguely, then nodded.

'Madness indeed,' Claude muttered, taking a last look at the corpse which lay congealing in front of its daughter. 'Shall I prepare the horses, sire?'

'Yes. Light tack. Against this pitiful creature we'll need speed more than power. François, are there any hounds here?'

As Claude turned to ready their horses, he heard the bitterness of the disappointment that edged his master's words. But he realised that above the sobs that still wove through the mist he alone had heard it, and for that he was thankful.

* * *

THE DAY'S HUNT was a futile affair. The only hounds to be found in the village were a trio of aged boar hounds, gaunt beasts whose stiff movements and swollen joints made Claude wince in sympathy. Sir Gilles, still hiding his disappointment behind a flawlessly polite mask, had decided to leave the motley pack behind, overruling François's attempts to press the dogs into service by explaining that speed of horse and clarity of vision would suffice to hunt down the fugitive.

It had proved to be a foolish boast. The beast of Celliers, although only a man and a crazed one at that, had vanished with all the ingenuity and cunning of any other animal. As Claude followed Sir Gilles out of the village the impossibility of their task struck him. What chance did they stand of finding the fugitive in the mighty swathe of forests and crevasses that covered this, his native territory?

By the time they had cleared the fields and broken into a canter the old man had begun to wonder why the same thought hadn't occurred to his master. It wasn't until Sir Gilles, with a wild cry that ignited frustration into exhilaration, closed spurs that Claude finally understood.

Their task here was complete. Jacques was gone. They might catch him, they probably wouldn't. Either way it made little difference to the lunatic. Alone and unarmed against the predators and dark races of this savage land he wouldn't last long.

He gave his own horse its head, allowing it to race along behind the knight's charger. Holding on to his mount with aching knees, branches slashing over his head and the wind stinging his eyes, Claude listened to the rolling thunder of their horses' hooves and felt a rush of excitement course through him.

By the Lady this was the life! Ahead of him, pulling away as swiftly and as surely as a stag from a drunken orc, Sir Gilles crested a low hill. By the time Claude had reached the spot the knight was already disappearing into the arms of the wood that lay beyond. Just before he was lost to sight the armoured figure turned in the saddle and called back.

'The pass. Meet me at the pass.'

'Aye, sire, the pass it is.' Claude bellowed his reply as Sir Gilles vanished. As if sensing that the race was lost

Claude's horse slackened its pace from gallop to canter to brisk walk.

'Lazy beast,' he muttered affectionately as they plodded along. The blood was still racing briskly through his veins after the impromptu charge and, despite the continuing grey dampness of the day, his spirits were high. And why not? Celliers's problems had been resolved, the beast had been vanquished. Even if he did return to the village, the madman, now that he had been unmasked, would find little chance of repeating his atrocities. For the people of this valley, at least, the winter would hold no more than the usual dangers. For himself and his master, though...

Claude sighed, his high spirits draining away at the thought of the coming months. 'I'm too old for this,' he told nobody in particular and spurred his mount into a canter.

By the time he reached the high saddle of the pass, Sir Gilles's horse was already grazing contentedly. The knight himself sat perched atop a boulder, dark eyes scanning the valley below. His aquiline nose and deep, predatory stare made him look a little like a beast himself, Claude thought as he toiled up the final approaches to the pass.

'It seems the king has more than one hippogriff,' he muttered to himself, the words lost beneath the clatter of scree underfoot.

'I'll take that as a compliment,' Sir Gilles called out as his man approached. Claude bit back on the expression of mortification he knew had crept treacherously across his weathered features and shrugged.

'And how else would I have meant it, sire?' he asked ingenuously.

Sir Gilles barked with laughter and jumped lightly from the boulder. The tension of the preceding days seemed to have melted away leaving the young man full of fresh energy. It was almost as if the conclusion of Celliers's problems, bloody and seedy as it had been, had lifted a weight from his shoulders – almost as if his task had been accomplished.

Claude hardly dared to ask, but the sudden rush of hope within his chest was too much to be denied.

'Sire...' he began, then hesitated, not quite knowing how to put the question. A moment's confusion passed before he shrugged and ploughed on: 'Is our quest complete?'

The knight's brows shot up in amazement as he studied his old retainer.

'No, of course not. Why should it be?'

'You seem… rejuvenated,' Claude explained, trying to keep the weight of disappointment out of his voice, out of his posture. It was hard work.

'I thought maybe you had seen the Lady after, you know, saving the village,' he continued with another shrug.

Sir Gilles's brow cleared with sudden realisation.

'I understand,' he nodded. 'But no, I have done nothing yet. And yet I do feel as if a burden has been lifted. I've come to a decision. I'm going to exchange greaves and bucklers and lances for furs and push on into the heart of these mountains. It is only there that I can be sure of proving the strength of my belief in the Lady and continue slaying the evil that would devour her people.'

Claude felt a moment's unease as he watched the features of the knight harden, straightening into a mask of fanaticism stronger than any steel. Even after all these years this transformation of his masters from men into something… something *more*… still sent a cold shiver racing down his spine.

But then his master was once more just Sir Gilles. His expression softened as he turned his attention from the jagged spikes of distant mountains to his faithful old retainer. 'The other decision I've made is that you'll stay in Celliers until I return. Or until the summer, whichever comes first. I'll leave you gold and a letter of safe conduct in case I am found, um, wanting.'

Now it was Claude's turn to look amazed. 'Sire, I will not leave you. I am sworn to follow you on this quest. My honour is at stake as much as yours.'

'You are sworn to *obey*!' the knight snapped, his tones suddenly harsh. 'And by the Lady you will! I'll not take any ill man into the ice and snow of mountains in the winter. And I'll certainly not throw your life away.'

In a gesture that looked strangely guilty Claude thrust his reddening knuckles behind his back.

'Sire, I–'

'You'll obey my orders,' Sir Gilles cut him off. 'Apart from anything else I don't want to waste one of my father's best men. You will stay here.'

The old man, who suddenly looked much, much older, dropped his eyes and slumped his shoulders. Without another word he turned back to his horse.

With a last resentful look towards his master Claude led his mount down the shifting carpet of scree and tried not to let his anger get the better of him. To be cast aside now, left in safety like a woman whilst his knight rode off into bitter danger! Was he an idiot or a cripple to be left on the roadside like a piece of useless baggage? It was an outrage.

What made it even more difficult to bear was the treacherous sense of relief that even now buoyed up his steps. But that, at least, proved to be short-lived.

'WHAT DO YOU mean you're leaving? Are you mad?' Sir Gilles barely controlled his exasperation, but at a cost. His windrouged cheeks reddened further and a small vein began to pulse a warning above his brow. If the village elder noticed these small chinks in his guest's composure he gave no sign of it.

Without taking his eyes off the two men who continued to overburden his haywain, François sighed and shook his head. 'No, we're not mad. Madness would be to stay.

'We found something after you went, ah, hunting this morning.' The elder flicked a glance almost contemptuously over the mud flecked flanks of the knight's horse. Her mighty chest heaving in great lungfuls of air and the heavy organic smell of horse sweat radiated off her in waves. After Claude had returned, his foul temper buried under consternation at the sight of Celliers packing up to go, Sir Gilles had ridden back here as hard as he could, sparing neither his horse nor himself.

'What did you find?' the knight finally asked, successfully keeping the irritation to himself.

'Jacques.' François said the word softly, almost reverently, and Sir Gilles wondered at his tones. What terrible vengeance must these villagers, his erstwhile comrades and erstwhile prey, have meted out to make them now sound so compassionate about the lunatic?

'Oh. Well, that's good. I take it he's dead?'

The pained expression on François's face deepened and Gilles could almost imagine that tears glinted beneath the craggy overhang of the elder's brow.

'How did the village execute him?' the knight asked gently, choosing his words now with the care of a surgeon choosing his instruments. A village execution. How clean that sounded. How impersonal.

François, however, had obviously being pushed beyond the niceties of not just diplomacy but even common sense. With a sudden start he wheeled on the knight, the fury in his eyes no longer hidden.

'Nobody *executed* him,' the elder hissed, lips drawn back in a snarl as he pronounced the word. 'He was murdered, horribly murdered, just like all the rest.'

The sudden vehemence of the elder's words sent Sir Gilles stepping automatically backwards into a defensive stance. His hand fell to the hilt of his sword before he realised what he was doing. He dropped his empty fist guiltily, but it was too late. François had already seen the gesture. The elder laughed bitterly, hopelessly.

'Oh yes, the protection of your knightly virtues,' he sneered mockingly, pulling himself to his feet and lurching towards the armoured man who towered above him. One of the lads who had been loading the cart appeared at his elbow to offer a supporting hand. The elder shook him off angrily as he stalked towards Sir Gilles.

'The only difference you've made is to double the number of this cursed thing's kills,' he said, the anger in his voice twisting into an accusation. Once more the youth, with a terrified glance at the knight, grabbed the elder's arm and tried to pull him away. Once more the old man shook the anxious hand off, this time turning his ire on the youngster who hovered nervously at his grandfather's side.

'Get away. What's the great knight going to do? Kill me? Ha!' He spat a gob of contemptuous phlegm onto the ground an inch away from Sir Gilles's boots, then turned away with a grunt of disgust.

Claude had watched his master flush beneath the old peasant's tirade, the vitriolic fusion of shame and rage burning on his cheeks. Now, as the villagers went on with their wary preparations, Claude saw the colour drain away from Sir Gilles's face, leaving him pale and shaking with emotion. The retainer opened his mouth to say something, anything, that might be of comfort to the stricken young knight. But before he could think of a single thing to say it was too late.

The muscles in Sir Gilles's jaw bulged with sudden determination and he strode forward after François. The old man's hunched back was still turned towards his guest. He must have seen something reflected in his grandson's widening eyes, though, for he turned when the knight had approached to within a dozen paces. Claude saw the rigid mask of defiance still etched across the elder's features. There would be no apology, of that he was sure, no more bowing. And behind the stubborn old fool a dozen of his sons and grandsons had noticed events unfolding.

As the steel giant closed in on their ancestor they fumbled for knives, hoes and pitchforks. In their shaking hands and round eyes Claude saw the same desperate courage that will drive a ewe to attack the wolf pack that has cornered her lambs. He felt his heart plummet at the tragedy he knew was about to unfold.

Sir Gilles, reaching out one gauntleted hand towards the old man, seemed oblivious to all this. His whole attention was focused on the elder. As the mailed fist fell towards him the old man's only response was the small straightening of posture that was all an aged skeleton would allow. The first of the villagers lowered his pitchfork and started forward. Claude, mind frozen by the speed of events, wished futilely that what was going to happen wouldn't.

Then the metalled talon of Sir Gilles's hand swept past his host's neck and landed gently upon his shoulder.

Bowing down to peer into the astonished elder's eyes the knight said: 'I am truly sorry to have so failed you. I am sorry that you are frightened enough to leave your village. I have failed in my duty to the Lady and to you, her people. My father would not have failed. Nor would my brother, Leon. But I have and I have no excuse.'

Suspicion chased astonishment off François's wizened features. By the time the knight had finished his apology the sincerity of the words had melted away even that.

'No, no, lord. I should apologise to you,' he replied warily, voice softened now with grudging compassion. 'I had no call to blame you. Since the black hail fell on these hills in my grandfather's day much has happened here, much that has proved beyond man's power to change.'

'Yet I would be more than a man,' Sir Gilles smiled bitterly. 'And perhaps I still can be. All I ask is that you give me one more night. Give me one more chance to find the monster that would prey upon the Lady's people.'

François hesitated for barely a moment before giving the shallowest of nods and turning to address his flock.

'We'll leave tomorrow,' he told them. Then, with a stiff bow towards Sir Gilles, he turned and hobbled back into his hut. The knight returned the bow and walked stiffly back to his horse.

'What will we do now, sire?' Claude asked, hurrying to catch up.

'I go to beg for the Lady's aid. There was a pool a little way into the woods we rode through this morning. It seemed like a goodly place.'

'And will I come with you?'

'No, you'll stay here. I want you to organise these people into three regiments and make sure they stay in them. I leave you in charge of the details.'

'Yes, sire, of course.' Claude bowed subserviently whilst his master climbed back into the saddle and cantered back out of the village. He waited until Sir Gilles was out of sight before crossing to François's hut. He ducked below the heavy oaken lintel of the door and instructed the elder.

'I want you to organise your people into three groups,' he told the old man urgently. 'All of them are to carry their weapons at all times. None of them are to leave their groups for any reason. Any that break these rules are to be fined half of their wealth. Do you understand?'

As soon as François had grumbled his assent Claude took his leave and went to fetch his horse. He had carried out his orders. Now he would go to watch his knight's back, as was proper for an equerry. There was nothing underhanded about that, he thought, as he carefully scanned the horizon. Nothing underhanded at all.

SIR GILLES WAS not difficult to follow, especially to one as skilled at reading the land as Claude. He had followed the path of crushed moss and snapped twigs through the forest just as easily as he had followed the great crescents of the charger's hoofs through the mud of the road.

He had tethered his own mount some way back and continued stealthily on foot beneath the great damp overhangs of beech and birch and twisted ancient oak. The undergrowth was thick here, heavy with moisture and dying brown leaves. As Claude pushed through it his nose wrinkled at the acrid smell of decay. In most parts of Bretonnia, he reflected, such a bulk of vegetation would have been cropped back by deer or boar, but here it seemed untouched.

And come to think of it the forest did seem strangely quiet, almost as if it had been cleared of life by something, perhaps even something that left human bite marks in the raw flesh of its prey. The thought sent a sliver of ice down the old man's spine and he found himself walking faster.

'Don't be such an old woman,' he scolded himself, consciously slowing his pace. 'A small wood in a small valley is easily over-hunted. There's nought more mysterious here than greedy peasants.'

Even so he was more than a little relieved when he finally reached Sir Gilles. Only the fact that the knight was so obviously immersed in prayer stilled the cry of greeting that rose to his retainer's lips.

Sir Gilles knelt silently before a wide pool, his attention lost in its cool depths.

Overarching trees shone and glimmered in the calm surface, one world reflected by another, and around the banks rushes swayed gently to some ancient and inaudible rhythm.

Claude sank to his haunches at the edge of the clearing, lulled by the peace of the scene. The only real movement was the light fall of autumn browned leaves. He watched one as it spiralled down onto the placid mirror of the water and began to float away, pulled by some invisible current.

Leaning back against the bole of a willow, the old man half-closed his eyes. In his imagination the leaf became a ship, bound for distant Cathay or even mythical Lustria. The stem became a mast, the withered edges the gunwales. And when the first splash of water sent thick ripples rolling towards the little craft he saw only waves riding before a storm.

A moment later he began to wonder what had caused such a disturbance in the water. Surely this pool was too isolated to contain trout to rise and leap. He looked up with a frown. For a moment he saw nothing but the enveloping mass of trees and shadows that encircled them, and the stooped form of his master's back.

Then he saw her and his heart leapt.

It was *her*, there could be no doubt of that. How many times had he seen her form, revered in stone or glass or on parchment? How many times had men whispered of her in the depths of the night or called upon her in the midst of battle? He'd even met her before in dreams and amongst the labyrinths of his imagination and felt her sacred presence, a comforting hand in the depths of hardship or a playful ripple of light on the water.

Yes, it was her. As she glided through the pool Claude's eyes caressed the skin that glowed paler and more precious than Araby pearl. Her hair cascaded down onto her shoulders, framing a face both girlish and ancient, wise and forgiving. And her eyes! How they sparkled and shone with a healing warmth of green fire.

Claude felt a moment's dizziness and realised that he had been holding his breath. He managed to tear his eyes away from the Lady for long enough to glance at Sir Gilles.

The knight still sat slumped in prayer, lips moving silently even as his goddess approached. The light gossamer of her dresses flowed around her, shining with a ghostly luminescence against the dark backdrop of rotten forest. For a moment Claude considered calling out to his master, of heralding her approach, but somehow he lacked the courage. In the presence of such divine beauty he felt too unworthy to speak. Instead he gazed upon her and let every detail of her magnificence burn itself into his memory.

She had almost reached Sir Gilles before he looked up. He rose to his feet, then started as though stung. The Lady smiled at his astonishment, a beatific expression of love and compassion speeding slowly across her face, and he sank back down to his knees.

'My Lady…' he whispered as she approached, arms opening and hands outstretched in benediction. Sir Gilles, head bowed, watched her glide through the last few feet of water and step onto the bank. He saw the water dripping from the hem of her dress, the white of it now speckled with the green of pond weed.

'My Lady…' he repeated breathlessly as she laid a perfect hand on his shoulder and stooped down to brush cold lips across his brow. She smiled again, revealing teeth as white and hard as bones and lowered her lips to kiss his neck.

'*My Lady!*' he said a third time, his voice suddenly full of fire as he sprang backwards. With an evil hiss of steel against leather, his sword was free of its scabbard, the burnished metal of the blade dull despite the divine light that surrounded the goddess. Then, before the enormity of the knight's actions could penetrate through Claude's shock, he watched his master slice his sword backhanded across the smooth, cream-coloured flesh of her neck.

It was a killing stroke. The blade spat out a bright plume of blood as it sawed effortlessly through the cords and tendons of her neck, almost decapitating her where she stood.

Claude watched as she crumpled backwards into the mud and filth of the forest floor. After a moment he walked numbly over to where the body lay and gazed down stonily at the ruined flesh that had once lived, once breathed… had once been a goddess. Now it was no more than meat cooling on the forest floor.

And bad meat at that. He watched as the flowing silk of its hair withered and died, shrinking back into a malformed skull. Already the supple grace of her frame had collapsed into something ruined and hunched, the skeleton twisted out of shape by who-knew-what dark sorcery?

Claude shivered and hugged himself as the fair pigment of her skin darkened and mottled, turning into a sickly grey leather before his very eyes. Even worse was the thing's face.

How could those evil and wizened features have resembled anything even the least bit fair? Only the colour of the eyes remained unchanged, but the green now seemed rotten and cancerous and so very cold.

He remembered the expression she had worn. He remembered how beautiful it had been, how alluring. Suddenly, for the first time since the brooding of his first battle, Claude's stomach clenched itself into a fist that doubled him up with nausea. With hardly a backwards glance he stumbled away into the undergrowth, leaving Sir Gilles still standing pale and trembling over his foe.

THE NEXT MORNING they crested the pass above Celliers for the last time. Below them the valley was laid out like a map. Claude turned in his saddle to take a last look at the village, the forest, the smoke from the great bonfire upon which the beast's body had been burned so gleefully the night before.

Where had it come from, he wondered for the dozenth, the hundredth time. Had it been made, or born, or ensorcelled by Chaos? And how long had it lived here, silently haunting the edges and dark places of this land before hunger drove it in to the village and the addictive taste of man-flesh?

Claude found his gaze shifting from the valley floor to the distant rock spires that were the heart of the Massif Orcal. Beyond them, peering from between the granite peaks, towering clouds waited blue and heavy with the year's first snow.

The old retainer shivered and thankfully turned his back on them. By the time they caught up with him he would be back beside the great fireplace of Castle Moreaux, a horn of spiced wine steaming in his hand.

Only one thing still bothered him. It hung in a leather bag from Sir Gilles's saddle, a diminutive, evil smelling lump that still sweated a disgusting grey slime. It had no scales, this head, no savage teeth or needle-sharp fangs. Its jaws were weak, lacking even the knots of muscle any man might boast. In fact when it had been cleaned the thing would be scarcely bigger than two clenched fists.

'Well, sire,' Claude began, knowing that he would have to broach the subject before they went much further. 'I'm sure we'll be able to pick up that boulder of an orc's head tomorrow afternoon. I lashed it to a lone pine tree for the birds to clean. It should look good mounted in the great hall, don't you think?'

'What do you mean?' the knight asked, turning in his saddle to regard his servant. 'I have my trophy here.'

'Yes, of course. Your real trophy. But for the family gibbet…'

'This is for the family gibbet. This thing is the beast that tested my faith to the utmost. It is this that will hang amongst the rest of my family's great trophies.'

Claude, sensing the strength of purpose that lay behind his master's words, sighed as he realised it would be pointless to continue.

'How… how could you be so sure that thing wasn't the Lady?' he dared to ask, changing the subject.

Sir Gilles smiled wistfully for a moment before he replied.

'The eyes,' he said at length. 'In the old tales she is always dark, a real Bretonnian woman. Brown hair. Brown eyes.'

'Tales, yes,' Claude nodded. 'But when your brother saw her she had green eyes. As green as your mother's, he said.'

'Yes,' Sir Gilles nodded, 'I know.'

Then, for no apparent reason, he began to laugh until his sides shook and tears glinted in his eyes.

Claude lapsed back into silence and shook his head. *Knights!* He would never understand them.

# A CHOICE OF HATREDS

## by C.L. Werner

ON THE OUTSKIRTS of the small town of Kleinsdorf, a group of raucous men gathered in a fallow field. Before them stood an inverted anvil upon which a burly man garbed in a heavy blacksmith's apron set a second anvil. The man's bearded face split into a booming laugh as one of his comrades lit a hemp fuse that slithered between the anvils to reach a small charge of gunpowder. A hushed silence fell upon the men as the smouldering flame slowly burned its way to the explosive. Suddenly a tremendous boom echoed across the barren fields and the uppermost anvil was thrown into the sky to crash into the ground several yards away. A great cheer erupted from the group and the blacksmith set off at a lumbering jog to retrieve the heavy iron projectile, even as one of his friends prepared another charge.

'It looks like we have chanced into a bit of a celebration, eh, Mathias?' commented a stout, bearded rider on the road overlooking the anvil-firing party.

The man wore a battered and ill-mended pair of leather breeches; an equally battered jerkin of studded leather struggled to contain the man's slight paunch. Greasy, swine-like

eyes peered from either side of a splayed nose while an
unkempt beard clothed his forward-jutting jaw. From a scabbard at his side a broadsword swayed with each step of his
horse.

'We come here seeking rest, friend Streng, not to indulge
your penchant for debauchery,' replied the second rider. A
tall, grim figure, the second man was his companion's senior
by at least a decade. Where Streng's attire was shabby and
worn, this man's was opulent. Immaculate shiny leather
boots rose to the man's knees and his back was enveloped by
a heavy black cape lined with the finest ermine. Fine calfskin
gauntlets garbed slender-fingered hands while a tunic of red
satin embroidered with gold clothed his arms and chest. The
wide rounded brim of his leather hat cast a shadow upon the
rider's features. Hanging from a dragonskin belt with an
enormous silver buckle were a pair of holstered pistols and a
slender-bladed longsword.

'You are the one who has taken so many fine vows to
Sigmar,' Streng said with a voice that was not quite a sneer. 'I
recall taking no such vows.'

Mathias turned to look at his companion and his face
emerged from the shadow cast by the brim of his hat. The
older man's visage was gaunt, dominated by a narrow, dag-
ger-like nose and the thin moustache that rested between it
and the man's slender lips. A grey arrow of beard stabbed out
from the man's chin. His eyes were of similar flinty hue but
burnt with a strange intensity, a determination and zeal that
were at odds with the glacial hue.

'You make no vows to Sigmar, yet you take the Temple's
gold easily enough,' Mathias locked eyes with his comrade.
Some of the glib disrespect in Streng's manner dissipated as
he met that gaze.

'I've not seen many monks with so fine a habit as yours,'
Streng said, turning his eyes from his companion.

'It is sometimes wise to remind people that Sigmar rewards
service in this life as well as the hereafter.' Mathias looked
away from his henchman and stared at the town before them.

A small settlement of some thousand persons, the simple
wooden structures were close together, the streets narrow and
crooked. Everywhere there was laughter and singing, music

from mandolin and fife. A celebratory throng choked the streets, dancing with recklessness born more of joy than drink, at least in this early hour of the festival. Yet, none were so reckless as not to make way for Mathias as he manoeuvred his steed into the narrow streets, nor to make the sign of Sigmar's Hammer with the witch hunter's passing.

'I shall take room at the inn. You find a stable for the horses,' Mathias said as he and Streng rode through the crowd.

'And then?' asked Streng, a lustful gleam in his eyes and a lecherous grin splitting his face.

'I care not what manner of sin you find fit to soil your soul with,' snarled the witch hunter. 'Just see that you are in condition to ride at cock's crow.'

As they talked, the pair did not observe the stealthy figure who watched their exchange from behind a hay-laden wagon. They did not see the same figure emerge from its hiding place with their passing, nor the venomous glare it sent after them.

GUSTAV SIPPED AT the small glass of Tilean wine, listening to the sounds of merriment beyond the walls of his inn. A greedy glint came to the innkeeper's eyes as he thought of the vacant rooms above his head and the drunken men who would fill them before the night was through. The Festival of Wilhelmstag brought many travellers to Kleinsdorf, travellers who would find themselves too drunk or too fatigued to quit the town once the festivities reached their end. Few would be lucid enough to haggle over the 'competitive' fee Gustav charged his annual Wilhelmstag guests.

Gustav again sipped at his wine, silently toasting Wilhelm Hoess and the minotaur lord which had been kind enough to let itself and its horde of Chaos spawn be slaughtered in the streets of Kleinsdorf two centuries past. Even now, the innkeeper could see the gilded skull of the monster atop a pole in the centre of the square outside, torchlight from the celebratory throng below it dancing across the golden surface. Gustav hoped that the minotaur was enjoying the view, for tomorrow the skull would return to a chest in the town hall, there to reside until next Wilhelmstag.

The opening of the inn's front door roused the innkeeper from his thoughts. Gustav smiled.

The first sheep comes to be fleeced, he thought as he scuttled away from the window. But the smile died when Gustav's eyes observed the countenance of his new guest. The high black hat, flowing cape and expensive weapons combined with the stern visage of the man's face told Gustav what this man was even before he saw the burning gleam in those cold grey eyes.

'I am sorry, my lord, but I am afraid that I have no rooms that are free.' Gustav winced as the witch hunter's eyes stared into his own. 'The… the festival. It brings many guests. If you had only come on another night…' the innkeeper stammered.

'Your common room is also filled?' the witch hunter interrupted.

'Why, no,' Gustav said, a nervous tic causing his left eye to twitch uncontrollably.

'Then you may move one of your guests to the common room,' the witch hunter declared. Gustav nodded his agreement even as he inwardly cursed the man. The common room was a long hall at the side of the inn lined with pallets of straw. Even drunkards would be unwilling to pay much for such lodgings.

'You may show me my room,' the witch hunter said, his firm hand grasping Gustav's shoulder and pushing the innkeeper ahead of himself. 'I trust that you have something appropriate for a devoted servant of Sigmar?'

'Yes, my lord,' Gustav said, altering his course away from the closet-like chamber he had thought to give the witch hunter. He led the way up a flight of stairs to one of the larger rooms. The witch hunter peered into the chamber while the innkeeper held the door open.

'No, I think not,' the witch hunter declared. The bearded face moved closer toward Gustav's own and one of the gloved fingers touched the twitching muscle beside the innkeeper's eye.

'Interesting,' Mathias said, not quite under his breath. The innkeeper's eyes grew wide with fright, seeming to see the word 'mutation' forming in the witch hunter's mind.

'A nervous twitch, nothing more,' Gustav muttered, know-ing that even so slight a physical defect had put men to the stake in many backwater towns. 'I have a much nicer room, if you would follow me.' Gustav turned, leading the witch hunter to a second flight of stairs.

'Yes, this will do,' Mathias stated when Gustav led him into a large and well-furnished room at the very top of the inn. Gustav smiled and nodded his head nervously.

'It is my honour to serve a noble Templar of Sigmar,' the innkeeper said as he walked to the large oak wardrobe that dominated one corner of the room. Gustav opened the wardrobe and removed his own nightshirt and cap from it.

'I will dine here,' Mathias declared, settling into a large chair and removing his weapon-laden belt. 'A goose and some wine, I think.' The witch hunter stroked his moustache with his thumb and forefinger.

'I will see to it,' the innkeeper said, knowing better than to challenge his most-unwanted guest. Gustav paused a few steps away from the witch hunter. Mathias reached into a pocket in the lining of his tunic and tossed a few coins into the man's hands. Gustav stared stupidly at them for several seconds.

'I did not come for the festival,' explained Mathias, 'so I should not have to pay festival prices.' The witch hunter sud-denly cocked his head and stared intently at Gustav's twitching eye.

'I shall see about your supper,' Gustav whimpered as he hurried from the room.

THE STREETS OF Kleinsdorf were alive with rejoicing. Everywhere there was dancing and singing. But all the laugh-ter and joy in the world could not touch the figure that writhed its way through the crowd. The dark, shabby cloak of the man, meant to keep him inconspicuous, was at odds with the bright fabrics and flowers of the revellers and made him stand out all the more. Dozens of times Reinhardt von Lichtberg had been forced to ward away garishly clad towns-people who thought to exorcise this wraith of melancholy in their midst with dance and drink. Reinhardt spat into the dust. A black-hearted murderer had descended upon this place and all these idiots could do was dance and laugh. Well, if things turned out as Reinhardt planned, he too would have cause to dance and laugh. Before they stretched his neck from a gallows.

Hands clasped Reinhardt's shoulders and spun the young man around. So lost in thoughts of revenge was he that he did not even begin to react before warm, moist lips closed about his own. The woman detached herself and stared up into the young man's face.

'I don't believe that I know you,' Reinhardt said as his eyes considered the golden-haired, well-built woman smiling impishly at him and the taste of ale that covered his lips.

'You could,' the woman smiled. 'The Festival of Wilhelmstag is a time for finding new people.'

Reinhardt shook his head. 'I am looking for no one new.' Reinhardt found himself thinking again of Mina and how she had died. And how her murderer would die.

'You have not seen a witch hunter, by any chance?' Reinhardt asked. The woman's smile turned into a full-lipped pout.

'I've met his surrogate,' the girl swore. 'Over at the beer hall, drinking like an orc and carrying on like a Tilean sailor. Mind you, no decent woman had better get near him.' The impish smile returned and the woman pulled scandalously at the torn fringe of her bodice. 'See what the brute did to me.'

Reinhardt grabbed the woman's arms in a vice-like grip.

'Did he say where Mathias Thulmann, the witch hunter, is?' Reinhardt snarled. The coyness left the woman's face as the drunken haze was replaced by something approaching fear.

'The inn, he was taking a room at the inn.' The girl retreated into the safety of the crowd as Reinhardt released her. The nobleman did not even notice her go, his mind already processing the information she had given him. His right hand slid beneath the shabby cloak and closed around the hilt of his sword.

'Soon, Mina,' Reinhardt whispered, 'soon your murderer will discover what suffering is.'

GERHARDT KNAUF HAD never known terror such as he now felt. The wonderful thrill of fear that he enjoyed when engaging in his secret activities was gone. The presence of the witch hunter had driven home the seriousness of discovery in a way that Knauf had never fully comprehended before. The shock and looks of disbelief he had visualised on his neighbours' faces when they realised that the merchant was more than he seemed had become the frenzied visages of a bloodthirsty mob. In his imagination, Knauf could even smell the kindling as it caught flame.

The calf-eyed merchant with his beetle-like brow downed the contents of the tankard resting on the bar before him in a single bolt. Knauf pressed a hand against his mouth, struggling to keep the beer from leaving his body as quickly as it had entered it. The merchant managed to force the bile back into his stomach and let his head sway towards the man sitting beside him.

'Mueller,' croaked Knauf, his thin voice struggling to maintain a semblance of dignity, even as he struggled against fear and inebriation. The heavy set mercenary at his side looked away from the gob of wax he had been whittling into a lewd shape and regarded the merchant.

'You have done jobs for me before,' Knauf continued.

'Aye,' the mercenary cautiously replied, fingering his knife.

'And I have always paid you fairly and promptly,' the merchant added, his head swaying from side to side like some bloated reptile.

'That is true enough,' Mueller said, a smirk on his face. The truth of it was that Knauf was too timid to be miserly when it came to paying the men who protected his wagons. A cross look from Rall, or Gunther, or even from the scarecrow-like Hossbach, and the mercenaries would see an increase in their wages.

'Would you say that we are friends?' Knauf said, reaching for another ceramic tankard of beer. He swallowed only half the tankard's contents this time, spilling most of the remainder when he clumsily set the vessel back upon the table.

'Were you to pay me enough, I would even say that we were brothers,' Mueller replied, struggling to contain the laughter building within his gut. But the condescending sarcasm in the mercenary's voice was lost on the half-drunken Knauf. The merchant caught hold of Mueller's arm and stared into his face with pleading eyes.

'Would you murder for me?' the merchant hissed. This time Mueller did laugh.

'By Ulric's fangs, Gerhardt!' the mercenary swore. 'Who could you possibly hate enough to need killed?' Mueller laughed again and downed his own tankard of beer.

'The witch hunter,' whispered Knauf, his head swaying from side to side to ensure that no one had overheard.

'Have you been reading things you shouldn't?' Mueller asked, only half-seriously. The look of fear in Knauf's eyes killed the joke forming on the mercenary's lips. Mueller rose from his chair and stared down at the merchant.

'Forty gold crowns,' the mercenary declared, waving away the look of joy and hope crawling across Knauf's features. 'And as far as the boys are concerned, you are paying us ten.' Mueller turned away from the table and started to walk into the main room of the beer hall.

'Where are you going?' Knauf called after Mueller in a voice that sounded unusually shrill even for the merchant.

'To get Hossbach and the others,' Mueller said. 'Maybe I'll see if I can't learn something about our friend as well.' The mercenary turned away. He only got a few steps before Knauf's drunken hands were scrabbling at the man's coat.

'How are you going to do that?' Knauf hissed up at him with alarm.

Mueller extracted himself from the merchant's grip. He pointed a finger to the far end of the beer hall where a bawdy song and shrieks of mock indignation marked the crowd gathered in morbid fascination around the man who had rode into Kleinsdorf with the witch hunter.

'How else? I'll speak with his lackey,' Mueller shook his head as Knauf started to protest. 'Leave this to me. Why don't you go home and get my gold ready?' The mercenary did not wait to see if Knauf would follow his suggestion, but continued across the beer hall, liberating a metal stein from a buxom barmaid along the way.

'Sometimes they confess straight away,' Streng was saying as Mueller inconspicuously joined his audience. 'That's the worst of it. There's nothing left to do but string them up, or burn them if they've been particularly bad.' Streng paused to smile at the woman sitting on his knee.

'So how do you go about finding a witch?' Mueller interrupted Streng's carousing. The lout turned to Mueller and regarded him with an irritated sneer.

'I don't. That's the Templar's job. Mathias finds them and then I make them confess. That way everything is above board and the Temple can burn the filthy things without anybody being upset.' Streng turned away from Mueller and returned his attention to his companion.

'So your master has come to Kleinsdorf looking for witches?' Mueller interrupted again.

Streng shook his head and glared at this man who insisted on intruding on his good time.

'Firstly, Mathias Thulmann is not my master. We're partners, him and me, that's what it is. Secondly, we are on our way to Stirland. Lots of witches down in Stirland.' Streng snorted derisively. 'Do you honestly think we'd cross half the Empire to come here?' Streng laughed. 'I wouldn't cross a meadow to come to this rat nest,' he said, before adding, 'present company excepted, of course,' to the locals gathered around him.

As Streng returned his attention to the giggling creature seated on his knee, Mueller extracted himself from the hangers-on and made his way toward the beer hall's exit. The mercenary spied a familiar face in the crowd and waved the man over to him. A young, wiry man with a broken nose and a livid scar across his forearm walked over to Mueller. The mercenary took the flower-festooned hat from the man's head and sent it sailing across the crowded room with a flick of his wrist.

'Go get Gunther and Hossbach,' Mueller snarled. 'I found us some night work.' The angry look on the young man's face disappeared at the mention of work. Rall set off at a brisk jog to find his fellow sellswords. Mueller looked at the crowd around Streng one last time before leaving the beer hall.

The mercenary had found out all that he needed to know. The witch hunter was only passing through Kleinsdorf; he would not be expecting any trouble. Like all the other jobs he had done for Gerhardt Knauf, this one would hardly be difficult enough to be called 'work'.

* * *

A CHEER WENT up from the crowd below as a small boy shimmied up the massive pole standing in the centre of the square and thrust a crown of flowers on the gilded skull at its top.

At the moment, Reinhardt von Lichtberg envied the boy his agility. The nobleman was gripping the outer wall of the inn, thirty feet above the square. To an observer, he might have looked like a great brown bat clinging to the wall of a cave. But there were no eyes trained upon Reinhardt, at least not at present. The few revellers who had lifted their heads skyward were watching the boy descend the pole with a good deal less bravado than he had ascended with. Still, the threat of discovery was far too real and Reinhardt was not yet ready to see the inside of a cell.

Slowly, carefully, Reinhardt worked his fingers from one precarious handhold to another. Only a few feet away he could see the window that was his goal. It had been easy to determine which room the murderer occupied; his was the only window from which light shone. Somehow it did not surprise Reinhardt that the witch hunter had taken a room on the inn's top floor. One last trial, one final obstacle before vengeance could be served.

At last he reached the window and Reinhardt stared through the glass, seeing for the first time in six months the man who had destroyed his life. The murderer sat in a wooden chair, a small table set before him. He cut morsels from a large roasted goose, a wicker-shrouded bottle of wine sitting beside it.

Reinhardt watched for a moment as the monster ate, burning the hated image of the man into his memory. He hoped that the meal was a good one, for it would be the witch hunter's last.

WITH AN ANIMAL cry, Reinhardt crashed through the window, broken glass and splintered wood flying across the room. Landing on his feet, the sword at his side was in his hand in less than a heartbeat. To his credit, the witch hunter reacted swiftly, kicking the small table at Reinhardt an instant after he landed in the room while diving in the opposite direction to gain the pistols and longsword that lay upon the bed. But Reinhardt had the speed of youth and the martial training of one who might have been a captain in the Reiksguard on his side. More, he had purpose.

The witch hunter's claw-like hand closed around the grip of his pistol just as cold steel touched his throat. There was a brief pause as Thulmann regarded the blade poised at his neck before releasing his weapon and holding his hands up in surrender. Both arms raised above his head, Mathias Thulmann faced the man with a sword at his throat.

'I fear that you will not find much gold,' Mathias said, his voice low and unafraid.

'You do not remember me, do you?' Reinhardt snarled. 'Or are you going to pretend that your name is not Mathias Thulmann, Templar of Sigmar, witch hunter?'

'That is indeed my name, and my trade,' replied Mathias, his voice unchanged.

'My name is Reinhardt von Lichtberg,' spat the other, pressing the tip of his blade into Mathias's throat until a bead of crimson slid down the steel. 'I am the man who is going to kill you.'

'To avenge your lost love?' the witch hunter mused, a touch of pity seeming to enter his voice. 'You should thank me for restoring her soul to the light of Sigmar.'

'*Thank you?*' Reinhardt bellowed incredulously. The youth fought to keep himself from driving his sword through the witch hunter's flesh. 'Thank you for imprisoning us, torturing us? Thank you for burning Mina at the stake? Thank you for destroying the only thing that made my life worth living?' Reinhardt clenched his fist against the wave of rage that pounded through his body. He shook his head from side to side.

'We were to be married,' the nobleman stated. 'I was to serve the Emperor in his Reiksguard and win glory and fame. Then I would return and she would be waiting for me to make her my wife.' Reinhardt pulled a fat skinning knife from a sheath on his belt. 'You took that from me. You took it all away.' Reinhardt let the light play across the knife in his left hand as he rolled his wrist back and forth. The witch hunter continued to watch him, his eyes hooded, his face betraying no fear or even concern. Reinhardt noted the man's seeming indifference to his fate.

'You will scream,' he swore. 'Before I let you die, Sigmar himself will hear your screams.'

The hand with the knife moved toward the witch hunter's body... And for the second time that evening, Mathias Thulmann had unexpected visitors.

THE DOOR BURST inwards, bludgeoned from its hinges by the ogre-like man who followed the smashed portal into the room. Three other men were close behind the ape-like bruiser. All four of them wore a motley array of piecemeal armour, strips of chainmail fastened to leather tunics, bands of steel woven to a padded hauberk. The only aspect that seemed to link the four men was the look of confusion on their faces.

'The witch hunter was supposed to be alone,' stated Rall, puzzled by the strange scene they had stumbled upon. Reinhardt turned his body toward the mercenaries, keeping his sword at Mathias's throat.

'Which one is he?' asked Rall, clearly not intending the question for either of the men already in the room.

'Why don't we just kill them both?' the scarecrow-thin figure of Hossbach said, stepping toward Reinhardt.

Like a lightning bolt, the skinning knife went flying across the room. Hossbach snarled as he dodged the projectile. The mercenary did not see the sword that flashed away from Thulmann's throat to slice across his armour and split his stomach across its centre. Hossbach toppled against the man who had dealt him the fatal wound. His sword forgotten on the floor, the mercenary clutched at Reinhardt, grabbing for the man's sword arm. Reinhardt kicked the dying man away from him, sending him crashing into the foot of the bed, but Hossbach had delayed him long enough. The brutish fist of Gunther crashed into Reinhardt's face while his dagger sought to bury itself in the pit of Reinhardt's left arm. The nobleman managed to grab his attacker's wrist, slowing the deadly blade's strike. The blade pierced his skin but did not sink into his heart. His huge opponent let a feral smile form on his face as he put more strength into the struggle. Slowly, by the slightest of measures, the dagger continued its lethal passage.

Suddenly the sound of thunder assailed Reinhardt's ears; a stench like rotten eggs filled his nose. One moment he had been staring into the triumphant face of his attacker. In the next instant the mercenary's head was a red ruin. The hand on the dagger slid away and the mercenary fell to the floor like a felled tree. Reinhardt saw one of the attackers run through the shattered doorway. The other lay with a gory wound on the side of his head at the feet of the only other man still standing in the room.'

A plume of grey smoke rose from the barrel of the pistol Mathias Thulmann held in his right hand. The other pistol, its butt bloody from its impact against the mercenary's skull, was cocked and pointed at Reinhardt von Lichtberg's own head.

'It seems the last of these yapping curs has not seen fit to remain with us,' Thulmann said. Although he now held the upper hand, the witch hunter still possessed the same air of cold indifference.

'Go ahead and kill me, butcher,' Reinhardt swore, his heart afire with the injustice of it all. To come so close… 'You will be doing me a service,' he added.

'There are some things you should know before I decide if you should live or die,' the witch hunter sat down on the bed, motioning Reinhardt to a position from which the pistol could cover him more easily.

'Have you not wondered what brought me to your father's estate?' Mathias asked. He saw the slight look of interest surface amidst Reinhardt's mask of hate. 'I was summoned by Father Haeften.' Reinhardt started at the mention of the wizened old priest of Sigmar who led his father's household in their devotions. It was impossible for him to believe that the kindly soft-spoken old man could have been responsible for bringing about Mina's death. The witch hunter continued to speak.

'The father reported that one of his parish was touched by Chaos,' Thulmann paused, letting the distasteful word linger in the air. 'A young woman who was with child, whose own mother bespoke the irregularities that were manifesting beneath her skin.'

Stunned shock claimed Reinhardt. With child. His child.

'Upon my arrival, I examined the woman and discovered that her mother's fears had proven themselves,' Thulmann shook his head sadly. 'Her background was not of a suspicious nature, but the Darkness infects even the most virtuous. It was necessary to question her, to learn the source of her affliction. After several hours, she said your name.'

'Hours of torture!' Reinhardt spat, face twisted into an animal snarl. 'And then you took me so that your creature might "question" me!'

'Yes!' affirmed Thulmann, fire in his voice. 'As the father, the source of her corruption might lie within you, yourself! It was necessary to discover if there were others! Chaos is a contagion, where one is infected others soon fall ill!'

'Yet you released me,' challenged Reinhardt, the shame he felt at his own survival further fuelling the impotent rage roaring through his veins.

'There was no corruption in you,' the witch hunter said, almost softly. 'Nor in the girl, not in her soul at least. It was days later that she confessed the crime that had been the cause of her corruption.' The witch hunter stared into Reinhardt's blazing eyes.

'Do you know a Doktor Weichs?' he asked.

'Freiherr Weichs?' Reinhardt answered. 'My father's physician?'

'Also physician to his household. Your Mina confided a most private problem with Weichs. She was worried that her condition would prevent you from leaving the von Lichtberg estate, from joining the Reiksguard and seeking the honour and glory that were your due. Weichs gave her a potion of his own creation which he assured her would dissolve the life within her womb as harmlessly as it had formed.'

Mathias Thulmann shook his head again. 'That devil's brew Weichs created was what destroyed your Mina, for it contained warpstone.' The witch hunter paused again, studying Reinhardt. 'I see that you are unfamiliar with the substance. It is the pure essence of Chaos, the black effluent of all the world's evil. In the days before Magnus the Pious, it was thought to possess healing properties, but only a fool or a madman would have anything to do with the stuff in this more enlightened age. Instead of destroying the life in the girl's belly, the warpstone changed it, corrupted woman and child. When I discovered this, I knew you were innocent and had you released.'

'And burned her!' Reinhardt swore.

The witch hunter did not answer the youth but instead kicked the figure lying at his feet.

'There is life in you yet,' Thulmann snarled, looking back at Reinhardt to remind his prisoner that his pistol was yet trained on him. 'Account for yourself, pig! Who sends you to harm a dully-ordained servant of Sigmar?'

Mueller groaned as he rolled onto his side, staring at the witch hunter through a swollen eye. Carefully he put a hand to his split lip and wiped the trickle of blood from his mouth.

'Gerhardt... Knauf,' Mueller said between groans. 'It was Gerhardt Knauf, the merchant. He was afraid you had come to Kleinsdorf seeking him.'

Mathias Thulmann let a grim smile part his lips. 'I am looking for him now,' he stated. The witch hunter smashed the heel of his boot into the grovelling mercenary's neck, crushing the man's windpipe. Mueller uttered a half-gargle, half-gasp and writhed on the floor as he desperately tried to breathe. Thulmann turned away from the dying wretch.

'This Knauf has reasons to see me dead,' Thulmann told Reinhardt, as though the noble had not heard the exchange between witch hunter and mercenary. 'Reasons which lie in the corruption of his mind and soul. If you would avenge your beloved, do so upon one deserving of your wrath, the same sort of filth that destroyed the girl long before I set foot in your father's house.'

Reinhardt glared at the witch hunter. 'I will kill you,' he said in a voice as cold as the grave. Mathias Thulmann sighed and removed a set of manacles from the belt lying on the bed.

'I cannot let you interfere with my holy duty,' the witch hunter said, pressing the barrel of the pistol against Reinhardt's temple. Thulmann closed one of the steel bracelets around the youth's wrist, locking it shut with a deft twist of an iron key. The other half of the manacles he closed around one of the bed posts, trapping the bracelet between the mattress and the wooden globe that topped the post.

'This should ensure that you do not interfere,' Mathias explained as he retrieved the rest of his weapons and stepped over the writhing Mueller.

'I will kill you, Mathias Thulmann,' Reinhardt repeated as the witch hunter left the room. As soon as the cloaked shape was gone, Reinhardt dropped to his knees and stretched his hand toward the ruined body of the mercenary who had almost killed him – and the small hatchet attached to the man's belt.

GERHARDT KNAUF PACED nervously across his bedchamber. It had been nearly an hour and still he had had no word from Mueller.

Not for the first time, the merchant cast his eyes toward the small door at the top of the stairs. The tiny room within was the domain of Knauf's secret vice, the storehouse of all the forbidden and arcane knowledge Knauf had obtained over the years: the grimoire of a centuries-dead Bretonnian witch; the abhorred *Ninth Canticle of Tzeentch*, its mad author's name lost to the ages; a book of incantations designed to bring prosperity, or alternately ruin, by the infamous sorcerer Verlag Duhring. All the black secrets that had given Knauf his power made him better than the ignorant masses that surrounded him, who sneered at his eccentric ways. Before the black arts at his command, brutish men like Mueller were nothing; witch hunters were nothing.

Knauf took another drink from the bottle of wine he had removed from his cellar. The sound of someone pounding on the door of his villa caused the merchant to set his drink down. 'Finally,' he thought.

But the figure that greeted Knauf when he gazed down from his window was not that of Mueller. Instead he saw the scarlet and black garbed form of the mercenary's victim. With a horrified gasp, Knauf withdrew from the window.

'He has come for me,' the merchant shuddered. Mueller and his men had failed and now there was no one to stand between Knauf and the determined witch hunter. Knauf shrieked as he heard a loud explosion from below and the splintering of wood as the door was kicked open. He had only moments in which to save himself from the witch hunter's justice, to avoid the flames that were the price of the knowledge he had sought.

A smile appeared on Knauf's face. The merchant raced for the garret room. If there was no one who would save him from the witch hunter, there was *something* that might.

MATHIAS THULMANN PAUSED on the threshold of the merchant's villa and holstered the smoking pistol in his hand. One shot from the flintlock weapon had been enough to smash the lock on the door, one kick enough to force open the heavy oak portal. The witch hunter drew his second pistol, the one he had reloaded after the melee at the inn and scanned the darkened foyer. No sign of life greeted Thulmann's gaze and he stepped cautiously into the room, watching for the slightest movement in the darkness.

Suddenly the witch hunter's head snapped around, his eyes fixating upon the stairway leading from the foyer to the chambers above. He could sense the dark energies that were gathering somewhere in the rooms above him. Somewhere in this house, someone was calling upon the Ruinous Powers. Thulmann shifted the pistol to his other hand and drew the silvered blade of his sword, blessed by the Grand Theogonist himself and grimly ascended the stairs.

GERHARDT KNAUF COULD feel the eldritch energies gathering in the air around him as he read from the *Ninth Canticle of Tzeentch*. The power was almost a tangible quantity as it surged from the warlock and gathered at the centre of a ring of lighted candles. A nervous laugh interrupted the arcane litany streaming from Knauf's lips as he saw the first faint glimmer of light appear. Swiftly, the glow grew in size, keeping pace with the increasing speed of the words flying from Knauf's tongue. The crackling nimbus took on a pinkish hue and the first faint suggestion of a shape within the light was visible to him.

No, the warlock realised, there was not a shape within the light; rather, the light was assuming a shape. As the blasphemous litany continued, a broad torso coalesced from which two long, simian arms dangled, each ending in an enormous clawed hand. Two short, thick legs slowly grew away from the torso until they touched the wooden floor. Finally, a head sprouted from between the two arms, growing away from the body so that the head was between its shoulders rather than above them. A gargoyle face appeared, its fanged mouth stretching across the head in a hideous grin. Two swirling pools of orange light stared at the warlock.

The daemon uttered a loathsome sound like the wailing of an infant, a sound hideous in its suggestion of malevolent mirth. Knauf shuddered and turned his eyes from the frightful thing he had summoned. In so doing, his gaze fell upon his feet and the colour drained away from his face as the horror of what he had done became known to him.

The first thing Knauf had learned, the most important rule he had found repeated again and again in the arcane books he had so long hoarded, was that a sorcerer must always protect himself from that which he would have do his bidding. In his haste to save himself from the witch hunter, to summon this creature of Tzeentch, Knauf had forgotten to draw about himself a protective circle, a barrier that no daemon may cross.

Knauf's mind desperately groped amongst its store of arcane knowledge seeking some enchantment, some spell that would save the warlock from his hideous mistake. Before him, the daemon uttered its loathsome laugh again. Knauf screamed as the pink abomination moved towards him with a curious scuttling motion.

Thoughts of sorcery forgotten, Knauf clenched his eyes and stretched his arm in front of his body, as though to ward away the monstrous horror even as the fiend advanced upon him. The daemon's grotesque hands closed about the warlock's extended arm, bringing new screams from Knauf as the icy touch seared through his veins. Slowly, the daemon raked a single claw down the length of the would-be wizard's arm, a deep wound that sank down to the very bone. Knauf's cries of agony rose still higher as the daemon's fingers probed the wound. Like a child with a piece of fruit, the horror began to peel the flesh from Knauf's arm, the warlock's howl of torment drowned out by the monster's increasing glee.

MATHIAS THULMANN reached the garret in time to witness the warlock's demise. No longer amused by the high-pitched wails escaping from Knauf's throat, the pink hands released the skeletal limb they clutched and seized the warlock's shoulders, pulling Knauf's body to the daemon's own. The daemon's giant maw gaped wide and with a formless undulating motion surged up and over Knauf's head and shoulders. The pseudo-corporeal substance of the daemon allowed a horrified Thulmann to see the warlock's features behind the ichorous pink jaws that engulfed it. He could see those still-screaming features twist and mutate as the flesh was quickly dissolved, patches of muscle appearing beneath skin before being stripped away to reveal the bone itself. The hardened witch hunter turned away from the appalling sight.

The daemon's insane gibbering brought Thulmann back to his senses. The witch hunter returned his gaze to the loathsome creature and the fool who had called it from the Realm of Chaos. Atop Gerhardt Knauf's body, a skull dripped the last of the warlock's blood and rivulets of meaty grease; the body beneath had been stripped to the breastbone. The whisper of a scream seemed to echo through the garret as the last shards of the warlock's soul fled into the night. The pink daemon rose from its gory repast and turned its fiery eyes upon the witch hunter.

Thulmann found himself powerless to act as the daemon slowly made its way across the garret room. The preternatural fiend moved in a capering, dance-like manner, its glowing body brilliant in the darkness, sounds of lunatic amusement emanating from its clenched, grinning jaws. The daemon stopped just out of reach of the witch hunter's sword, settling down on its haunches. It trained its fiery eyes on the scarlet-clad Templar, regarding him with an unholy mixture of hatred, humour, and hunger.

Thulmann forced himself to meet that inhuman gaze, to stare into the swirling fires that burned from the pink face, forced himself to match his own faith and determination against the daemon's ageless malevolence. Thulmann could feel the orange light seeping into his mind, clouding his thoughts and numbing his will.

With an oath, the witch hunter tore his eyes from those of the daemon. The horror snarled, no longer amused by the novelty of the witch hunter's defiance.

The daemon launched itself at Thulmann, its mouth still wet with the warlock's blood. Thulmann dodged to his left, the quick action sparing him the brunt of the daemon's assault, but still resulting in the unearthly creature's claws scraping the witch hunter's ribs. Clenching his teeth against the painful wound and the daemon's icy touch, Thulmann lashed out at the beast as it recovered from its charge.

A grip of frozen iron closed around the wrist of Thulmann's sword arm even as the heavy butt of the witch hunter's pistol crashed against the leering head of the horror. The daemon glared into Mathias's face and uttered a sinister laugh. Again, the witch hunter dealt the monster a blow that would have smashed the skull of any mortal creature. As Thulmann brought his arm back to strike again at the grinning daemon, his nightmarish foe swatted the weapon from his hand, sending the pistol hurtling down the stairway.

The daemon's gibbering laughter grew; it leaned forward, its grinning jaws inches from Thulmann's hawk-like nose. The witch hunter pushed against the daemon's frigid shape with his free hand, desperately trying to keep the ethereal jaws at bay, at the same time frenziedly trying to free his sword arm. Thulmann's efforts attracted the daemon's attention and, as if noticing the weapon for the first time, it reached across Thulmann's body to remove the sword from his grasp. Luminous pink claws closed around the steel blade.

The smell of burnt metal assaulted Thulmann's nostrils as the keening wail of the daemon ripped at his ears. As the horror's hand had closed about the witch hunter's blade, the daemon's glowing flesh had started to burn, luminous sparks crackling and dancing from the seared paw. The daemon released its grip on Thulmann and scuttled away from the witch hunter, a new look in its fiery eyes. A look Thulmann recognised even in so inhuman a being: *fear*.

The daemon's left hand still gave off streams of purplish smoke, its very shape throbbing uncontrollably. The daemon looked at its injured paw then returned its attention to its adversary. The daemon could see the growing sense of hope, the first fledgling seed of triumph appearing in the very aura of the witch hunter. The sight incensed the daemon.

Thulmann slowly advanced upon the beast. The witch hunter had gained an advantage, he did not intend to lose it. But he did not reckon upon the creature's supernatural speed, or its feral rage. Before Thulmann had taken more than a few steps towards it, the daemon sprang from the floor as though it had been shot from a cannon. The monster crashed into Thulmann sending both man and fiend plummeting down the stairs.

Mathias Thulmann groggily tried to gain his feet, ears ringing from his violent descent. By some miracle he had managed to retain his sword. It was a fact that further infuriated his monstrous foe. The daemon scuttled toward the witch hunter. Thulmann struck at it, but the attack was a clumsy one, easily dodged by the luminous being. The horror responded by striking him in the chest with a powerful upswing of both its arms. The witch hunter was lifted off his feet, hurled backward by the tremendous force of the daemon's attack. Thulmann landed on the final flight of stairs, tumbling down them to lie broken and battered in the foyer.

At the foot of the stairs, the witch hunter struggled to rise, groping feebly for the sword that had landed beside him. He watched as the giggling pink daemon capered down the stairs, dancing in hideous parody of the revellers of Kleinsdorf. Mathias summoned his last reserves of strength as the daemon descended toward him. With a prayer to Sigmar, the witch hunter struck as the daemon leaped.

A shriek like the tearing of metal rang out as Thulmann's sword sank into the daemon. The blade impaled the horror, its body writhing in agony before bursting apart like a bubble rising from a fetid marsh. A squeal of venomous rage rose from the daemon, shattering the glass in the foyer's solitary window. Tiny sparks of bluish light flew from the point of the daemon's dissolution. Thulmann sank to his knees, thanking Sigmar for his deliverance.

Daemonic laughter broke into Thulmann's prayers. The taste of victory left the witch hunter as he saw the two daemons dance towards him from the darkness of the foyer. They were blue, goblin-sized parodies of the larger daemon Thulmann had vanquished, and they were glaring at him with looks of utter malevolence.

The foremost of the daemons opened its gigantic mouth, revealing the shark-like rows of serrated fangs. The blue horror laughed as it hopped and bounded across the foyer with frightening speed. Holding the sword before him, Thulmann prepared to meet the monster's attack.

Thulmann cried out as a torrent of pain wracked his body. Swift as the first daemon's movements had been, the other had been swifter still, circling the witch hunter as he prepared to meet its companion's attack. Unseen, the blue horror struck at the witch hunter's leg, sinking its fangs through the hard leather boot to worry the calf within. The intense pain made Thulmann drop his weapon, his only thought to seize the creature ravaging his leg.

The blue thing gave a hiccup of mock fright as Thulmann's hands closed around its scintillating form. The witch hunter tore the creature away from his boot and lifted the daemon over his head by its heals, thinking to dash its brains against the floor. In that instant he realised the trickery the beasts had employed. Scuttling across the floor, its over-sized hands dragging the sword by the hilt, was the other daemon. The monsters had taken away his only weapon.

The horror in Thulmann's hands twisted out of his grasp with a disgustingly boneless motion, raking its claws across his left hand as it fell to the floor. Giggling madly, the blue daemon danced away from the witch hunter's wrath, capering just beyond his reach until its companion returned from secreting his sword.

The two monsters circled Thulmann, striking at him from both sides at once, slashing his flesh with their claws before dancing away again. It was a slow, lingering death, like a pack of dogs tormenting a tethered horse because they do not know how to make a clean kill. Thulmann bled from dozens of wounds. Most were only superficial, but the pain caused by their infliction was intense. Every nerve in his body now writhed at the slightest touch from one of the daemons.

Thulmann's eyes fell upon an object lying upon the floor, its metal barrel reflecting the unearthly bodies of his tormentors. The pistol their unholy parent had taken away from him. If it had not discharged or otherwise been fouled by its violent descent, perhaps the witch hunter could find escape from his agony. Trembling with pain, Thulmann reached for the gun.

One of the daemons slashed the man's cheek as he stooped to retrieve the weapon. Dancing away, the creature laughed and brayed. It licked its fanged mouth and turned to rejoin its comrade in their amusement. It did not see the figure emerge from the darkness, nor the brilliant steel blade that reflected the light of its own glowing body.

The second monster sank its teeth into Thulmann's wrist. How dare the human think to spoil its fun? The blue fiend kicked the pistol away, turning to rake its claws through the shredded cloak that covered Thulmann's mangled back. The daemon leapt away in mid-stroke, turning to the source of the sight and sound that had alarmed it. In the darkness, the sparks and spirals of luminous smoke rising from the death of the other blue horror were almost blinding. The beast scrambled toward the being it sensed lurking in the shadows, eager to rend the flesh of this new adversary who had vanquished its other half. A rusted wooden hatchet sailed out of the darkness, smashing into the snarling daemon.

'The sword,' gasped Thulmann, again reaching for his pistol. 'Use the sword.'

The remaining fiend rose swiftly, its fiery eyes blazing. The daemon lunged in the direction from which the attack had come. It was a fatal mistake. The small creature's hands closed upon the naked blade, sparking and sizzling just as its its parent's had. As the blue horror recoiled from its unpleasant surprise, its attacker struck at its head with a sweep of the blade, finishing the daemon in an explosion of sparks and shrieks. Unlike the pink monster, no new horrors were born from the deaths of its lesser offspring.

'You are mine to kill, Thulmann,' a cold voice from the shadows said. 'I'll not lose my vengeance to anyone else, be they man or daemon!' The witch hunter laughed weakly.

'You shall find your task much simpler now, avenger. My wounds prevent me from mounting any manner of capable defence.' A venomous note entered the witch hunter's voice. 'But you would prefer butchery to a fair duel. That is your idea of honour?'

Reinhardt glared at him, tossing the witch hunter's sword to Thulmann. Thulmann shook his head as he gingerly sheathed the weapon with his injured hand.

'I could not hold that blade with these,' Thulmann showed the enraged noble his bleeding palms and wrist, 'much less combat an able swordsman.'

Reinhardt glared at the witch hunter contemptuously. His gaze studied Thulmann before settling upon the holstered pistols on the witch hunter's belt.

'Are you fit enough to use one of those?' the youth snarled.

'Are you skilled enough to use one?' Mathias countered, slowly drawing one of the weapons and sliding it across the floor. Reinhardt stooped and retrieved the firearm.

'When you see hell, you will know,' the youth responded. He waited as the witch hunter lifted himself from the floor and slowly drew the remaining gun. As soon as he felt the witch hunter was ready, the youth's hand pointed at Thulmann and his finger depressed the pistol's trigger. There was a sharp click as the hammer fell upon an already expired cap.

'Never accept a weapon from an enemy,' Thulmann said his voice icy and emotionless. There was a loud explosion of noise as he fired the weapon he had retrieved from the base of the stairs and holstered while Reinhardt still fought the last daemon. Reinhardt was thrown to the floor as the bullet impacted against his shoulder. Thulmann limped toward the fallen noble. The witch hunter trained his eyes upon the man's wound.

'With a decent physician that will heal in a fortnight,' the witch hunter said, turning away from his victim. 'If we meet again, I may not be so restrained,' Thulmann added as he made his way from the house.

Reinhardt von Lichtberg's shout followed the witch hunter into the street.

'I will find you, Mathias Thulmann! If I have to track you to the nethermost pits of the Wastes, you will not escape me! I will find you again, and I will kill you!'

And the people of Kleinsdorf continued to dance and laugh and sing as they celebrated the triumph of light over Chaos.

# TYBALT'S QUEST

## by Gav Thorpe

THE STENCH OF death hung heavily in the cloying fog. The broken shadows of twisted trunks and branches swayed fitfully in the lacklustre breeze. Tybalt dismounted from his great black stallion, his armour dripping with moisture from the swirling mist. Casting his gaze around to find something to fix his horse's reins to, the Bretonnian knight spied what looked to be an old hitching post by the cemetery's gate. As he led his steed towards it, the heavy footfalls of his armoured boots and the horse's iron-shod hooves muffled by the dense fog, Tybalt's eyes and ears strained to sense any other sound. All was still and silent. Even the hoots of owls and the baying of dogs from the village had fallen quiet.

Quickly tying the reins to the rotted post, Tybalt unsheathed his longsword and took one last look around. Above him, the light of the new moon could barely be seen through the misty blanket surrounding the hilltop. The twinkling lights of Moreux had been left far behind as he had made his way to the ancient graveyard overlooking the whole of the valley. Up here, in one of the narrower passes of the Grey Mountains, the air was thin, and even the fit and

youthful Tybalt was finding himself short of breath. With a
deep inhalation, the knight laid a gauntleted hand on the
cemetery gate, the curled ironwork of which stretched several
feet above his head, and pushed it open.

The shrieking of rusted hinges rent the air, causing Tybalt to
freeze involuntarily . His heart was hammering in his chest,
and it was a few moments before he realised that he had been
holding his breath. Letting it out slowly, he eased the gate
open further, an action accompanied by erratic squeaks and
grinding noises. When he'd opened a gap just wide enough
for him to pass, he turned sideways and slid himself through
the opening, looking up at the gargoyles on the flanking
gateposts. Both had probably been identical when sculpted,
but now the one to the left had only one of its three twisting
horns left, while the lolling tongue of the other had been broken off just outside its fanged mouth.

Treading carefully to avoid the deepest puddles in the
uneven path, Tybalt made his way further up the hill, heading towards the blocky, dark shadows of the largest and
oldest crypts at the summit. Something scuttling through the
darkness banged into his foot, causing Tybalt to stumble in
fright. As he fell to one knee, he came face to face with the
evil, yellow eyes of a black rat. The verminous scavenger
hissed at him and then scampered out of view.

Heaving himself to his feet once more, Tybalt wiped the
mud from his left hand on his scarlet and azure quartered
surcoat. For a moment, Tybalt wondered if he should go
back to his horse to fetch his shield, but decided that a free
hand would be more valuable in these treacherous environs.
Pausing to collect his thoughts, Tybalt peered through the
mist at the looming shapes of the old mausoleums at the
cemetery's highest point, wondering which belonged to
Duke Laroche, the resting place of the ghost who had
appeared to him in a dream five months earlier.

The long-dead duke had warned Tybalt that a great evil was
disturbing his rest, and that he should undertake a quest to
halt this darkness spreading through the realm. It had taken
four months of searching the length of Bretonnia, examining
the oldest heraldic records, to identify the arms of the ghost
who had appeared to him: a black eagle on a plain yellow

field. Duke Laroche was one of the founders of Mousillon, a man whose family dated back to the settling of Bretonnia in the time of Gilles le Breton, the first king. For the last month, Tybalt had searched far and wide for the old duke's resting place, until finally he had come across the answer in the chapel records in the small mountain village of Moreux.

When they had learned that Tybalt was heading up to the old graveyard, the commoners back in Moreux had warned him against going to the ancient cemetery. Local superstition was rife with tales of ghouls and spectres haunting the heights of the mountains. Hearing these accounts had done little to ease the knight's nerves.

TYBALT'S THOUGHTS WERE interrupted by rustling behind him and he spun around, sword at the ready. Taking a few steps back down the path, his grey eyes tried to pierce the gloom. Shadows drifted in and out of focus with the rolling fog, and Tybalt heard more rustling. Taking another cautious step forward, the knight brought his sword back over his shoulder, ready to strike at a moment's notice. More scuffling swung his attention to his left, and he stepped off the muddy path into the wet grass, which reached up to his thighs. Tybalt could hear an inhuman snuffling noise, accompanied by deep breathing and intermittent grunting. Something was approaching slowly towards him; he could see its vague shadow only a few paces away now.

'Reveal yourself, rascal!' challenged Tybalt, trying to speak with a confidence his shaking hand betrayed he did not have. There was an unearthly squeal and the shadow leapt at him from the darkness.

'Die, spawn of blackness!' Tybalt cried, stepping sideways and bringing his heavy sword flashing down. The blade bit deep into flesh, and blood fountained through the mist, splashing across Tybalt's surcoat and armour. Ensuring the beast was no longer moving, Tybalt took a closer look. At first he thought it some hideous mutant, but as he bent down to look into the thick weeds, he saw that the long tusks did not belong to some creature of the netherworlds and were in fact those of a wild boar. Tybalt straightened up slowly and the tension suddenly released from his body.

'Lady, protect me from fears and nightmares of my own creation,' he laughed quietly to himself, turning quickly and striding back to the path. The sudden action and its mundane end had eliminated all of the knight's trepidation now, and as he looked about, he saw nothing more unnatural than the heavy mist of the mountains, hanging over a place where the dead quietly rested in eternal sleep. With more of a spring in his step, he walked up the twisting path towards the summit.

TYBALT FOUND DUKE Laroche's tomb towards the centre of the hilltop, identifying it by the deep inscription and the coat of arms whose yellow and black paint had been all but obliterated by the ceaseless march of the centuries. Hacking away at the twining ivy and stubby bushes surrounding the crypt, Tybalt made his way around to the back of the tomb, away from the cemetery gates, where ancient tradition dictated the entrance stone would be.

On turning the corner, Tybalt was momentarily taken aback. The portal was already half open! The young knight's ears could hear nothing from inside the tomb, and so he ventured forward once more. Peering into the darkness of the mausoleum's interior, he could not discern anything untoward, and he quickly set to with his tinder and flint to make a torch from one of the many broken branches scattered across the ground. The brand sputtered and smoked badly. The wood was dead but wet from the recent rains and the vapours swirling around the graveyard.

As he was about to step over the threshold of the tomb, Tybalt glanced down and stopped. Muddy footprints could be seen quite clearly leading into the darkness. Kneeling for a closer look, he saw that there were several sets, all overlapping but made by the same pair of boots. Judging from the length of the strides, Tybalt guessed that the man was fairly short. He then noticed scuffing on the imprints of the right boot which could mean that he either had a limp or perhaps was carrying a heavy burden. Tybalt was glad that he had spent much of his childhood with his father's personal huntsman, learning some of the man's tracking secrets. Deciding there was no more to be deduced, Tybalt stood up and took a few steps forward, into the tomb itself.

Looking around in the ruddy, flickering glow of his torch, he could see the walls were hung with ancient tapestries, each depicting some event from Duke Laroche's life. Here was the duke repelling the green-skinned orcs from his castle walls near to what would become the city of Mousillon. Another showed the duke winning the Tourney of Couronne, claiming the silver helm from the Fay Enchantress herself. Another showed Laroche at court with the king of that age, his armour almost white with the brilliance of its polish. There were also scenes from his daily life, such as the duke out hawking in the mountains, his wedding to the Lady Isabon and the knighting of his son. The largest tapestry, almost a dozen paces in length, depicted various tableaux from his Grail Quest. It showed the duke driving forth foul beastmen of Chaos from the hallowed woods of Lapelle, his founding of the Grail Temple at Mousillon and his solitary two-month vigil in the Grey Mountains during which the Lady of the Lake had guided him to one of the Grail's resting places.

Spurred on by the visitation of the duke's ghost, who had given him such dire warnings of evil to come that Tybalt had woken with a shudder and covered in sweat despite the autumn night chill, the knight had vowed to his father that he would seek out this evil, wherever it would be found. It was his father who first directed him to the massive heraldic library at Couronne. During his research, Tybalt had learnt much of the duke and had come to see him as a shining example of the true Bretonnian knight. Records told of a man who was pure and holy, pious in every way, noble to his servants and his peers. His humility had been near-legendary in his time and his ultimate sacrifice, saving the Queen's life from a traitor's blade, had been a glorious end to a glorious life. And now the duke had appeared to Tybalt, asking him for help. Tybalt was honoured that such a hero of his lands had faith in him.

Tybalt noticed that the tapestry at the far end of the chamber was hanging askance, obviously moved by someone. Combined with the footprints by the entrance, this convinced Tybalt that someone had been down here. Or perhaps they were still down here, Tybalt realised with a start. Easing his sword from its scabbard, Tybalt stepped cautiously towards the skewed tapestry, pushing it to one side with the tip of his sword. There was an archway beyond, and in the fitful light he could see that the burial chamber on the other side was empty of life. Glancing up, Tybalt noticed an inscription in the stonework above the arch. Raising the torch above his head, Tybalt read the epigraph: *'In Life I protected thee; In Death I shall Watch over thee.'*

It is true, thought Tybalt. Even from beyond death, the duke has returned to warn us of a growing peril to the realm of Bretonnia.

The inner tomb was unadorned, and in the middle sat the duke's sarcophagus. His shield and sword were laid upon it, along with the silver helm given to him by the Fay Enchantress so many centuries ago. None of his arms showed any sign of the many years that had passed. Looking around, Tybalt could see nothing amiss, but that only served to worry him further. If it had been crude graverobbers who had disturbed the duke's eternal resting place, they would have surely have taken the treasures atop the coffin.

The young knight then noticed something on the floor near to the coffin. It was faint and scuffed, but he could see a tracing of lines and sigils. As he followed them, he realised that they formed some kind of pentagram with the tomb at its centre. They had a reddish-brown tinge to them and Tybalt knew instinctively that they had been drawn in blood. Perhaps human blood, he suddenly found himself thinking, his skin prickling with goosebumps. To his eyes, the enchanted matrix appeared to have faded, the blood at least several days old.

Tybalt was at a loss for a moment. He had finally reached the duke's place of eternal rest, but now what was he to do? Would the duke appear to him again, or was there some ritual he must perform first? Laying his sword to one side and placing the impromptu torch in one of the several brackets hanging from the walls, Tybalt knelt on both knees, bowing his head to the stone coffin.

'By the Lady of the Lake, our eternal guardian, I have sought out this place. I am here to fight whatever dangers await my land. My sword and my life are yours to command, ancient duke. What will you have me do?' he asked, his voice barely above a whisper.

For a moment, nothing happened, but then something stirred in the red-tinged gloom. A faint whispering noise echoed off the walls; a gentle wind sighed around the room. Looking up, Tybalt gasped in surprise. There, no more than two paces from him, stood the shade of Duke Laroche. He looked exactly as he had in the dream, dressed in flowing, yellow robes, the black eagle embroidered onto the left breast, over his heart. A small circlet of gold was placed over his shoulder-length hair, and his dark-brown eyes stared peacefully at Tybalt. The duke's face radiated a knightly air, his hooked nose and strong jaw echoed in most of the aristocratic families of the present day. His face was stern but kindly.

The image was only half-present though. Tybalt could clearly see the coffin and the far wall through the shimmering apparition. A nimbus of white light played around the edges of the ghost, twinkling like distant starlight.

'My lord, I am your humble servant,' Tybalt managed to say. The duke remained silent, beckoning with his right hand for Tybalt to stand. Finally the duke spoke, the words echoing and distant, as if he were speaking from a long way away and some large chamber was magnifying his words.

'I knew thou wouldst come, young Tybalt,' the duke said with a warm smile. 'I knew one of thy great-great-great-great-great-great-great-great-great grandsires! He was a good man, and I knew his blood runneth thick in thy veins. Thou wilst be a fine duke when thy father finally passeth into the care of Our Lady.'

'Thank you, milord,' Tybalt replied, blushing at such praise.

'I expect thou wonderest why I have brought thou here, knight,' the apparition said.

'There is some great evil stirring in this place,' Tybalt answered. 'That is what you have warned me of.'

'Yea,' the ghost agreed, 'a great evil indeed. It hast been long forgotten now, but the ground thou treadst upon is one of the most holy places in all of the sacred kingdom.'

Tybalt stared down at the stone floor of the tomb in astonishment.

'This hilltop is that very spot where Gilles himself rested the night before he descended to claim the lands south of the mountains for his people,' explained Laroche. 'Here is the place that our First King did witness the first visitation of the Lady of the Lake, and from here did all his knowledge and power spring. Even before the coming of the King, this land was a holy one, for our ancestors beyond the founding of the realm of Bretonnia did labour hard here to build the cairns for their dead lords. The very hill itself is but a gigantic tomb of the resting dead, from the time when the elves and dwarfs ruled the lands and our people were but scattered hunting tribes.'

Tybalt gulped heavily in amazement.

'How could such a place be forgotten, milord?' he asked, shaking his head in disbelief.

"Tis the way of things, young knight,' the old duke replied simply, stroking an incorporeal hand through his dark hair. 'Ages pass, the world changes, the old ways are replaced by new ways; the ancient secrets and beliefs give way to the wonders of the modern age. It is the duty of the Grail Knights to keep that true wisdom alive, but there are fewer of us with every passing generation. A darkness threatens all of our lands, and the realms of others to the north, south, east and west. A time of great change is coming, young knight, a time of war and disorder. We shall need men such as thyself. Verily, there shall be such need of heroes, the like of which time has never seen before!'

Tybalt was about to ask what darkness was coming, but the duke held up a hand to silence him. The knight saw that the duke's gloves were made from the blackest velvet, and on every finger was a golden ring bearing the crests of the eight great families of the founding of Mousillon.

'But that is the future, not thy current quest, valiant Tybalt,' the apparition finally said. 'For now, you must fight against the hideous attentions of a dabbler in the black arts of necromancy.'

'Necromancy, milord?' Tybalt asked, unsure of the word's meaning.

"Tis the power to summon the forces of Death and Undeath, and bind them to thy bidding,' the duke answered, his ghostly form stepping back to lean against the coffin. 'Tis the power to raise corpses from thy graves to dance in unholy rites and march to war against the living. 'Tis the power to steal life with a touch of the finger. 'Tis the power to gaze past the gates of Death itself and peer at that which lies beyond. 'Tis the power to forever forestall the coming of the eternal sleep, so that thou might never know Death.'

The duke stood up once more, his fists clenched by his sides in anger.

'One who has these powers hath come here,' he spat. 'To this site, that which is the most holy of places. He hath disturbed mine own slumber and that of others of your great ancestors. He yet will raise the bodies of the dead to sweep all before him, his vile blackness spreading like spilt ink across a clean parchment. Thou must stop him, Tybalt; that is why I brought thee here.'

'I should have brought my father's army!' exclaimed Tybalt, raising his hand to his mouth in horror. 'This foul creature would have no chance against a hundred sturdy men and knights.'

'Thou canst not defeat such an evil with battle alone, young Tybalt,' Laroche answered. 'They feed on fear, thrive on thy terror. From the fallen ranks, he wouldst summon more from their graves to do his bidding. Nay, an army is not needed, for is not a knight of Bretonnia strong enough to overcome all obstacles? Is not the Lady the most powerful of allies? 'Tis faith that will break this darkness, and faith does not come from an army, but from one knight who will stand alone against the perils of the world.'

'I do not understand, milord,' Tybalt protested. 'What can I do against a man who can raise an army from the very ground at my feet?'

'You can fight him,' the duke replied shortly, his eyebrows raised in humour. The duke then paused a moment, his head turning as if to look through the wall of the tomb.

'The beast cometh now!' he hissed. 'Gird your arms, and do battle, brave knight. Take mine silver helm, for it wilst protect thee from the worst of the devil's magicks. The Lady is with you, brave Tybalt, so look to your faith for strength, and you will endure and overcome.' With a reassuring smile, the ghost of Duke Laroche began to waver and then was gone.

* * *

STANDING ON THE crest of the hill, Tybalt could just make out a faint lightness in the mist, moving slowly towards him. As it grew closer, he saw that it was the glow of a flame, and it was not long before he could make out the figure of a man walking lopsidedly along the path. He had wisely extinguished his own torch, fearing he would reveal his presence too soon, and as the stranger came closer, the knight stepped behind one of the nearby tombs. Another dozen heartbeats passed before he could hear the scuffing of the newcomer's twisted leg as well as the intruder's laboured wheezing and a constant whispering in a tongue the knight did not understand. Pushing himself even further into the shadows, Tybalt waited for his adversary to come closer. The shuffling footfalls stopped at the summit, no more than a dozen strides from his hiding place. Tybalt eased his sword into a position ready to strike, and he waited for his foe to limp within easy reach of his blade. He heard the man give a hacking cough, and then a voice called out in accented Bretonnian.

'Show yourself, knight! I know you are here waiting!'

Tybalt felt his stomach tighten with fear, and he fought down the sick feeling. Blinking quickly to clear the moisture in his eyes, he took a deep breath and then stepped out of the shadows to confront the stranger.

The man was indeed short, no more than five feet tall. His right leg was crooked below the knee, splaying his foot outwards. He was dressed in a heavy, grey robe fastened with a frayed length of rope. In one hand, he held a knobbled wooden staff, the tip of which was glowing with an unnatural flame. Under the other arm, the man carried a heavy book bound in leather and brass. The man was looking the other way, and all Tybalt could see of his face was a bulbous nose surrounded by a wild shock of greasy, grey hair. The stranger then turned to face him, his face old and lined with many deep wrinkles like a carelessly discarded blanket. A scraggly growth of beard sprouted from his chin and cheeks, but the eyes that stared at him from under thick bushy brows were bright and lively.

'There you are!' the figure said, taking several steps closer. 'I came as quick as I could. Did not want you to get cold waiting for me.'

'Approach no closer, creature of evil,' Tybalt warned, brandishing his sword towards the necromancer, who took a step back.

'Creature of evil?' the necromancer replied. 'Who told you such things?'

'The duke has warned me of the vile deeds you are committing,' Tybalt said proudly, lowering his blade slightly.

'The duke?' the magic user replied excitedly, his sharp gaze meeting Tybalt's own defiant stare. 'Then it is true, a spirit can come back across the void! Oh, wondrous!'

'Leave, and never trouble these lands again,' Tybalt told the man facing him in his most commanding voice.

'Leave?' the necromancer replied incredulously, his head tilted to one side in astonishment. 'When I am so near to finishing my work here? I do not think so! Get out of my way, and I will spare you.'

'You shall not pass me while I draw breath!' Tybalt threatened, bringing his sword up once more.

'So be it,' the necromancer sneered, pointing his staff towards the knight. The foreigner spoke two words in a harsh, clipped voice – and a white-hot flame roared out of the staff to engulf Tybalt.

The knight felt Laroche's silver helm growing colder and the flames licked around him without touching, keeping him safe from harm. The flames continued, but the necromancer took a step back in dismay when the uninjured Tybalt strode from the magical fires, his eyes filled with murderous intent, his sword still stained with the boar's blood, raised for a lethal strike. With surprising speed, the evil wizard lashed out with the staff, cracking it against the side of Tybalt's helm.

Dizzied, the knight lurched to one side, his outstretched hand finding the wall of a tomb to brace himself against. When he looked around, the necromancer had disappeared into the mists, the glow of the staff nowhere to be seen. Tybalt could feel a small trickle of blood running down his left cheek from where his helm had broken the skin, and his jaw felt numb. Blinking back tears of shock, he pushed himself upright and began searching for the fleeing sorcerer.

\* \* \*

*Lords of Valour*

TYBALT HAD WANDERED aimlessly for some time, trying to find the necromancer's hiding place. He had walked back along the length of the path and was sure his prey had not left the cemetery. It was at the gate that he had another revelation. The necromancer had only known he was in the cemetery because of the black stallion he'd tied up by the gate! There had been nothing mystical about his knowledge at all. The man's magic was hardly as all-powerful as the knight had at first believed. Checking on his horse, the knight found it unharmed, and Tybalt suspected that the vile wizard had decided to steal the fine steed once its owner had been killed.

'This is fruitless!' Tybalt hissed to himself in frustration. The graveyard was large, and in the dense mist it was impossible to see anything at all beyond two dozen yards. What was it the duke had said? Faith would see him victorious? Shrugging, Tybalt stuck his sword in the ground, knelt on one knee and bowed his head to its pommel.

'Oh glorious Lady of the Lake, who watches over our king and lands, guide me to this evil man so that I may slay him in your name,' he prayed, eyes still flickering from side to side, alert from danger.

He knelt for almost thirty heartbeats, but nothing happened. With a sigh, he closed his eyes for a second, and suddenly his mind was filled with a vision. Blinking, Tybalt closed his eyes once more and concentrated. In his mind's eye, he could see the necromancer in a narrow depression which the knight somehow knew was on the other side of the hill. The wizard had his spellbook open on the top of a low tomb in front of him and was chanting verses of magic from its pages. The air around him was shifting and changing, ruffled and rippled by the movement of unquiet spirits. Focusing his mind even more, Tybalt caught the noise of the wizard's words and, as he opened his eyes once more, he found he could still faintly hear them. Following his ears, Tybalt began to move around the base of the hill, staying close to the high, dry stone wall that served as the cemetery's boundary.

TYBALT WAS CREEPING up the hillside, closing in on the necromancer's ritual. Stealthily he wove his way through the mass of gravestones, glad that his armour was well oiled and did not make too much noise. As he made his way between the graves, Tybalt's foot caught in something, pitching him forward onto his hands and knees. Thinking it a bramble or similar, he tugged hard, but to no avail. Glancing back he gave a high pitched yelp. A bony hand protruded from the ground and was grasping his ankle!

As the knight tried to wrench his leg free, another arm broke through the surface, and then the skeleton's skull pushed free, its fleshless grin leering at the knight from the dead creature's grave. Tybalt smashed the skull in two with his sword, and the dead thing's grip relaxed.

Pushing himself up, Tybalt realised other shapes were pressing through the mist towards him. Preferring not to be trapped in the tightening ring of dead creatures, he jumped towards the nearest, lashing out with his blade. The sword crashed through the skeleton's ribs and spine, toppling it to the ground in two parts. Turning to face the others, he counted four more adversaries. Dodging to one side, he realised that three of the four were armoured and armed with ancient-looking axes and maces. One still carried a shield on its left arm, while all four wore scattered fragments of mail armour.

'Lady, give me strength!' Tybalt hissed as the nearest undead creature lashed out with its rusty-bladed axe, the blow falling wide as Tybalt swayed to his left. Tybalt brought his sword around in a long, backhand sweep, smashing the skeleton several feet backwards. Tybalt stepped forward, thrusting out with the point of his blade, embedding it deep into the creature's chest. The magic binding it to the world of the living severed, and the thing collapsed into a pile of mouldering bones. Fleshless hands grabbed at Tybalt's neck and he spun on the spot, ramming his elbow into the face of the skeleton which had attacked him, its jaw flying into the fog. Too close to use his sword, Tybalt brought his knee up sharply and was rewarded by the sound of splintering ribs.

Tybalt was staggered sideways as a mace crashed into his shoulder, and as he stumbled he brought the pommel of his sword down onto the skull of the unarmed skeleton, crunching through the time-worn bone and smashing it asunder. His next blow crashed against the other's shield and Tybalt was forced to sway backwards as the mace rushed inches in front of his face. With a grunt, Tybalt grabbed the skeleton's shield, pulling the thing's face forward onto the brow of his helm with bone-shattering force. As it flailed backwards under the impact, Tybalt gripped his sword in both hands and cleaved it from right shoulder to pelvis with an arcing, overhead chop.

Tybalt felt something ragged dig deep into his right thigh and he fell to his left knee, the axe in his leg wrenched from the dead grip of the skeleton. Its fingers clawed at his closed helmet, trying to twist his head off. Tybalt grabbed its neck in one hand, battering the thing's temples with the quillions of his sword. The skeleton would not let go though, and with a cry of pain, Tybalt forced himself to his feet, his hand still tightly gripping the creature's neck, blood pouring down his leg from where the axe still hung.

'You died once, you can die again!' Tybalt spat, dropping his sword and thrusting the fingers of his free hand into the skeleton's eye sockets. As its clawed fingers scraped deafeningly against his helm, Tybalt stretched his right arm forward with all his strength, pushing the unnatural monster's head further and further back. He felt the thing's bony fingers scratching at his exposed throat and a flicker of fear struck him when they slid across the veins and arteries which were standing out from his neck with the effort of pushing the skeleton away.

Suddenly shifting his weight to one side, Tybalt pulled the skeleton towards him, throwing it over one hip so that it landed back-first on the ground. Its grip had been broken and Tybalt stamped down on its chest, his heavily armoured boot crushing the unlife from the creature.

Panting with exhaustion and pain, Tybalt grabbed the handle of the axe stuck in his leg and pulled it free, a cry of agony torn from his lips. Tossing the ancient weapon aside, he retrieved his sword from the long grass. Using the blade of his sword, the knight cut a rough bandage from his surcoat and wrapped it around the injured thigh, pulling it painfully tight over the wound to stem the bleeding. Glancing around to ensure that no more unholy denizens were nearby, he started to limp up the slope towards the necromancer.

* * *

THE WIZARD'S FACE was a picture of almost comical shock when Tybalt staggered through the mist towards him. He had one hand outstretched, the other pointing towards his grimoire, where he had obviously been following the lines of writing. Around him stood a dozen more animated corpses, all of them ancient and yellowing skeletons. The summoner of the dead quickly masked his surprise.

'Still walking, yes?' he said, a cruel smile playing briefly across his thin, cracked lips.

'I am,' Tybalt replied simply, taking another step towards the necromancer, his sword held across his chest.

'It does not matter, I have more minions to deal with you,' the wizard said glibly, gesturing left and right to the skeletons stood around him.

'And I will destroy them in turn, before I destroy you,' Tybalt answered with utmost sincerity, momentarily surprised at his own confidence.

The sorcerer hesitated for a second, and once again Tybalt noticed doubt creeping into the old man's eyes. The knight took another step forward.

'You think you can stop me? On your own?' sneered the necromancer, but Tybalt caught more than just a hint of false bravado about the wizard's defiance.

'One Bretonnian knight is enough for any evil creature, be it griffon, elf-thing, orc or man,' Tybalt assured the necromancer. A shadow of fear passed briefly across the evil wizard's face. Behind the magic user, two of the skeletons began to sway back and forth and then collapsed into a pile of bones. Tybalt thought he saw a flicker of soul-light and heard a distant cry of joy of a spirit set free once more. The necromancer turned and looked over his shoulder before his horrified gaze settled on Tybalt once more.

'Your power is fading, old man,' Tybalt said menacingly, pleased with the metallic ring given to his voice by the closed visor of his helmet. He saw the necromancer swallow hard, eyes darting left and right, searching for an escape route. Another three skeletons crumbled into grave dust to the knight's left.

'No, no, no, no...' the foul wizard whispered harshly and then began to babble something in a strange tongue. But this was no otherworldly language of magic, for Tybalt recognised it as the Reikspiel of the Empire, even though he did not understand the words.

'It seems your creations are sparing me the exertion of slaying them again,' Tybalt joked, marching slowly through the long grass. He levelled the point of his sword at the necromancer.

'Your death will be brief,' the knight assured him with all earnestness. With a clatter of bones the magic animating the remaining skeletons was broken, and the necromancer was left standing alone in the thinning fog. Tybalt saw that his foe was visibly shaking with fear now, as the knight stalked across the shallow dell. Once more, the necromancer looked for somewhere to run, but there was no way out. Even wounded, the knight would catch the crippled wizard with ease.

'What powers of magic have you that you can destroy my creations so easily?' asked the wizard, eyes pleading beneath his grey brows.

'I have no magic other than the blessing of the Lady,' Tybalt answered him. 'It is your own weaknesses that have destroyed them, your own lack of will to keep them animated. Your magic is powerful, but you are weak. Without your magic, you are nothing!'

'Have mercy, knight,' the necromancer begged, eyes filling with tears. 'Please do not kill me!'

'Mercy?' Tybalt sneered, stabbing his sword towards the wizard to emphasise his scorn. 'Mercy for the creature who has despoiled and profaned one of the most sacred places of all Bretonnia? Mercy for the beast who would wake the heroes of our past from their eternal sleep to be slaves to his vile purposes? Mercy for a creature that would sweep away the living with his own tide of death? There can be no mercy for such crimes!'

'Please kill me not!' begged the other, falling to his knees in the long, wet grass. 'I cannot bear the thought of death!'

Tybalt paused in his rage-driven advance.

'Scared of death?' the knight asked scornfully. 'Is that all you have in your defence? You have plagued the living and the dead because of your own fear of death? Your fear is the root of your weakness. The very thing that drove you to seek such dark powers has unmanned you.'

'I cannot bear the thought of the final ending of my life,' the necromancer admitted, his squinting eyes streaming with tears of fear and loathing. 'I had to find some way to escape. I did not mean harm. That I will one day not be anymore fills me with terror that I cannot face.'

'But death is not an ending,' Tybalt growled, stepping towards the wizard, through the thick weeds once more. 'As the duke has shown me, death is merely a gateway to another place. If we live well, we shall be rewarded: the Lady will take care of us, and we shall be beside her for the rest of time.'

'How do you know of such things?' the sorcerer demanded, his face filled with anguish.

'I do not know such things. I believe in them,' Tybalt answered, standing over the cowering necromancer. 'I have faith that what I have been taught is true. I need no evidence of the land beyond death, for it is faith in its existence that will take me there.'

'And what of those who have no faith?' the necromancer asked fearfully.

'I do not know,' the knight replied, drawing his sword back. 'Perhaps we all get what we believe in. Perhaps you will just simply cease, or perhaps your soul will be trapped in a limbo between realms. Or maybe there is a hell, and devils will rend your soul for all eternity.' Tybalt stepped to one side of the necromancer and braced his legs in the soft ground.

'You will know, sooner than I!' he cried, his sword arm bringing his blade swiftly across the necromancer's neck, sending the head tumbling into the overgrown grass.

As TYBALT RODE back along the single road of Moreux, a crowd of peasants began to gather around him. He must have been a fearsome sight, his armour scratched and bloody, his face a grim mask. Reaching the open space that served as town square, he halted his steed.

'Foul things have come to this land because we have allowed them to trespass,' he called to the assembled throng. 'We have forgotten that which should be remembered. Hear this, and heed it well. As a knight of Bretonnia, I command you all to send men to the graveyard along the pass, to clear away the ruin of centuries. It shall be your duty to see that it is maintained with dignity and pride. I lay this honour upon you. Do not fail in this task, for I shall return, and I shall demand to know who is responsible if my commands fall on deaf ears!'

As the peasants began to drift away, Tybalt turned to look back at the hill at the top of the pass. The sun was just now reaching over its crest, its golden light spilling down the slope and lending it a beauty it had not had in the dark mists of the night before. He wondered for a moment if the duke was still there looking down on him.

'Farewell, milord,' the knight said to himself. 'You have earned your rest.'

# WHO MOURNS
# A NECROMANCER?

## by Brian Craig

THE FUNERAL CART made its slow and steady way up the hill towards the Colaincourt Cemetery. The day was grey and overcast, and a cold wind blew from the east. The man who drove the cart and the companion who sat beside him both bore sullen scowls upon their faces, and the two dappled black mares which pulled it held their heads very low, as if they too had lost all enthusiasm for the work which was their lot. Behind the cart walked a solitary mourner, incongruous in his isolation.

The lone mourner was Alpheus Kalispera, High Priest of Verena and Magister of the University of Gisoreux. When he went about his normal business he commanded respect and was treated with due deference, but in his present role he drew hostile glances from all those who watched the cart go by. There were not many; although Lanfranc Chazal had been an important and well-respected man in his prime, that prime was now long past, and Chazal's reputation had been badly tarnished in his later years.

Kalispera walked rather painfully. He was old and his joints were very stiff. He kept his hands carefully within the

79

folds of his cloak, for the cold made his gnarled fingers ache terribly.

When the cemetery gates finally came into sight a company of small boys ran from one of the side-streets, hurling mud and stones at the coffin which rested on the cart, crying: 'Necromancer! Necromancer!'

Kalispera rounded on them, and would have spoken angrily, but they hared away as fast as their thin legs would carry them. To abuse an alleged necromancer was to them an act of great daring, even if the man be dead in his coffin, unable to answer the charge in any way at all.

A sallow-faced priest of Morr waited by a freshly-dug grave, quite alone. Even the sexton had taken care to absent himself from the ceremony of interment. Kalispera frowned – there should have been two priests, at least. He had been here many times before to see officers of the University laid to rest, and had been witness to occasions when scholars of far less status had been laid to rest by three officiating priests, attended by half a hundred mourners.

The magister took up a position opposite the priest, who stared at him while the two carriers manhandled the coffin down from the death-cart on to the ropes, then lowered it with indecent haste into the pit which had been made ready for it. It was all too obvious from the man's manner that the priest was here under protest, bound by the vows he had taken – which would not let him refuse to conduct a funeral service if he were so instructed. Kalispera felt the man's stare upon him, full of hostility, but he would not bow his head yet. Instead, he met the gaze as steadily as he could.

The priest took objection to this refusal to be ashamed. 'Who mourns a necromancer?' he asked bitterly. 'It would be best if I were left to do this sorry task alone.'

'I was his friend,' Kalispera said evenly. 'I had known him since childhood.'

'Such a man forsakes all claims of friendship and amity when he delves into forbidden lore,' the priest answered him. 'This man has sought to deal unnaturally with the dead, and should be shunned by the living – especially those who deem themselves priests of Verena.'

'He himself has joined the ranks of the dead now,' Kalispera observed, refusing to be stung by the insult. 'He is but a memory to the living and, of all the memories which I have of him, by far the greater number are happy ones. I have come to say farewell to a man I have known all my life, and I will not permit the fact that he has lately been abused by foolish and malicious men to prevent me from doing so.'

'But you have come alone,' the priest replied sourly, gesturing about him. 'It seems that all the others who knew him when they were young have a keener sense of duty to the cause of righteousness.'

Kalispera could not help but look around, though he did not expect to see any others hurrying to the place. He sighed, but very quietly, for he did not want the priest of Morr to know how disappointed he was. All but a few of the magisters of the university had known Lanfranc Chazal for many years, and had liked him well enough before the evil rumours had taken wing like a flock of Morr's dark ravens. He had thought that a few might be prepared to set aside the vilifications and accusations, for the sake of remembrance of better times. But the university was, as ever, a fever-pit of jealousies and intrigues, in which reputations were considered very precious things, not to be risked on such a chance as this.

Kalispera felt a moment of paradoxical gratitude for the fact that he was old and far beyond the calls of ambition. It was all too probable that the next Magister of Gisoreux to ride up the hill on the creaking death-cart would be himself.

'Please proceed,' he said to the priest. 'You will be glad to get it over, I know.'

The priest frowned again, but consented to let the magister have the last word. Sonorously, he began to intone the funeral rite, consigning the body of unlucky Lanfranc Chazal to the care of his stern master.

But Morr's officer was barely half way through the ceremony when there was a sudden clatter of hooves in the gateway of the cemetery, and though propriety demanded that neither of them should look up, both priest and magister glanced sideways with astonishment.

A huge bay, liberally flecked with sweat, was reined in not thirty feet from the grave. A man leapt down, patting the trembling horse upon the neck to offer thanks for its unusual effort – it was obvious that it had ridden far and fast. The newcomer was a man in his late twenties, plainly dressed, without livery or ornament – but he strode to the graveside with the pride and grace of an aristocrat. He favoured the priest with a single glance of haughty disapproval, but looked at Kalispera longer and far more respectfully. In fact, he nodded to the magister as if he knew him and expected to be recognised in turn, but Kalispera could not immediately put a name to the face.

*Who mourns a necromancer?* Kalispera thought, echoing the priest's words with a hint of ironic triumph. Two men at least, it seems, are not so cowardly that they dare not show their faces here. I thank you, young sir, with all my heart.

Before he bowed his head again, he favoured the younger man with a discreet smile. The priest of Morr saw, and disapproved, but there was nothing he could do save resume the ceremony with all due expedition.

As soon as it was all finished, though, the priest graced the newcomer with a scowl more hateful than any he had previously contrived. Then he hurried off, leaving the grave gaping like a fresh wound in the green hillside.

THE SEXTON, WHO must have been almost as old as Alpheus Kalispera, and every bit as feeble in wind and limb, shuffled from his hiding place to begin the work of filling in the grave.

The need for a respectfully bowed head now gone, Kalispera looked long and hard at the second mourner – and suddenly found the name which had momentarily eluded him. 'Cesar Barbier! As I live and breathe!' he said.

Barbier smiled, but thinly, as though he had not the heart for a proper greeting. 'Aye, Magister Kalispera,' he said. 'You did well to remember me at all, for it's a fair while since I was a student here – and I have not been in Gisoreux for some years, though I have not been far away.'

'In Oisillon, perhaps?' Kalispera said. 'I remember that we thought you destined to be a luminary of His Majesty's court.'

Now the magister had the name, the rest was not too hard to remember. The Barbiers were one of the great families of the region, more celebrated for breeding soldiers than scholars. But Cesar had been a clever student, more attentive than many to what his teachers had to tell him. Young men of his class came to the university primarily to sow their wild oats at a safe distance from home, and in truth Barbier had certainly done his share of that, but his interests had eventually extended at least a little beyond wine, women and the dance.

Barbier shook his head. 'I have been in Rondeau,' he said, naming a small town some miles to the south of the great city. Kalispera frowned, trying to remember whether Rondeau was part of the Barbier estate – and, for that matter, whether Cesar had yet succeeded to his father's title. A good Bretonnian was supposed to know such things, even if he were a high priest of Verena and a magister of a university, devoted by vocation to more permanent kinds of wisdom. Cesar Barbier certainly did not look like a Tilean nobleman, for he wore no powder and no wig, and his clothes were honest leather – but if he had come to Gisoreux on horseback he might easily have consigned his finery to a saddlebag.

'I am glad to see you here, my lord,' Kalispera said guardedly. He dared not ask whether Barbier had really come to Gisoreux simply to attend the funeral – or, if so, why.

Barbier gave another slight smile when he heard the magister call him 'my lord' – an appellation to which custom had not entitled him while he was a student. 'And I am glad to see you, sir,' he replied in turn, 'though I must confess to a little disappointment that I find you alone. I came as soon as I heard that Magister Chazal had died, but I fear that the news had made slow progress in arriving at Rondeau. Still, it seems that I came in time.'

As he spoke he looked at the ancient sexton, who was shovelling earth as fast as he possibly could, clearly no more anxious than any other to be too long in the company of a corpse of such evil repute.

'Aye,' Kalispera said, 'you came in time. But I doubt that you would have come at all, had rumour of Lanfranc's last years reached Rondeau before the news of his death. I am alone because no other would come. It has been rumoured of late that my friend was… was a necromancer, and I dare say that you know as well as any other what damage such rumours can do. I am glad to see you, as I said – but perhaps I should rather be sorry that you have taken the trouble, if you came in ignorance.'

'I did not come in ignorance, I assure you,' Barbier said solemnly. 'I came because I knew, far better than any other, what kind of man he really was.'

Kalispera felt tears rising to his eyes, and he bowed his head.

'Thank you for that,' he said.

'Oh no,' replied the other, reaching out to take the older and frailer man by the arm. 'It is for me to thank you on his behalf – for you stood by him when no one else would.'

They stood together, silently, for two or three minutes more. When the sexton was finished, Barbier gave him a suitable coin, which the old man accepted without any word or gesture of thanks.

'Is there somewhere we can go?' the young nobleman asked gently. 'I think we both stand in need of the warmth of a fire and a cup of good wine.'

'Of course,' Kalispera said quietly. 'I would be most honoured if you would be my guest, and would share with me in the remembrance of my friend.'

'I will do it gladly,' Barbier assured him. The two went down the hill together, quite oblivious to any inquisitive eyes which may have stared after them.

ALPHEUS KALISPERA TOOK Cesar Barbier to the room where he worked and taught. The sun had set by the time they arrived there, but the autumn twilight always lingered in the room, because its latticed window faced the south-west. Kalispera had always found it to be a good room for reading – and an excellent place for deeper contemplation.

At Barbier's request, Kalispera told him about the shadow which had been cast over Lanfranc Chazal during the last years of his tenure at the university.

'No charge was brought against him in any court, sacred or secular,' he was at pains to explain. 'He was condemned exclusively by scurrilous gossip and clandestine vilification. I have even heard it said that his death was a manifestation of the wrath of Verena, delayed for so long only because Verena was a calm and patient deity who loved her followers of wisdom just a little too well. That was terrible, truly terrible.

'Alas for poor Lanfranc, he had the misfortune to age less gracefully than he might, and he came to suffer from a certain disfiguration of the features which his enemies took to be evident proof of his dabbling with forbidden knowledge. One expects to hear such folderol from common peasants, of course, but I had thought better of Gisoreux and the university. If the men who call themselves the wisest in the world can so easily fall prey to such silly suspicions, what hope is there for the future of reason?

'Long before he was consigned to the grave where we saw him laid today, Lanfranc had begun to take on the appearance of a dead man, with whited skin and sunken eyes. I tried in vain to persuade our colleagues that it was merely an illness of old age, with no dire implication, but my ideas on the subject had always been considered unorthodox, and no one would listen to me. Even his friends were content to accept his disfigurement as evidence of a secret interest in the practice of necromancy. "All illness comes from the gods," they said, "and is sent to educate us." Lanfranc Chazal never believed any such thing, and neither do I, for we had seen too many sick men and women in our time. Alas, we were the only two remaining who remembered the great plague of forty years ago, and how dreadfully it used the magisters of the day. Now there is only me.'

Kalispera realized that his tone had become very bitter, and stopped in embarrassment. The twilight had faded while he spoke and the room was now as gloomy as his mood, so he covered his embarrassment by looking about for the tinderbox in order that he might light a candle. He had mislaid it, and was forced to get up in order to conduct a scrupulous search.

Cesar Barbier did not say anything to him while he searched for the box, found it and struck a light. But when the candle finally flared up, he saw that the younger man was watching him very quizzically from his place by the fireside.

Kalispera resumed his own seat, then smoothed his white beard with his right hand as if to settle himself completely. 'You are probably astonished to hear all this,' he said.

'On the contrary,' Barbier replied with a guarded look. 'There is nothing in it which is news to me, but I am glad to hear your account of it. He would have been very pleased and proud to know that his truest friend did not desert him, even at the end.'

'You knew!' Kalispera exclaimed. 'But you said that you have not been in Gisoreux for some time. How could you know about Lanfranc's illness, the changes in his appearance?'

'He visited me in Rondeau,' the young nobleman said. 'We have seen one another frequently over the years. I always regarded him as my mentor – he was ever the man to whom I turned for advice and help, and he never failed me. He told me more than once how grateful he was for your amity, and I know that it weighed upon his conscience that his claim upon your good opinion was not as honest as he would have wished.'

Alpheus Kalispera started in his seat and his eyes grew suddenly wide. 'What are you saying?' he cried, angrily. 'Do you mean to insult my grief?'

Barbier sat upright as well, but then leaned forward to reach out a soothing hand. 'No, magister!' he said. 'Anything but! Lanfranc Chazal was the best and noblest man I ever knew. I came here to share my grief, not to insult yours.'

Kalispera stared at him angrily for a moment, but then relaxed with a sigh. 'I do not know what you mean,' he said. 'Lanfranc said nothing to me about visiting you in Rondeau – nothing at all. And I cannot believe that he deceived me, even in a matter as small as that.'

'Alas, sir,' Barbier said, 'he did deceive you, even in matters much weightier. I can assure you, though, that it was not because he doubted you that he kept his darkest secrets from you, but only because he doubted himself.'

There was a long moment's silence before Kalispera said in a horrified whisper, 'Do you mean to tell me that Lanfranc Chazal *was* a necromancer, after all – and that you were party to his experiments?'

'That is what I mean to tell you,' the other confirmed, in a low voice. 'But I beg you not to condemn me – and certainly not to condemn Magister Chazal – until you have heard me out.'

Alpheus Kalispera felt that the features of his face were firmly set in a mask of pain, and that his heart was unnaturally heavy in his breast. Nevertheless, he made every effort to speak boldly. 'Explain yourself, my lord,' he said. Despite the title, it was the patronising command of the instructor, not the humble request of the commoner.

'I intend to explain, magister,' said the young man, quietly, 'and I beg you to forgive my clumsiness in going about it. You will remember, I am sure, that I was not the best of students. I was, after all, one of those sent by a pretentious father to acquire the merest veneer of culture and learning, not one intended to learn the skills of a scrivener or the training of a priest. I was something of a noble fool in my early days, and although Magister Chazal taught me in the end to be less of a fool than I was, still my wisdom is of a very narrow kind. Let me tell you my story in my own way, so that we may mourn together the passing of a great and generous man.'

Kalispera had to admit that this was a pretty speech, and he believed that he could hear within its phrases the influence of his friend Lanfranc Chazal. But there was another thought echoing its derision inside his head: *Who mourns a necromancer?*

Could it be, he wondered, that the world had been right after all, and he the lone fool?

'I am sorry, my lord,' he said, however, with honest but troubled humility. 'Please say what you have come to say. I will listen patiently.'

'Thank you, sir,' Cesar Barbier said, relaxing again in his turn. He paused for a moment, collecting his thoughts, and then he proceeded to tell his story.

'YOU KNOW MY name,' Barbier began, 'and I assume that you know whose son I am. Perhaps you remember my father from his own student days, when I am sure he impressed you with his command of those aristocratic virtues befitting a man whose service to our king has been of the military kind. He is now as he undoubtedly was then: bold in word and deed, with a will and stomach of iron. Neither wine nor passion has the power to disturb his firmness of mind, and I dare say that you found his head quite impregnable to wisdom or sophistication.

'When I first became a student here I set out to do my best to be like my father, and I think that for a while I succeeded well enough to convince almost everyone that I was a perfect example of that kind, save only for Magister Chazal. He saw through my facade of reckless intolerance to the, well, the gentler soul within. He knew what a creature of dishonesty I was, and helped me to use my years here to become a better man.

'In public he never gave evidence by word or gesture that he knew what a poseur I was, but in private he talked to me in a different way. He taught me to trust him, and be honest in what I said to him. With him and him alone I was my true self: full of doubt, full of passion and tender of sentiment – all traits which my father despised, and despises still. Magister Chazal never advised me to break down my public pretence, but was content to give me an opportunity to lay it aside. I cannot tell you how much it meant to me to have that relief.

'When the time came for me to leave Gisoreux and take up the business of accepting the responsibilities of my position, I quickly began to use the gift of lettering – which was one of the valuable things which I had learned within these walls – in the writing of letters to Magister Chazal. I was his guest here in Gisoreux on numerous occasions. He was the one and only person to whom I confided my true feelings, and by degrees I won his confidence too, so that he began to say to me those things which he dared not say to people of his own kind.

'It was from Magister Chazal that I learned about your beliefs, Magister Kalispera. He told me that you had drawn conclusions about the nature of disease which were, if not openly heretical, at least unorthodox. He told me about your sceptical attitude to the medicines and treatments established by custom. He told me too about your insistence that disease and suffering make no discrimination between the guilty and the innocent, and are far less often the result of magic or divine intervention than we are prone to believe. He respected you for holding those beliefs, and for setting what you believed to be the truth over the advantages to be gained by conformity. He thought that you might respect his own opinions, but hesitated to burden you with any more unorthodoxy than you had already accepted.'

Alpheus Kalispera had begun to see where this account was leading, but he kept silent while Barbier paused, and looked at him very gravely.

'It is the common belief,' the younger man continued, 'that any magic but the pettiest is inherently good or evil. Any magic which involves trafficking with the dead or the undead is held to be supremely wicked. Magister Chazal was prepared to doubt that. His view was that although any knowledge might be used for evil ends by evil men, knowledge as such is always good. Ignorance, he used to say, is the greatest evil of all.'

Kalispera nodded his head then, for he had certainly heard Chazal say that on many an occasion.

'For that reason,' Barbier went on, 'Magister Chazal had studied the arcane language of necromancy and had read books written in that language. His intention in so doing was not to become a master of necromantic magic, but to learn more about the mysteries of death – to enhance his understanding. He was not a man to play with the conjuration of ghosts or the reanimation of corpses; for him, the written word was enough. He valued enlightenment far more than power.

'The story of these researches he confided to me by degrees, over a period of more than a year. In return, I talked to him about my own very different problems, which arose from friction between myself and my father as to the managements of our estates and our lives.

'I found myself in disagreement with my father on many matters of principle – on the matter of the unhappiness which he caused my mother and my sisters, for instance, and on the matter of the relentless tyranny which he exerted over his tenants and his bondsmen. But I could not successfully oppose him because I was still forced by convention and circumstance to pretend to be like him. I had begun to hate my father, and in so doing had begun to hate myself too, for being so obviously his son.

'Then, quite out of the blue, disaster struck me. I fell in love.

'Love was not a factor in my father's calculations of advantage, and he had already contracted marriages for my two sisters on the basis of his commercial interests. It would have been bad enough had I fallen in love with a woman of my own class, had it not been the one which he considered most useful to the family interest, but in fact I fell in love with a commoner, who was very beautiful but of no account whatsoever in my father's scheme of things.

'To my father, the very idea of love is bizarre. He has not an atom of affection in his being. I, by virtue of some silly jest of the gods who determine such things, am very differently made, and my honest passion for the girl – whose name was Siri – was quite boundless. I could not envision life without her, and life itself came to depend in my estimation upon my possession of her. By possession I do not mean mere physical possession – my father would have raised no word of objection had I been able simply to rape and then discard the girl – but authentic union. That, of course, my father would never tolerate, and yet it was what I had to have.

'When I said all this to Magister Chazal, he did not presume to tell me what to do, but he gave me every assistance in dissolving my confusion and seeing clearly what kind of choice I had to make. He helped me to understand that the time had come when I must either break completely with my father or utterly destroy the secret self which I had so carefully preserved for many years. I could not cut out and burn my own heart. And so I eloped and married Siri in secret, resolving never to see my father again.

'I anticipated that my father would disown me and forbid my name ever to be mentioned again in his house or his estates. That was what I expected, and was prepared to accept. But I had underestimated him. Perhaps it would have been different had he had another heir to put in my place, but I had no brother and nor had he. He could not face the thought of allowing his lands and his titles to become subservient to another name in being diverted to one of my sisters.

'He sent his servants to search me out, and then to bring me home by force, my… my young wife with me.'

* * *

CESAR BARBIER PAUSED again in his account – but not, this time, to measure the attitude of his listener. Until now he had been quite calm and very scrupulous in his speech, as befitted a nobleman of Bretonnia, but now his breathing was clotted by emotion, and there were tears in his eyes: tears of anguish, and of rage.

When it seemed that the young noble could not go on, Alpheus Kalispera said, very quietly: 'He had her killed?'

'Had her killed?' answered Barbier, as though the words had been forced out of him with a hot iron. 'Oh no, he did not have her killed! You do not know what manner of man my father is! He killed her with his own hands, while his servants forced me to watch.

'He destroyed her, and the unborn child she carried within her, without any trace of feeling – not because he hated her, but simply because she stood in the way of his calculations. He felt no guilt, nor any fear of retribution. Had she killed him it would have been a fearful crime, for which she would have been burned alive as a petty traitor, but for him to kill her was merely a matter of business, for her father was his bondsman, and she an item of inconvenient property. I saw her die, Magister Kalispera – I saw her *die!*'

Kalispera did not know what to say. He could not imagine that Lanfranc Chazal had known what to say, when the poor man had run to him with the same dreadful tale, four or five years earlier.

'I wanted to kill him,' Cesar Barbier said, when he was capable of continuing his tale. 'And the folly of it all is that if I had been what he wanted me to be, I would have killed him. With a sword or a cudgel or a poisoned cup I would have snuffed out his vile existence, and sent our title to oblivion by surrendering myself to the law and going gladly to the gallows. If his way had been the right way, I would have taken my revenge, and happily so.

'Perhaps I would have done it, had it not been for Magister Chazal – for he it was who persuaded me that I must not waste my own being in destroying my father's, on the two accounts that it would be both futile and false to my own true nature. He implored me to find a better way – and in my turn, I implored him to show me one.'

*Lords of Valour*

Kalispera drew in his breath, deeply and painfully. It was all too obvious to him what the result of this mutual imploring must have been. Barbier saw that he had guessed.

'Will you tell me that it was unlawful?' said the young man angrily. 'Will you tell me that it was lawful and just for my father to murder my wife and unborn child because they did not suit him, and a horrid crime to undo the act, as far it could be undone? Will you tell me that Magister Chazal was evil, and my father's soul quite stainless? Tell me then, Magister Kalispera. Tell me, in so many words, where the right of it lies.'

Kalispera shook his head. The darkness in the corners of the room seemed to close in around them. 'Tell me,' he countered in a steely voice, 'what it was that Lanfranc did, and what its consequence has been.'

'I had not dared to bring the body of my wife into the precincts of the university,' Barbier said, 'nor even through the gates of Gisoreux. I had taken her instead to the house in Rondeau which I had bought, intending that we should live there when we returned from the Empire – for we did not expect to spend our whole lives in exile from our homeland. Magister Chazal accompanied me there and begun his work.

'He had told me that he could not bring my Siri back to life, for if such a thing could be done at all it was beyond his skill. He could not restore her flesh to me, but her spirit was a different matter; he believed that he had knowledge enough to bring back her ghost from the realm of the dead, and protect it from the dissolution which ordinarily overtakes such beings.

'Spectres, he told me, are often bound to our world in consequence of curses, doomed to haunt the spot where they died. What he intended to do was to summon Siri as a ghost, and ask her whether she would be bound of her own free will, not to the place where she had died but to the place where she had hoped to live. If she consented, he said, then he would try to bind her to the house in Rondeau.

'He was not sure that he had knowledge enough to accomplish more, but he promised that he would try firstly to give her a voice that she might speak to me, and secondly to allow her to take on at intervals a certain frail substance which

would allow us to touch. For this latter purpose he required
to combine together something of her substance and something of mine, and I allowed him to remove from my left
hand that finger upon which I had placed my wedding ring.'

Barbier held up his left hand, and Kalispera saw for the first
time that the finger next to the smallest had been neatly cut
away.

'He bound that finger to hers before we laid her in a tomb
beneath the house,' continued Barbier, his voice hushed. 'And
he used my blood to write the symbols which he used in his
conjuration. When I first saw her ghost I was overtaken by
such a terror that I nearly cried out to him to stop, to send her
back where she belonged, but I bit my tongue. And when he
asked her whether she would rather go to her appointed
place, or be bound to this world with me, I felt a tremendous
surge of joy which overwhelmed my terror on the instant –
for her answer was yes.

'Her answer was *yes*.

'I could not tell what powers Magister Chazal drew upon in
order to complete what he had begun. I know that he sacrificed more than I, for I only lost a finger and a little blood,
while he seemed to draw upon his own inner life and
strength in such a way as to leave them forever depleted.

'What words he spoke, or what dark daemons may have
moved to do his bidding, I cannot begin to understand. But
his work was successful, and the ghost of my wife now lives
in my house, carrying within her the ghost of my unborn
child. And whenever Morrslieb is at its brightest in the night
sky, she takes on substance sufficient to allow her to caress
me, and receive caresses in return.'

ALPHEUS KALISPERA BOWED his head slightly, and said: 'I had
thought the change in him was the effect of an affliction
which he had in no way invited. I was sure of it.'

'And are you sure now that it was not?' Barbier demanded,
with sudden passion. 'Are you so certain, now that you know
what you had not guessed before, that he was marked by the
evil of his deeds? I tell you that he worked no evil, but exer-
cised his knowledge only to help his friend. If it was
judgment on his necromancy which engraved the death-mask

on his features, then it was a cruel and stupid judgment, for he did not deserve it. If there was a debt to be paid, then I should have paid it, and would have done so willingly!

'Have you no faith in your own beliefs, that you would lose them now because of what I have told you? If that is so, I cry shame on you, Magister Kalispera! The man you saw buried today was a man as good as any in the world, and whatever disfigured him was no fault of his, but an undeserved misfortune.'

Kalispera laid his head back and stared off into infinity, before he finally said: 'I do not know what to believe.'

Barbier rose to his feet and looked down at the older man. 'You had best make up your mind,' he said harshly. 'If you will not understand, you must at least keep silent about what I have told you.'

The magister met his visitor's gaze then, and felt a slight shock of fear – but then he remembered that this had once been his pupil, and Lanfranc's friend, and that there was no need to be afraid of him.

'Sit down, my lord,' he said tiredly. 'This is no one's business but our own. I would not denounce you for what you have done, nor would I ever have denounced my friend for helping you. But I cannot say that it was a good thing to do, for it is the most unnatural thing of which I have ever heard.'

Barbier took his seat again, but did not relax. 'Oh yes!' he said. 'Unnatural, to be sure. When a father is utterly without love or compassion – that is natural! When a father murders his son's innocent bride – that is natural! But when a son opposes his father's will and undoes his father's evil – why, that is surely repulsive in its defiance of the laws which the gods have made!

'Tell me, my white-haired philosopher, is it natural for the fops and philanderers of our good King's court to parade themselves in silk and velvet? Is it natural that they should live in gaudy luxury while the peasants who work the soil to produce their wealth go hungry? Are their measured dances natural, or the games which they play with quoits and skittles? Are their manners and hypocrisies natural – or are these noblemen natural only when they ache and bleed like common folk?

'Instruct me, magister, I implore you. Tell me, I pray, why men like you and I should respect and revere what is natural, when everything we are and do is artifice? Your own belief is that disease and illness are but natural shocks to which our fragile flesh is heir, not supernatural punishments sent by the gods or inflicted by the ill-wishing of witches. Lanfranc Chazal's belief was that knowledge of life and death is only knowledge of nature, and that magic is merely control of nature, like other arts and crafts. You could not see a differ-ence between yourself and your lifelong friend this morning – can you really see one now?'

For fully half a minute, Kalispera did not reply. And when he did, it was not with an answer but with a question. 'What will happen,' he asked, 'when you die in your turn, and go to the realm of the dead?'

Barbier laughed, very briefly. 'I cannot tell,' he said. 'If I have the power to curse myself to be a spectre, then I will exert that power with my dying breath, and will be all the closer to my love for sharing her insubstantiality whenever Morrslieb is pale in the sky. And if I have not... then I must wait for her release, as she would have waited for mine, had I not found a necromancer to cast off the chains of nature!'

'And what if you fall in love again?' said the magister, in a low whisper. 'What if you should one day hope for a better child than the ghost of one unborn?'

Barbier shook his head as though to rule the questions impertinent, but Kalispera could see that the man was not untroubled by them. He was a man, after all, and he knew that love is not always eternal, nor the call of duty entirely impotent.

'What will happen when your father dies?' Kalispera said, speaking now as the High Priest of Verena which he also was. 'Will you inherit his title and his estate? And if you do, will you be content to stay in Rondeau, or will you want to show the world how a demesne's affairs could be managed by a better man than your father was? Ten years have passed since you came here as a student, I think, fully seven of them since you left these cloisters – but what did you truly learn, in the three years or the seven, which makes you sure that you are finished and complete, as changeless as your love-deluded

wife? What right did you really have to demand of Lanfranc
Chazal that which he did for you?'

Barbier was confused now, and taken aback. Whatever he
had expected of the old magister, it was not this. 'He was my
friend,' he said. 'And a far better father to me than my own
parent ever was.'

'Aye,' Kalispera said sadly, 'no doubt that was what he
wanted to be. He was my friend, too, but I did not need him
as a father. When you combined your catalogue of challenges,
you might have asked whether it is natural for priests and
magisters to be celibate, so that the only sons they have are
those of other men.'

The younger man said nothing.

'Do you love your ghostly wife?' Kalispera asked abruptly.

'I do,' said Barbier boldly. 'With all my heart.'

'And do you think that you can love her forever?'

'I do.'

Alpheus Kalispera shrugged his shoulders, and said: 'Let us
hope that your boldness will not let you down, and that your
heart is as constant as your father's, after its own very different fashion.'

Barbier bowed his head, and said: 'Thank you for that, magister.' Then he looked up again, and said: 'I hope that you will
not think any worse of your friend, because of what I have
told you. I did not mean to injure him in your estimation.'

'You have not done that,' Kalispera assured him. 'And I am
grateful to know that I am not the only man who will mourn
him. If the only epitaph he will have is that which is graven
in the memories of other men, I am glad that there are two of
us to share the burden of the truth.'

'So am I,' Cesar Barbier said. 'So am I.'

Kalispera got up from his seat and went to the window. He
unlatched the glazed lattice, and pushed it back to let in the
cool night air. It was not so very dark, for Mannslieb was full
and Morrslieb, though by no means at its brightest, was shining from another sector of the vault of heaven. The stars, as
always, were too many to be counted. The streets of the city
were lit by tiny flames which were similarly numberless, for
in a city as munificent as Gisoreux even the poor could afford
candles to keep the dark at bay.

'Where is his spirit, do you think?' he asked of the younger man.

'Close at hand,' said Barbier softly, 'or far away. Does it matter which?'

'It is said that the spirit of a necromancer is bound to its rotting hull,' the magister said. 'It is said that such a spirit cannot escape from the hell of that decay, but can sometimes animate the body as a liche with glowing eyes, which spreads terror wherever it goes, and leaves suffering in its train.'

'Do you think that he feared such an end?' Barbier asked, with such faint anxiety that it seemed a mere politeness.

'No man truly knows what he has to fear when he dies,' Kalispera replied. 'Even a man like you, who has brought another back from the life beyond life. No man truly knows.'

Alpheus Kalispera looked at his hands, then. They were gnarled and stiff, and the pain in their swollen joints gave him little rest nowadays. Might it reduce his pain, he wondered, to cut off those fingers which he did not really need? Or was the pain a divine punishment after all, and not – as he had always believed – a mere accident of happenstance?

He had, after all, given succour and sustenance to a secret necromancer!

'He was a good man,' Kalispera murmured, not for the first time. 'He was a good friend.'

'In truth he was,' Cesar Barbier said.

And though neither man could know the other's thoughts, both shared at that particular moment in time an identical hope. Each of them was praying, silently and fervently, that whatever god or daemon now had charge of the spirit of Lanfranc Chazal would hear their words, and echo their merciful disposition.

# SON AND HEIR
## by Ian Winterton

'BY THE GRACE of the Lady!' The Grail Knight's voice echoed throughout the forest clearing. The heads of the four beast-men at the entrance to the shrine turned to look at him, claws reaching for weapons. Drawing his own blade, Sir Gilles Ettringer, Knight of the Grail and champion of Baron Gregory de Chambourt, spurred his steed towards the hated abominations.

How dare they tread upon this holy place?

Though righteous anger burned in his heart, he did not let it consume nor cloud his mind, for he was a loyal servant of the Lady of the Lake. Nourished by the water of the holy chalice, his soul was as strong and sure as the steel in his mailed hand. These defilers would pay dearly for their trespass.

The first was dispatched before it even had chance to bring its sword to bear. The second's head, that of a half-starved dog, flew from its shoulders, crashing into the undergrowth.

A goat-headed enemy came at him from the side, baring foam-flecked teeth, scrawny arm preparing to throw a crude spear. Sir Gilles tugged sharply at the reins, sinking his spurs deep into his mount, and manoeuvred it round. The warhorse, rocking forward onto sturdy forelegs, kicked sharply backwards, its iron-clad hooves snapping the beast-man's neck.

A spiked mace was swung vainly. Sir Gilles brought his shield up, absorbing the blow, then flicked his blade deftly out, its point sinking for a fatal second into the breast of his final foe.

Hardly out of breath, Sir Gilles surveyed the carnage he had wrought. The only sound was the pounding of his horse's hooves as it pawed the blood-soaked ground.

Darkness came prematurely to this part of the forest, the sun blocked out by the plateau that was Sir Gilles's home. Though the base of the Chambourt was only an hour's ride distant, to be alone in the forest at this time was far from desirable, even for a warrior of his stature.

Before he could resume his journey, there was something he had to be sure of.

Armour clanking, Sir Gilles dismounted. He raised the visor on his helm, revealing the face of a middle-aged man, lined and white-whiskered. He walked towards the entrance of the shrine and knew immediately that his task was not yet over.

From inside he could hear the buzzing of flies.

LYING AT THE heart of Bretonnia, the Chambourt was a vast shelf nestling in the foothills of the Orcal Massif, thrusting high above the crag-filled oaks of the Forest of Charons.

From the window of his chamber, the baron gazed out at his realm with a contented heart. Set against the monotonous, cloud-wisped expanse of the forest, the Chambourt glowed beneath the last rays of the setting sun. Squares of corn caught the fading sunlight, intersected with pasture, dotted with healthy cattle. Irrigated orchards flanked the river that flowed down from the snow-capped peaks of the Massif, cutting a life-giving path through the land.

There was a light knock at the door.

'Enter,' the baron said, turning from the window.

Pagnol, his ageing manservant, shuffled into the room, gaze respectfully averted. The baron shuttered the window.

'The banquet hall is prepared, my liege,' said the old man. 'We wait only for your presence.'

'Any word from Sir Gilles?'

'No, my lord. He has not yet returned.'

Taking a robe from his bed, the baron fastened it at his shoulder and stepped towards the doorway, held open by the faithful Pagnol. 'No matter. It is not to be helped.'

At twenty-five the baron was entering the fifth year of his rule. A robust warrior, he was much loved by the people, like his father before him. The year had also seen a record harvest, the best the old farmers said, since they were but boys. The barrels were full of new wine, and along the river the mills ground a ceaseless supply of wheat into flour. Baskets seemingly overflowing with fruit could be seen stacked on every doorstep or rattling to market on the back of wagons.

The baron was overjoyed with his realm. Everything seemed vital and alive, imbued with an astonishing fertility. This, it transpired, included his young wife, the Lady Isobella. A pleasingly attractive princess of the Estalian nobility, she was about to give birth to their first child.

Her labour pains had started that morning. Ensconcing her in a specially constructed birthing chamber, the midwifes attended to her while the priests prayed to the Lady of the Lake for the baby to be born healthy, untainted and, most importantly, male. The baron, as was the tradition, was to spend the time in the banqueting hall. It was a shame that his old friend, Sir Gilles, would not be present. Still, with a wench on each arm and a never-ending supply of wine, the baron felt sure the birth would be over in no time.

ELSEWHERE, THE SEEDS of the baron's undoing were not only sown, but had taken root.

The baron had a sister, ten years his junior. Named Juliette, she was of the same healthy stock as he, though born of a different mother. It was universally agreed by approving men and envious women that she was possessed of great beauty. Always immaculately attired in gowns of flowing silk, she was elegant, demure and slim of waist. Her pale face was delicately featured, painted at the lips and eyes like the finest of masques. With her modest and chaste nature, she was the

model of obedient womanhood, sought after by every
unmarried nobleman in Bretonnia and beyond.

The baron forbade her to attend banquets, for fear that the
sight of such debauchery and routine debasement would
corrupt her valuable innocence. Some would say later that
this was not a little ironic. Counting Juliette amongst his
many blessings, the baron looked forward to the day of her
marriage and the excellent alliance it would surely cement.

He could not have known then that his sister was already
wed.


ABOVE THE DRONE of the flies there was a chanting: clipped,
harsh syllables, of no language Sir Gilles understood, but
they possessed a rhythm he recognised, a dread cadence that
pierced him to his heart with its evil intent.

The entrance gave way to a wide corridor that led in turn
to the main chapel. Within, the knight could see insubstantial shadows, cast by candlelight, slowly writhing. A stench
assailed his nostrils, the scent of damp and decay and aban-
donment. For how long had these fiends been desecrating
this holy place? So close to the Chambourt itself, it was not
often used by travellers and pilgrims. He himself, amongst
the most pious, had not ventured this way in over a year.
However long it had been, it would end today.

Shield up, sword at the ready, Sir Gilles stepped into the
chapel.

Dead animals. Rats, goats, dogs, sheep, all in varying stages
of decomposition, piled high around the room. Dead
priests, male and female, lay among them, some not long
dead, others grey and rotting. The abominable centre-piece
of the sculpture was the lone priestess of the chapel. A thin,
middle-aged woman, her body hung by the neck from a rope
fastened to one of the roof-beams. Stripped of her robes, the
skin had been flayed from her bones, stopping only at the
ligature that bit tightly into the skin beneath her chin. A gaping expression of pure terror was stamped on her ashen face.
From the glistening blood on her muscle tissue, Sir Gilles
guessed that she had been the last to die.

Standing beside her, stroking the priestess's cheek in a
mockery of affection, was a man.

A solid block of muscle, he was naked, blasphemous symbols daubed in blood on his body. Long, jet-black hair flowed over his taut shoulders. Eyes lightly closed, he continued to murmur foul homage to his Dark Gods. A blood-soaked, cruelly curved dagger lay at his feet.

With a cry, Sir Gilles launched himself at the fiend.

Eyes snapping open, the man moved with unnatural speed.

Sir Gilles found his blade biting into the marble floor. Recovering his balance, he turned to face his foe.

The man, if man he truly was, was standing a little way off, close to the rotting carcasses, rocking from side to side on the balls of his feet like a wrestler preparing to fight. He made no attempt to reach for the dagger. His dark eyes flashed with venom. An amused smile played on his lips.

Cautiously, Sir Gilles squared up to the man. He was naked, unarmed and yet seemed more sure of himself than any opponent he had ever faced. Was it madness that produced such self-belief, or something else?

Sir Gilles brought his sword back, then struck, this time anticipating the man's agile dodge. The blade hit the man on the side just above his top rib, cutting him open.

Clutching his wound, blood bubbling up between his fingers, the man staggered, knocked against the priestess, setting her gently swinging, and fell on his side. As blood pumped out of him, he started laughing gently, as though the blow had but tickled him.

Kicking the dagger safely out of reach, Sir Gilles moved in to settle the matter. Something leapt at him from behind. From the shrill screams, he could tell that his assailant was a woman. She was unarmed, also, and wearing only a thin cotton robe. She clung with one hand to Sir Gilles's back, while trying to claw at his face with the other. He shifted his weight and effortlessly threw her over him. She smacked against the hard floor, a bone in her leg snapping.

She lay groaning, twisting in anguish on the floor. Nearby, her companion was still shaking with mirth. His wound, Sir Gilles noted with concern, no longer bled and was healing up. This man was well protected by his foul gods. The fire would be the only sure way of ending his evil.

Working quickly, afraid that his quarry would soon recover, Sir Gilles set about tying him up, so as to deliver him to the baron. Considering her of little threat, he did not pay the woman much attention. She continued to squirm in pain, moaning softly.

'Make it stop, make it stop…'

The voice. The voice seemed familiar. Pulling the last of the knots tight, Sir Gilles stood up and crossed the chamber. He knelt by the woman, brushed the hair from her face and lifted her head up.

The old knight caught his breath and whispered a prayer on the holy chalice.

Staring at him with hatred and a snarl on her fair lips, was the Lady Juliette.

LEAVING HIS TWO prisoners with the castle's militia, Sir Gilles strode into the banqueting hall. A grave expression on his face, his tabard flecked with the blood of beastmen, revellers heads turned to stare at him as he walked the length of the table. By the time he had reached the baron all merry-making and conversation had ceased.

'If I may speak with you, my lord…'

FULL OF WINE, the baron refused to believe the knight at first. 'My sister sleeps in her room,' he guffawed. 'As she has done every night.'

Sir Gilles laid a hand on his master's shoulder.

'Not every night, I fear,' he said.

The baron understood the situation soon enough when he was shown to the cell holding his sister. She was huddled in the corner of the room, broken leg lying at an unnatural angle, hateful eyes shining from the gloom. When the baron approached, she hissed and spat like a cat.

'Show me the fiend responsible for this outrage,' the baron said, his voice shaking with anger. 'And I will have his head.'

THE DARK-HAIRED man was altogether calmer than his bride. Clothed now in sack-cloth, he sat against the wall of his cell, a serene smile on his lips. Flanked by crossbow-wielding guards, the baron confronted him.

'What manner of daemon are you?'

'None, sir.' The man spoke in a deep, steady voice. 'I am a man like yourself.'

'That I doubt. From where do you hail, witch?'

The man gave a vague wave of his hand.

A headache banging behind his eyeballs from the wine, the baron massaged his temples with one hand. 'Do you, then, have a name?'

The man gave no answer.

The baron was not one to pander to such games. 'No matter,' he said, coldly. 'My torturers will have it from you before long. And after that, you will burn.'

THE WITCH FINDERS set about their task with consummate zeal and efficiency. When the stranger was next brought before the baron, his body was broken, if not his spirit. His long hair had been shaved down to the scalp with a blunt knife. Dried blood congealed over his face and ears. He was missing his top row of teeth. His back flapped open, raw from flogging. But, like the wound in his side, of which no sign remained, the man's body appeared to be healing rapidly. Of small consolation to the baron were the two fingers that the shears had taken. Although hours had passed, they remained stubborn stumps. So he could be hurt. He would be hurt.

The baron, gazing levelly from his throne at the wretched sight before him, ordered the two guards holding the man by his arms to relinquish their grip. The witch did not topple forward as expected, but stood, swaying, his eyes regarding his tormentor defiantly. He spoke mockingly in a clear voice.

'Sir, I feel I must thank you. The pain your lackeys have inflicted upon me is but a small price to pay for the months of nocturnal pleasure your sister has bestowed upon me.'

The baron leapt from his seat, half jumped down the steps and struck the witch across his face, hard with his gauntleted hand. The man staggered back, laughing, fresh blood pouring from a cut over his eye.

'I would kill you here with my bare hands,' bellowed the baron, 'if the law did not demand that you, like all your diseased kind, should be put to the fire.'

'Oh, sir, sir...' the witch cooed. 'Rest assured I will not burn. My master's game will not allow it. I am to be the bane of your life. You do not even begin to comprehend the horror of which I am capable.'

The baron found himself unable to look for long upon the man's face, lest he catch sight of himself in eyes as jet-black and soulless as a viper's.

The witch cupped his hand to his ear as though listening for something. A childish grin spread across his face. 'Oh, sir. I believe congratulations are in order. You are a father at last. And it is a boy.'

In the wake of the terrible events, the baron had forgotten about his wife's confinement. Before he could react, a lad, son to one of the midwives, came scampering into the throne-room. He gave a hurried, unpractised bow and said, excitably, 'My lord, my mother bids me come tell you the glad tidings: that my lady has been delivered of a son.'

Ordering the guards to clamp themselves back onto the prisoner, the baron strode towards the door. Struggling against his captors, the witch started to laugh once again.

'Baron! Hear me!' he screamed. 'By the Dark Gods I lay a curse upon your house! I will take everything from you, in time. First, though: your wife!'

The baron started to run.

'Go!' the witch shouted after him. 'But you are too late. My master's work is already done.'

THE MIDWIVES AND servant-girls crowded round the newborn, cooing in adoration. None of them thought to check on the baroness.

The baron burst into the chamber.

Responding to his presence by casting their eyes to the floor, the women curtsied and murmured respectfully.

Rushing to his wife's side, the baron took her hand in his. Her head turned slowly to face him. Though drawn and tired from her ordeal, she wore a contented smile.

It was then that he noticed the blood at the corner of her mouth. It trickled out, a small amount at first, but grew steadily. The baroness appeared not to notice, but continued to stare beatifically at her husband.

'Help her,' he said, unable to raise his voice above a hiss. The servant-girls looked up. 'Help her.'

Her head fell onto one side, a dead weight. Blood seeped slowly out, soaking into the pillow and onto the sheet. Her body went limp. But for the soft whimpering from the servant-girls, there was no noise.

The baron freed his hand from his wife's lifeless fingers. Numb and shaking, he crossed the room and picked up the child. He held it to his breast. A boy, thanks be to the Lady. A son. An *heir*.

THE BARON WENT immediately from the chamber, channelling his grief into thunderous anger. In the cell, he rained blow after blow against the witch's body. Throughout it all, the fiend made no sound.

At last, breathing hard, exhausted, his knuckles scuffed and bleeding, the baron stopped.

The witch sat up, as though refreshed, one eye completely closed with bruising.

'You have a healthy son, my lord,' he said. 'Such a shame that his life will be so short.'

Powered by grief and fear, the baron launched himself again at the witch, pinning him to the wall by the throat.

'You will speak no more!'

From his belt he took a dagger and, forcing the witch's jaws apart, worked his way inside the mouth, cut and carved for a second, then stepped back.

The witch slumped against the wall, blood cascading from his mouth. His face was slack but his eyes still shone with mirth and malice.

WHILE THESE EVENTS had been unfolding, a crowd of the kingdom's finest scholars had been gathered about the Lady Juliette. By now almost mad with grief, the baron received their report in a state of great agitation.

'How fares my sister?'

All reluctant to speak, Blampel the beak-nosed physician was nudged forward. One hand adjusting his skull-cap, he muttered a curse intended for his craven colleagues.

'I fear the news is not good, my lord,' he said at last.

The baron nodded at him to elaborate.

'The lady has lost her mind. Human speech and reasoning are beyond her. Never before have I seen madness consume a person so swiftly.'

Stroking his neatly-trimmed beard with a hand still spattered with the witch's dried blood, the baron said, 'And what of her dabbling in witchcraft? Is she an innocent party or am I to put my own flesh and blood to the flame?' He looked across. 'Tertullion?'

The portly mage, who had been hiding at the back of the group, guzzling from a wineskin left over from the banquet, shuffled drunkenly forward. He dabbed at his food-encrusted whiskers and steadied himself against a pillar. 'My lord. As my friend, the learned man of medicine, has already rightly diagnosed, the Lady Juliette is quite insane. I am of the opinion that because of this, her innocence or otherwise in this matter is now an irrelevance. Any of the Dark Ways that may have been imparted to her by her foul consort are now surely lost, along with the rest of her humanity.'

This was typical of Tertullion. Long-winded, wordy. And wrong.

For come the dawn, the guards found within the cell, not the witch but the Lady Juliette, her state of mind greatly improved. Somehow fully clothed, she stood holding the trail of her silken dress up, so as to avoid the filth of the floor. Giggling like a young girl, she uttered a single dark word.

Two of the guards fell, screaming, to their knees, eyeballs liquefying, bubbling from the sockets. The third guard, swinging blindly with terror, lopped her head neatly from her body. Escaping from her neck with a hiss like steam, blood sprayed the dirty walls and showered the straw-strewn floor.

Blinking blood out of his eyes, the petrified guard stared at the crumpled body before him as it twitched its last. Juliette's head lay at an angle, partly obscured by the straw, her fine, dark hair framing an expression of surprise.

The witch, her master, was not to be seen for many years.

* * *

THOUGH HE WAS born into a house of sorrow, the baron's son, also named Gregory as had been the custom for the first-born son for ten generations, grew into a healthy and well-adjusted boy. His father put at his disposal the finest academics. He soon became the first male member of the line who could read and write, and in several languages, too. But it soon became apparent that the warrior-blood burned brightly within. As adolescence approached, it was to jousts and sword-play that he turned. Even the books he read were tomes dealing with tactics and warfare.

Eager to encourage this aspect of his son's life, the baron put him under the tutelage of Sir Gilles. Though already into his fourth decade at the boy's birth, his sword skills knew no equal and, in the trials, he could still keep several far younger opponents at bay. But it was his tales that made Gregory love him.

Gilles's questing had taken him all over the Old World and beyond. He had fought alongside dwarfs against orcs and goblins in the World's Edge Mountains, done battle with Sartosan pirates, slaughtered beastmen and mutants within the forests, even driven a skaven horde back into the heart of its foul subterranean nest. Every time Gilles spoke of these adventures, Gregory's face lit up in rapt attention.

Shortly before his twelfth birthday, he asked Gilles why he was not allowed to leave the castle.

'That is your father's decision,' Gilles said in his soothing, deep voice. 'And you would do better not to question it.'

But something in the Grail Knight's pale, blue eyes, told the young heir to do exactly the opposite.

'YOU HAVE BEEN filling his head with your tales!' the baron roared. Gilles, kneeling before the throne on the flagstones, lifted his bowed head.

'I meant no harm by it, my liege.'

The baron, about to shout again, felt suddenly foolish. He put one hand against the side of his head, where the hair had already grown prematurely grey.

'Get up, old friend,' the baron said, sadly. 'I am sorry.'

Gilles got to his feet and looked his master steadily in the eyes. 'No apologies are necessary,' he said. 'But I must ask you why you are so opposed to your son's request?'

'Because I will not allow him to leave this castle,' said the baron. 'And this hunting party he craves? Into the forest? No.' He sighed wearily, adding, 'It is for his own protection.'

'That is as maybe,' Gilles said. 'But do you not think it more dangerous to cosset the boy, to leave him ill-prepared for the dangers he may face?'

'I have made my decision,' the baron rumbled.

THE HUNTING PARTY took place a week later, on the occasion of Gregory's birthday. Though he had relented, the baron was leaving nothing to chance. A retinue of men-at-arms and bowmen, as well as Gilles and his company of knights and squires, all accompanied the noblemen down into the forest. Also, for his magical abilities only, the old bore Tertullion was carried on a litter with the party, his white, oval face flushed with the wine he drank.

They rode away from the shadow of the Chambourt, to an area where direct sunlight broke through the canopy of leaves. Riding between Gilles and his father, Gregory jabbered with excitement.

'Will we hunt boar, father?'

'Yes,' the baron said. 'With the lance.'

The boy turned to Gilles. 'And deer? I would like to test my archery skills on a moving target. Will we hunt deer?'

'Undoubtedly,' Sir Gilles said with a laugh. He flashed a smile across at the baron, and was pleased to see that he shared his good humour.

Tertullion, his goblet refreshed by a servant-girl, bobbed alongside on his cushion.

'I must say, my lord,' he slurred, 'that the effect of this hunting party upon the young prince, already a fine figure of burgeoning manhood, can only be beneficial.' He raised his drink. 'A capital idea.'

It was to be the last wrong thing he said. The arrow entered through his eyeball, cracked his skull apart, and left through the back of his head.

He was but the first.

'Beastmen!' cried one of the soldiers from the front. Horses whinnied as a volley of arrows came from the trees. Screams. The thud of arrowheads on shields.

Pulling the reins of his steed in tight, Sir Gilles quickly assessed the situation. Arrows were coming from all around. They were surrounded. He spurred his house through the confusion of panicked noblemen, to the men-at-arms.

'Form up! Form up!' he yelled. 'Shields high!'

At his word the bowmen scurried forward, taking up places behind the pikes. They fired a volley into the trees. Bestial cries of their victims rang out. Pulling his visor down, Gilles peered into the murk. The shadows moved; suggestions of horns and hooves, tentacles and twisted, Chaos-tainted limbs. This was no opportunist beastman raid, he realised. They were well organised. And there were hundreds of them.

Screaming in their foul, ululating tongue, the enemy burst forth from the trees. Wave after wave fell to the bow and the pike, but each time a gap was left. Under Gilles's command, the soldiers shored up, but the protective circle was getting ever smaller. And the arrows kept coming from all around.

Gilles looked across at Gregory. To the boy's credit he showed no fear. His face, as he kept close to his father, was fixed with a look of stoic determination. He was calm. He had his wits. He would make a fine warrior.

A clamour of clashing armour from one side of the circle announced another attack. The beastmen were concentrating on one area. They hacked at it, burst through, splintering shields and cleaving skulls, cutting down bowmen. They were in.

His horse rising onto its hind-legs, Gilles raised his sword skywards, gave a rallying cry and went to join the fray. An arrow found a gap in his mount's armour-plating, piercing its side. It fell sideways. Unable to free his foot from his stirrups in time, Gilles went with it.

He heard the crunch as his leg dislocated. His sword snapped in two as it connected with a rock. Fighting against the pain, Gilles was unaware of the beastman, a stocky hunchback with the head of bull, standing over him with a club. Raining blow after blow against his armour, it beat him into the blackness.

GILLES AWOKE TO find himself bound. He had been stripped of his armour and was lying on a slab of stone, his arms and legs pinioned by ropes. He was covered in bruises. Blood had dried over his head. His broken leg was numb and would not move. From a torch set on the wall, he could see that he was in some sort of cave. The vicious points of stalactites jutted out of the darkness above him.

'Sir Gilles?' a voice called. It was hoarse as though from sobbing.

'Gregory?'

Gilles craned his head, wincing against the pain. The lad, tied to another slab of rock, appeared unharmed. He was trembling, his face once again that of a frightened boy.

A man entered the room. Towering, his head almost touching the jagged roof, Sir Gilles recognised him of old. He had grown his long hair back. The witch.

He lowered his disfigured face, his hair brushing against Sir Gilles's face. He hissed, opening his tongueless mouth, a string of saliva winding its way down onto the knight's forehead. Sir Gilles gazed defiantly upon the witch, unflinching.

The witch stood up, a rattling, gurgling laugh coming from his throat. He clicked his fingers. Two beastmen lumbered in, hooves clattering on the rock, and took Gregory up from his slab. He started to cry, kicking uselessly against them as they took him from the cave.

'Where are you taking him?' Gilles cried out. 'I warn you now, witch! Do not harm that boy!'

The witch stood in the centre of the room, facing Sir Gilles. He pulled out a knife. Wide-bladed and so sharp its edges shone, it was inscribed with the eldritch signs of the witch's evil master. He held it above his head in both hands, stumps knotting with the fingers that remained, blade facing the floor. He brought it down, plunging it into an imaginary victim. His body shook with deranged, guttural laughter.

The witch strode from the room, dagger at the ready.

Desperately, Sir Gilles began to struggle against his bonds.

IN THE FOREST, the cries of the wounded and dying filled the twilight. Soldiers busied themselves digging graves for the dead men. A pyre was stacked high with slaughtered horses, the stench of burning meat all pervading. Subdued and utterly defeated, the men performed their grim duties like automatons. None of them spoke of the likely fates of those men whose bodies could not be found.

Amidst this pitiful scene, surrounded by a circle of troops, the baron sat on a rock, staring into space, his grief by now impenetrable.

'The head-count has been completed, my lord,' the sergeant-at-arms said quietly.

Barely registering the man's presence, the baron waved a cursory hand at him to continue.

'Upon the field are the bodies of thirty men, five of them of name. Ten more are severely wounded and are not expected to live long.'

The baron shuddered, closing his eyes slowly. It was all his fault.

'There is one more disturbing detail,' the sergeant went on. 'As well as your son and Sir Gilles, we could not find the bodies of a further ten retainers. From the testimony of the men, confused by the chaos of battle though it is, they appear to have been taken away alive.'

'But why?' the baron demanded, as much of the darkening forest as the sergeant.

A horse came galloping from the forest, carrying on its back one of the baron's scouts. The man pulled his mount to a halt and dismounted. He stood, panting, trying to find his voice, sweat dripping from his head.

'My lord,' he said, breathlessly. 'My lord, I think I have found them!'

SITTING UP ON the slab, Sir Gilles untied the last of the bonds around his feet. He swung round and planted his good foot on the cave floor. Wincing, he limped up the rough slope in the direction the witch had taken. Supporting himself on the limestone wall, he looked down into another chamber, beyond which could be seen a moonlit clearing in the forest. A bonfire was burning and the unholy mutterings of the beastmen could be heard. Somewhere, drums were being pounded.

Sir Gilles crept out of the cave, hoping that the night and the flickering shadows of the fire would provide enough cover to prevent his detection. It was then he heard the first scream.

Squinting in the darkness, Sir Gilles could make out a terrible sight.

With several flat-topped stones arranged around him in a circle, each with one of the baron's soldiers lying upon it, the witch stood in his robes, his knife in one hand, a severed head in the other. Blood trickled down his arm, glistening in the flames. He moved on to his next victim.

Issuing a silent prayer to the Lady, Sir Gilles called upon his last reserves of strength and courage and took action. He deftly broke the neck of the nearest beastman, took its weapon – a rusted broadsword – and went to work.

Swinging rhythmically, lopping off heads, opening throats, he hobbled forward, screaming out the ancient battle-cries of his order. The beastmen, drunk and distracted by the blood-letting ceremony, were slow to react. And Sir Gilles had his righteous anger on his side. Wounded though he was, he was unstoppable.

More screams rang out as the witch continued to add new heads to the pile at his feet.

Sir Gilles was by now on the other side of the bonfire and could see the witch and his unholy ritual clearly now. The prince was tied to a tree, slumped unconscious, arms above his head and feet crossed over like a martyr of old. The witch was working on the last of the men. The knife, blunted on the other victims, hacked laboriously through windpipe and bone, sending blood rising through the darkness. Occupied with fending off beastmen, Gilles could only listen helplessly to the strangulated cries of the man's prolonged agony.

Standing back, the last of the heads in his hands, the witch held both arms aloft, the power of his sacrifices flowing through him. He moved towards Gregory.

A beastman came out of the darkness at Sir Gilles, its large hooves kicking up cinders and dead twigs. One arm was a lashing tentacle, the other a thick, almost-human arm, wielding a large club. Its head was that of a horse. Deep-set eyes glowed with rage. Its mouth was crowded with needle-sharp teeth. Expertly side-stepping Sir Gilles's first lunge, it retaliated with an unexpectedly swift upswing that caught the knight in the stomach. Winded, he staggered backwards. The beastman leapt at him.

Beyond the horse-creature, Sir Gilles could see that the witch had not yet harmed Gregory. He stood instead by the tree, freeing Gregory from his bonds, no doubt in preparation for moving him to one of the plinths.

Blocking club with sword, Sir Gilles pulled his arm back ready to punch, but found it held fast by the tentacle. The beast dropped the club and gripped the knight's sword arm instead. Its strength was too great. Sir Gilles felt the blood fleeing his fingers. He dropped his weapon.

A cracking noise. The beastman let its lower jaw dislocate like a snake's, the bone hanging loose in stretching skin. The teeth, coated in spittle, glistened in the flames.

Sir Gilles tried to struggle but the beast held him fast. He prayed to the Lady. *Not this way. Not like this.*

With a roar the horse-head sank its teeth into his neck and bit down hard. Then stopped.

The tentacle uncoiled itself, and the fingers around his sword arm went slack. The beastman pitched forward, a dead weight.

Scrabbling back out from under the monstrosity, one hand to his neck to stem the flow of blood, Sir Gilles saw that an arrow protruded from the back of the creature's neck, lost in the mane.

Not having time to question his good fortune, and losing blood fast, Sir Gilles drew on the last reserves of strength and pounded across to the witch.

Lowering Gregory to the ground, the fiend did not see him. Gilles knocked him to the side, rolled over with him, pinned him to the ground. One punch destroyed his nose.

Choking on blood that flowed down his throat, the witch stared up at the Grail Knight. His eyes were wild with shock and, though Sir Gilles dare not think it, what looked like fear.

Starting to lose consciousness, Sir Gilles brought his fist down once again. The witch went limp.

More arrows flew out of the darkness, bringing beastmen down as they closed in on Sir Gilles. The others stopped to sniff the air.

Clambering off the witch, Sir Gilles went to Gregory. Felt for a pulse. The boy still lived.

The beastmen started baying in alarm. A crashing of undergrowth. Horses' hooves. The clank of armour. The glint of weapons in the flames. The baron had arrived.

The slaughter was great. Not a beastman was permitted to live. Though the fire burnt still in the centre of the clearing, the baron ordered that their bodies should be left to rot, their heads put upon spikes as a warning to others of their kind. To prevent desecration, the bodies of the ten sacrificed soldiers were taken back to the Chambourt, together with the witch. For him, the flames awaited.

IT WAS A STARK, cold morning. The entire town was assembled outside the castle grounds. For a week now, the pyre that would claim the life of the witch had been under construction. Every household had contributed wood. Many trees had been felled. It towered above the crowd, in competition with the castle itself, a man-made cousin to the peaks beyond. A scaffold had been built around it, enabling the chaos-worshipping fiend to be marched up to the stake at the summit.

Having been put to the torture for the entire time his execution was being prepared, he was at last a broken figure. Pale and hunched, head scabbed over where his hair had been burnt off in a bucket of hot coals, he stumbled upwards, each step an agony. From a platform at the base of the pyre, the baron noted with grim satisfaction that the witch's eyes, where defiance had burned so long, now seemed confused and bovine.

'HELP ME TO the window, Gregory,' Sir Gilles said in a faint voice. 'I wish to watch the monster's final moments.'

Pale, drawn and confined to his bed, the Grail Knight's health had deteriorated since his ordeal. His leg had not set well and the bite mark, through which he had lost a lot of blood, was not healing satisfactorily. That morning, Blampel, the old fool, had muttered something indistinct about a possible infection.

In contrast, Gregory, his cheeks ruddy with the flush of youth, was as sturdy as ever before.

He lifted the old retainer from his bed and supported him while he hobbled on his broken leg to the window. Sir Gilles rested himself against the sill, his breathing shallow, his thoughts scattered and vague. If this was a taste of old age, he said to himself, then he prayed that his end would not be long in coming.

Tapestries lifted in the wind as Gregory opened the windows. A low rumble of conversation drifted upwards from the crowd. The occasional cry of a hawker advertising his wares.

The window was level with the top of the pyre, towards which the crippled figure was being marched. The gaoler tied the witch to the stake and made his way back down the steps.

Sir Gilles stared, unblinking, at his hated enemy.

The monster strained forward from the stake, feebly struggling, the filth on his face streaked with tears. A distressed shrieking came from his empty mouth. He seemed more like a child than a man.

THE GAOLER HANDED the baron a flaming brand. All chatter in the crowd died. The witch was screaming down at the baron, neck fully outstretched, eyes bulging, demented. Though his words could not be understood, it was clear he was pleading for mercy. At last, thought the baron. At last.

Making sure he maintained eye contact with his enemy, the baron slowly put the torch at the base of the pyre.

With a crackle of dry tinder, the hungry flames leapt up.

At the sight of the orange glow far beneath him, the witch hysterically started to repeat the same word over and over.

THE SAME WORD, over and over… Sir Gilles felt the hairs on the back of his neck and arms bristle. A prickling sensation came to his face.

The word. The word sounded like–

He turned to look at Gregory. He stood, arms folded, impassively surveying the grim scene. His mouth was curled into a sneering smile.

Sir Gilles started to shake.

The wind brought the scent of burning flesh into the room.

Arms still folded, Gregory waved a dismissive hand at the knight. 'Die,' he commanded.

* * *

THE FLAMES licked up. The baron forced himself to keep his eyes on the witch. The fire seared his flesh now, billowing through his clothes. Still he screamed out the same word, rasping and harsh.

SIR GILLES STAGGERED back from the window. He dropped to his knees. Felt the air fleeing his lungs. A sharp pain in his head. Tears in his eyes. Blood in his mouth.

Deadly malice flashing in his eyes, Gregory paced around him in a circle.

'Old fool. You did not think to question the nature, the purpose of the ceremony.'

The Grail Knight started to shake.

'The ceremony, the deaths of those ten men, wasn't merely to satisfy my blood-lust. It had a purpose.'

'No…' Sir Gilles croaked. 'No…'

'That night, by the unholy power of my dark master I took the body of the baron's son.' The man that called himself Gregory came close to Sir Gilles's ear. 'And bequeathed him mine.'

Outside, the screaming had stopped. Framed by the small window, Sir Gilles could see all that remained of the witch's body, a column of black smoke.

The darkness of death crowding in on his mind, Sir Gilles locked his hands together in desperate prayer.

He knew now what the word had been.

IT WAS OVER. The people were still silent, awe-struck by the terrible sight they had witnessed. The flames roared on, hungrily consuming the last of the wood.

Suddenly exhausted, the baron let his head drop. The acrid smoke stung his eyes. He moved towards the edge of the platform, his guards stepping aside to allow him onto the steps.

The crowd cheered him as he walked, but he barely heard it. An inexplicable sorrow hung heavily on his heart. He cared nothing for his land, nor his faithful subjects. Only one thing mattered to him now. His son, his heir: Gregory.

* * *

WATCHING THE DEAD knight, his aged face contorted with the anguish of his final moments, the witch's eyes flashed with triumph.

The sound of the baron's approaching footsteps on the cold stone echoed along the corridor.

Transforming Gregory's features into a suitable mask of sorrow, the witch opened the door and fell into his father's arms.

Seeing the knight's fallen form beyond the doorway, the baron gave a cry of grief and pulled his son tightly to him.

Face pressed into the baron's tunic, Gregory's muffled voice repeated the same word over and over. Though the sadness was almost too much to bear, the baron took comfort at the word. It was all he had left.

He pulled his son closer, rocking him gently, one hand cradling the back of his head.

The same word, over and over.

'Father.'

# THE JUDAS GOAT
## by Robert Earl

MOLLENS SNARLED WITH surprise and leapt backwards. He tried to ignore the blood-red slash across his forearm and snatched for his knife. The hulking Reiklander advanced towards him, his own glistening blade held downwards. Mollens licked his lips nervously, more worried by the man's wide grin than the blade in his hand. What had got into him?

With a speed and grace which belied his hefty frame, the Reiklander leapt with a savage howl. Mollens twisted and struck in one fluid, thoughtless motion. For one terrible moment the two men gazed helplessly into each other's eyes, then the Reiklander collapsed into the cold mud.

Ignoring the horrified silence and the ring of shocked faces, Captain Gustav Mollens stooped and retrieved his knife from the corpse's side. Brandishing the gory weapon, he glared, white-faced, at the others.

'Anyone else?'

The recruits edged backwards. Their commander, knife still at the ready, watched them closely for any further sign of rebellion. Only one of their number seemed unaffected by the sudden, murderous violence.

'That won't help your recruitment drive much,' he said.

Mollens was surprised into a bark of laughter by the swarthy, dark-haired man's callous indifference. 'No, I guess not,' he admitted, stooping to wipe his knife on the dead man's tunic. When he was satisfied that the blade was clean, he sheathed it and started issuing orders as though nothing untoward had occurred.

'You and you, build a pyre. We'll burn this and then make camp for the night. You four, box the compass until I work out a roster for guard duty. Now,' he concluded, turning back to his sardonic companion, 'what's your name, soldier?'

'Gevalt, sir. Why are you burning him?' A smirk still played across the man's lips. Mollens decided it was no wonder the man's nose had been broken, more than once by the look of it.

'Well, when I was in the southlands...' His voice trailed off. Best not to mention those whispering horrors here, with the skeletal limbs of the forest reaching out over his little band of innocents.

'Ah, zombies you mean,' Gevalt finished for him.

Well, Mollens thought, perhaps not all such innocents.

'You should tell them about the deathless ones,' Gevalt continued, gesturing casually at the rest of the band, who were by now all busy assembling tents and the fire. 'Might stop the desertions.'

Mollens regarded the man with something approaching respect. Callous and manipulative, he thought; useful traits. He's also confident enough to speak his mind, so he's not intimidated by the scars and the stories. Most of these lads are as nervous of me, as I am of...

The captain tugged his earlobe thoughtfully, then took Gevalt aside.

'I've thought of telling them something like that,' he admitted quietly. 'But start telling this bunch of clodhoppers what they're really going to have to contend with and how many do you think we'll get to Nuln? No, better to leave them to their dreams of glory and the only desertions we'll get will be a few of the most homesick. Not that it isn't a glorious life in the Emperor's army, of course,' he added quickly, on seeing Gevalt's blank expression.

The man winked conspiratorially and smiled. 'I'm sure you're right,' he said. 'But I don't mind taking the night watches with you for a while. Perhaps if I can catch some of these rabbits before they run, I'll have more of a squad to lead when we get to Nuln. Under yourself, of course, captain.'

It was Mollens's turn to smile. He had been right to confide in this man. If nothing else, it meant he wouldn't have to sleep with one eye open every night.

'Well, Acting-Sergeant Gevalt,' he said decisively, 'I think we are agreed.'

In the gathering darkness of the night the two men shook hands, then turned back to the funeral pyre.

MOLLENS TWISTED IRRITABLY under his blankets. It was going to be one of those nights, he knew it. As soon as he had lain down in this relatively comfortable spot, dog-tired and with a full belly, he had started to slip into the warm embrace of sleep. But the horror was there again.

It was worse in his imagination than it had ever been in reality, he knew – but knowing didn't help. The twinned yellow fangs; the cloying, sulphurous stench of filthy fur. Worst of all were the paws, bearing incongruously nimble fingers and thumbs. When the nightmares came it was always those mutant fingers that he felt closing around his throat in the second before he jerked awake, sweating and bloodless.

And the last of his gin was gone. On nights like this it was the only escape he could find. He had grown to love the acrid smell of the clear liquid, the way it stung his gums but soothed away his fears. Most of all, he loved the rising tide of peace that the anaesthetic of raw alcohol brought. It drowned the daemons which lurked in the tangled labyrinths of his memory with a solid, chemical efficiency that was always reliable.

Of course there was a price to pay. Mornings became monotonously painful; afternoons became increasingly thirsty. And although he cursed his colonel for wasting him, a seasoned veteran, on these damnable recruitment marches, he knew that the alcohol was really to blame. It had driven him into making too many mistakes, getting into too many brawls. He'd even been banned from the Reiksguard's mess in Nuln, quite a feat in an Empire army barracks.

Mollens shifted again beneath his blankets and scratched listlessly. It had seemed like a good idea to ration himself to a single canteen on this trip but then he had been drunk when he'd made the decision, and now he cursed himself for a fool. Since his supply had run out he'd become irritable, flying into fits of rage at the slightest mistake by the new recruits. It was no wonder so many of them had taken the advantage of darkness and an exhausted officer to slip away, out of the noose of the Emperor's commission.

The old soldier rolled onto his side and stared at the flickering fire. Here and there one of the troops would turn beneath his rough blanket, snore or murmur through the fog of sleep. One of the men, who lay completely swathed but for his grubby pink toes, called from the depths of slumber for his mother.

Men? Be truthful, Mollens thought; they are only boys fresh from their families and farms. They don't have a clue about what they've let themselves in for. But then, neither did I. You can't afford to feel sorry for them, not in this game. Even if they might end up patrolling the sewers. Looking for rats... By Sigmar, now he would *never* get to sleep.

THE COLD BRIGHTNESS of dawn found Mollens curled up and snoring. Gevalt, threading his way through the awakening camp, approached him with a mug of tea. The sergeant shook the sleeping bulk of his commander through the grey dampness of his dew-soaked blanket, wafting the fragrant steam of the drink into his face.

Mollens sat up, a grimace on his face, and gratefully accepted the mug, clasping it between his hands like a poor man's grail. Grunting his thanks he drank greedily, smacked his lips in appreciation, then clambered stiffly to his feet.

'It's a fine morning,' Gevalt said cheerily, taking the emptied mug that Mollens handed back to him. He heard one of the officer's joints pop as he stretched; the sound reminded him of a twig snapping.

'Yes, it is a fine morning,' replied the captain, and looked suspiciously at his companion. The man seemed obscenely cheerful for this time of day. 'Did we lose any more last night?'

'Not one,' Gevalt said happily. 'Counted 'em myself. Mind you, I've been up all night. Do you suppose I could sleep during exercises this afternoon?'

Mollens grunted, exasperated more by the sudden cessation in desertions than by his new sergeant's request. There were almost forty men here. If the instinct to escape became strong enough they could always find a way to follow it past their single officer. That was how things were supposed to be – the Nuln regiments were no place for the faint-hearted – but Mollens had already lost a score a men. Quite a record. Had he really become such a bad commander?

'I'll decide after I've called the roll,' Mollens consented, turning away and bellowing the order to fall in. The roll call confirmed Gevalt's boast. The troop, although still too undisciplined to be called correct, were at least all present. Mollens smiled and turned to his sergeant.

'Well done. You can rest up this afternoon. But first we march.'

And march they did. Packs that would have driven mules to mutiny dragged the men down, turning the muscles in their backs and legs and necks into twists of agonised meat. Boots, new and unbroken, raised crops of blisters across unfamiliar soles, constantly bursting and reforming into fresh lines of pain. By the time the column had reached the next campsite in a clearing burned from the heart of the forest, they felt as stooped and frail as their grandfathers.

Mollens watched them steaming in the frosty winter air and found himself remembering a herd of beef cattle he'd seen a month or so ago. They too had created their own warm mist of sweat and exhaustion. They too had stood with this same air of worn out passivity, seemingly grateful at being allowed to rest. It had been in a butcher's yard on the outskirts of Nuln. The recruits, some of them still panting, looked to their captain with trusting, hopeful eyes. Mollens found that the thought of cattle being led to the slaughterhouse made it strangely difficult for him to meet their collective gaze. But at least he could give them the order they must all be praying for.

'We'll stop here for the day and eat. This afternoon is spear practice,' Mollens told them, dropping his pack and biting down on the groan of relief that came to his own lips. It wouldn't do to let the men know that he was tired. Instead he posted four sentries and settled down to eat.

As he bit through the iron-hard crust of his bread, he watched the petty bartering that preceded all of their meals. Apples were swapped for bread, a measure of beer for a slice of mutton. Some of Mollens's charges still had the remnants of parcels prepared by their tearful families. The captain noticed that the owners of these were reluctant to swap now that the food was the only link they had left with their homes. He was surprised by the pang of sentimentality the thought brought, and began to plan the afternoon's drill to drown it out.

There was always something reassuringly sane about drill; if only the rest of life could be so clear cut and orderly. There had been a time not so long ago when it had been, or at least seemed to be. He had known, for instance, that Emperor Karl Franz had been fighting a just war. It was the duty of every man in the Empire to fight in the Emperor's armies. And didn't everyone know that a glorious death was infinitely preferable to a quiet life? Even the priests said so. So why, then, did bringing these farm lads in to bolster the Elector Countess of Nuln's army seem like treachery?

Perhaps, whispered his subconscious unpleasantly, it's because nobody who knows anything about the sewers would willingly go down there. You've managed to avoid it for the past five years, haven't you? After all, when you're choking on filth, cut off from the sun and buried amongst the rotting intestines of the city, there's no room for drill. Or glory. And if you believed in duty so much you wouldn't have–

'Shut up!' Mollens snapped, pulled himself from the terrible mire of this reverie. For a moment he was sure he'd spoken aloud. But a guilty glance left and right reassured him. The men were sprawled around the clearing with a languid contentment that the captain found difficult not to envy. Gods, but he needed a drink!

Instead he allowed himself one long, deep sigh then pulled himself to his feet and called them to order. 'Very well! We'll spend the rest of the day learning more about our comrade the spear,' he barked, falling easily back into the familiar role of drill-master. He was pleased by the appreciative murmur that ran through the troop. They were obviously keen, even if it was only because they were tired of marching.

'As you progress through training,' he continued, 'you will be tested with halberds or bows, or perhaps even those new-fangled black powder weapons. But to learn the spear is to begin to understand them all, for it was the first weapon of the Empire and it will be the last. Today, then, we will learn the rudiments of attacking, parrying and fighting in ranks. The rudiments, in other words, of war.'

The afternoon passed swiftly. Mollens enjoyed losing himself in the comforting routine of weapons instruction and the men were revitalised by their eagerness to learn. When they were split into competing pairs, the competition was fierce, much to their captain's approval. Desertions so far had been too high, but at least those that remained genuinely wanted to be warriors.

Mollens heard a sudden howl and span to find a flushed looking youth had dropped his weapon to staunch his bleeding nose with both hands. His opponent looked away guiltily as the captain approached.

'Why have you dropped your weapon?' Mollens gently asked the injured man.

'Hurt my nose, sir,' he replied, holding out a blood-smeared hand in corroboration. The captain examined it, then stepped to one side to peer intently at his charge's profile. The youth began to blush under this merciless scrutiny, and by the time the rest of the troop had gathered around curiously his face was burning with itching self-consciousness.

'I can see why you're worried about your profile,' Mollens said at length, allowing concern to surface in his voice. 'Who'd worry about fighting with such a fine bone structure to protect?'

A ripple of nervous laughter spread through the ranks like a breeze through corn. Without the slightest warning Mollens's hand scythed through it, to slam into the injured

man's nose. It broke with a grisly snap of crushed cartilage
and the youth stumbled backwards. Mollens followed him, a
cold light burning in his eyes.

'Never drop your weapon!' he hissed, but resisted the
temptation to strike the recruit again. The boy, deathly pale
apart from the rivulet of fresh blood which streamed from
his nose, nodded mutely. Mollens glared ferociously at him,
then realised that his charge was fighting back tears. His
anger evaporated in a sudden wash of self-reproach.

'I'm sorry I had to do that,' he said, trying not to sound
defensive. 'But if you lose your weapon in combat you're
dead. And your comrades won't be far behind you.
Understand? Never allow yourself to be disarmed.'

'What if your weapons break?' The questioner, thick-set and
heavy browed, had moved to stand beside his bleeding comrade, the offer of support evident in his stance and voice.
Mollens was taken aback by the recruit's tone, but the profes-
sional in him was pleased to hear it. Esprit de corps was always
preferable to blind obedience. Even so, he stared angrily at the
youth, pretending annoyance at the interruption.

'You find another one,' the captain replied, waiting until
the questioner could no longer hold his gaze. 'Even if it's just
a club or a rock. Any weapon is better than none. Now, back
to practice. We've only an hour of light, so let's make the
most of it.'

RED-EYED AND crawling with the fidgets, Mollens gave up on
his attempt to sleep. He had learned long ago that it was no
use trying to force it. Against the hot and cold claws of
insomnia, even mindless self-discipline was useless. Against
the horrors of the past, though, it sometimes worked.

Again and again he forcibly dragged his mind's eye away
from images of that last, lethal patrol. He tried not to think
about the hungry sucking sound the rats had made when
they had buried their fangs into Muller. He ignored the desperate chorus of screams that had rung out beneath the
tranquil streets of Nuln five miserable years ago, screams that
still echoed within the tortured confines of his dreams.

But as soon as he had blanked that memory another, even
worse, jostled into its place. This time it was of Ferdinand

staggering along behind him as they fled towards the exit. Even in the pathetically inadequate light of the guttering lamp, Mollens could see the flaps of shredded skin that hung obscenely down from his ruined body like torn rags. Behind them, echoing and multiplying in the cold brick tube of the sewer, came the sounds of the pursuing foe. The rattle of sharp claws against stone, the sliding tidal hiss of packed furry bodies, the occasional muffled squeak. At every step the sound came closer. They had almost made it back to the surface, could even smell the freshness of the night air, when Ferdinand had stopped. The last of Mollens's comrades, the most loyal of his friends, listened to the enemies' quickening approach with his head to one side in a familiar, curiously childish gesture. Then he had looked to Mollens, his face unreadable through the mask of pain and blood, and nodded.

And Mollens, Sigmar help him, had nodded back and ran on. The next patrol hadn't even found Ferdinand's bones.

Mollens gazed upwards at the stars, then past them into the chilled depths of the void. As always the memory of that last betrayal seemed to empty him of everything but a deep, aching tiredness. Perhaps that, combined with his inability to sleep, was Sigmar's way of punishing his cowardice.

The staccato sound of a cracking twig startled Mollens, pulling him out of his self-pity. He lay still, eyes straining against the darkness, until he saw a familiar swarthy shadow detach itself, bat-like, from a tree and steal away into the night.

Cautiously Mollens slid out from beneath his blankets and pulled on his boots. A quick glance around the camp perimeter told him all he needed to know. Gevalt was nowhere to be seen. So much for him catching rabbits.

Mollens stalked quietly through the camp, seething with an anger fuelled by insomnia. He felt betrayed, and foolish for it. As he slunk into the darkness he loosened his knife in its scabbard. He would cut this particular deserter a smile that would serve as an example to the rest. Things had been sliding too far out of control lately and for tonight, at least, he had found someone to blame.

Under the dark canopy of the forest the captain stopped and waited for his night vision to come. He'd catch Gevalt eventually. No point walking into a trap; the bastard was certainly cunning enough for it. Despite the delay there was no chance of him losing his prey. Whatever Gevalt had been, he was no woodsman. In front of him Mollens heard a dull thump followed by a muffled curse. With a wolfish grin playing about his scarred features he stooped and scurried forward on fingers and toes well versed in the arts of silence and stealth.

The stumbling Gevalt was almost within striking distance when Mollens, his senses amplified tenfold by this familiar game, froze. A few yards ahead there was a faint, hardly noticeable green glow, and as Mollens waiting on rigid, frozen limbs, his nose caught the smell. It reminded him of Nuln and its ancient catacombs, and the sickening horror that lurked within that nightmare underworld. It reminded him of the *rats!* Sweat started to trickle lazily over his cold, tingling skin. Blood hissed and pounded in his ears, racing to the wild beat of his heart. In the darkness he waited, alone with his terror.

'You came. Why? Speak-speak!' squeaked a voice from the darkness. Mollens almost screamed before he realised that it was Gevalt and not himself who was being addressed.

'My lord,' Gevalt whined. 'I am here only to serve you. I have an idea, probably worthless it is true, but I thought I should give it to you as I give everything to you.'

A bubbling, squeaking laugh cut through the night. 'Everything but the gold, yes? So, speak, man-thing, or I feed my pet.'

A flash of sickly green fire bloomed and its ghastly light confirmed the worst of Mollens's suspicions. This was his nightmare, tearing through into the waking world to finally claim him just as it had claimed Ferdinand, Muller and the rest, those five years ago.

A bundle of dark and filthy rags lurked under a burning staff. From amidst this shambling heap protruded a long, whiskered snout. Its obscene pink tip wrinkled and twisted back and forth, gleaming in the corrupted light. From beneath the decaying cloth, hidden from Gevalt, a revolting hairless tail writhed around the haft of a knife, its crescent blade glistening beneath a coating of pale, treacly fluid. This hideous apparition, though, was nothing compared to the monstrous form which stood silently behind it.

The thing stood at least eight feet tall from black taloned feet to ragged ears. The guttering flare its master held aloft threw its twisted features into sharp relief. The slimy razors of its fangs, the corded muscles which twitched beneath its lice-ridden pelt, the vicious spikes and filthy pits that encrusted its rusting armour – all were picked out and magnified by the green light.

'My liege,' Gevalt grovelled, his whimpering tones pulling Mollens from out of his trance, 'I can bring you the whole pack of slaves now, instead of just one or two of the most foolish here and there. When I kill the leader–'

An angry squeal cut across Gevalt's words, shocking him into silence.

'Stupid! What do you think will happen when all man-things disappear?'

'Yes, of course, you're right, master,' the traitor gulped, trying a wide, toothy, placating grin. It was almost the death of him.

In a confused explosion of movement the scaly tail whipped forward, the blade a blur in the shadows. Before Gevalt had time to even register the movement, the tip came to rest on the soft skin of his throat.

'So, it shows its teeth, does it? I'll show its filthy liver!'

'Please, master...' Gevalt whispered. 'I didn't... Let me live... to help you.'

The cloaked figure bubbled and hissed again. Laughter, thought Mollens; that's laughter.

'Once more you will send a slave, yes? Tomorrow.'

Before his trembling servant could reply, the rat-man brandished its flaming staff. There was a blinding, too-bright flash of luminescence. Then there was nothing but total darkness and gruesome after-images cavorting across Mollens's eyes.

He waited for an age, as still as a corpse in the cold dampness, his blood whispering terrifying echoes in his ears. Eventually the dark edges of the trees and the pale glimmer of distant stars reappeared and he could hear nothing except the breeze curling through the branches above him and the occasional rustling of some small beast.

Then he heard Gevalt: a pitiful sob, followed by a low moan of private agony. For one fleeting moment the captain felt a twinge of pity for the miserable wretch. Then he remembered all the 'deserters' and felt his heart close in a convulsion of rage. Gevalt stumbled away into the night. After a few thoughtful moments Mollens stood and strode soundlessly back the way he had come.

'CAPTAIN, WHERE HAVE you been?' Gevalt asked from his seat beside the campfire, as Mollens strolled back. If he noticed his new sergeant's strained tone, or the vein that pulsed a warning in his forehead, Mollens gave no sign of it.

'Just watering the trees,' Mollens said with a manufactured smile. 'You can turn in now; I'll not be able to get back to sleep.'

'Thank you, sir,' Gevalt croaked and stumbled towards his blankets.

Mollens watched him go, then stirred the dying embers of the fire back into life. He fetched his cloak, wrapped it around his shoulders and sat staring into the flames.

A few hours later and the troop was ready to move off. It was another crisp dawn, made all the more refreshing by the optimistic chatter of the woodland birds. Under the blue vault of the sky the dew sparkled on the verdant sweeps of the forest. Mollens breathed in the smell of sap in the clear, cool breeze. He almost believed that last night must just have been a nightmare. Gevalt, for one, looked like a man without a care in the world as he shouldered his pack and started the first of the day's marching songs. But as the column stamped off along the narrow woodland track the captain realised that he was trying to deceive himself about the night's events. He had seen what he had seen, and to try to deny it would be little more than a slow form of suicide.

*Your speciality*, gloated his subconscious, but the captain ignored the voice and examined his plan for the tenth time.

After six hours of strenuous marching they reached a wide, undulating meadow. The troop crunched doggedly through the yellow remains of winter wheat that stubbled the field, stumbling into each other when they crossed the occasional barren slick of mud, before Mollens called the day's halt.

Perhaps the relieved joy the men felt at this decision was contagious, or perhaps it was the quickening pulse of the forest in early spring, but for some reason the captain felt almost happy. The afternoon's spear practice buoyed his spirits even more. His men displayed a remarkable aptitude for the weapon, their nerves and sinews already half trained by shovels and pitchforks and from the occasional hunt.

Mollens prowled around the practice ring, barking a warning here or bestowing a word of praise there. By the time the cooks had prepared the evening's communal meal he had begun to realise that many of his recruits had more to offer than he had thought.

They were fitter than the usual gutter-scum the Nuln sewer guard took, certainly. But more than that, they were possessed of a certain straightforward savagery that the soldier in Mollens delighted in. Many of these men, he sensed, had joined up not to escape from the gallows or poverty, but because they were keen to fight. For some reason the notion gave him a peculiar floating sensation. It felt as if a weight, carried for so long as to be almost a part of him, had sloughed off.

Gevalt, meanwhile, had appeared calm and cheerful all day, his mask not slipping for a moment. Mollens hated him all the more for it. He had kept one eye on the traitor ever since last night and had twice almost surrendered to the urge to kill the man, to smash him down and finish him there and then. But he knew that even his rank would not allow him to act without real evidence.

As the campfire smoked and crackled, Mollens stretched out on his back, by turn first tensing and then relaxing his various muscle groups. It was an old campaign trick, one of a hundred he knew he should have been teaching his charges over the past weeks instead of wallowing in self pity. Still, he would have plenty of time to make good his negligence when they got to Nuln. *Sigmar willing.*

He savoured the smell of wood-smoke, and the rich aroma of boiling meat and vegetables. Above him the stars started to appear, shining in anticipation of their nightly dance, and the last pink rind of sunlight faded away from the western horizon. As the world spun away into darkness Mollens was surprised that for the first time in an age he felt totally relaxed. It had always been thus in the heart of a battle, when all that could be done had been done and his fate was in the hands of the gods. How long, he wondered, since he had felt this? How long since he had been so at peace?

It wasn't until the sleeping blankets were laid out that Gevalt finally approached him. A ball of hatred tried to claw itself up from the pit of Mollens's stomach, but even that couldn't totally destroy his new-found sense of peace.

'Thank you for concluding my watch last night,' Gevalt said with an easy grin. 'If you want to turn in, I'll return the favour.'

'Don't mind if I do,' Mollens replied, trying to sound genuine. 'You seem to be able to stop the rabbits running, sergeant. When we reach Nuln I'll certainly tell the colonel of it.'

Gevalt bowed slightly, seeming pleased.

'I'll turn in then. Wake me up before the rest, won't you?' Mollens, feeling the heat of his anger beginning to burn through his friendly façade despite his best intentions, hastily buried himself beneath the blankets.

It was a long, tense night. Much to his chagrin Mollens found that the insomnia that had tormented him for so long chose this, of all nights, to depart. Throughout the monotonous hours of the watch he kept from beneath his blankets, sleep waited, a hungry predator waiting in ambush. As time crawled past he dozed, sometimes for frighteningly indeterminate periods, before waking with a jolt. Every time he jerked back to his senses, a feeling of doom washed through him, but each time it was dispelled by the sight of Gevalt sitting cross-legged and watchful near the trees.

Strange how circumstances could make such a loathsome, dangerous man a source of comfort. In Bretonnia, Mollens's first campaign, the laughter of the enemy archers across the fields had also soothed him. While they had laughed, their bowstrings had been silent, and that was a thought to bring warmth to any soldier of the Emperor in those days. They were a colourful foe, the Bretonnians; in his mind he could see their bright tunics, shining armour, flowing banners. From amidst a sea of them Mollens, with mild surprise, picked out the face of old Ferdinand. He laughed at the sight of his dead friend's face, the familiar lines and furrows that marked it like duelling scars were twisting into a warm, forgiving smile. How different from the last time he had looked, down in the sewers. With the rats. The ambush. The blood-stained teeth and claws reaching out for him–

Mollens awoke, gasping from the horror of the images. He looked frantically around for Gevalt and felt a rush of relief when he saw the man sitting spider-like barely a dozen paces away. Then he noticed a second figure sitting beside the traitor, and relief became anticipation.

Mollens, his eyes still at ground level, couldn't tell which of the troop it was. As he watched Gevalt passed a flask to his companion, metal glowing with a dull, blood coloured sheen in the firelight. In the moment before the lad raised it to his grateful lips Mollens felt that he must surely lose control. What a relief it would be to spring up, knock the poisoned cup away from the recruit's mouth, and finish Gevalt. Not in anger or vengeance but just quickly, the way one would kill a scorpion.

But the moment passed. Mollens watched the flask tilt upwards. One gulp was enough. The flask clanked as it hit the ground, loosened by a spasm which shook the victim's fingers. The lad sat stiff and trembling as Gevalt, his face a gargoyle's mask of watchful cunning, leaned forwards and whispered an indiscernible suggestion to his prey. The lad groaned faintly, then began to hoist himself off the ground.

Mollens rose wraithlike from his bed and stalked towards the two men. Not until the drugged victim of Gevalt's treachery took his first lurching step towards the south did the captain speak.

'Evening, sergeant. Where's he off to?'

Gevalt sprang to his feet, face white, and reached instinctively for his dagger. Just in time he remembered himself and forced his pale features into a ghastly smile.

'Going for firewood, sir,' he managed. Mollens noted the sudden sheen of sweat that bathed the man's face and the hand which hovered uncertainly by the hilt of his knife.

'No need. I've decided that we could use some night exercises. Let the troops know that the glory of serving the

Emperor doesn't stop at dinnertime, eh?' His savage smile was genuine enough now. Let him guess that I know, he thought. Let him try to silence me.

For a moment Gevalt's features were twisted in fearful indecision. In the end, much to Mollens's disappointment, he chose to continue his bluff.

'You, lad,' the man said, placing a hand on the recruit's twitching shoulder. 'You heard the captain. Go and wake the troop.'

As the lad turned back towards the campfire, Mollens noted his wide pupils and the peculiar tautness of the muscles in his face. He remembered the young Reiklander, now nothing more than ash in the woods, and made a sudden decision. The time for bluff and silence was past, but he wouldn't cheat the witch hunters in Nuln of their vile pleasures by taking his own vengeance now.

When the last of the recruits was roused to stand groggily with the rest of his fellows, Mollens gestured at Gevalt, who stood hovering by his side, and spoke.

'You have no uniforms and scant enough training but tonight you will become soldiers of our great Emperor. You will face many dangers in the years to come, from steel to disease, but always the most lethal will be the traitorous knife in the back. This man, your sergeant–'

He got no further. Gevalt had been listening to his words in an agony of apprehension and now his control snapped. With a piercing cry he leapt towards his captain with open jaws, forgetting even his knife in his terror. Mollens, surprised, managed to lift his forearm in time to keep the teeth from his throat, but Gevalt bit down into the flesh with shocking strength.

The captain screamed as he felt his muscles tearing. Instinctively he fell back beneath the momentum of his enemy's charge, twisting as he fell in order to trap Gevalt beneath him. He grabbed for his knife and felt a flare of horror when his groping fingers clutched Gevalt's fist, already clasped around the hilt. With a vicious tug Gevalt freed the blade and Mollens screamed again as his palm was sliced open.

Wounded or not, he caught his enemy's wrist in a bloody grip. The agony of his split hand paled beside that flaring along his arm as Gevalt's jaws closed tighter, releasing a stream of blood. Mollens raised his head to look into the traitor's frenzied eyes, then snapped his forehead down onto his crooked nose. There was a satisfying crack, but before he could repeat the manoeuvre he felt fingers closing around his throat. He twisted and struggled away from the lethal grip, but it was no use. Gevalt hung onto him with a cold, iron tenacity that was born of complete desperation.

His strength bled away as a red veil fell across the captain's vision. He could feel himself starting to fade, even the passions of rage and fear that had burned so brightly within his chest withering away, smothered by the cold ashes of frustration and apathy. Eyes dimming, Mollens could see the ring of worried faces gathered around them, confused and afraid.

Poor sods, he thought regretfully. Suppose they never stood a chance. It was his last thought before the darkness reached out to claim him.

HE AWOKE WITH a splutter, choking from the water somebody was pouring down his throat. The broad, heavy browed face that hovered above him broke into a wide, gap toothed grin, dispelling any illusion that it was one of Sigmar's angels.

'Captain, praise be you're all right,' the recruit said. His companions pushed closer, but he shoved them back impatiently. Gradually the spinning world slowed down enough for Mollens to sit up, his aching eyes searching for Gevalt.

'Where is he?' he asked the youth thickly, his throat still bruised and aching.

'We tied him up over there,' came the reply. 'He kept screaming and trying to bite us, then he tried to get us to sup some potion. Shall we kill him?'

Mollens smiled wearily at the lad's enthusiasm. He remembered him now from the previous day's weapons training. He'd been the one to stand up for his comrade.

'Time enough for that, soldier. How long have I been out?'

'Only a few moments, captain. We could have taken the daemon sooner but we were waiting for your order.'

'Which of you took the decision?'

'I did, sir. Rifka Henning,' the youth said, holding out his hand and grinning in pride.

'Congratulations on your promotion, Acting-Sergeant Henning.' Mollens took his hand and grinned back. 'Now show me the traitor.'

He followed the man through the cluster of recruits and immediately saw Gevalt. His captors hadn't taken any chances. He lay awkwardly against a tree trunk, his wrists tied painfully behind it. His legs were bound by another coil of rope and a noose had been tied around his scrawny neck, the free end hanging over a branch, ready for use.

Mollens noted the cuts and bruises that covered the traitor's body with some satisfaction, then he looked at the man's tormented face and realised that he was suffering a pain far worse than the physical. Once more the captain felt a wave of unwanted compassion for the agonised soul in front of him. But, well, the wretch was no longer his problem. Best leave him to the authorities.

Mollens turned back to his troop and stood for a moment gazing silently into their young, fearful faces. He gathered his thoughts for a moment before speaking.

'Gevalt was no daemon, just a traitor. Have you heard of the skaven, the rat-men?' He could tell by their expressions that some of them had. 'Well, he has been selling you to them. The deserters weren't cowards. They were drugged and sent to their deaths... or worse.'

He could see the fear and horror sweeping through them now, uniting them in the face of the common enemy. Then, to his relief, he saw anger take its place. A few of them started purposefully towards Gevalt. The captain waved them back.

'He's just their pawn. Tonight we'll catch the real monsters. I'll walk into their trap. You will follow me, silently. When you hear my call, charge towards the sound, keeping together at all times. Sergeant Henning here will be in charge until you rejoin me. It's a simple plan – which means it will work. Any questions?'

There were none. After just a moment's hesitation, Henning plucked a spear from the stack and one by one the others followed his example. Even thus armed they huddled close together, peering uncertainly into the darkness of the forest or back towards their captain.

How easy it would be not to do this, thought Mollens, how easy to just close ranks and head back to Nuln. Who would blame me? The troop certainly wouldn't. The Colonel wouldn't. Sykes at the tavern wouldn't as he poured one measure, then another, and another–

Abruptly, without fully realising what he was doing, Mollens started off towards the treeline.

'Give me five minutes, then follow,' he told Henning as he passed. 'Remember, don't throw your spears.'

'Sir.' Henning saluted.

Mollens was warmed a little by the respect he saw in his troops' eyes. But as the firelight faded behind him and he continued striding forward into the night the warmth faded, extinguished by the tide of dread that poured relentlessly through him. He could feel it eating away at his resolve like storm waters against a dam. A weird feeling of unreality washed through him. He couldn't quite believe that he was doing this. The cold sweat that poured off him threatened to spoil the comforting grip he had on the haft of his spear. The tightly clamped muscles in his jaws spasmed uncontrollably, and he had to bite down to stop his teeth from chattering. All the while his unwilling legs carried him further into the forest.

Eventually the terror started to fade. He had been walking for a long time and there was still no sign of the enemy. Surely they would have taken him by now if they had been going to. Perhaps they had spied on the camp and fled, or maybe they had been driven off by some other terrible beast.

In spite of himself the captain began to feel a cautious relief. He stopped for a moment and listened. Hearing only the soft background patter of the woods he began to smile, then turned and started back.

A swathe of sickly green light burst through the darkness. The captain sobbed at the horrible tableau it revealed, and for a moment he stood, paralysed with horror, at the sight in front of him.

The giant rat-thing stood a scant five paces in front of him, lips drawn back in a foam-flecked snarl. It was hunched forward, tail whipping the ground behind it impatiently, its beady red eyes skewering Mollens with blind animal hatred. Skulking beside the hulking form of the beast was its vile master. It let out a shrill squeak and from the shadows amongst the trees half a dozen figures lurched forwards in response.

The were foul. In gait and appearance they were like zombies, the slack grey flesh, the untended wounds. Mollens had seen their like before. But the things that came crashing towards him now were no zombies. Their eyes reflected a mute pleading for release that was all too human. As they came for him Mollens recognised the deserters.

These were the boys whom he had lured from their mothers and sweethearts. They had left their safe, comfortable lives for dreams, chasing the mirage of glory that Mollens had helped to create. And this was where it had led them. As their fingers reached towards him, Mollens found that his throat was locked too tight to scream.

His mind reeling, the captain found odd details in his last few moments standing out with a bright, unreal clarity. He noticed every chip and crack on the nearest of the creatures' shattered fingernails. He noticed the shift of the breeze, picking up now. Then he noticed an amulet hung around the neck of one of the things, and remembered the wizened old crone who had put it around the neck of her grandson. It had been such a touching gesture of hopeless, naïve faith that Mollens had felt awful as he had led the boy away – to this.

The bitter memory became a spark, a light amidst the utter, despairing darkness of his soul. And the spark ignited a white hot ball of pure hatred in Mollens's chest. It burned with a maddening intensity, fed as it was by fear and loss, and five long, tormented years. With a keening, inhuman scream Mollens sprang through the feeble forms of his lost men towards the rat-ogre before him.

The beast loomed above him, its foul reek an almost physical armour. But Mollens was unstoppable. The rat-ogre's expression changed from hatred to dumb surprise as Mollens's spear-tip smashed through its throat and out of the back of its skull in a spray of blood. Taloned hands reached upwards to grasp the haft of the spear as the monster toppled backwards into the decaying litter of the forest floor.

A piercing shriek cut through the noise of its fall, and from the corner of his eye Mollens saw a bundle of darkness and steel launch itself at him. He grabbed for his knife with a snarl and stepped back, only to trip over the huge, twitching body of the skaven's beast. A paroxysm of rage seized him, and within its grip he forgot the most basic rule of all. He threw his knife.

The blade spun through the night, sparkling with flashes and whorls of light as it flew towards the bounding shape of the enemy. But the creature twisted sideways, cast aside its cowl, and leapt eagerly forwards towards its prone adversary. The flame from its burning staff streamed forwards now into a sharp fang of fire, its light gleaming on the poisoned dagger held in its tail.

Mollens struggled across the verminous body, ignoring the lice that swarmed beneath his fingers, and reached for his spear. He grasped the haft but his hands, slick with blood and sweat, slipped as he tugged at it. With a moan he glanced back and saw the rat-thing, its lips drawn back in a gleeful grimace, preparing to strike. There was a savage flare of blinding light, then darkness.

He lay tense, waiting for the blow to fall. But instead of the agonising bite of cold steel it was a shove, followed by a muffled curse, that sent Mollens leaping backwards. Sparks started striking around him like fireflies in the darkness, then a dozen torches burst into life. The captain bathed in their yellow glow until a hand reached down and he gratefully allowed a pair of troopers to help him to his feet. They stared past him, awe-struck by the monstrous corpse at their feet. Their spears stuck it again and again, until it lay still. One of them ventured to kick it, then sprang away in shock as a cry rang out behind him.

Sergeant Henning stood reluctantly in front of the cowering troop, his spear wavering uncertainly before him. A dozen slumped figures took step after uncertain step towards him as he backed away. Torchlight flickered across their wasted features, leaving dark caverns of night in hollow

cheeks and between protruding bones. One of the
shambling horrors gave a low rasping moan as it reached
forwards.

Mollens, moving quickly, was there to meet its clammy
grip with his own. He held the creature's withered hand
still and gazed into the gleams of light that were reflected
back from its sunken eyes. Not daring to turn, the captain
barked the order to Henning to take the troop back to the
camp.

In the darkness they left behind, a dagger glittered in the
pale moonlight. It lashed out once, twice, a dozen times. The
one remaining figure stood stooped over the bodies for several long moments, then forced himself to turn and follow
his fellows. The sound of his boots faded away, and soon
there was nothing left in the clearing but for the keening of
the wind.

WHEN MOLLENS, red-eyed and numb, returned to the camp,
he found the troop gathered around Gevalt's lifeless form.
He pushed his way through the silent huddle and felt his
stomach turn at the sight of the traitor's butchered remains.

'It wasn't us, sir,' Henning blurted, worried by his captain's
expression.

'I know,' Mollens said, his eyes glued to the body. Here and
there jagged pink shards of bone, splintered like twigs during
the traitor's final convulsions, had torn through frail parchment skin. Worse was the face, a frozen mask of agony. The
eyes, as pink and blind as a new-born rat's, stared wildly into
the great beyond. Blood had cascaded from the mouth in a
great stream, the gore flecked with shreds of cheek and
tongue. And, most horribly of all, the man had died with an
almost gleeful rictus grin spread across his twisted features.

'I know,' repeated Mollens to himself. He knew that the
will, let alone the ability, to do this to a man was far beyond
the capability of these farm lads. No, he told himself, not
farm lads. Not any more.

'Wrap him in a blanket We'd better take him with us.'

'Yes, sir… erm, captain? What's that?'

Mollens glanced down at the makeshift sack he carried in
his left hand. The folded cloak was already dripping with

dark crimson fluid. He hefted it in his hand and smiled, suddenly proud of himself and his men.

'It's our first trophy. Look.' Out of the bag he spilled the head of the rat-ogre. It rolled onto its side, dead eyes glaring accusingly at them.

'It's horrible,' Henning said vaguely. Then he grinned, wonder writ large across his broad features. 'And we beat it, didn't we?'

'We certainly did,' Mollens nodded. He watched his men, studied their faces. He saw fear and horrified fascination warring for ascendancy across their young features, and then the sudden joyous rush of victory hit them. A moment later the cheering started.

Four days later, they reached the final camp outside the walls of Nuln. Mollens, yawning contentedly after another sound night's sleep, awoke first. Leaving the slumbering camp behind him he waded through the cold, grey shoals of morning mist to the summit of the last hill.

The great ancient city lay sprawled out beneath the blanket of fog below him. From this distance it was still and silent apart from the chattering symphony of the dawn chorus, but Mollens knew that such a city never really slept. Already the farmers would be trudging along the twists and turns of the city streets with their loads of eggs or milk or apples. The dung collectors, finishing for the night, would be returning to their hovels on the outskirts, tired and hungry for breakfast. Apprentices, squinting with sleep, would be lighting fires or opening shops.

And meanwhile, in the stinking depths beneath the city there would be another sort of life, secret and poisonous. Mollens thought of the traps and the pitfalls, the claustrophobia and sudden, boiling masses of the enemy. He thought of his men, of poor Ferdinand and of five, long tormented years. Then he smiled a wolf's smile, savage and full of teeth.

It was good to be back.

# THE SOUND WHICH WAKES YOU

## by Ben Chessell

You NEVER HEAR the sound which wakes you. It remains in the realm of sleep while you enter the world of wakefulness.

Tomas sat up like a bending board and willed his eyes to open. He slept on the smooth, black stones beside the forge; a good place to sleep, especially when the winter chills rolled down like waves from the Grey Mountains, leaving a coating of frosty brine come morning. One night a spark from the forge had spat out and ignited his bed of grass and bracken while he slept but, unlike his father, Tomas was not a heavy sleeper.

His father! Pierro was smith to the people who lived in the village of Montreuil, under the jagged shadow of the Grey Mountains, in the north of Bretonnia. Tomas came to the realisation, as he did every morning, that the sound which had woken him must have been that of his father's first hammer stroke for the day, which was closely followed, with mechanic inevitability, by the second.

Each blow of the hammer bid Tomas an ungentle good morning, before departing the smithy to wake the creatures of the forest, and reminded him sternly of the amount of brandy he and Luc had consumed the previous evening. Tomas prised open his eyes and, through the narrow slit which he managed in his visor of sleep, located his smock and boots.

Manoeuvering around his father, Tomas began slowly to dress. Neither acknowledged the other. Tomas pulled his smock over his head and squeezed into his boots while Pierro bent over the forge, puffing great blasts of air from his lungs with every swing of his hammer: a set of human bellows. Tomas's father worked hard and never left the smithy, unless it was to tend to the grove of ancient oaks which stood at the edge of the forest beyond the common pasture land.

It had been his father's responsibility, and so on down to the very roots of the family tree. One day, Tomas supposed, it would be his. Tomas left the smithy as soon as he was ready, as he did every morning.

In the doorway he met Marc, who was Pierro's apprentice and had held the post ever since Pietre. Tomas's elder brother had been the most promising young smith Montreuil had seen since the brighter days of Pierro's youth and the old regime. Marc was capable enough in his own steady way, and he and Tomas were friendly, accounting for the fact that Marc held the job which might have been thought most rightly to belong to Tomas. When his time had come, Tomas had refused to take up the position as his father's apprentice and it was only because of the prayers of his mother who had lost one son already, that Tomas was permitted to continue to live under Pierro's roof. Tomas brought in a little money to the family through different jobs for farmers in the district and Marc became the smith's apprentice. The two exchanged a polite greeting and Tomas plunged into the bright, grey world.

MANY IN THE forest-edge village saw fit to comment about the estranged family, wondering whether it was Tomas who refused to meet his inherited responsibilities or Pierro who refused to fulfil his parental ones. Whatever the facts of the matter (and actually it was both), it was fortunate for Montreuil that young Marc, whose father had perished in the cells of the Marquis, could step in and fill the need.

These things wandered through Tomas's mind as he rounded the back of the smithy and stuffed his head and torso into the barrel of ice and water. Tomas practiced this routine every morning almost as though it might harden him as his father tempered a glowing blade. Tomas had need of the hardness of iron, if he was going to rid Montreuil of Gilbert: Gilbert de la Roserie, Marquis, holder of the King's commission – and tyrant.

Montreuil was a political enigma, a political embarrassment. Squeezed like a stone between the toes of a giant, the village lay in the foothills of the northern Grey Mountains. Further north even than the great spa city of Couronne, Montreuil had almost no value to the thriving rural heart of Bretonnia many days to the south.

The King, however, who wielded the complicated feudal system like a well-weighted blade, had found a use for Montreuil. He made a grant of land there to one of his lords whose outspoken militaristic opinions had become unfashionable in these times of détente. This commission, this putting out to pasture, had been bestowed on Gilbert Helene, who had become the Marquis Gilbert de la Roserie more than thirty years ago, after he had served the king faithfully, if a little bloodily, in the wars of their youth.

Most of the villagers guessed, quite rightly, that the King had entirely forgotten about the existence of Montreuil and the man who ruled there. Marquis Gilbert certainly behaved as if the village was his own private kingdom and the troop of border guards – a dozen aging career soldiers and petty officers – was his royal army.

THIS WAS THE sad situation that Tomas was determined to upset. Approaching his twentieth year, Tomas was brimming with the rebelliousness of youth and the sense of invincibility which comes with it. He dreamed constantly of calling the hundred or so villagers to arms and ousting the tyrant with his twenty men. There were practical problems of course. The soldiers, called 'sergeants' by the villagers because most of them had held at least that rank in the national army before their ambition had got the better of them, were the only armed folk in the village. One of the

Marquis's many laws prevented the villagers from owning anything more warlike than a bow for hunting and a knife for cutting meat.

What made this restriction all the more unbearable for Tomas was the fact that his own father forged the swords and spears with which Gilbert's men enforced his laws. Every helmet, every breastplate had begun life in the forge at the end of Tomas's house, beside which he slept each night and yet not one blade remained there.

This alone would have been enough to estrange father and son but the situation was aggravated for Tomas by the fact that his own father, Pierro, refused to talk about any aspect of his work with Tomas since Tomas had declined to become his apprentice. Pierro was a talented smith and on Gilbert's own hip hung a rapier, hilted in fine gold set with uncut topaz, made by Tomas's father. Besides which, the villagers of Montreuil were an infuriatingly peaceful people and took each new injustice as simply another trial to be borne in silence.

Lost in such thoughts, Tomas broke free of the woods and began the climb up the slope above the village. Sheep and goats picked among the scree for the meagre spring grasses, having only recently made the trek from their winter quarters themselves. Tomas headed toward the shepherd's hut, made from dark pine logs lashed with the innards of stock unfortunate enough to be chosen for the table. Tomas knew that, after last night's drinking episode, Luc would still be sleeping while his sheep strayed where they chose, unprotected from wolves, bears or rustlers.

The brandy had hit Luc a little harder than it had Tomas and besides, Luc loathed to leave his bed without the strongest provocation. He was just like any other villager, Tomas reflected as he chose a large stone with which to announce his arrival: happier sleeping, but waiting for the right signal to rouse him. Tomas heaved the stone overarm and watched with satisfaction as it bounced from the side of the hut with a loud thump. He sat on a rock to wait.

Luc stumbled out soon enough and, having realised how seriously he had overslept, looked about frantically for the source of the danger. Tomas sent another, smaller rock sailing in a graceful arc toward the younger boy. It struck him on the hip and he spun to discover his laughing assailant. His relief was clear to see and it occurred to Tomas that Luc was more worried that he might have to confront one of the owners of the sheep, come to check the flock, than a wolf come to eat it.

Luc was a simple enough lad as far as Tomas was concerned though there was something about him the older boy could never quite grasp. The two breakfasted together among the stones and picked up their conversation of the previous evening. The plans they had made seemed less practical in the grey light of morning than they had by the lively dance of the fire the night before.

'Firelight makes all things seem possible, Tomas'.

'But did we not agree that all that is needed to begin this thing is for the right spark to be set to the tinder?'

'Tomas we did, but we had the confidence of the brandy then', Luc paused to consume a piece of bread, 'and besides we do not know how to set that fire, where to place the spark.'

'I hear you, I hear you', Tomas gestured, stabbing the air twice with his piece of bread, 'but what if I told you I had discovered where the spark should be set, what if I told you I will not wait any longer?'

'I would not believe you, and I would say you were still drunk.'

'But we do nothing! Even when my brother is killed my father does nothing. He accepts the blows of fate with the meekness of one of your sheep, in the jaws of a wolf.'

'Tomas, your brother killed a sergeant…'

'Who killed his lover…'

'Who poured wine over his head and threw him from the tavern…'

'This is senseless Luc, what matters is that nobody here does anything but work, eat and sleep. And I will be different.'

'Well that is what I want too Tomas, but…'

'Good, then bring your flint.'

'Now?'

Luc stopped chewing as the conversation which he had had many times with Tomas became something else altogether. 'Now.'

'But my sheep–'

'The sheep can see to themselves, we have a more important flock to tend.'

Tomas leading, Luc following, the pair descended from the mountainside down the path to Montreuil. The view afforded by the summer pastures mapped out the tiny village, clustered around a green common from which a tree-lined avenue led to the manor. The large house, more in some ways a small castle, was surrounded by a thick hedge of briar and roses, thus 'The Roserie'. The hedge was more decorative than defensive, although it would take a determined attacker to hack through its thorns, and in spring, as it now was, it bore a crop of white and pink roses of notable beauty.

It was forbidden for any villager to pick a rose with which to adorn their own dwelling, or to make a cutting from the ancient tangle. Occasionally the Marquis would make a gift of a small bunch of the blooms to some young woman of the district he had chosen for his amusement, but otherwise he enjoyed his exclusive hold on beauty. It was towards this hedge, and the dwelling it concealed, that Tomas led an increasingly dubious Luc.

Although there would be no guard set at this time of day, Luc pulled Tomas up behind the last copse of trees before the rose hedge. Luc said nothing but looked hard at Tomas, perhaps willing him to reconsider, perhaps something else. Tomas returned the stare, expecting to find uncertainty, and saw instead a testing glance, questioning. Whatever the truth of it, Luc solemnly handed over his flint and tinder and climbed up into the oak to observe the crime.

'If you are not back in half an hour I will come looking.'

Tomas nodded, watched him climb in silence, and then turned toward his objective. A large brown arm descended from the tree and signalled to Tomas. Sufficiently comforted, Tomas sprang into a low run. There was a part of the hedge at the back corner of the manor which was particularly wild and Tomas headed for that now. It concealed the beginning of a tunnel which led through the vicious thicket and which was a dangerous children's challenge in Montreuil. Tomas had made the run many times as a youth, winning ale, sweets or merely admiration. The punishment if caught depended on which of the sergeants found you, and how drunk they were on that particular day. Having never been caught, Tomas had become something of a village champion at the game and in his later years had taken to making the trip around the hedge for his own sake, seeking no accolades. Today those journeys of childish rebellion seemed like the memories of another boy.

He found the entrance to the tunnel with little difficulty though it had been some years since he had last been here. Indeed the architecture of the place had changed as does the shape of any childhood haunt when revisited. The dimensions shift, not just because the viewer is taller, but also because of the years spent away from the place. Certain things were more important to Tomas now than when last he had navigated the spine-wrought passageway and these things changed the very shape of the tunnel through the hedge.

He crawled in and lay still. The sounds of the manor drifted across the lawns which lay in between. Marquis Gilbert would still be asleep, but the maids and gardeners were at work. The sergeants slept in a long, low barracks on the other side of the house and Tomas wasn't sure how many of them would be awake. A few maintained notions of martial excellence and practised drills regularly with his father's swords upon the well-cut lawns which ringed the manor like a bright, green moat. Tomas listened hard for the sound of metal on metal, one the smith's son knew very well, but heard nothing. He began his work.

The driest fuel in the hedge was high in the branches but the best place to set a fire is low to the ground so Tomas set himself the task of fetching some down.

Climbing up through the hedge was a process best undertaken slowly and carefully, and ensured a certain amount of scratching nonetheless. After four trips up and back and about a half an hour's work, Tomas had a pile of kindling which reached his waist, topped by an old bird's nest.

At this point he paused and sat, sucking his arm where a thorn like a doornail had dug deep. With his other hand he took out the sheepskin pouch which contained Luc's flint and laid it on the mat of thorns and leaves which formed the floor of the rose-hedge.

Certain actions, certain distances are, when it is you that must travel them, very much greater than they appear. Such was the tiny fall which the sparks made to the tinder as Tomas struck steel against grey stone. He had set many fires in his time, every night before bed until the age of fifteen, but none so hot as this.

At first he thought it wasn't going to catch. The fuel was dew-laden and in some cases had been lying for a long time, but it did begin to burn. Tomas nursed his fire to the fulcrum point, beyond which it could take care of itself, coaxing it with small twigs and grass from the nest. In a final poetic gesture he pulled a hair from his head and added it to the blaze, watching it curl and snarl, the acrid smell lost in the sweet aroma of burning rosewood. Tomas accepted several deep scratches on his arms and cheeks as he made his way forcefully from the hedge, already breathing smoke, his eyes seeping tears. The final part of the plan was simply to run, low and quick, and climb the hill to watch the drama unfold.

Tomas began his run, flat and hard, toward the tree where he had left Luc. He heard his name called. Luc's voice, not from in front but from behind. Tomas spun and fell, rolled and regained his feet. Looking back he was first struck by how quickly his work was taking effect. The fire had moved quickly upward and fifteen foot high flames now claimed the top reaches of the hedge. Rose blooms dropped to the ground in a burning rain as the upper limbs of the hedge bent, snapped and plunged backwards into the hungry blaze. Then Tomas saw Luc.

It is often something totally simple and yet totally unpredictable which undoes a great plan, or even a modest one and Tomas watched in horror as Luc stood as near as he could to the base of the blaze and called 'Tomas!'.

Tomas hesitated. The sergeants, were any awake, would be at the fire any moment and Luc would be seen. He ran back, driving the ground with his legs, and felt the intense heat of the fire. He dared not call Luc's name in case the sergeants heard. That Luc had called his could not now be helped, both of them need not be revealed.

The younger boy was almost blinded by the fire and would not see Tomas until he was close. Coughing out the smoke which invaded his lungs with each breath, Tomas watched the manor gate as he reached Luc. Two sergeants ran out, buckling their belts and fanning smoke away in order to better gauge the extent of the blaze.

Tomas shouldered Luc in the back and both hit the ground hard. The two rolled away from the fire, Luc following Tomas, and rounded the corner of the hedge. There they stood and sprinted for the relative safety of the woods which backed the manor. Reaching the trees they crouched and Tomas wiped black tears from his eyes while striving to regain his breath.

Luc lay in the bracken and looked up at Tomas. 'I'm sorry. I was scared. There were men in the grounds. I came to warn you.'

Tomas did not look at Luc when he spoke but instead kept his gaze fixed on the fire, which now consumed the entire east corner of the hedge and was almost at the gate. He bit down hard on his lip and said nothing.

Above the gate, a span of almost twenty feet, there was a thin archway of hedge fronds and thorn-bush. The fire snaked out one end of the span while one of the sergeants tried to hack it down with his sword. The work was too much and the heat too great and as he fell back the fire made the journey across the bridge and the entire hedge was doomed.

Tomas had seen enough and took Luc's hand to lead him away. He was surprised to hear himself accuse, 'Luc, you said my name.'

BY THE TIME the two parted company the news was all through the village. So was the smoke. Tomas joined the steady stream of spectators walking cautiously up to the manor to see the fire and soon most of the inhabitants of Montreuil stood by as the rose-hedge collapsed inwards into a pile of coals and ash. At one point the blaze threatened the manor itself but a few of the younger sergeants managed to keep it at bay, filling buckets from the stream. Noon came, grey and dull; the show was over and the talk had begun.

Tomas mingled and listened with satisfaction to the rumours as they evolved. Some said it was out-of-towners, others that it was one the many lovers Gilbert had jilted and a third tale conjured enemies from the Marquis's past. Tomas joined some of the conversations enthusiastically, encouraging whatever theory held sway. He was relieved to hear no mention of his own name on anybody's lips.

As the crowd dispersed Tomas turned to leave – and walked directly into the leather apron which his father wore, dawn until sleep, at work or abroad. He did not know how long Pierro had stood there, his face golden in the glow from the hedge. Tomas's name was on his father's lips and Pierro's hand was firmly on the boy's shoulder. 'Tomas, come with me. Now.'

His father propelled Tomas away from the crowd which had begun to disperse and marched him back to the smithy. Tomas felt no fear from what was about to happen. He had more serious concerns than familiar discipline, and besides, the actions of the early morning had hardened him to the point where his father's leather belt was no more than a light switch of rush grasses. Pierro pulled the hide across the door of the smithy and turned around. Tomas cocked his head to one side and planted his hands on his hips. He waited for his father to unbuckle his belt and administer the punishment. Instead Pierro looked at his son, long and deep. Tomas found himself able to meet the gaze but the beginnings of confusion stirred in his stomach. His father had not looked at him in such a way before.

When Pierro finally spoke it was not with the tone, nor indeed the words, that Tomas expected. 'Go and say farewell to your mother.'

'My mother?'

'Did you not hear me, Tomas?' Normally his father called him 'boy'. 'She is mourning your loss already.'

'What loss?'

'They will be here soon.'

'How do you know? How could you know that?' Tomas's anger came from fear but also from losing control of the conversation.

'I have friends among the sergeants.' His father's calm certainty frightened Tomas even more. He hit back.

'Because you are their friend, because you help them to hurt all who live in Montreuil, because you are a traitor even to your own family!'

Pierro sighed, his apron rising and falling with his bellows lungs. 'No, Tomas. Because an uprising such as the one of which you dream must be planned properly and with patience, otherwise good people have to die.'

Tomas tried to grasp the meaning of this last and very unexpected answer. He failed, drowning in uncertainty, and waited desperately for his father to throw him a rope.

'Did you think, Tomas, that I bore this injustice willingly, that I befriended tyrants for my own betterment?' Tomas's head was suddenly light and he leant against the forge, warm clay against his back.

'The blood which flows in your veins, my son, was my blood before it was yours. That is the reason that I cannot be quite as angry as I might. In some ways, Lady forgive me, I am proud.'

Pierro stopped as they both heard voices from outside the smithy. The smith peered through a hole in the hide door and turned back to Tomas with a grave expression. Without saying anything he picked up his son and placed him on top of the forge like he had many times when Tomas had been a young lad, to warm the soles of his feet on winter mornings. He removed his leather gloves and handed them over. Tomas put them on without understanding why.

'Go to the grove and wait for me there. I must think what is best to do.'

The sound of several riders dismounting could be heard clearly from outside. Pierro looked hard into Tomas's eyes and then, touching the hot metal pipe which was the chimney of the forge, said one word: 'Climb.'

Tomas watched the ensuing scene from the thatched roof of the house in which he had spent his entire life. The events which occurred seemed even more unreal framed by this most normal of settings. The surprise Tomas might have expected when his father produced a sword from underneath a stack of raw iron ingots and bundled it with the apron in his right hand, never occurred. Neither did the shock register when the Marquis himself, with four of his men, stood in Tomas's front yard. He wriggled to the apex of the roof, where he himself had knitted the thatching together and saw his father approach the men. By the time the exchange began he felt himself ready to witness anything and remain unsurprised. He was wrong.

Tomas could not hear the conversation in detail and voices reached him only when they were raised. His father faced away, leather apron folded and hanging from his right hand. Tomas could hear none of Pierro's words.

The Marquis remained mounted, untouchable on his black perch, while his men spread out, their hands never far from their sword hilts. They were clearly looking for Tomas. How they knew, with such certainty, that he was responsible for the rose-scented smoke which still clung to the valley, he could never be sure. Perhaps they had heard Luc's cry; maybe Tomas had made one too many drunken speeches on sunny festival afternoons. Whatever their source of information they were only angered by his father's denials. The Marquis stabbed the air with his gloved hand and early in the exchange augmented his gesturing by drawing the rapier which Pierro had made for him. The blade was dull in the grey light but Tomas knew that the edge would be well honed. His fingers clutched handfuls of straw and he breathed moss and dust as he watched the scene unfold. Two of the men entered the house while the others kept Pierro from following.

The Marquis rested his blade on the smith's chest and pushed to emphasize a heated point he was making. Pierro stepped back, between the two sergeants who crushed him between their shoulders. The others returned from the house, having failed to find Tomas. Both had their blades drawn; one also carried a red-hot iron from the forge. Tomas strangled a squeal.

WHEN RELATING THE details of his father's last moments, as he later had to do many times, Tomas could never exactly account for what happened.

At the Marquis's signal, the two men behind Pierro grabbed his arms and, with some effort, pulled them from his side. The apron fell to the ground, revealing Pierro's sword. Gilbert shrieked hysterically and pointed with his own blade. The sergeants looked with open mouths and one pounced to retrieve the blade. He was rewarded with Pierro's boot in his face and he rolled backwards into the Marquis's horse. Tomas's father swung his huge arms in front of him and his captors crashed together, bone on bone. He twisted his hands from theirs and sprang back, claiming his sword and apron from the dirt. Pierro backed cautiously toward his house, and the sergeant who remained uninjured followed up hard. Gilbert's man crouched and stretched his arms, willing them to remember the long lost training grounds and infantry manoeuvres of his youth. He lunged and Pierro beat the attack away with his left hand, wrapped in the heavy leather apron. With a booming cry Tomas had never heard his father utter before, the smith covered his attacker's head with his apron and smashed his knee out and away. The man fell and Pierro looked up to consider his options.

The Marquis sat safely on his horse behind his men who moved slowly forward, trapping Pierro against the wall of the smithy. Tomas crept further up the roof as his father retreated under the eaves. He couldn't see him anymore, only the expressions on the faces of his foes. At a command from the Marquis the three rushed Pierro in an unsophisticated charge. All combatants disappeared from Tomas's view and all he could see now was Gilbert's face wearing a feral snarl. One sergeant reappeared immediately, one hand grasping the other to stem the wellspring of blood which gushed there. Tomas didn't see his father die – but he heard it.

As he slid off the roof behind the house he tasted blood and realised he had bitten down on his tongue. The sound of his father dying was still in his ears, the cry and the unholy punctuation of the body meeting the ground. Tomas dropped from the straw eaves and set off for the woods at a barely controlled scamper.

Tomas wasn't sure whether they had heard him or not and he didn't care. He kept running, weaving between the trees like a fox before the chase. He rested only when he reached the grove of oaks, heavy and dark in the late afternoon sun. Tomas propped his back against the largest of the trees and slid to the ground, the shadow of the canopy reaching down and embracing him in its lattice. Tomas cried then. He sat and cried and watched the shadow grow and twist and finally fade as the pale sun faltered. He thought about his father. He thought about their final conversation and the sound his father had made as he fell to the ground. He felt like a little boy. Tomas decided what he had to do and only then could he fall asleep.

HE WOKE IN the pre-dawn hour when the deep-green canopy of the oaks gathered the mist and distilled it into crystal drops. A drop landed on Tomas's nose and rolled down, pooling between his lips. He opened his eyes and adjusted slowly to the flat, grey light. Standing at the other end of the grove, barely visible through the curtain of fog, were four figures. Tomas drew breath. He lay still and examined the group. They did not appear to be sergeants; the outlines were too slim and lacked weapons. They were talking quietly to each other and occasionally one would glance in Tomas's direction. He lay still, nestled between the bony roots of the oak. The figures knew he was there but not that he was awake. He determined to lie still until he could learn who they were.

The four became six with the arrival of a pair from the direction of the village. The two newcomers came in at a run and spoke to the others in breathless tones. Their message was clearly urgent though Tomas could catch none of its detail. The smaller of the arrivals grabbed the shirt of the figure he addressed with both fists to add emphasis to his news. Tomas studied the silhouette of the messenger against the growing dawn. He recognized the shape of the shoulders and neck and wondered hard what it was that had roused Luc from his bed before the sun itself. By the time dawn was undeniably upon them the six had become nine, and then twelve, and Tomas could see who they were: men from the village, men he knew, farmers, shepherds and Ludo the tavern keeper. They were deep in discussion. Suddenly a decision was reached and all turned their faces toward the tree at whose feet Tomas lay.

'Tomas, wake up.'

Tomas stood slowly and looked around the group. Their faces were grim and not altogether friendly. They seemed to be sizing him up.

'That you have done this thing you have done is brave, we acknowledge.' The speaker was Paul, a lean farmer and a friend of Tomas's father.

'What we need to know is how brave you will be now.' The group seemed to move closer to Tomas, blocking the morning sun.

'What does it matter what I do?'

'It matters a great deal.'

'I don't understand any of this. I am the one who must run and hide. It is my father who is dead, Lady watch over him.'

'Did you speak with him before he gave his life to save you? Have you opened your eyes just a little?' Now Tomas was addressed by a younger man, whose anger was palpable. Gerni the miller pressed his questioning further. 'Did he give you his blessing?'

'He told me to come here.'

There was a general murmur concerning what this might mean. Some thought that Pierro's last request was of great significance and that the smith had intended and foreseen the conversation which was taking place. Others were more skeptical, citing the less than perfect relationship between father and son. Tomas was almost forgotten for a moment.

Luc stepped from the huddle and asked him in a low voice. 'What will you do?' Tomas looked at him, hard.

'Have you always been part of… part of whatever this is?'

'Don't be angry, Tomas. Your father always wanted to know what you were thinking, what you were saying.'

'And you told him?'

'Everything.'

'What was my father to these people?'

'He was our leader.'

'He was what?'

'From the very beginning.'

'Leader, leader in what?'

'Are you so very blind, Tomas?'

'What is this meeting? What are you here for?'

'To decide what should be done.' Luc looked away. He might have been about to say more but Paul turned back to Tomas.

'What would you have us do, boy? What would you do?'

No response of Tomas's would have satisfied the group. Their expectations were based on their respect for and memory of a dead man, and their palpable disappointment with his replacement.

'I am going to the manor to kill the Marquis, or I will join my brave father, that is all.'

The men thought for a moment. Before one of the more senior figures could respond, Luc spoke up.

'We could come with you. Perhaps you need not die.'

'That would mean war. We can't fight soldiers with sticks, Luc.'

'The village is already full of sergeants, looking for us, and besides…'

Gerni choked a little laugh and walked past Tomas to the oak under which he had slept. The miller reached up into a hole near the bole of the tree and his hand returned with a large hessian sack, sewn shut at both ends. He lay the bundle heavily at his feet and cut a careful, longitudinal slash with his knife.

Tomas still could not understand what he was seeing as the bright blades spilled onto the grass. Something about the simple, elegant ironwork was familiar but a part of him still refused to understand. 'Where did these come from?'

'Your father, boy. Pierro forged these over years of crafty, secret work. An ingot of iron here, a few spare hours there. Paid for by the Marquis and crafted by his own smith. Intended for his downfall. There aren't quite enough but we will have to make do. That is, unless you have a better idea.' The bitterness in Paul's speech cut Tomas and his eyes stung with salt.

'My father?'

'Your father.'

The men distributed the weapons and made final repairs to the leather handles. They sharpened the blades on stones among the trees which seemed to be too well placed in the grove to have lain there by chance. Others spent the day practicing, or preparing a meal for the group. By nightfall they were ready. There had been no discussion, no decision and there was no plan, but a general consensus had spread through the group that they would move at night. It was agreed that the sergeants would know something was up but would not be anywhere close to ready for exactly what was. Tomas felt unable to claim a sword when others were without them, and he gripped his knife as if someone was trying to wrest it from his grasp.

THE FIRES WERE well and truly out around the manor and the huge house lay strangely naked in the moonlight when the mob arrived. They hid at the edge of the woods and watched for long enough to establish that four sergeants were out in the grounds, patrolling, and that fires burned in many of the manor's hearths. What they didn't know was how many of the sergeants remained in the village and how many were in the barracks. Facing all the armed men at once they would be fatally outnumbered. Their only hope was to deal with their enemy piecemeal. The distance between the forest and the manor, only about a third of a mile, seemed an uncrossable chasm of open ground.

Tomas heard himself give what sounded like an order and thought only later about how easily it had come to him. 'This way. Follow me.'

Tomas, Paul, Gerni and Luc went ahead, the others waiting in the woods for their signal. The four scouts crept as far as the scar of the hedge and hit the ground. Nothing remained but a few twisted black bones of the great growth and a two-foot deep ditch of coals and ash. Tomas felt the warmth of it on his face, even now, and took some comfort from that. They waited for two of the sergeants to pass further away and then Tomas demonstrated his idea. He found a deep pile of ashes and took a double handful. With this he painted his face and clothes black and grey and almost disappeared into the background of the burnt hedge. The others followed suit and the four crept up the hedge-line, keeping low, almost invisible towards the main gate where the two men stood guard. The gates looked forlorn and foolish with their stone gateposts standing alone and no hedge to justify them.

Tomas, Paul, Gerni and Luc crept as close as they dared and halted again, looking briefly into each other's eyes and waiting for what must come next. Tomas looked at Luc's blackened face and saw his brown eyes brighter than the ash, wide and fearful. Gerni wriggled over to Tomas, making too much noise for Tomas's liking.

'What's your plan now, boy?'

Tomas didn't like the diminutive but could only agree that the doubt on the older man's part was justified. He thought quickly.

'I will gain their attention while you and Paul rush them from behind.' A sound enough plan.

'What about me?' Luc whispered.

'You can go back and bring the others to the hedge, what's left of it.' Luc was clearly relieved by this job. He pulled his sword quietly from his belt.

'Give me your knife, Tomas. You will have more need of this.'

Tomas took the sword and felt its cool weight. He looked briefly at the simple, sturdy ironwork in the moonlight and thought of his father. 'Not now', he told himself, 'not now.'

They watched Luc crawl away down the hedge-line and melt into the black scar, one more grey lump, and turned to their allotted task. Paul looked up at the moon.

'Time to move, Tomas.' Tomas was grateful not to be called 'boy' this one time. 'How do you mean to get their attention?'

'Be ready and you will know soon enough.' Tomas wished he had a better answer but he did not. Paul, however, took his brusqueness as evidence that he had everything under control. Paul and Gerni moved quietly into position.

Tomas crept toward the front of the hedge and the gate. He could see the two men clearly now, he even thought he knew one of their names. Alain, an older sergeant, had come to the smithy more than once to have his armour adjusted to suit his expanding girth. Tomas willed a clever idea to come into his head but none did, so he fell back on the only notion he had. He stood up, walked several steps away from the hedge and began to stroll toward the gate. He tried to whistle but his mouth was shaking so much that he couldn't form the proper shape.

ALAIN AND HIS colleague didn't see him until he was quite close. 'Who's there?'

'It's me, Tomas, I've come to see the Marquis.'

'You've what?'

'Gilbert. I've come to pay him a visit.' The soldiers peered into the night to ascertain whether Tomas was alone. Alain stepped forward a little and peered at the boy in the darkness.

'Let me get this right. You've come to see the Marquis. We've been looking for you all the last night and day, and you waltz up here, bold as you please, asking to see the boss?'

'That's right.'

'Well you got balls on you, boy, even if you don't have brains.' In a strange and somewhat terrifying development to Tomas, he was beginning to enjoy himself.

'Please don't call me "boy". My name is Tomas.' He hoped Paul and Gerni would not take too much longer and his ears were rewarded with the sound of a stealthy footfall. If he could just hold the attention of the guards for a moment longer… Alain's companion joined the conversation.

'Well, boy, the Marquis will be very pleased to see you, but not with that sword at your hip. Where did you get it?' Tomas had forgotten the weapon stuffed through the rope which held his trews up. Tomas still couldn't see Paul or Gerni but decided that if they didn't arrive soon he was in serious trouble anyway.

'This sword?' One last stall.

'Yeah, boy, that sword. What are you going to do with it?'

'I'm going to stick this sword into Gilbert's soft belly and watch his bright blood spill out.'

The men stopped for a second and looked at each other. They reached for their own blades and Tomas dragged his from his belt. For a brief moment he found himself facing two experienced fighters with a weapon he had never wielded before. He bit his tongue and opened the wound from the day before, tasting iron.

Had Paul and Gerni synchronised their attacks a little better it would have been over instantly. As it was, the younger sergeant went down under a double handed stroke to his neck, not pretty swordplay by any means but brutally effective. Alain had a breath after this had happened to turn and put his arm in the way of Gerni's upward thrust. The tip of the blade pierced his much repaired chain-mail vest at the bottom of the ribcage and both men fell to the ground. Alain was a big man and had taken wounds before, though not for many years. He punched Gerni in the mouth with a mailed glove and the miller rolled away spitting blood and teeth.

Paul was still engaged and so Tomas grabbed his weapon tightly and approached the panting Alain. The fat soldier was having trouble getting his sword out of its scabbard which had fallen underneath him and he was concentrating on this task when Tomas arrived. He looked up at Tomas's face. 'Now, boy…'

Tomas stamped hard on his sword hand and kicked at his face. Looking down at the older man, cradling his broken fingers against his bleeding face Tomas paused, but he quickly realised he had come much too far for remorse. He reversed the sword in both hands and struck downward as hard as he could. The brief battle was over and the three men fought to regain their breaths.

Hardly had they drawn three lungfulls each when they heard Luc cry, 'Tomas!'

The distance and the dark made it hard to discern the situation but this is how it seemed to the three at the gate. Luc must have run into the other patrol and now fled across the open ground toward the forest with the two sergeants on his heels. The unarmoured Luc was faster but was done for if the soldiers caught him.

Paul grabbed Tomas, 'Quickly! We must help.' Tomas was torn.

'No, wait.'

'There will be more men.'

'We knew we'd have to fight. Wait.'

LUC ALMOST REACHED the eaves of the forest before he fell. He rolled and tried to stand but he had hurt his leg or his ankle and he pitched forward again. The men were on him. From the trees which offered him safety came a roar and eight villagers sprang out, charging toward the soldiers who stood over Luc. The sergeants did a quick head count and attempted a rapid about face. The farmers caught them and

Tomas lost the details in a whirl of bodies and blades. He counted eight men standing at the end of it and that seemed to be a comforting thing. He couldn't tell if any of them were Luc. A door at the end of the house burst open and six armed sergeants carrying torches ran out and down the hill towards the forest. Paul gripped Tomas's arm again.

'They need us. Them's trained soldiers.' The door stood open and firelight spilled out.

'We'll never get a better chance to get inside the house.' Tomas heard the sound of raised voices from the barracks on the other side of the manor.

'They'll be cut to pieces.'

'It's now or never.'

In the end Paul ran back to help the others and Tomas and Gerni made a dash for the house.

They ran hard, bent double, and plunged without hesitation into the fire-lit kitchen whose door stood open. Tomas led and Gerni followed. Had they stopped to think at the door Tomas might never have found the courage to go in at all. The kitchen was empty as they discovered after picking themselves up off the wooden floor. Gerni had slid all the way under the table and stopped against a sack of flour. A cloud of white snow settled in his hair. Tomas's elbow caught on the door frame and sent him spinning against the stone trough in the corner. He splashed his face and combed a handful of water through his hair with his fingers. If he strained his ears Tomas could hear the sounds of a battle from outside in the grounds. Inside the house it was silent. Gerni and Tomas shared a 'you first' look before gripping their swords and going further into the house.

Heavy carpets lay on the floor and hung on the walls eating the sound of their footfalls so that Tomas and Gerni rounded a corner and found themselves almost seated at a table with two sergeants before either group was aware of the other. One of the men was almost asleep and the other strained to read by the guttering stub of a candle. A bottle lay on its side, resting against the book. Their position stood sentry over the main staircase of the house which swept up to the private apartments of the Marquis. The four men looked at each other, unsure of what might happen next.

Had Gerni or Tomas been a competent assassin the outcome would have been simple and quick but the struggle in the dark at the gate had not prepared them for striking in cold blood. The sergeant with the book, a young man with reading spectacles, woke the other with one hand while folding his spectacles and replacing them with his sword in the other. The sleeper stirred and made an inquisitive snort as his eyes opened. He grasped the situation quite speedily and stood, clearing space as he drew his blade.

Tomas and Gerni circled away from each other a little and exchanged a nervous glance. The odds were hardly even. The sergeants were veterans and the older one wore armour, Tomas and Gerni were farmers with weapons they had never, until recently, even held in their hands. Neither side seemed willing to make the first move. Tomas realised that the sergeants had everything to gain by waiting, and he much to lose. It was unlikely the battle outside would go his way and soon more soldiers would return to the house. Tomas swallowed the urge to run and hide. An indistinct shout made its way in from outside and he could wait no longer. The soldiers continued to stand at the table, blocking the stairs. Gerni hung back, the point of his sword wandering aimlessly in front of his face.

In what he was sure would be his last and most foolish action, Tomas leapt forward with his sword in front of him, almost closing his eyes in silent supplication to the memory of his father.

YOU NEVER HEAR the sound which wakes you. He was fairly sure something was amiss in his house, however, and so Marquis Gilbert sat up, letting the satin sheet slide down his naked, hairless chest. He heard something then, a thud and a crash from outside his room. He dressed quickly but clumsily, missing the aid of his dresser who had left for the evening. In the polished silver mirror he frowned at his paunch as he did every morning. He had to admit to himself that he was not the lean and dangerous man he had once been, but there wasn't much that could conceivably be in his house which could cause him to raise a sweat. He buckled on his rapier, which hadn't struck a blow in all its elegant life, and composed himself, risking one more glance in the looking glass before unbolting the door and walking onto the landing.

At the top of the stairs stood two boys. One, the elder of the two, was bleeding seriously from a cut in his cheek. Gilbert looked to the bottom of the staircase. Two of his men lay there, probably dead, certainly on the way. On the table the stub of a candle illuminated one of his books, some spectacles and an empty bottle which would once have contained port, his port.

He snorted. His useless soldiers spent more time drunk than sober. Gilbert's eyes climbed the stairs and settled again on the boys. They held swords in their hands. They held them far from their bodies, as if the blood on the blades might poison them. A good swordsman loved his blade, especially when bloody. Gilbert walked quietly towards the pair. One of them, the younger one, yelled something indistinct and charged along the balcony toward him. The other, the bleeding one, stayed put. Gilbert sank into a fencing stance and waited patiently. The charger realised he was alone about three quarters of the way to his objective and spun around, exposing his back. The older boy was clearly too scared to charge; clever boy.

Gilbert lunged forward, hopping on his back foot first for extra distance, and whipped his blade across the younger boy's back. It raised a welt from waist to shoulder and the lad fell, screaming. Gilbert gently broke his nose by stepping on the back of his head with his boot heel and walked over to attend to the frightened one.

He seemed to find a morsel of courage as he squared up and faced the Marquis rather than run down the stairs as he clearly wanted to. Gilbert feinted low and the boy followed like a trout to a fly. The Marquis's knee connected with his face and the lad cart-wheeled backward and down the stairs, taking every third one as if he were eager to reach the bottom. He lay still and Gilbert turned around.

The young boy had got up again. Bravo. Gilbert assumed a dueling stance with all of the proper flourishes and detail, and signaled as was proper that his opponent might begin when he was ready. As the boy looked into his eyes, with

some anger it must be said, Gilbert noted with amusement
that it was the wretch they had all been looking for. How fit-
ting that he might kill him here, with the sword made by his
own father. Gilbert doubted that the child would appreciate
the irony.

The Marquis set about playing with his victim a little. He
stepped out of the way of the increasingly desperate attacks,
spinning and pirouetting like a dancer. In between each of
the boy's sorties he gave him a little cut, on the face or the
arm, with the tip of the blade. Eventually Gilbert tired of the
game and it occurred to him he should find out if there were
other intruders in his house. He imagined with a certain
amount of grim glee the retribution he would exact from
whoever was responsible for this little insurrection. He
turned to his opponent.

The boy lunged, straight and unimaginative, slow and
clumsy. Gilbert was an enthusiastic user of the stop-hit, a
manoeuvre in which one fencer, instead of parrying his
opponent's offence, attacks instead, hitting before the original blow lands. He employed it now, bringing his blade
inside the boy's, and placing the tip accurately at the base of
his ribcage. The golden-hilted rapier cut the boy a little, bent
– and then snapped.

Gilbert had a brief, very brief, moment to comprehend his
mortal danger before the boy's sword penetrated deep into
his stomach. Both fell to the floor and blood poured from
two wounds. Only the boy managed to stand, however.

It occurred to Gilbert, only in his very last moment, that in
truth he had never fully trusted the smith, and had been
unsurprised when he had discovered that the smith's son
was a troublemaker.

*Like father, like son*, he thought, as he died.

THE AFTERMATH OF the battle at the manor was a sad time in
Montreuil. The surviving sergeants, which turned out to be
most of them, drifted away when it was discovered that the
Marquis would no longer be paying their wages. One stayed
on and married a village girl, when their affair was made
public, and another downed his weapons and installed himself at the mill, now that Gerni was gone.

Tomas didn't stay long in Montreuil and not all were sad when he left. Though nobody was sorry to see the end of the Marquis, many thought that the cost in lives was too steep, and that things had been bearable as they were. Tomas didn't say where he was going, though perhaps he told his mother.

The manor house stood mostly empty at one end of the village and fell quickly into disrepair. It became custom in Montreuil, when a roof was leaking, or a hinge fell off a door, for the villager in need to make a trip to the manor and to take what he sought to make the repair.

The rose hedge slowly grew back, but was kept to a modest height, perhaps the waist of a tall man, and on festival days in honour of the Lady the village was covered in a garland of roses.

It was purely speculation on the behalf of some villagers that the new flowers were brighter and more fragrant than those which had grown there before.

# PORTRAIT OF
# MY UNDYING LADY
## by Gordon Rennie

'A COMMISSION, you say? What kind of commission?'
Giovanni Gottio leaned across the table, wine slopping from
the cheap copper goblet in his hand. It would soon be
replenished, he knew, in just the same way as his new-found
friend sitting opposite had been steadily refilling Giovanni's
goblet all night.

'A portrait,' answered his new-found friend. 'In oils. My
employer will pay you well for your time.'

Giovanni snorted, spilling more wine. Absent-mindedly he
dabbed one grimy finger in the spilled mess, painting imaginary brush strokes on the rough surface of the bar table.
Faces. Faces had always been his speciality. Strangely,
though, he had been sitting with the man for hours, drinking his wine and spending his money, but if the stranger got
up and left this minute, Giovanni would have been unable
to say what exactly he looked like. His was more a blurred
impressionistic sketch of a face – eyes cold and cruel, mouth
weak and arrogant – than any kind of finished work. The
most memorable thing about him in Giovanni's mind was
the way the emerald ring on his finger caught and held even
the dim candlelight of this grimy back street taverna.

'Haven't you heard?' Giovanni slurred, becoming gradually aware that he was far more drunk than he should be this early in the night, even after those three pitchers of wine the stranger had bought for him. 'The great Gottio doesn't do portraits any more. He is an artist, and artists are supposed to show truth in their work. The trouble is, people don't want the truth. They don't like it. That fool Lorenzo Lupo certainly didn't, when he commissioned the great Gottio to paint a portrait of his wife.'

Giovanni realised he was shouting now, that he was drawing sniggering glances from the other regular patrons of the taverna. Not caring, he reached out to angrily refill his goblet once more.

'Did you see it, my portrait of that famed beauty, the wife of the Merchant Prince of Luccini? Not many people did, for her husband had it destroyed as quickly as he could. Still, those few that did see it said that it captured the woman perfectly, not just in its reflection of her exquisite beauty but even more so in the way it brought out all the charm, grace and personality of the hungry mountain wolf that lurked beneath that fair skin.'

Giovanni drained his goblet and slammed it down, stumbling as he got up to leave. This drunk after only three pitchers, he thought. The great Gottio truly has lost his touch...

'So, thank you for your hospitality, sir, but the great Gottio no longer paints portraits any more. He paints only the truth, a quality which would sadly seem to be in little fashion amongst this world's lords and masters.'

Mocking laughter followed him out of the taverna. Outside, he staggered along the alleyway, leaning against a wall for support. Shallya's mercy. That cheap Pavonan wine certainly had a kick to it!

A welcome night breeze sprang up, carrying with it the strong scent of the fruit orchards that grew on the slopes of the Trantine Hills overlooking the city, and Giovanni took several deep breaths, trying to clear his head. From behind, he heard quick, decisive footsteps following him out of the taverna; clearly his new-found friend wasn't a man prepared to take 'no' for an answer.

Giovanni turned to greet his persistent new friend for the night, but instead of the ingratiating smile he expected, he saw a snarl of anger. A hand reached out, grasping him by the throat and lifting him off his feet. Claws sprang out where there had only been fingernails before, and Giovanni felt their sharp edges dig into the skin of his exposed throat. The hand held him there for long seconds as he struggled, unable to draw breath, never mind cry for help. And then it suddenly released him. Senses dimming, Giovanni fell to the ground, only half-conscious as his supposed friend effortlessly dragged him through the shadows towards a nearby waiting coach. There was the sound of a coach door opening, and a face as bright and terrible in its unearthly beauty as that of the Chaos moon of Morrslieb looked down at him as Giovanni finally slipped into unconsciousness.

'No matter, Mariato,' he heard it speak in a voice as cold as glacial ice. 'This way will do just as well…'

GIOVANNI AWAKENED, immediately recognising in the pain throbbing behind his eyes the all-too-familiar signs of the previous night's excesses. Mind still numbed by the copious quantities of wine he had no doubt cheerfully downed, it took him several seconds to register the fact that this was not the hovel-like garret that the recent downturn in his fortunes had reduced him to calling home. Nor were his clothes – a shirt of finest Cathay silk and breeches of pure Estalian calf-skin – the same threadbare and patchy garments that he had put on the previous morning.

Previous morning? he thought suddenly realising that it was still night, a silver sliver of the waxing Morrslieb moon visible through the barred window above his bed. He ran a hand to his face, feeling the rough stubble of what felt like two days' beard growth that had not been there earlier. Shallya's mercy. How long had he been unconscious?

There was a rattle of keys at the only door into the room. Giovanni tensed, ready to… what, he wondered. Fight? Overpower his gaolers and try to escape? Half a head smaller than his average countryman – the stature, or more precisely lack of it, of the inhabitants of the Tilean peninsula was the basis of many jokes amongst the other nations of the Old

World – and with something of a paunch that the long months of penury since his fall from grace had still so far mostly failed to diminish. Giovanni knew that he was hardly the stuff that dashing dogs of war mercenary hero legends were made of. The only wound he had ever suffered was a broken nose inflicted during a heated taverna dispute with some fop of a Bretonnian poet over the favours of a young and curvaceous follower of the arts. The only blade he had ever wielded was a small knife used to sharpen the charcoal pencil nubs he sketched with.

The heavy door swung open, revealing two black-robed figures standing in the corridor outside. Faceless under their hooded robes, it was impossible to determine anything about them. A hand, pale and skeletal thin, appeared from within the folds of one of the robes, gesturing for the artist to rise and come with them. Shrugging with an attempted air of casual nonchalance that he wished he truly felt, Giovanni did as commanded.

He found himself in a wide, stone-walled corridor, falling into step between his faceless gaolers. Stars shone through breaks in the wood-raftered ceiling, and, glancing up, Giovanni saw the shattered ruins of a burned-out upper storey above him. The floor at his feet had been hurriedly swept clean, with piles of rubble and ancient fire debris piled up at its sides, and Giovanni could just make out blackened and faded frescoes under the grime and soot on the corridor walls. They showed nymphs and satyrs at play and were of a pastoral style that went out of fashion over a century ago. The night breeze drifted in through the breaks in the ruined ceiling, and Giovanni caught the faint but familiar scent of distant fruit groves.

With a shock of recognition, he realised that he was probably in one of the abandoned villas that dotted the countryside hills above Trantio. There were many such ruins, Giovanni knew, for in safer and more prosperous times it had been the fashion amongst the city's wealthy merchant families to build such palaces in the surrounding countryside, as both an ostentatious display of wealth and a retreat from the squalor of the city. A downturn in mercantile fortunes and the steadily increasing numbers of greenskin savages stealing over the Apuccini Mountains had brought an abrupt end to the such rural idylls, and the survivors abandoned their countryside retreats and fled back to the comfort of their counting houses and the safety of high and well-guarded city walls. Since then, the abandoned villas had become notorious as lairs for the predators that hid out in the wilderness areas beyond the limits of the Trantine city guard's horseback patrols.

Predators such as bandit gangs, or orc warbands, or–

*Or what?* Giovanni wondered with a shudder, his lively artist's imagination painting a series of vivid nightmare images of all the things bad enough to scare bandits and even orcs away from such a place.

Something rustled at Giovanni's feet and he jumped back as a large rat scampered out of a hole in the floor and ran across the corridor, running right over the top of his booted feet. There was a blur of movement from behind him, followed instantly by a harsh squeal of pain and an abrupt wet tearing sound. Giovanni turned, catching a glimpse of the scene beneath the hooded cloaks behind him – long skeletal fingers crammed something squealing and still alive between jaws distended horribly wide open – before a warning hiss from his other gaoler urged him to keep moving. Suitably inspired, Giovanni's imagination mentally erased the previous portfolio of nightmare images and began work on a new gallery of even greater horrors.

The corridor ended in an open doorway, soft light spilling out from the open doorway there. Urged on by a low angry grunt from one of the gaoler creatures, Giovanni gingerly stepped forward into the room beyond.

The chamber was how he imagined the villa would have looked in its heyday. It was opulently furnished, and his gaze passed over a tempting platter of fruit and a crystal decanter of wine laid out on a nearby table – did his captors seek to trick him into poisoning himself after having him at their mercy for at least a day as he lay insensible in his cell, he wondered? – and also the oddly disquieting sight of a painting easel with a blank canvas upon it. But it was the paintings on the walls all around that drew his immediate attention.

There were a full dozen of them, and they were by far the greatest collection of art that Giovanni had ever seen.

There he recognised the brushwork of the legendary da Venzio, whose monumental frescoes decorating the ceiling of the great Temple of Shallya in Remas were still one of the great wonders of the Old World. And beside it was a canvas bearing the distinctive Chaos-tainted style of the mad Estalian genius Dari, whose work had been condemned as heretical two hundred years ago and was still banned throughout the Empire to this day. Hanging on the wall opposite the Dari was a work bearing all the hallmarks of the work of Fra' Litti. There were only eight known Litti paintings still in existence, all of them in the possession of the richest merchant princes of Tilea who competed with each other in bitterly fought bidding wars to purchase only the rarest and most exquisite works of art. If this really was a ninth and until now unknown Litti, then its potential value was truly incalculable.

Giovanni's senses continued to reel at the wealth of artistic riches that surrounded him. Over here a work by Bardovo, whose epic depiction of Marco Columbo's discovery of Lustria spawned a whole school of lesser talented imitators. Beside it hung a canvas bearing the disturbing scratch-mark signature of the mysterious Il Ratzo, who some historians now whispered may not even have been fully human.

It was only then, as he reached out to touch the da Venzio canvas, his fingers reverently tracing the maestro's brushstroke patterns, that an even greater and more profound realisation about all the paintings collected here occurred to him.

They were all portraits, and they were all of the same subject: an alabaster-skinned noblewoman of striking but glacial beauty.

Giovanni gazed from portrait to portrait, his eyes confirming what his mind would not yet accept. No matter the artist, no matter the difference in their individual styles, each had painted the same subject, and from life too, if the telltale details in each painting were to be believed. Here he saw the same glint of forbidden promise in the dark pools of her eyes, there the same hint of unspoken secrets behind the faint mocking smile on her lips. But while each artist had found the same qualities in their subject, each also found in her something different. In da Venzio's portrait she was a beguiling angel of darkness, his painting a blasphemous twin piece to the images of the blessed goddess of mercy on the temple ceiling in Remas. Bardovo's work showed her as a lonely spectral figure standing against a backdrop of a corpse-strewn battlefield.

How could this be, Giovanni wondered? Da Venzio had lived three hundred years ago, Bardovo more than a thousand and Fra' Litti and one or two others even longer than that.

A faint breeze passed through the air of the room, sending flickering shadows over the faces of the portraits as it disturbed the flames of the many candles which lit the chamber.

'How could artists that lived centuries apart all come to have painted the same subject?' said a voice from somewhere close behind Giovanni, completing the thought that his mind dared not yet ask itself.

He turned to face the figure reclining on the couch behind him, a figure who had not been there moments ago, he was sure. She was even more beautiful in person, he thought. More beautiful and more terrible than any portrait – even one by the great da Venzio himself – could ever do full justice to. Her eyes were endless pools of mystery that drank in everything, surrendering nothing in return. Her blood-red lips were full and of the same colour as the burning scarlet rubies which hung at her plunging neckline, revealing flawless skin that glowed like soft moonlight, skin that had not felt the kiss of sunlight in centuries.

'I am the Lady Khemalla of Lahmia,' she said in a voice that whispered like the shifting desert sands of her long-dead homeland. 'I bid you welcome to my home.'

'Then I am not a prisoner here?' asked Giovanni, surprised at his directness of his own question.

'You are my guest,' she smiled. 'And, while you are my guest, it pleases me for you to paint my portrait.' She gestured at the paintings around them. 'As you can see, I have a taste for art. And occasionally for artists too.'

She smiled at this last comment, blood-red lips curling back to show the subtle points of concealed fangs.

'Why me?' asked Giovanni, pouring himself a generous measure of wine from the decanter. Doomed as he was, he saw no need to deny himself a few final pleasures.

'If you know what I am, then you must understand that it has been many years since I have gazed upon my own face in the glass of any mirror. To never again see the features of your reflection, to live so long that you perhaps forget the image of your own face, can you begin to imagine what that might be like, mortal? Is it any wonder that so many of my kind give themselves fully over to madness and cruelty when they have nothing left to remind them of their own humanity? I can only see myself through the eyes of others, and so I choose to do so only through the eyes of the greatest artists of each age.'

She paused, favouring him with a look from the deep desert oases of her eyes as she again gestured at the paintings hanging on the walls around them. 'You should be honoured, little mortal. After all, consider the company I am including you in here.'

'You know that I have a reputation for only painting the truth as I see it.' Nervous, he reached to refill his already empty glass, concentrating hard to quell the involuntary tremor in his hands. 'It is a trait of mine that found little favour with my previous patrons. I have discovered to my cost that people wish only to have their own flattering self-image of themselves reflected back at them.'

She smiled at his show of bravado. 'I chose you because of your reputation. You say you only paint the truth, the true soul of your subject. Very well, then that is what I want, brave little mortal. The truth. Look at me and paint what you see. To try and capture on canvas the soul of one of my kind; what greater challenge could there be for an artist?'

'And afterwards, when the work is complete? You will let me leave?'

'You will be free to refuse my hospitality when you have gifted me something that I deem worthy of your talents. If your work pleases me you will be well rewarded for your troubles, I promise you.'

'And if it does not, what then?'

The question hung unanswered in the air between them.

Giovanni set down his goblet and went over to the easel and blank canvas set up nearby. As he had expected, there was a palette of every imaginable kind of artist's materials. He rummaged amongst them, selecting a charcoal pencil for sketching and a knife to sharpen it with. A challenge, she had called it, and so it was. To paint the soul of a creature of the darkness, an age-old liche-thing, and yet to paint only the truth of what lay beneath that perfect ageless skin while still producing something that would please this most demanding of patrons. This would either be the greatest work of his life, he thought, or merely his last.

He turned back to his waiting subject, his practised eye seeing her at this earliest stage as merely a vexing collection of surfaces, angles, lines and subtle blends of light and shadow. The fine detail, in which lay those crucial insubstantial elements that would determine whether he lived or died here, would come later.

'Shall we begin?' he said.

LIKE THE VILLA'S other inhabitants, he worked only at night now and slept by day. Each night after sundown they came for him, and each night she sat for him. She talked while he worked – he always encouraged his subjects to talk, the better to understand them and their lives, for a portrait should speak of far more than its subject's mere outward physical appearance – and as he worked he heard tales of her homeland. Tales of gods, heroes and villains whose names and deeds are remembered now by none other than those of her kind; tales of mighty cities and impregnable fortresses now reduced to a few ancient crumbling ruins buried and forgotten beneath the desert sands.

Some nights they did not come for him. On those nights, she sent apologies for her absence, and gifts of fine wines and food, and books to let him pass the time in his cell more easily. The books, usually works of history or philosophy, fascinated him. Several of them were written in languages completely unknown to Giovanni – the languages of legendary and far Cathay or Nippon, he thought – while one was composed of thin leafs of hammer-beaten copper and inlaid with a queer hieroglyphic script which he doubted was even human in origin.

He knew that there were other occupants of the villa, although besides his silent faceless gaolers and his patron herself he had seen none of them. But as he lay in his cell reading on those work-free nights, he heard much activity going on around him. Each night brought visitors to the place. He heard the clatter of rider's hooves and the rumble of coach wheels and the jangle of pack team harnesses, and once he thought he heard the beating of heavy leather wings and perhaps even saw the fleeting shadow of something vast and bat-like momentarily blotting out the moonlit window above his bed.

There were other sounds too – screams and sobs and once the unmistakable cry of an infant child – from the cellars deep beneath his feet. At such times Giovanni buried his face into the mattress of his bedding or read aloud from the book in his hand until either the sounds had ceased or he had convinced himself that he could no longer hear them.

ONE NIGHT HE awoke in his room. The sitting had been cut short that night. One of the black-cloaked servant things had entered and fearfully handed its mistress a sealed scroll tube. As she read it her face had changed – transformed, Giovanni thought – and for a second he saw something of the savage and cruel creature of darkness that lay beneath the human mask she presented to him. The news was both urgent and unwelcome and she had abruptly ended the night's session, issuing curt orders for him to be escorted back to his room. He had fallen asleep as soon as he lay down on the bedding, exhausted by the continued effort of keeping up with the night-time schedule of his new employer.

Again, he heard the sound that had awoken him. There was someone in the room with him.

A face detached itself from the shadowy gloom of the cell, leaning over the bed and glared angrily down angrily at him. Jagged teeth, too many of them for any human mouth, crowded out from snarling lips. It was her servant, Mariato, the one that had approached him in the tavern that night. He had obviously just fed, and his breath was thick with the slaughterhouse reek of blood.

'Scheherazade. That is what I shall call you,' the vampire growled, glaring down at him with eyes full of hate and the madness of bloodlust. 'Do you know the name, little painter? It is a name from her homeland, a storyteller who prolonged her life for a thousand and one nights by entertaining her master with tales and fables.'

The vampire raised one bristle-covered hand, pointing at the half-face of Mannslieb in the sky above. The ring on his finger flashed green in the moonlight.

'How many nights do you think you have left, my Scheherazade? Her enemies are close, and by the time Mannslieb's face shines full again, we will be gone from here. Will your precious painting be finished by then? I think not, for such things take great time and care, do they not?'

He paused, leaning in closer, hissing into Giovanni's face, stifling him with the sour reek of his carrion breath.

'She will not take you with us, and she cannot leave you here alive for our enemies to find. So what is she to do with you then, my Scheherazade?'

The vampire melted back into the shadows, its voice a whispering promise from out of the darkness.

'When Mannslieb's face shines full again, then you will be mine.'

'YOUR SERVANT MARIATO, he doesn't like me.' She looked up with interest. This was the first time he had dared speak to her without permission. She lay reclining on the couch in the position that he had first seen her in. A bowl of strange dark-skinned fruit lay on the floor before her. The main composition of the piece was complete, and all he needed to concentrate on now was the detail of the face.

'He is jealous,' she answered. 'He is afraid that I will grow bored with him and seek to make another my favourite in his stead.' She looked at him sharply. 'Has he disturbed you? Has he said or done anything to interrupt your work?'

Giovanni kept his eyes on his work, unwilling to meet her keen gaze. 'Has he a right to be jealous?'

She smiled, favouring him with a look of secret amusement. 'Perhaps,' she mused. 'His kind always have their place at my side, but they are always dull and unimaginative.

Perhaps I will take a new consort, not a warrior or a noble-man this time. Perhaps this time an artist? What do you think, little mortal? Shall I make you my new paramour and grant you the gift of eternal life in darkness?'

She laughed, picking up a fruit from the bowl and biting deep into it, enjoying the taste of his fear. Thick juice, obscenely scarlet in colour, bled out of the fruit as she ate it.

Giovanni studied the lines and contours of the painted face on the canvas in front of him. A few brushstrokes, a subtle touch of shading, and he had added an extra element of sardonic cruelty to the line of her smile.

THE NEXT NIGHT he returned to his cell at dawn to find a small tied leather pouch sitting on his bed. He opened it, pouring out a quantity of powdered ash. Puzzled, Giovanni ran his fingers through the stuff, finding it strangely unpleasant to the touch. There was something amongst it. Giovanni gin-gerly picked it up, discovering it to be a ring. He held it up, the light of the rising sun catching the familiar emerald stone set upon it.

It seemed that Mariato no longer occupied the same posi-tion amongst his mistress's favours as he had once done.

GIOVANNI KNEW THAT their time together was coming to an end. Mannslieb hung high in the night sky, almost full, and for the last few nights there had been more activity than usual in the villa. He heard the sound of heavy boxes – earth-filled coffins, he supposed – being dragged up from the cellars and loaded into wagons. He worked in daylight hours too now; foregoing sleep and working on the painting alone in his cell, making changes so subtle that he doubted anyone other than he would notice the difference. Adding new details and taking away others. Revising. Reworking. Perfecting. He was haggard and gaunt, exhausted from too little food and sleep, looking more like one of her pale ghoul-thing servants than the portly florid-faced drunk who had been brought here just scant weeks ago.

All that mattered now was the painting itself. The greatest work of his life, that is what he had said he would have to produce, and that is what he had done. After that, he discovered to his surprise, nothing else really mattered.

SHE SENT FOR him the next night, with Mannslieb shining full-faced in the night sky. The painting too, was now complete.

She stood looking at it. The room had been stripped almost bare, and the easel that the canvas stood on was the most significant item left in it. There were faint outlines on the walls where her portraits had hung.

'You are leaving?' he said, more in statement than question.

'We have many enemies, my kind. Not just the witch hunters with their silver and fire. We wage war amongst ourselves, fighting over sovereignty of the night. It has become too dangerous to remain here.'

She gestured towards the painting. 'It is beautiful, master Gottio. I thank you for your gift. What do you call it?'

'*Unchanging Beauty*,' he answered, joining her to look at his masterpiece. It showed her standing regally against a backdrop of palatial splendour. Giovanni's talent had captured all her cruel and terrible beauty as the others before him had also done, but the real artistry was in the detail of the trappings around her. Look closer and the eye was drawn to the tarnished gold of the throne behind her, the subtle patterns of mildew creeping across the wall tapestries, the broken pinnacles of the palace towers seen through the window in the far background. It was a world where everything other than her was subject to change and decay. Only she was unchanging. Only she was forever.

'Then my task here is done. I am free to leave now?' He looked at her, half in hope, half in dread.

'I had thought to keep you here with me as an new diversion to replace poor Mariato.' She looked at him, trying to gauge his reaction, toying with him yet again.

'But, no, you would make a poor vampire, master Gottio,' she reassured him, relishing one last taste of his fear. 'There is something in our nature that destroys any creative ability we may have had in our mortal lives, and I would not deny the world the great works still within you. So, yes, you are free to go.'

'And my reward?'

She gestured towards a small open casket nearby. Giovanni glanced at it, silently toting up the value of the gold and precious stones it contained and coming to a figure comparable with a minor merchant prince's ransom. When he looked back, she was holding a goblet of wine out to him.

'What is it?' he asked, suspecting one final cruel jest.

'A little wine mixed with a sleeping draught, the same one that Mariato tried to lull you with. Call it a final precaution, for your own safety. When you awaken, you will be safe and in familiar surroundings, I promise you. I could compel you to drink it, but this way is easier.'

He took it, raising it to his lips and drinking. She watched him intently as he did so. The wine was excellent, as he expected, but mixed in with it, the taste of something else, not any kind of potion or sleeping draught. Something dark and rich, something that rose up to overwhelm his senses.

'An extra gift,' she said, seeing the reaction in his eyes. 'With your painting, you have given me a part of yourself. It only seemed fair that I give you something equally valuable in return. Farewell, little mortal, I look forward to seeing what uses you will put my gift to.'

She reached out with preternatural reflexes to catch him as he fell, as the darkness rushed in to envelop his numbed senses...

HE AWOKE IN blinding daylight, crying out in pain as the unaccustomed sunlight stabbed into his eyes. When he recovered, he realised that he was in the pauper's attic garret he called home. The precious casket lay on the floor beside him.

It took him several hours to realise the nature of the additional gift she had given him.

He sat inspecting his reflection in the small cracked looking glass he had finally managed to find amongst the jumble of his possessions. Days ago he had been a haggard wreck, now there was not a trace of the ordeal left upon him, none of the exhaustion of the last few weeks. He looked and felt better than he had in years. In fact...

*Shallya's mercy*, he thought, studying the reflection of his face in the mirror. *I look ten years younger!*

He thought of certain legends about her kind, about the gifts they granted to their loyal mortal servants and about the restorative powers of...

Of vampire blood. Only the smallest portion, but he could feel it flowing in his veins, feel her inside him. Her life-force added to his own. Had she done this with the others, he wondered, and then he remembered that the da Venzio had been reputed to have lived to over a century in age – blessed by the mercy goddess, they said, in reward for the work he had done in her great temple in Remas – and of how Bardovo had lived long enough to paint not just the portrait of the Marco Columbo but also that of the legendary explorer's merchant prince great-grandson.

He wondered how long he, Giovanni Gottio, had, and about how he would put his time to best use.

He looked around his squalid attic, seeing only the detritus of his former miserable life: smashed wine bottles and pieces of cheap parchment torn up in anger and thrown in crumpled balls across the room. He picked one up, smoothing it out and recognising it as the abandoned portrait sketch of a local tavern girl. The workmanship was poor and he could see why he had so quickly abandoned the piece, but looking at it with fresh vision he could see possibilities in its line and form that had not been there to him before.

He found his drawing board and pinned the parchment to it, sitting looking at it in quiet contemplation. After a while, he searched amongst the debris on the floor and found the broken end of a charcoal pencil.

And with it, he began to draw.

# THE PLAGUE PIT

## by Jonathan Green

A CHILL GUST of wind whipped across the twilight landscape. It tore over the desolate moorland and rode the contours of two long-overgrown burial mounds, full of the promise of a harsh winter to come. It swirled around the age-weathered standing stone and buffeted the huddle of men crouched around the dancing flames of a small campfire. Leaving the mercenary band pulling their thick, Kislev cloaks even tighter about them, it continued on its way up the gently rising slope until, at last, it reached the dilapidated windmill standing at the summit, tugging at the sails that in turn groaned in protest at the wind's attentions.

Torben Badenov, raven-haired leader of the band, looked up at the building's black silhouette half a mile to the south on the crest of the hill. The windmill stood out stark against the darkening sky. To Torben it looked like some mysterious sentinel studying his party, as if they were invading its territory, and watching over the scholar's work at the monolith with dark interest. The builders of the windmill had chosen the spot well. The wind scoured these desolate moors relentlessly. And yet despite the ideal location, the

187

wild unforgiving land had proved almost impossible to tame, man and nature instead living in an uneasy truce that could be overturned at any moment. Time and the weather had taken its toll on the mill too. Here and there a sail baton was splintered or missing, the brickwork was crumbling and there were holes in the roof.

Here as much as anywhere, Torben was reminded of the fact that civilisation was only to be found in small pockets across the Old World. Karl Franz might claim this wild country as his Empire but in reality, it belonged to indomitable nature and the rough elements. It was in places such as this that it became apparent that the greatest battle the peoples of the Empire had ever fought was with their environment. The early winter chill cut him to the marrow, even through his bearskin cloak, and with the rising wind the air pressure was rising also.

A lean figure, crouching close to the fire, his cloak clenched tightly about him, broke the silence with a bitter request: 'Just remind me why we're here again.'

Torben straightened, rubbing the small of his back with one hand while running the other through his black hair. He swallowed hard, trying to relieve the pressure in his ears that was making them ache. 'The same as always,' the tall mercenary said bluntly, 'because of the money.'

'You really think he's going to pay up?' a slim, mop-haired young man asked, looking towards the rough-hewn monolith, fifty yards or so from the campfire. Hunched at the foot of the granite obelisk was Johannes Verfallen, scholar of Ostermark and currently the employer of Badenov's band.

'I do, Yuri,' Torben replied. 'He came up with the first half of our fee, didn't he?'

'That he did,' said the fourth member of the party. Stanislav was a huge bear of a man, deft at the use of a battleaxe. Strong as an ox and yet as gentle as a kitten when occasion allowed – that was Stanislav.

'But only half,' the weaselly, rat-faced Oran Scarfen pointed out. 'Half on hiring, the rest on finding the mound, just to ensure our loyalty. I mean, how desperate for money do we look?'

'Pretty desperate, by the looks of you,' Alexi, the old solider, said with a grin, adjusting the jerkin of his leather armour.

Rubbing his neatly trimmed beard Torben cast his mind back to the smoke-filled bar of the Slaughtered Troll in Ostermark and remembered with a shiver the warmth of the alehouse compared to the bitter cold of the moorlands. Krakov, the last member of his mercenary band, had failed to show up after driving the Lady Isolde of Ostenwald to petition the Lord Gunther, commander of the city's militia, for his aid in ridding her demesne of a deathless threat. No doubt Krakov, the debonair, style-conscious Kislevite, had found the attentions of one of Gunther's chambermaids more appealing than the prospect of meeting up with his companions. Either that or he was still too embarrassed at having lost the party's horses to show his face again for a while. He would be propping up the bar again by the time Torben and the others returned, with drink-fuelled tales of the escapades he had been involved in during their absence, the hearts he'd broken and the money he'd lost at the gaming-house. He wouldn't see any of the gold from this latest venture, however: if he couldn't be bothered to turn up for a job he certainly wasn't going to get paid for it!

But it was while waiting for the errant Krakov that Torben had been approached by the gaunt Verfallen. In Torben's considered opinion, Johannes Verfallen was a typical man of learning: nervous, pale-skinned, and with a sparrow's physique hidden under a black cowled robe two sizes too big for him. Before explaining the reasons he had for wanting to hire Badenov's band, the young scholar was at great pains to expound his credentials to Torben. The mercenary had to hear every last detail of how Verfallen had studied first at the University of Altdorf. How he had gained a degree in Ancient History with particular focus on the beliefs and practices of the tribes of the Old World, before making the move to Ostermark. There he continued his research under the sup-posedly renowned sage Heinrich the Grey. But then you'd want to mention every last qualification you had earned, Torben thought, if you had no scars or battle stories to testify to the achievements of your life.

And yet despite Verfallen's apparent youth there was something prematurely old about him. His face was gaunt, fleshless skin stretched taught over the sharp contours of his skull, and a sharply receding hairline revealed blemishes not unlike liver spots on his balding pate. Beady eyes, sunken into shadow-ringed sockets, twinkled from behind severe pince-nez glasses and Torben noticed that when he lifted his cup of watered-down wine to his thin, colourless lips, Verfallen's hand shook tremulously – and his breath stank.

Torben would be the first to admit that at times, particularly the morning after a heavy drinking session, his mouth smelt like something akin to a latrine, but Verfallen was something else. His breath reeked of dental decay, gum disease and the promise of an agonising visit to the nearest barber-surgeon for some serious tooth pulling. In fact, extreme as it might sound, Torben could only liken it to an odour he had smelt when his chosen career in life had caused him to break into charnel houses or exhume corpses from their graves – the stench of death.

Torben wasn't surprised that the scholar came to him with his somewhat peculiar request, for his band of mercenaries to accompany Verfallen as bodyguards onto the moors east of Ostermark, while he searched for the burial mound of some ancient king. He wasn't ashamed of what he did and saw no point in keeping it a secret in the presence of others. In fact, Badenov was rather proud of his career as a mercenary. Like so many others who sold their sword-arms to others for a living, he had cut his teeth in the art of killing as a soldier. In Torben's case, it had been in the army of old Tzar Bokha himself. That was where he had met Alexi and Yuri, having joined up with the weasely Oran Scarfen as the result of a foolish, beer-fuelled bet. Then circumstances had changed and they had decided to try their hand as mercenaries and the risk had been worth it.

In those days – how many years past was it? seven? eight? – Arnwolf, Lars, Manfred and Berrin the Dwarf had been part of the company. But they were gone now: the life of a sellsword was not without its pitfalls. Manfred had been the first to leave the band, an orc's arrow protruding from his stomach as he fell from the battlements at the Siege of Galein's Gate. Arnwolf had fallen victim to a troll's vile appetite – if only he hadn't gone to answer the call of nature alone! A skaven assassin's weeping blade had done for Lars the Norseman while Berrin had left alive, of his own choice, muttering something about now being the last of his line and the ancestral hall calling him home. The heavy-drinking Stanislav and eye-patched Krakov had joined them later – Alexi still felt a twinge on cold nights as a result of wrestling the gentle giant Stanislav on their first meeting.

Then there was the newest member of the party, Pieter Valburg. Torben looked at the well-dressed nobleman's son sitting with his back turned to the fire, staring out into the encroaching night.

'Everything all right with you, Pieter?' he asked.

'The wind's picking up. There's a storm brewing,' the glum young man replied, directing Torben's gaze towards the massing black billows to the south.

He could be right, Torben thought. Since dusk had fallen there had been a distinct rise pressure in the air. It could be the reason for Torben's earache. Slightly unnerved by Pieter's manner, Torben felt some sort of reply was needed to break the tension in the atmosphere. 'Hmm... looks like rain.'

Torben still hadn't worked Pieter out. The only son of the mayor of Schwertdorf, he had given up his former life to pursue a personal vendetta against the creature responsible for the death of his childhood sweetheart. But once vengeance had been claimed, his morbid air had remained. He was almost permanently quiet and sombre. At times his dark, sullen moods worried the others: that one man could carry such a sense of doom about him! It made their lives, and all the lives they had taken, seem so insignificant and futile in the scheme of things. In Torben's often-voiced opinion, the nobleman's son thought about things too much.

Yet Torben couldn't fault Pieter's courage, loyalty, ardour and skill as a swordsman – but then he had been trained by the best fencing coach his father could afford. Pieter Valburg had a purpose to his actions like none of the rest of them. He wasn't in this business for the money. He was a man with a mission and at times, it seemed that his mission was to wipe out every evil thing and servant of the Dark Powers in the Empire and beyond.

A low chanting drew Torben's attention back to their client. Verfallen was muttering almost continually under his breath in a monotonous drone. Torben would never understand scholars and sages. They were weak specimens, more like women than men, and that was demeaning to a good number of the fairer sex he had encountered in his life. So what if Badenov's band were effectively no more than playing nursemaids to a scholar at present? They had seen the colour of Verfallen's money and he paid very well for such simple work. It was worth putting up with the cold, the wind and the rain for a night or two in return for another five hundred crowns. That would see them clear to replacing the steeds that preening fool Krakov had managed to lose for them.

Verfallen was hunched in front of the dark monolith, as he had been since long before dusk fell. The stone itself was ancient. The scholar had said it had been set in its place on the hillside by a tribe of primitives in times long past. The carvings that covered the surface of the ancient stone were weatherworn and pitted with age before the founding of the Empire. It was almost impossible to make out the strange runic script that wound over the granite in a serpent-like trail. Torben should know, he had tried for a full two minutes before giving up. Verfallen had been at it for hours. Rather than stop as the light began to fade, he insisted on continuing with his transcription. A lantern provided flickering illumination, while he peered through his spectacles at the impressions left by the chiselling tool of some prehistoric hand, the tip of his nose almost touching the lichen-covered stone.

Learned men! Torben had to admit that at times, knowledge could prove a valuable weapon against the dark but when it came to the conclusion of things, it was the sword, the axe, the dagger and the bow that won the day. He would trust his survival to strength of muscle and cold steel.

'What's he doing again?' Alexi enquired, pausing mid-way through sharpening his sword.

'He said he'd got to translate the carvings on that ages-old stone to find the site of some old burial mound,' Torben explained once again. 'Apparently, this whole area was once the territory of some ancient human tribe. The barrows around here are the resting-places of the tribe's chieftains.' Torben was quite getting into his role as historian and his opinion of scholars, for now, was forgotten. 'As I'm sure you know already, it was the practice in those days to bury the chieftain with all his worldly possessions. Most were looted long ago but Verfallen reckons the barrow of one ancient king – Verfallen calls him Morroot, or something like that – is still intact and you know what that means?'

'Ah, they're all the same, these so-called learned men,' Oran interrupted. 'They make out they're concerned with things on a higher plane, only interested in increasing the depth of their knowledge, but they're just like the rest of us. They're only in it for the money or the power! In this case, the money.'

Now it was Pieter's turn to speak up: 'You don't know that he isn't searching for forgotten wisdom!' Of all of the mercenary band, it was Pieter who held the greatest sway by the research of academics.

'Trust me,' Oran spat, scowling at the young nobleman, looking even more like a rat than usual in the flickering light of the fire. 'Money or power, simple as that! Bloody hypocrites!'

'What was that?' A hush fell over the party at Torben's interjection. Then they all heard it: the sound of someone being violently sick.

'Sounds like our scholar's not feeling so well,' Oran said with obvious delight.

The retching came again accompanied by the splatter of a half-digested meal regurgitated over the ancient monolith. It sounded as if Verfallen were throwing up his intestines.

'That doesn't sound good,' Torben said, surprised at the concern apparent in his voice. 'That doesn't sound good at all!'

INSTINCTIVELY WITH ONE hand on the hilt of his sword, Torben moved at a jog towards the monolith and the hunched figure of Verfallen. As he neared the stone Torben could see the scholar picked out in the circle of light cast by the lantern.

He was doubled up, leaning against the obelisk with one hand supporting his weight while his other hand clutched at his midriff. A convulsion passed through Verfallen's body and he vomited again. By the lantern's light, Torben could see that the scholar was throwing up great gouts of blood and black bile.

The mercenary captain was joined by the rest of the party, muttering and troubled. But Torben had noticed that something else had started to happen. At first he thought it was merely an effect caused by the bunched folds of the scholar's robe but now it was unmistakable – Verfallen's stomach was starting to swell. As the retching man struggled to stay on his feet, with the convulsions wracking his body, his belly was rapidly blowing up like an inflated pig's bladder.

'Shouldn't someone help him?' Yuri suggested feebly.

'Why, are you offering?' Oran threw back as a retort. The stomach continued in its seemingly inexorable swelling.

'I'm not touching him,' Alexi said. There was a ripping sound as the strained fibres of cloth covering Verfallen's expanding gut began to tear apart.

'Nor me,' Stanislav added. 'I'm not going anywhere near him.'

As one, the party turned their eyes away from the vomiting scholar and onto their raven-haired leader.

'Well don't look at me!' Torben exclaimed. There was a wet ripping sound. Turning back to the sickening scene before them Torben added in a horrified gasp, 'By all the gods!'

The others were too shocked to comment.

Verfallen collapsed in front of the monolith, blood pooling beside him and mingling with the puddle of vomit. It was too revolting a sight to behold but Torben found himself unable to tear his eyes from it. The man's distended stomach was split right across its middle. A mass of bloated, yellow maggots spilled from the rent as worms writhed in the great open wound. Torben found himself mentally comparing the injury to a twisted red smile.

'Maybe it was something he ate,' Oran said darkly. Nobody laughed.

'It's like he was rotten to the core,' a stunned Yuri managed to utter.

'Is he dead?' asked Stanislav.

As the mercenaries watched, the body spasmed again. Torben noticed that the fingertips of Verfallen's hand were still just touching the snaking line of runes. A glittering shimmer passed through crystalline formations in the rock. It was as if they followed the line of runic script, culminating at the point where Verfallen's hand made contact with the granite obelisk. The impression only lasted for a second. Then, as they watched, the fingers twitched.

'What's going on?' Yuri asked, trying to suppress the quaver in his voice.

'I don't like this at all,' Stanislav stated firmly.

'We must destroy the body.' It was the first thing Pieter had said since leaving his place at the fire.

The party turned to look at the serious young man who had given them the order. He stared back at them from darkly hooded eyes.

'Why do you say that?' Alexi asked, disconcerted.

There was a terrible sucking, stretching sound as skin tore, muscles elongated and bones twisted themselves into new, unrecognisable shapes. Verfallen was transforming before their very eyes, growing as some embryonic life form might over several months, only at a grossly accelerated rate.

Impossibly rising from the hips, the thing that had been Verfallen rose to its hoofed feet, adjusting the stance of its triple-jointed legs to get its balance. The scholar's distorted body was now over three yards tall. Verfallen's face was unrecognisable, the pallid skin and flesh having split and stretched to accommodate the equine qualities the scholar's skull had taken on. The thing looked down at them from black-pitted eyes.

'That's why!' Torben declared, his sword already out of its scabbard.

Illuminated by the tumbled lantern and distant campfire, with a glance Torben took in every detail of the foul creature's physique. Its elongated skull; the extended arms ending in three-clawed talons, Verfallen's finger bones having fused together; the beginnings of a bony tail; the multi-jointed hindquarters. The creature's body was covered in the stretched skin of the scholar and where it had torn under the pressure of the mutating body, knots of wet, red muscle had been exposed.

Torben suddenly realised that they had all unwittingly taken several steps back.

Opening its malformed mouth, blunt teeth splitting the gums, the creature that only moments before had been Johannes Verfallen let out a neighing cry like that of a horse being slaughtered. It was like nothing that would come from a human throat. A guttural roar that issued from the creature's stomach echoed the howl. Where Verfallen's gut had torn open sharp teeth now lined the ragged, bleeding edges of a monstrous second mouth.

With a roar that was as much to boost his own resolve as to terrify the enemy, Torben charged at the aberrant beast. A great three-fingered talon lashed out, striking him fully across his chest and sending him flying. The mercenary captain had fallen into the trap of expecting the horror to move more slowly because of its increased size but it had struck like lightning, lashing out with the speed of a striking serpent.

Torben's fellows helped him to his feet but were in no rush to imitate their leader. He grunted, a look of angry disdain on his face.

'Come on! Attack! What are you afraid of?'

'What do you think?' Oran yelled back.

'What is it?' Yuri demanded, holding back.

'Chaos spawn,' Pieter hissed, half to himself under his breath. 'A creature formed from mortal flesh by the twisted powers of darkness and disorder that threaten to overwhelm us!'

Yuri hesitated still further, as if Pieter's explanation was almost more shocking than the gangling horror before them.

'It doesn't matter what it is!' Torben shouted incredulously. 'We're going to kill it anyway! We've fought worse than this. What about that beastman horde outside Tierdorf? By Queen Katarin's sword, we've even routed a whole nest of vampires! What are you waiting for? Are we dew-eyed milkmaids or Badenov's band?'

Their leader's rousing speech had the desired effect. 'Badenov's band!' the mercenaries cried as one, apart from the reticent Pieter. As one they rushed the horror.

The foul monstrosity kicked and struck, jerking its dispro-
portionately long neck forward in an attempt to bite the
mercenaries. Sword, axe and dagger made contact with pli-
able, newly rendered flesh. The second terrible mouth
snarled and hissed uselessly as the men did their best to give
the monster a wide berth between lunges. And yet for every
wound laid against it, with the incline of the hill aiding it,
the monstrosity still managed to advance on the mercenaries, driving them back towards the campfire.

As they fought the Chaos-spawned beast the wind
whipped more fiercely about them. Howling in fury, the
enraged fiend lurched forward. Stanislav's double-headed
battle-axe bit deep into a shin bone, splintering it and bringing the monster down on one knee with a baleful braying. As
Alexi lunged at the beast, intending to plunge his sword deep
into its chest where he supposed its dark heart to be, the
mutant snaked its neck down sharply. Its hot, moist breath
caught him full in the face, the noxious stench making him
gag and lose the initiative. Only a swift up-thrust from
Pieter's sword into what had once been Verfallen's sternum
saved Alexi from losing his head to the champing jaws.

Pushing down on the ground with its great knuckled
hands the spawn hefted itself back into an almost upright
position. In its determination to stand, it seemed to shrug off
the continued attacks of the mercenaries. It soon became
apparent, however, that each well-placed hit had taken its
toll. The monster hobbled forward, Oran sidestepping out of
the way to avoid having his foot crushed by a large, bony
hoof. As it tried to support itself on both legs again, its broken limb gave way and the horrific mutation crumpled into
a heap on top of the campfire.

Not pausing for a second, Torben snatched up a burning
brand and thrust it into a dark-pitted eye-socket. The creature screamed but this only made the mercenary captain
push all the harder, driving the blazing branch into the monster's skull. His work finished, Torben stepped back from the
blaze as the corrupted form of Johannes Verfallen began to
burn.

For a few, long, panting seconds the only sound they were
aware of was the hissing and sizzling of the creature's

Chaos-mutated flesh cooking on the fire, orange-white coals melting its already warped bones. Then the roar of the gale broke into Torben's consciousness.

Throughout the battle with the monstrosity, the wind had continued to rise. What had started as an evening breeze had become a howling gale that showed no sign of abating. Black clouds scudded across the midnight blue of the sky, drawn into the swirling turmoil centred over the hilltop. The roiling storm clouds had blotted out the moon long ago. Beneath the centre of the tempest stood the dilapidated windmill, its ragged sails spinning freely in the racing air currents.

Torben looked around at the circle of faces lit by the flickering flames of Verfallen's funeral pyre. Beyond them the hillside was black, the stone was black, everything apart from the campfire, the deep blue of the distant horizon and their anxious faces was an amorphous mass of darkness. Over the keening of the wind around the monolith and the crackling of the fire there was a wet popping sound and the darkness moved.

Shadows, blacker even than the blasted, night-time landscape, stirred and scampered at the foot of the standing stone. Above the roar of the gale the popping sound continued and was joined by a high-pitched, unintelligible gibbering which was getting louder. More shadows moved to either side of the mercenaries. Whatever was emerging from the night was increasing in number and very rapidly.

A distant rumble rolled across the moors towards the hill and then something came within range of the flickering firelight. Torben caught the gleam of a claw, the wicked grin of discoloured teeth and the glistening of mucus on green skin.

'What was that?' Yuri exclaimed, pushing the black tangle of his fringe from his eyes.

Then with one concerted movement the darkness advanced towards them. The forms at the vanguard of the scurrying mass broke from the shadows and Badenov's band took another step back.

The creatures were the colour of bruises. Haemorrhage purples, greens and yellows, dribbling strings of silver spittle and oozing night-soil brown fluid from pores and unnatural orifices on their small swollen bodies. They were all studying the soldiers with darting jaundice-yellow eyes.

'Ugly little bastards, aren't they?' Alexi stated unnecessarily.

Pointed ears pricked up at the words and several of the creatures snarled through curling lips.

'Oh, well done,' Oran muttered, 'now you've upset them.'

'I don't think they're that bothered about making friends,' Torben assured his companion as the mass of tiny green monsters waddled forward, clawed hands raised menacingly. There wasn't a single one of the creatures that was more than two feet tall and yet each one looked as if it was quite capable of taking a man down, having gone for the throat.

'So what do we do now?'

Torben hesitated, scouring the area around them. The discoloured, bloated bodies surged towards them like a rippling tide of corruption.

'We run,' Pieter stated simply. 'We can't fight them, there are too many of them. We would appear to be surrounded on all sides but to the south. The windmill will provide us with a better position. So we run.'

They didn't need telling twice: Oran was already a good fifty yards ahead of the rest of them. Torben didn't like it. He was a fighter but he knew when we was up against the odds and liked the idea of being eaten alive by these disgusting things even less. With a firm grip on his drawn sword, he sprinted after the fleeing mercenaries.

TORBEN WAS THE first to burst through the unlocked door into the windmill. 'Anybody here?' he called out, half-expecting the startled face of the miller to greet him. There was no reply. There wasn't a sound. The mill was dark and empty. It stank of mildew. 'No? Good.'

Puffing and panting, the mercenary band staggered into the mill. The run through the night, fuelled by fear and adrenaline, had taken its toll. A lantern was found, lit, and hung from a beam in the centre of the room.

Alexi sat down heavily on a bulging sack of corn. 'I'm exhausted,' he managed to say between gasps.

'You can't sit down yet,' Torben said, closing the door and barring it. 'Now that we're in, we've got to make sure that nothing else can follow us. Something tells me those things out there aren't going to give up too easily.'

'Did any of you see where they came from?' Yuri asked, a shocked expression on his face after witnessing one horror after another that night.

'It was dark,' Oran pointed out, 'and I was busy at the time, fighting a monster from children's nightmares!'

'It was like they came out of the night itself, I mean out of thin air, right in front of us,' Yuri continued, as if he hadn't heard a word Oran had uttered.

The chamber they found themselves in was effectively one storey of the mill. A thick wooden shaft emerged from a hole in the floor above and was connected to large cogs and other pieces of mill machinery, culminating in the grindstone at the centre of the room. On the other side of the building, a heavy-looking trapdoor covered the entrance to a cellar. Various pieces of furniture stood around the chamber, including a rough wooden pallet draped with a blanket. More curiously, what seemed like half a library was strewn about amongst the mill workings. Someone had been living here recently and it didn't look like it had been the miller.

Torben grabbed the end of a table covered in books and papers. As he dragged it in front of the doorway, with Stanislav's assistance, several scrolls and open tomes fell onto the floor. The rest of the party began making the wind-mill as siege-proof as they could but Pieter was more interested in the clutter covering the table.

'Look at all this,' he said gesturing to the piles of papers.

'What about it?' Oran said, gruffly.

'Well it's hardly the sort of thing you'd expect to find in a mill is it?' He picked up a slim black volume and studied the gilt-embossed words on the spine. 'How many millers do you know who read Braustein's *Ancient Tribes of the Ostermark Region*? Or, Lempter's *Necrotic Diseases of the Body*. Most of them can't even write their own name, let alone read *La Lune d'Enfer* in the original Bretonnian.'

He exchanged the book in his hands for a battered bundle of pages held together with knotted string. The others listened to his almost unhealthily excited ranting, as they barricaded themselves into the tower.

'The *Albergoeren Almanac* has been declared a heretical text. I remember old Walter telling me about it. It contains a list of all the feast days observed within the Empire, including those of the Fell Powers. He had a copy until the Edict of Verbrenner decreed that copies of the book should be destroyed, after the razing of Krachzen.'

As well as the books, rolls of parchment had been spread out on the table, the corners held down with anything that had come to hand: a curious looking device of brass and mahogany, a pestle, a stoppered flask. There were maps here, of the heavens as well as the lands of the Ostermark Marches, and charts for calculating the movements of the moons.

'I shouldn't read that, if I were you,' Pieter said anxiously, eyeing Stanislav, who was holding a large grimoire that seemed to be bound in some kind of dark, scaly hide.

'Why, what is it?' the great bear asked suspiciously.

'I believe in the scholar's script it's called the *Liber Pestilentia*. It's said, if you're not an acolyte of the Dark Gods and you're not protected by various talismans and charms, reading that will drive you insane and make you go blind.'

The heavy book fell with a thump onto the table.

'Ah, now what's this?' Pieter said, the excitement in his voice unmistakable and unnerving.

Despite themselves the more poorly read members of the band gathered around the erudite youth.

'Yes, I do believe it's Johannes Verfallen's journal!' he exclaimed. Pieter began intently scouring the slanting spider scrawl that covered page after page of the book open in his hands with closely packed notes. Not a square inch of paper had been wasted. There were diagrams and lines of runes, as well as a thickly inked, unreadable script that Torben didn't recognise and yet spoke to him of dark yearnings, bodily corruption and spiritual depravity. What was it about scholarly types that made them want to write down every little thing they did? Why couldn't they just be satisfied with living their lives rather than writing about them?

Beyond the walls of the windmill the wind whistled while the sails creaked and groaned. Inside all was silence as Pieter scanned page after page of the insane scholar's journal, gradually piecing together all the parts of the puzzle. At last he looked up at the huddle of expectant faces around him.

'So what's it say?' Torben voiced the question they were all thinking.

'In a nutshell?' Pieter looked grim. 'If you thought things were bad so far, they're about to get a whole lot worse. What happened at the standing stone was only the beginning. Apparently, from what I can make out from this,' he said, tapping the journal with a finger, 'the monolith was some sort of "keystone". It was set up centuries, probably even thousands of years ago, by a primitive marauder tribe, like those who dwell beyond the known world at the edge of the Chaos Wastes.

'This particular tribe worshipped the Plague God in the aspect of a monstrous, skeletal carrion crow. Their greatest leader was a shaman who went by the name of Moruut. It was his desire to attain daemonhood and it seems he would have succeeded, had he not been traitorously murdered by his own son.'

'What is this,' an incredulous Oran challenged, 'a bedtime story?'

Taking a deep breath, Pieter ignored the ignorant heckle and continued. 'The monolith was erected to collect and store magical energy. The runes covering it were a spell to release Nurgle's power in this area. Casting the spell would have given Moruut the power he needed to become a Daemon Prince!'

Gasps passed around the group.

'Surely such things are just legends?' Torben pointed out.

'Well, let's hope so,' Pieter replied, 'because Verfallen wasn't translating those runes: he was casting the spell.'

'And Grandfather Nurgle got a foothold in this world,' an anxious Yuri added. 'I didn't think that storm was natural.'

'Exactly, hence the appearance of the nurglings – those monsters outside. It seems Verfallen expected to be turned into some kind of Chaos champion himself but the Dark Gods are fickle, as we witnessed.'

Torben pushed a callused hand through his mane of thick black hair. 'So what's next? Plagues of flies? Crops failing for miles around? The pox?'

'Worse than that. As was the custom of the tribe, Moruut was buried in a barrow, like those we saw on our way to this forsaken place.'

'Oh, let me guess. I think I know this one,' Oran mocked. 'The barrow's under this hill.'

'Yes,' Pieter said coldly. 'Right under this windmill, according to Verfallen's notes.'

'So if Nurgle's power has been released in this area, could Moruut's dream still be fulfilled?' Yuri asked, desperately hoping to be wrong.

'Verfallen thought so. But the effects of the spell would have only awakened the daemon from what's left of Moruut's physical remains. To restore it fully so it can exist beyond its tomb, the daemon needs potent human sacrifices.'

'Don't they always?' Stanislav said uncomfortably.

'By Sigmar, we're exactly where that bastard wanted us!' Torben suddenly exclaimed angrily. 'He didn't hire us for protection. He hired us to be the sacrifices!' The mercenary captain slammed his fist down on the table. A stunned silence reigned inside the windmill.

With an ear-splitting crash and perfect dramatic timing, the storm broke directly overhead. The thunderclap resounded around the mill and shook the building to its foundations. Gale-force winds howled around the windmill with cyclonic force, driving horizontal rain against the solitary building.

'I haven't witnessed a storm like this since the night the old Tzar died,' Alexi said.

'I told you, it's not natural,' Yuri repeated. 'It's not the weather that's causing this, it's the power of Chaos!'

Then they heard them. Over the crackling booms of the storm raging beyond their erstwhile sanctuary they heard gibbering cries and howls; the scraping of tiny, yet insistent, taloned hands on the stonework, shutters and door of the windmill. Despite their best efforts, with cold realisation the mercenaries were suddenly very aware of how poorly protected they were inside the crumbling structure. Although there was only the one door in or out, there were also the shuttered windows on this level and the next. Against a larger attacker their barricade would have been adequate, although they would have still been prisoners inside the windmill. Against a small, determined foe, however, one that could scale the pitted exterior of the building with ease and one in such large numbers, their defences seemed pitifully inadequate.

There were narrow spaces between the boards that made up the shutters and a draughty gap under the door. The neglected state of the building didn't help. All around them there were countless tiny access ways into the mill: knotholes in the wooden planks; gaps between the stones where the mortar holding them together had disintegrated. Such holes didn't need to be big, not when it was tiny claws and bodies that were trying to break into the mill. Yet with the press of hundreds of bodies, the nurglings' size proved to be no disadvantage in terms of the force they could exert on rotten boards that should have been replaced years ago.

'Every man to an opening!' Torben commanded. 'We can't let them get in!'

Instantly each of the mercenaries took up a position at a window or in front of the mill door. The shutters shook on their hinges as clawing green hands reached through the gaps between the planks, trying to pull them apart, while the door bolts rattled in their fastenings.

Torben had fought ratmen, black-armoured warriors of Chaos and even the undead, in his time, but never had he encountered such an indomitable foe. It wasn't their strength or even their dogged determination: it was their numbers.

'Give me a mad axe-wielding minotaur any day!' he found himself blurting out aloud. 'Anything but these little buggers!'

Torben and his companions did their best to fend off the nurglings' onslaught but where one grasping limb was removed, or one hole jammed with a sword blade, three more taloned hands tore through elsewhere. Besides, the mercenaries' weapons were proving unwieldy in such confined conditions. Their swords and Stanislav's axe were for use in open combat where a soldier could swing his weapon freely, thrust and parry. At the windows inside the mill, their weapons had to be used more like spears or polearms, in a stabbing motion, which was proving to be hard work. Not only that, it brought them in reach of the clutching claws of the besieging nurglings.

The only one who seemed to be having any luck was Oran, whose slim dagger slipped neatly between the boards of the window he was defending. Every well-aimed jab resulted in a high-pitched squeal from the other side of the shutter.

Alexi gave a pained shout, distracting the others for a moment. Glancing round, Torben saw the old soldier hopping around on one leg. Hanging on to his other ankle by its teeth was one of the fat little daemons, while three more squeezed under the now undefended door, under the table and into the mill.

Then Stanislav was striding across the floor. In one fluid motion, which appeared incredible from a hulking bear of a man like him, he dropped his axe and picked up a long-handled scythe from its place against the wall. With his newly-appropriated weapon gripped firmly in his huge hands, Stanislav was able to keep his distance as he swept the long, curved blade under the door. The rusted and notched blade cut through daemonic flesh and bone. Four swift strokes left a brace of dismembered bodies oozing dark green ichor in its wake.

Crushing the nurgling attached to his ankle against the mill's grindstone, Alexi finally managed to kick the struggling creature free of his leg, although its sharp teeth tore a chunk of flesh away with it. The nurgling tumbled through the air, landing in a gibbering heap in front of the barricaded door. Extending his stride, Stanislav brought his foot down on top of the foul creature. There was a squelching pop as the daemon was squashed under the great man's booted heel.

Following Stanislav's example, Torben, Pieter and Yuri exchanged their more familiar weapons for the pitchforks, sickles and rakes the original occupant of the windmill had left behind, defending their positions all the more effectively as a result. Suddenly light-headed, Alexi sat down heavily on the broad grindstone, tying a hastily prepared bandage around his bleeding ankle.

For half an hour, the six mercenaries battled against the onslaught of innumerable nurglings as wave after wave of the Plague God's children assailed the mill. The strain was beginning to show. They had been fighting for their lives since sunset. First Verfallen's Chaos spawn, then the flight up the hill and now the incessant attacks of the nurglings.

Where the nurglings were inevitably beginning to break through the rotten wood of one window, Yuri had begun piling sacks of mouldy grain into the window frame in an attempt to block the daemons' advance.

Putrid green ichor running from the sills and the rapidly decomposing remains of the nurglings that had infiltrated the tower had mixed with the flour and chaff-dust that covered the floor of the mill, creating a thick, foul-smelling sludge that was treacherously slippery underfoot. Pieter and the limping Alexi both lost their footing on the ooze-slicked planks.

There was a sudden, loud thud from the floor above them. In a second Stanislav had abandoned his position by the door and was up the ladder. Almost as quickly, he was leaping down it again.

'They're in!' he yelled, looking desperately to his captain. 'They've got in upstairs!'

Torben opened his mouth as if to issue an order, but no order came. When it mattered most, he was at a loss about what to do.

'Then we go into the cellar,' Pieter said, grimly.

Turning from the window he guarded, the steely-eyed young man crossed the room to the heavy trapdoor set into the floor. Taking the great iron ring in both hands he heaved on the trap, lifting it up and sending a shower of wheat-dust and chaff into the air around him. Taking the lantern from its hook Pieter took his first step into the cellar. The lantern cast a weak halo of light into the depths as if unwilling to enter the subterranean chamber itself. Pieter peered ahead into the gloom beyond the lantern's circle of illumination.

'Are you mad?' Yuri yelled.

Scores of scrabbling green creatures were pouring down the ladder into the main chamber. Clawing, biting, howling nurglings surged towards the mill's defenders, a mass of bloated, suppurating bodies with snapping needle-like fangs and ripping talons. One of the creatures flung itself from the surge of daemons, latching onto Stanislav's unprotected face with its jaws. Ripping the nurgling from his cheek he cast it back into the mass of scrabbling bodies.

The giant turned to Yuri, blood streaming down his face. 'They're going to overwhelm us!' he said with brutal finality.

'We have no choice!' Pieter shouted back over the gibbering cacophony of the daemonlings and then added to himself: 'So into the jaws of hell we go.'

HOLDING THE LANTERN at arm's length ahead of him, Pieter looked into the darkened cellar. After the clutter of the mill, the cellar was spartan by comparison. As he crept down the stone steps into the space beneath the windmill, Pieter's lantern cast flickering shadows on the curved walls. The cellar was cold and damp. Slime and patches of pallid, strangely shaped fungi covered the walls. The underside of the mill floor was thick with mould. Pieter shivered, although whether it was from the cold or some deep-seated fear, he wasn't sure – or at least didn't like to admit.

Reaching the bottom of the steps, he steadied himself against the wall with one hand. It was clammy with condensation and cold to the touch. They were on bedrock here. The rough stone of the floor of the cellar was dangerously uneven. Pieter hung the lantern from a splintered beam above his head, trying not to disturb any of the fungi growing there and so release any toxic spores.

The rest of the party followed Pieter into the under-room, Yuri and Stanislav being the last, fighting back the nurglings as they came. With a final swipe of his reclaimed axe, Stanislav slammed the heavy trapdoor shut, crushing the skull of one of the tiny daemons and the grasping forelimbs of several others in the process. With a satisfying 'Shunk!' he slammed the bolts home. It wasn't until much later that Stanislav wondered why the trapdoor should have bolts on its underside – unless someone had wanted to be able to keep others out should matters so dictate.

The lantern-light reflected off gleaming yellow-white bone and Pieter found himself looking into the empty eye-sockets of what he took to be the former owner of the mill. The almost fleshless corpse lay slumped against the wall, a cluster of thin-stemmed toadstools growing through the exposed bones of his ribcage. Doubtless the miller had been the first sacrifice made by Verfallen to re-consecrate this place to Nurgle and to begin the process of awakening the dormant Moruut.

And yet, other than the algae and necrotic-loving fungi, there were none of the accompanying carrion-feeders that Pieter would have expected. Where were the beetles, the centipedes, even a lone rat? Where was the buzz of bluebottles, laying their eggs within the host corpse that would provide a feast for their larval young? Perhaps they had departed long ago. Or perhaps they were down there.

Pieter took a step forward to get a better look at the round metal grille set into the centre of the cellar's stone floor. Three or four feet in diameter, and with widely spaced bars practically rusted through, the grille was sunk into a dressed stone rim. Beneath it, all Pieter could see was utter blackness. It was as if the hole swallowed up any light cast into it. The stink of the grave and the sewer assailed his nostrils, making him gag.

Then a sound rose up from the bottom of the pit: the splashing of water, the splatter of filth and a faint mewling moan, horribly as if of something newborn. Something was sloshing around in the slime at the bottom of the pit. Something large, by the sounds of it.

Stepping back again he noticed for the first time the filth-encrusted grooves in the floor, partially hidden by rotting straw and other muck. He followed the narrow channels filled with congealed blood and other unspeakable fluids, tracing the pattern they formed. Yes, there were the three connected circles and the three arrowheads emerging from between them: the symbol of the Plague God as recorded in Verfallen's journal. Nurgle's rune had been chiselled into the bedrock before being filled with putrescent material pleasing to the Lord of Decay. The blasphemous symbol covered most of the cellar floor with the grilled pit at its very centre.

'This isn't a cellar,' Stanislav said with a sense of unease.

'No, this is a shrine,' Pieter said, 'dedicated to Nurgle.'

'How does that saying go again?' Oran started with a tone of contempt in his voice. 'Out of the frying pan–'

'Into the plague pit,' Torben finished.

'At least up there,' Oran complained, indicating the floor above, 'we could have got out of this ruddy place!'

'Oh yes, and into what?' Torben snarled turning on him. 'An agonising death at the hands of the hordes of Nurgle? At least down here we're still alive, for the time being, and right now that's all that matters!'

'And this could be our way out,' Pieter said with something approaching excitement, an intense look in his glazed eyes. He hadn't taken his gaze from the rusted iron grille.

'You are insane!' Yuri exclaimed, his voice raised in fear and anger.

Torben hushed him with a gesture. 'What do you mean?' he asked, his commanding tone demanding an explanation from the nobleman and silence from the others.

'Inside this hill, Moruut is growing, awakened by the spell inscribed on the monolith. His body is reforming from the sludge and slime of his mortal remains that has lain in his burial chamber for countless centuries.'

'If you say so,' Oran muttered.

'As Verfallen recorded in his journal!' Pieter fumed.

'Go on,' Torben said.

'Anyway,' Pieter said, composing himself again, 'before he can return to full strength on this earthly plane Moruut has to consume the lot of us, body and soul.'

'Doesn't seem too unlikely from where I'm standing,' Yuri moaned, continuing in his despairing vein.

'Ignore him,' Alexi said, the old soldier encouraging the young noble.

'Well, if we could destroy Moruut before he's fully re-formed, while he's still comparatively weak, Nurgle's power in this area will be broken and the nurglings will be banished back to the Realm of Chaos. They won't be able to maintain their physical form with the source of the corruption gone.' It seemed there was no stopping Pieter now he had settled on this train of thought. 'Moruut's still a daemon, so he'll still be pretty strong, but we should be able to do it.'

'It sounds like it could work, in principle,' Alexi said, pondering the plan.

'Sounds like a good plan to me,' Stanislav agreed.

Oran grunted: 'It's the only plan we've got!'

'I hate to spoil things,' the mercenaries' leader said, interrupting their musings, 'but as you said yourself, this thing's a

daemon – a Daemon Prince, no less! Something tells me
that our weapons aren't going to be enough. What are we
going to fight it with?'

'This.' Pieter reached inside his jerkin and pulled out a
small, leather-bound book. The cover was dark with age and
the grease-stained pages well thumbed. A number of scraps
of paper and strips of ribbon marked places in the book.

'What's that?' Yuri asked.

'You godless heathen!' the older Alexi suddenly bellowed.
'Don't you recognise a prayer book of Sigmar when you see
one?'

'It was given to me by my old manservant, Walter,' Pieter
explained, opening the book and turning the pages as if
searching for a particular passage.

'Sure, so how's that going to help?' Torben asked, his brow
furrowed in concentration as he tried to fill in the gaps.

'It is known that the holy might of Sigmar can smite the
creatures of Chaos, such as daemons. Walter told me tales of
such horrors when I was a boy. They cannot stand against the
purity and righteousness of the Heldenhammer. They are
repelled by his cleansing zeal.'

Pieter stopped on a page, scanning the verses printed
there before continuing. 'In this book, there is a ritual of
purification. With the charms I have in my possession and
a little time I think I can carry out the rite and purge this
place of evil. All we need is to hold to our faith in blessed
Sigmar.'

'Faith?' Oran scoffed. 'It's all very well talking about faith
in the safety of your churches and surrounded by a city wall
but I think you'll find there's precious little faith out here?'

'Really?' Pieter challenged. 'Verfallen had faith. His belief
in his Dark God is what got us into this mess! I am strong in
my faith. Will you be found wanting when your time
comes?' The resolute noble fixed the rat-faced mercenary
with his steely-blue eyes.

'If the scholar's journal was correct, this evil that you speak
of has probably been here longer than the Empire. To have
lasted that long it's got to be strong too,' Torben warned, 'and
we're just a bunch of desperate swordsmen who know little
of the ways of the priest.'

'Nurgle's power waxes and wanes like the moon, as out-breaks of plague and other epidemics rise and fall,' Pieter explained patiently. 'I am sure we can prevail here.'

'What, all of us?' The party turned to look at Alexi at the old soldier's words. Normally he was the last to speak of fail-ure. The hard-bitten veteran of a hundred campaigns, defeat wasn't a concept Alexi seemed familiar with. But then they saw the reason for his change of heart.

Alexi was sitting on the steps, one leg of his britches rolled up to the knee to expose his bitten ankle. The teeth marks were clearly visible as angry red puncture wounds, apart from where the nurgling had torn off a mouthful. The flesh around the bite was discoloured purple and green. As Alexi pressed the flesh with his fingertips yellow pus dribbled from the wound. It was already infected. Alexi's face was a pallid grey and he was starting to sweat despite the cold.

'We end this now!' Torben determined. 'Pieter, do what you have to and tell us how we can best help.'

Hastily the devout young man instructed the rest of the party to take up positions around the pit. He knew the dae-mon would not go back into the void without a fight. As the mercenaries spaced out equidistantly around the chamber, Pieter placed a superstitious trinket or holy charm at each of the points where the carved lines of Nurgle's rune inter-sected.

Stanislav and Yuri stood at the bottom of the steps, half expecting the attack to come from the nurglings that had over-run the windmill. Torben and Oran flanked Pieter, who knelt down in the filth at the edge of the pit, while the weak-ened, hobbling Alexi marked the fifth point of the pentagram. He leant heavily on his sword for support while the others took up a fighting stance, weapons at the ready.

Kneeling on the cold, wet floor, Pieter began the ritual of purification. All eyes, other than his own, focused on the grille. The rabid gibbering from the nurglings above had died down, as if the tiny monsters knew that their lord was on his way.

LIKE A BLOATED purple-green slug at first, and then more like a sinuous snake, a tentacle emerged from between the bars of

the grille. Slick with slime the lantern light caused oily rain-
bow spirals to swirl across its mucus-wet skin. Slowly it
began to uncoil towards the kneeling Pieter.

'Careful,' the mercenaries' leader said in a forced whisper.

Raising his sword, ready to fight, the lame Alexi took a
staggering step forward to balance himself. The tentacle suddenly froze and then just as quickly whipped backwards
wrapping itself around the rotund old soldier's waist. A look
of horror flashed across Alexi's face and then he was being
pulled through the air. With a sickening crunch he hit the
grille, arms and legs outstretched. The tentacle pulled tighter,
forcing out what little air he had left in his lungs.

Gasping, Alexi somehow found his voice: 'By the gods!
Help me! Help me!'

To Torben it seemed that his own movements suddenly
slowed to a snail's pace. Tensed muscles released, he was running towards Alexi as Pieter slowly intoned the words of a
prayer to Sigmar. But before he was even halfway across the
cellar, the disgusting, boneless limb tightened still further,
tugging at the rotund man. Alexi's screams were joined by a
mournful moaning from the bottom of the pit, and another
sound – the sound of twisting metal. Within two seconds the
protesting bars, half-eaten through by rust, snapped.

Torben reached out his hand to the flailing, screaming
Alexi only to see the old soldier fold impossibly in the middle as his spine snapped.

And suddenly Alexi was gone.

His screams of agony descended into the blackness of the
pit only to be cut off abruptly a second later. As the mercenaries stood in stunned silence around the cellar a new
sound came to their ears. At first it was almost inaudible, a
bass growl that vibrated through the bedrock and then rose
in pitch and volume until it became a daemonic roar of triumph that shook the ground and rung in their ears long after
it had ceased.

Torben stood where he was, in stunned shock. There was
nothing he had been able to do! He remembered Manfred,
clutching at the arrow protruding from his stomach as he
toppled from the battlements into the greenskin throng
below. There had been nothing he could do then either, but

this was different. Manfred's death had been in the midst of battle. Alexi had been lost in a cellar, under an isolated windmill on a bleak hilltop in the middle of the Ostermark Moors. This was no battle to be sung of later in mead halls!

Following the daemonic roar, Pieter's words became more urgent, the litanies and prayers of supplication tumbling from his lips as he desperately tried to complete the ritual. More tentacles emerged from the pit, lashing out at the mercenaries. The men dodged to avoid the muscular, rubbery flesh as they tried to lay their own blows with their keen-edged blades.

And then, rising from the pit amidst the mass of tentacles, Verfallen's face appeared. Torben caught sight of the grinning scholar and, momentarily distracted, only just managed to deflect a swipe from a squid-like limb with the flat of his sword blade. Only it wasn't Verfallen: it was a sickly-green facsimile of the Chaos acolyte's head, bony growths standing in for spectacles, bobbing on top of a scaly, serpentine neck.

The head spoke: 'I am Moruut the Festering, Daemon Prince of Nurgle, the Infecter, the Corruptor, the Plague Lord's Chosen One.' Verfallen's image surveyed the warriors beneath it struggling against the constricting tentacles, a malevolent smile on its thin purple lips. 'And you are all going to die!'

ONLY HALF-AWARE of what was going on around him, Pieter began reading the prayer of exorcism. 'Lord Sigmar, Defender of the Empire!' He spoke the words as boldly and confidently as he could but it suddenly seemed to him that his voice was like that of a feeble, pleading child. And then Moruut spoke again.

'Pieter Valburg,' it said, 'what do you hope to achieve?'

Pieter stumbled over the next line. He tried to focus on the book held open in his shaking, sweating palms and then repeated the invocation.

'You couldn't save your dead sweetheart from the Dark Kiss and you won't be able to save your pathetic friends now.'

Pieter struggled on but no matter how hard he tried to ignore the taunts spoken by Moruut's slimy, slug-like tongue, the incessant, blasphemous chatter of the daemon drowned out his own feeble pleas to Sigmar, distracting him from his vital task.

'It's no good, boy,' Verfallen's grotesquely grinning head seemed to be saying to him.

'…and let the glorious light of righteousness shine into the dark places…'

'Your god is dead. He cannot hear you.'

'…and let the corrupters turn from your beauteous face…'

'Stop this futile charade. Give in to the darkness.'

'…for as your arm is strong smite the daemons and creatures of Chaos with your hammer of truth…'

'You're exhausted, boy. We all go to the darkness in time. Go now and let your body rest.'

Verfallen's head glided down on its great neck until they were practically nose-to-nose. Pieter could feel the daemon's warm foetid breath on his sweat-cold skin and it pimpled at the contact.

'Let your body rest. You have fought enough.'

Pieter paused. The daemon's words sounded so reasonable. It even sounded human. There was no gurgling voice as though spoken by decayed vocal chords choked with sewer-slime. Just a clear, persuasive human voice, dripping with honey, sickly-sweet like the sickly-sweet smell of decay that lingered in the cellar.

Slowly Pieter looked up from the open page before him and was just in time to see Torben's sword connect with the sinuous neck. The force of the mercenary captain's cutting stroke was powerful enough to slice through the unnatural flesh, severing the neck from Verfallen's grotesquely grinning head. Foul fluid spurted from the stump and the neck lolled. The simulacrum of the scholar's head landed at Torben's feet with a wet thud and an unearthly howl echoed around the cellar. With one strong kick he sent the monstrosity flying into the pit.

'Come on, lad,' he said turning to Pieter. 'We need you now, more than ever, you're the only one who can get us out of this!' Taking a deep breath, Pieter resumed the ceremony.

Writhing tentacles emerged from the hole in the floor, snaking across the chamber towards the kneeling nobleman. Before any of the others could react, the squid-like limbs were coiling around his arms and legs, and even trying to tear the prayer book from his grasp. But this only had the effect of making Pieter even more determined to complete the ritual. He had almost given in once. The daemon was becoming desperate, scared. If it feared him, he must be winning. He wouldn't give in again.

Over Pieter's frenzied invocations yet another sound rose to the party's ears from within the pit. The buzzing rapidly increased in volume until the swarm burst into the cellar. Flies filled the air. There were so many of them that Pieter could hardly see the words of the page in front of him as the tightening tentacles tried to pull him and the holy book apart. And still they came, bloated, hairy black bodies bombarding the warriors incessantly. Their weapons were useless against such a foe. Cutting through the swarm had about as much effect as cutting through the air itself. All the while the buzzing bluebottles found their irritating way into the mercenaries' clothes, hair, ears, noses and mouths, distracting them as they desperately fought against the daemon!

'Bloody hell!' Oran spat through a mash of black bodies.

Pieter kept reading. Only a few more verses, a final prayer of benediction and the ritual would be complete. With each line, each word, Pieter fancied he could sense the daemon flinch and recoil as if his words themselves were like the touch of acid on its festering flesh.

'Don't give up now!' Torben was yelling over the infernal buzzing. Pieter wasn't going to. They were winning, he knew it, and he was going to see this thing through to the finish.

'Hold fast!' Torben barked as the battering tentacles assailed his beleaguered band once again. It was all the harder now. With Alexi gone there were only four of them left to hold off the daemon long enough for Pieter to complete the ritual of purification. Yuri had fallen back to the steps and the trapdoor where the nurglings had renewed their attack and were beginning to break in to the cellar.

Despite their best efforts Pieter was now ensnared in the tentacles but still he read on as his companions fought to break the daemon's hold on him. Oran darted in between the slimy pseudopods, stabbing his dagger into their thickest parts and twisting before withdrawing his blade, ready for another strike. Ducking a swipe from a tentacle, Stanislav swung his axe in a figure-of-eight, chopping more of the limbs into pieces. Seizing the initiative, Torben flung himself into the gap created by Stanislav's attack. Skewering another tentacle with his sword, he managed to get a hand on Pieter's shoulder.

'That was always your problem, Torben Badenov,' a familiar voice said behind the captain, 'you never did know when you'd lost.'

Torben looked round into Alexi's anxious face. He froze, shocked by what he was seeing. He knew it wasn't Alexi: they had seen their friend pulled into the pit; they had all heard his death-cry. Yet here he was again, ever the wise old soldier, Torben's mentor from years before, offering him words of gentle advice like a father. How could this be?

Alexi's face winced and a tremor shook the hill.

'You always were too stubborn and stupid to realise you hadn't a hope!' Alexi reiterated, the snake-like neck it was attached to recoiling suddenly. The ritual was nearing its end. Pieter had faltered once but now he would not be stopped: he had been duped himself in such a way before by his vampire lover, Rosamund. But Torben's moment of doubt was enough.

A tentacle twisted around the mercenary's arm, yanking his hand from Pieter's shoulder as the coils around the nobleman constricted and pulled. The last lines of the ritual became a scream as the daemon dragged the vainly struggling Pieter, along with his prayer book, into the hole. Then he too was gone.

In an instant Stanislav was next to Torben, his face red with anger. The first blow from the big man's axe opened the side of Alexi's head. The second removed it from the daemon's body and sent it flying across the cellar. The foul parody of their dead companion landed next to the skeletal remains of the miller with a splat. It started to scream.

The near-deafening blood-curdling howling tore through all of them, pounding at their eardrums, ripping through their minds and churning their stomachs. A bellowing roar from deep inside the hill joined the scream. In response to the daemon's death-howl the cellar began to shake. Dust rained down from between the boards above their heads. The shaking worsened as a deep rumbling rose through the rock beneath their feet. Torben and the others found themselves stumbling to keep their balance as the stone floor buckled and split. But the screaming didn't stop.

'He did it!' Yuri shouted. 'The daemon's dying!'

The lad was right, Torben thought as the tentacles thrashed uncontrollably and began to retract into the pit. Pieter had succeeded! His death had not been in vain. The buzzing cloud of flies dissipated, escaping from the collapsing cellar through holes in the floor above. With a sickening sound, the joists holding up the floor of the windmill splintered and began to give way.

'Go! Get out of here!' Torben yelled above the noise.

The four remaining members of the band staggered across the chamber, trying to stay on their feet and avoid the rifts appearing in the floor. Part of the cellar wall subsided as the party reached the steps, climbing up them on their hands and knees as earth and stones showered down around them. Stanislav hurled the trapdoor open and burst into the tower of the windmill. All around him, mewling nurglings writhed in torment, their bodies dissolving into slime before his eyes. With the Plague Lord's power broken in this place, the daemonlings were unable to maintain their physical form.

As Torben reached the top of the steps, the last to escape the cellar, he glanced back at the pit, set at the heart of the rune of Nurgle. The tentacles had gone: Moruut had returned to his burial chamber to die. Moruut, Daemon Prince of Nurgle, the Corrupter, killed by Badenov's band, but not before it had claimed two of their number.

The fingers of a filth-covered hand grabbed the dressed stone lip of the pit. Then a second hand reached over the rim. Knuckles whitening the fingers pulled and a filth-splattered face emerged from the hole. Torben leapt down the steps and, half-falling, half-running, reached the pit in a matter of strides. Grasping Pieter's wrist, Torben pulled the struggling nobleman from the pit. A fractured beam crashed down next to them as Pieter's feet found purchase on the edge.

Then the two of them were fleeing from the cellar, following the others out of the building. Either the earthquake or the nurglings had destroyed their makeshift barricade in front of the door that now hung open, the rest of the mercenaries having fled into the night beyond. Torben skidded across the room and, hearing a dreadful groaning, looked up in time to see the mill machinery shake free of its settings. The great cogwheels and drive shafts smashed through the floor into the cellar and into the walls. Masonry crashing down around them, the air thick with dust, Torben and Pieter made it through the doorway and out of the crumbling mill.

Adrenaline driving their exhausted bodies on, the two men found the strength to make their weary legs run. Torben was suddenly aware of pale moonlight bathing the view before him, the moon visible once again through the clouds. The storm had abated. Ahead of them he could see Oran, Stanislav and Yuri pelting down the shaking hillside but Torben couldn't help glancing back over his shoulder. Behind them great rents emanating from the base of the windmill at the summit split the ground open. He hurtled on, a fissure zigzagging its way down the slope to his right. He could hear the windmill collapsing behind them. With a whirling crash the mill's sails cartwheeled past him, bouncing off down the hillside.

Past the fallen standing stone, past the smoking remains of their campfire, right at the foot of the hill, Badenov's band gathered, hands on knees, protesting lungs heaving, and watched the windmill's demise. Its sails gone, its drive shaft broken, the whole structure toppled in on itself and was swallowed up by the earth, as the summit of the hill caved in.

MORNING CAME AND with it clear skies, the unnatural storm Verfallen had raised with his blasphemous spell having dissipated. The hill had a distinctly different outline against the horizon, the summit and the windmill both gone. Amongst Badenov's band there followed the usual ritual of dressing wounds. However, whereas after a victory there would normally be the cheerful banter of the mercenaries celebrating a job well done, on this morning they were silent as all mourned the loss of Alexi of Nuln and honoured his memory in their own private way – all except Pieter Valburg.

Pieter's thoughts were elsewhere. He stood away from the group. With his back turned to the others he removed something from inside his jerkin. The cover of the grimoire was as black as the heart of the scholar who had owned it. Daemon faces leered at Pieter from the sculpted leather, if leather it was, and a spiked ring rune, picked out in crimson, left no doubt as to the nature of the book.

As Pieter traced the pattern with his fingertips an old adage of his late manservant came to mind: *know thine enemy.*

# ANCESTRAL HONOUR
## by Gav Thorpe

THICK, BLUE-GREY pipe smoke drifted lazily around the low rafters of the tavern, stirred into swirls and eddies by the dwarfs sat at the long benches in the main room. Grimli, known as the Blacktooth to many, hauled another keg of Bugman's Firestarter onto the bar with grunt. It wasn't even noon and already the tavern's patrons had guzzled their way through four barrels of ale. The thirsty dwarf miners were now banging their tankards in unison as one of their number tried to recite as many different names of beer as he could remember. The record, Grimli knew, was held by Oransson Brakkur and stood at three hundred and seventy-eight all told. The tavern owner, Skorri Weritaz, had a standing wager that if someone named more beers than Oransson they would get a free tankard of each that they named. The miner was already beginning to falter at a hundred and sixty-three, and even Grimli could think of twenty others he had not mentioned yet.

'Stop daydreaming, lad, and serve,' Skorri muttered as he walked past carrying a platter of steaming roast meat almost as large as himself. He saw Dangar, one of the mine overseers, at the far end of the bar gazing around with an empty tankard hanging limply in his hand. Wiping his hands on his apron, Grimli hurried over.

'Mug of Old Reliable's, Dangar?' Grimli offered, plucking the tankard from the other dwarf's grasp.

'I'll wait for Skorri to serve me, if'n you don't mind,' grunted Dangar, snatching back his drinking mug with a fierce scowl. 'Oathbreakers spoil the head.'

Skorri appeared at that moment and shooed Grimli away with a waved rag, turning to Dangar and taking the proffered tankard. Grimli wandered back to the Firestarter keg and picked the tapping hammer from his pocket. Placing a tap three fingers' breadth above the lower hoop, he delivered a swift crack with the hammer and the tap drove neatly into the small barrel. Positioning the slops bucket under the keg, he poured off the first half-pint, to make sure there were no splinters and that the beer had started to settle.

As he wandered around the benches, picking up empty plates, discarded bones and wiping the tables with his cloth, Grimli sighed. Not a single dwarf met his eye, and many openly turned their back on him as he approached. Sighing again, he returned to the bar. A shrill steam whistle blew signalling a change of shift, and as the incumbent miners filed out, a new crowd entered, shouting for ale and food.

And so the afternoon passed, the miners openly shunning Grimli, Skorri bad tempered and Grimli miserable. Just as the last ten years had been. Nothing had changed in all that time. No matter how diligently he worked, how polite and respectful he was, Grimli had been born a Skrundigor, and the stigma of the clan stayed with him. Here, in Karaz-a-Karak, home of the High King himself, Grimli was lucky he was even allowed to stay. He could have been cast out, doomed to wander in foreign lands until he died.

Well, Grimli thought to himself, as he washed the dishes in the kitchen at the back of the tavern, perhaps that would be better than the half-life he was leading now. Even Skorri, who was half mad, from when a cave-in dropped a tunnel roof on his head, could barely say three words to him, and Grimli considered him the closest thing he had to a friend. In truth, Skorri put up with having the Blacktooth in his bar because no other dwarf would lower themselves to work for the mad old bartender. No one else would listen to his constant muttering day after day, week after week, year after year. No one except Grimli, who had no other choice. He wasn't allowed in the mines because it would bring bad luck, he'd never been taken as an apprentice and so knew nothing of smithying, stonemasonry or carpentry. And as for anything to do with the treasuries and armouries, well no one would let an oathbreaker by birth within three tunnels of those areas. And so, bottle washer and tankard cleaner he was, and bottle washer and tankard cleaner he would stay for the rest of his life, perhaps only two hundred years more if he was lucky.

That thought started a chain of others in Grimli's mind. Dishonoured and desperate for release, from this living prison of disdain and hatred, the dwarf's thoughts turned to the Slayer shrine just two levels above his head. He was neither an experienced nor naturally talented fighter. Perhaps if he joined the Slayers, if he swore to seek out an honourable death against the toughest foe he could find, then he would find peace. If not, then his less than ample skills at battle would see him dead within the year, he was sure of it. Grimli had seen a few Slayers; some of them came to Karaz-a-Karak on their journeys and drank in Skorri's tavern. He liked them because they would talk to him, as they knew nothing about his family's past. They would never talk about their own dishonour, of course, and Grimli didn't want to hear it; he was still a dwarf after all and such things were for oneself not open conversation even with friends and family. But they had talked about the places outside of Karaz-a-Karak, of deadly battles, strange beasts and mighty foes. As a life, it would be better than picking up scraps for a few meagre copper coins.

He was decided. When his shift finished that evening, he would go up to the shrine of Grimnir and swear the Slayer oath.

As HE STEPPED through the large stone archway into the shrine, Grimli steeled himself. For the rest of the day he had questioned his decision, looking at it from every possible angle, seeing if there was some other solution than this desperate measure. But no other answer had come to him, and here he was, reciting the words of the Slayer oath in his mind. He took a deep breath and stared steadily at the massive gold-embossed face of Grimnir, the Ancestor God of Battle. In the stylised form of the shrine's decoration, his beard was long and full, his eyes steely and menacing, his demeanour proud and stern.

*I am a dwarf,* Grimli recited to himself in his head, *my honour is my life and without it, I am nothing.* He took another deep breath. *I shall become a Slayer, I shall seek redemption in the eyes of my ancestors.* The lines came clearly to Grimli's keen mind.

'I shall become as death to my enemies until I face he that takes my life and my shame,' a gravely voice continued next to him. Turning with a start, Grimli was face-to-face with a Slayer. He had heard no one enter, but perhaps he had been so intent on the oath he had not noticed. He was sure that no one else had been here when he came in.

'How do you know what I'm doing?' asked Grimli suspiciously. 'I might have come here for other reasons.'

'You are Grimli Blacktooth Skrundigor,' the Slayer boomed in his harsh voice. 'You and all your family have been accused of cowardice and cursed by the High King for seventeen generations. You are a serving lad in a tavern. Why else would you come to Grimnir's shrine other than to forsake your previous life and become as I?'

'How do you know so much about me, Slayer?' Grimli eyed the stranger with caution. He looked vaguely familiar, but even if Grimli had once known him, his transformation into a Slayer made him unrecognisable now. The Slayer was just a little taller than he was; though he seemed much more for his hair was spiked with orange-dyed lime and stood another foot higher than Grimli. His beard was long and lustrous, similarly dyed and woven with bronze and gold beads and bands, which sparkled in the lantern light of the shrine. Upon his face were numerous swirling tattoos – runes and patterns of Grugni and Valaya, to ward away evil. In his hand, the Slayer carried a great axe, fully as tall as the Slayer himself. Its head gleamed with a bluish light and even Grimli could recognise rune work when he saw it. The double-headed blade was etched with signs of cutting and cleaving, and Grimli had no doubt that many a troll, orc or skaven had felt its indelicate bite.

'Call me Dammaz,' the Slayer told Grimli, extending a hand in friendship with a grin. Grimli noticed with a quiver of fear that the Slayer's teeth were filed to points, and somewhat reddened. He shuddered when he realised they were bloodstained.

*Dammaz*, he thought. One of the oldest dwarf words, it meant 'grudge' or 'grievance'. Not such a strange name for a Slayer.

He took the offered hand gingerly and felt his fingers in a fierce grip which almost crushed his hand. Dammaz's forearms and biceps bulged with corded muscles and veins as they shook hands, and it was then Grimli noticed just how broad the other dwarf was. His shoulders were like piles of boulders, honed with many long years of swinging that massive axe. His chest was similarly bulged; the harsh white of many scars cut across the deep tan of the Slayer's bare flesh.

'Do you want me to accompany you after I've sworn the oath?' guessed Grimli, wondering why this mighty warrior was taking such an interest in him.

'No, lad,' Dammaz replied, releasing his bone-splintering grip. 'I want you to come with me to Karak Azgal, and see what I have to show you. If, after that, you want to return here and be a Slayer, then you can do so.'

'Why Karak Azgal?' Grimli's suspicions were still roused.

'You of anyone should know that,' Dammaz told him sternly.

'Because that is… was where…' Grimli started, but he found he couldn't say the words. He couldn't talk about it, not here, not with this dwarf who he had just met. He could barely let the words enter his own head let alone speak them. It was too much to ask, and part of the reason he wanted to become a Slayer.

'Yes, that is why,' nodded Dammaz with a sad smile. 'Easy, lad, you don't have to tell me anything. Just answer yes or no. Will you come with me to Karak Azgal and see what I have to show you?'

Grimli looked into the hard eyes of the Slayer and saw nothing there but tiny reflections of himself.

'I will come,' he said, and for some reason his spirits lifted.

IT WASN'T EXACTLY a fond farewell when Grimli told Skorri that he was leaving. The old dwarf looked him up and down and then took his arm and led him into the small room next to the kitchen which served as the tavern owner's bed chamber, store room and office. He pulled a battered chest from under the bed and opened the lid on creaking hinges. Delving inside, he pulled out a hammer which he laid reverentially on the bed, followed by a glistening coat of chainmail. He then unhooked the shield that hung above the fireplace and added it to the pile.

'Take 'em,' he said gruffly, pointing to the armour and hammer. 'Did me good, killed plenty grobi and such with them, I did. Figure you need 'em more 'n me now, and you do the right thing now. It's good. Maybe you come back, maybe you don't, but you won't come back the same, I reckon.'

Grimli opened his mouth to thank Skorri, but the old dwarf had turned and stomped from the room, muttering to himself again. Grimli stood there for a moment, staring absently out of the door at Skorri's receding back, before turning to the bed. He took off his apron and hung it neatly over the chair by the fire. Lifting the mail coat, he slipped it over his head and shoulders where it settled neatly. It was lighter than he had imagined, and fitted him almost perfectly. The shield had a long strap and he hooked it over one shoulder, settling it across his back.

Finally, he took up the hammer. The haft was bound in worn leather, moulded over the years into a grip that his short fingers could hold comfortably. The weight was good, the balance slightly towards the head but not ungainly. Hefting it in his hand a couple of times, Grimli smiled to himself. Putting the hammer through his belt, he strode out into the busy tavern room. The conversation died immediately and a still calm settled. Everyone was looking at him.

'Goin' somewhere, are ye?' asked a miner from over by the bar. 'Off to fight, perhaps?'

'Perhaps,' agreed Grimli. 'I'm going to Karak Azgal, to find my honour.'

With that he walked slowly, confidently across the room. A few of the dwarfs actually met his gaze, a couple nodded in understanding. As he was about to cross the threshold he heard Dangar call out from behind him.

'When you find it lad, I'll be the first to buy you a drink.'

With a lightness in his step he had never felt before, Grimli walked out of the tavern.

FOR MANY WEEKS the pair travelled south, using the long underway beneath the World's Edge Mountains when possible, climbing to the surface where collapses and disrepair made the underground highway impassable. For the most part they journeyed in silence; Grimli used to keeping his own company, the Slayer unwilling or unable to take part in idle conversation. The night before they were due to enter Karak Azgal they sat camped in the ruins of an old wayhouse just off the main underway. By the firelight, the stone reliefs that adorned the walls and ceiling of the low, wide room flickered in ruddy shadow. Scenes from the great dwarf history surrounded Grimli, and he felt reassured by the weight of the ancient stones around him. He felt a little trepidation about the coming day, for Karak Azgal was one of the fallen Holds, now a nest of goblins, trolls, skaven and many other foul creatures. During the nights they had shared in each other's company, Dammaz had taught him a little of fighting. Grimli was not so much afraid for his own life, he was surprised and gladdened to realise, but that he would fail Dammaz. He had little doubt that the hardened Slayer would not need his help, but he fancied that the old dwarf might do something reckless if he needed protecting and Grimli did not want that on his conscience.

'Worried, lad?' asked Dammaz, appearing out of the gloom. He had disappeared frequently in the last week, returning sometimes with a blood-slicked axe. Grimli knew better than to ask.

'A little,' Grimli admitted with a shrug.

'Take heart then,' Dammaz told him, squatting down on the opposite side of the fire, the flames dancing in bright reflections off his burnished jewellery. 'For fear makes us strong. Use it, lad, and it won't use you. You'll be fine.

Remember, strike with confidence and you'll strike with strength. Aim low and keep your head high.'

They sat for a while longer in quiet contemplation. Clearing his throat, Grimli broke the silence.

'We are about to enter Karak Azgal, and I'd like to know something,' Grimli spoke. 'If you don't want to answer, I'll understand but it'll set my mind at rest.'

'Ask away, lad. I can only say no,' Dammaz reassured him.

'What's your interest in me, what do you know about the Skrundigor curse?' Grimli asked before he changed his mind.

Dammaz stayed silent for a long while and Grimli thought he wasn't going to get an answer. The old dwarf eventually looked him in the eye and Grimli meant his gaze.

'Your distant forefather Okrinok Skrundigor failed in his duty many centuries ago, for which the High King cursed him and all his line,' Dammaz told him. 'The name of Skrundigor is inscribed into the Dammaz Kron. Until such time as the honour of the clan is restored, the curse will bring great pain, ill fortune and the scorn of others onto Okrinok's entire heritage. This I know. But, do you know why the High King cursed you so?'

'I do,' Grimli replied solemnly. Like Dammaz, he did not speak straight away, but considered his reply before answering. 'Okrinok was a coward. He fled from a fight. He broke his oaths to protect the High King's daughter from harm, and for that he can never be forgiven. His selfishness and betrayal has brought misery to seventeen generations of my clan and I am last of his line. Accidents and mishaps have killed all my kin at early ages. Many left in self-exile, others became Slayers before me.'

'That is right,' agreed Dammaz. 'But do you know exactly what happened, Grimli?'

'For my shame, I do,' Grimli replied. 'Okrinok was sworn to protect Frammi Sunlocks, the High King's daughter, when she travelled to Karak Azgal to meet her betrothed, Prince Gorgnir. She wished to see something of her new home, and Prince Gorgnir, accompanied by Okrinok and the royal bodyguard, took her to the treasuries, the forges, the armouries and the many other great wonders of Karak Azgal. Being of good dwarf blood, she was interested in the mines. One day they travelled to the depths of the hold so that she could see the miners labouring. It was an ill-chosen day, for that very day vile goblins broke through into the mines. They had been tunnelling for Grugni knows how long, and of all the days that their sprawling den had to meet the wide-hewn corridors of Karak Azgal it was that one which fate decreed.'

Grimli stopped and shook his head with disbelief. A day earlier or a day later, and the entire history of the Skrundigors may have been completely different; a glorious heritage of battles won and loyal service to the High King. But it had not been so.

'The grobi set upon the royal household,' continued Grimli. 'Hard fought was the battle, and bodyguard and miners clashed with a countless horde of greenskins. But there were too many of them, and their wicked knives caught Frammi and Gorgnir and slew them. One of the bodyguards, left for dead by the grobi, survived to recount the tale to the High King and much was the woe of all the dwarf realm. Yet greater still was the hardship for as the survivor told the High King with his dying breath, Okrinok Skrundigor, upon seeing the princess and prince-to-be slain, had fled the fight and his body was never found. Righteous and furious was the High King's anger and we have been cursed since.'

'Told as it has been to each generation of Skrundigor since that day,' Dammaz nodded thoughtfully. 'And was the High King just in his anger?'

'I have thought of it quite a lot, and I reckon he was,' admitted Grimli, poking at the fire as it began to die down. 'Many a king would have had us cast out or even slain for such oathbreaking and so I think he was merciful.'

'We will speak of this again soon,' Dammaz said as he stood up. 'I go to Kargun Skalfson now, to seek permission to enter Karak Azgal come tomorrow.'

With that the Slayer was gone into the gloom once more, leaving Grimli to his dour thoughts.

THE STENCH OF the troll sickened Grimli's stomach as it lurched through the doorway towards him. It gave a guttural bellow as it broke into a loping run. Grimli was rooted to the spot. In his mind's eye he could see himself casually stepping to one side, blocking its claw with his shield as Dammaz had taught him; in reality his muscles were bunched and tense and his arm shook. Then the Slayer was there, between him and the approaching monster. In the darkness, Grimli could clearly see the blazing axe head as it swung towards the troll, cleaving through its midriff, spraying foul blood across the flagged floor as the blade continued on its course and shattered its backbone before swinging clear. Grimli stood in dumbfounded amazement. One blow had sheared the troll cleanly in two. Dammaz stood over the rank corpse and beheaded it with another strike before spitting on the body.

'Can never be too sure with trolls. Always cut the head off, lad,' Dammaz told him matter-of-factly as he strolled back to stand in front of Grimli.

'I'm sorry,' Grimli lowered his head in shame. 'I wanted to fight it, but I couldn't.'

'Calm yourself, lad,' Dammaz laid a comforting hand on his shoulder. 'Next time you'll try harder, won't you?'

'Yes, I will,' Grimli replied, meeting the Slayer's gaze.

FOR TWO DAYS and two nights they had been in Karak Azgal. The night before, Grimli had slain his first troll, crushing its head with his hammer after breaking one of its legs. He had already lost count of the number of goblins whose last vision had been his hammer swinging towards them. Over twenty at least, possibly nearer thirty, he realised. Of course, Dammaz had slain twice, even thrice that number, but Grimli felt comfortable that he was holding his own.

Dammaz had been right, it did get easier. Trolls still scared Grimli, but he had worked out how to turn that fear into anger, imbuing his limbs with extra strength and honing his reflexes. And most of all, it had taught Grimli that it felt good to kill grobi. It was in his blood, by race and by clan, and he now relished each fight, every battle a chance to exact a small measure of revenge on the foul creatures whose kind had ruined his clan so many centuries before.

They were just breaking camp in what used to be the forges, so Dammaz informed him. Everything had been stripped bare by the evacuating dwarfs and centuries of bestial looters and other treasure hunters. But the firepits could still clearly be seen, twenty of them in all, spread evenly across the large hall. Grugni, God of Smithing, was represented by a great anvil carved into the floor, his stern but kindly face embossed at its centre. Dammaz told him that the lines of the anvil used to run with molten metal so that its light illuminated the whole chamber with fiery beauty.

Grimli would have liked to have seen that, like so many other things from the days when the dwarf realms stretched unbroken from one end of the World's Edge Mountains to the other. Such a great past, so many treasures and wonders, now all lost, perhaps never to be regained and certainly never to be surpassed. Centuries of treachery, volcanoes, earthquakes and the attacks of grobi and skaven had almost brought the dwarfs to their knees. They had survived though; the dwarfs were at their fiercest when hardest pressed. The southern holds may have fallen, but the northern holds still stood strong. In his heart, Grimli knew that the day would come when once more the mountains would resound along their length to the clatter of dwarf boots marching to war and the pound of hammers on dwarfish anvils. Already Karak Eight Peaks was being reclaimed, and others would follow.

'Dreaming of the golden age, lad?' Dammaz asked, and Grimli realised he had been stood staring at the carving of Grugni for several minutes.

'And the glory days to come,' replied Grimli which brought forth a rare smile from the Slayer.

'Aye, that's the spirit, Grimli, that's the spirit,' Dammaz agreed. 'When we're done here, you'll be a new dwarf, I reckon.'

'I'm already...' started Grimli but Dammaz silenced him with a finger raised to his lips. The Slayer tapped his nose and Grimli sniffed deeply. At first he could smell nothing, but as he concentrated, his nostrils detected a whiff of something unclean, something rotten and oily.

'That's the stink of skaven,' whispered Dammaz, his eyes peering into the darkness. Grimli closed his eyes and focused his thoughts on his senses of smell and hearing. There was breeze coming from behind him, where the odour of rats was strongest, and he thought he could hear the odd scratch, as of clawed feet on bare stone, to his right. Opening his eyes he looked in that direction, noting that Dammaz was looking the same way. The Slayer glanced at him and gave a single nod of agreement, and Grimli stepped up beside him, slipping his hammer from his belt and unslinging his shield from his back.

Without warning, the skaven attacked. Humanoid rats, no taller than Grimli, scuttled and ran out of the gloom, their red eyes intent on the two dwarfs. Dammaz did not wait a moment longer, launching himself at the ratmen with a wordless bellow. The first went down with its head lopped from its shoulders; the second was carved from groin to chest by the return blow. One of the skaven managed to dodge aside from Dammaz's attack and ran hissing at Grimli. He felt no fear now; had he not slain a troll single-handedly? He suddenly realised the peril of overconfidence as the skaven lashed out with a crudely sharpened blade, the speed of the attack taking him by surprise so that he had to step back to block the blow with his shield. The skaven were not as strong as trolls, but they were a lot faster.

Grimli batted away the second attack, his shield ringing dully with the clang of metal on metal, and swung his hammer upwards to connect with the skaven's head, but the creature jumped back before the blow landed. Its breath was foetid and its matted fur was balding around open sores in places. Grimli knew that if he was cut, the infection that surrounded the pestilential scavengers might kill him even if the wound did not. He desperately parried another blow, realising that other skaven were circling quickly behind him. He took another step back and then launched himself forward as his foe advanced after him, smashing the ratman to the ground with his shield. He stomped on its chest with his heavy boot, pinning it to the ground as he brought his hammer smashing into its face. Glancing over his shoulder, he saw Dammaz was still fighting, as he'd expected, a growing pile of furry bodies at his feet.

Two skaven then attacked Grimli at once, one thrusting at him with a poorly constructed spear, the other slashing with a wide-bladed knife. He let his shield drop slightly and the skaven with the spear lunged at the opportunity. Prepared for the attack, Grimli deflected the spearhead to his right, stepped forward and smashed his hammer into the skaven's chest, audibly splintering ribs and crushing its internal organs. He spun on the other skaven but not fast enough, its knife thankfully scraping without harm along the links of his chainmail. He slammed the edge of the shield up into the skaven's long jaw, dazing it, and then smashed its legs from underneath it with a wide swing of his hammer. The creature gave a keening, agonised cry as it lay there on the ground and he stoved its head in with a casual backswing.

The air was filled with a musky scent, which stuck in Grimli's nostrils, distracting him, and it was a moment before he realised that the rest of the skaven had fled. Joining Dammaz he counted thirteen skaven corpses on the ground around the Slayer, many of them dismembered or beheaded.

'Skaven are all cowards,' Dammaz told him. He pointed at a darker-furred corpse, both its legs missing. 'Once I killed their leader they had no stomach for the fight.

'Kill the leader, I'll remember that,' Grimli said as he swung his shield back over his shoulder.

For the rest of the day Grimli felt the presence of the skaven shadowing him and the Slayer, but no further attack came. They passed out of the forges and strong rooms down into the mines. The wondrously carved hallways and corridors led them into lower and more basically hewn tunnels, the ceiling supported now by pit props and not pillars engraved with ancient runes. The stench of skaven became stronger for a while, their spoor was littered across the floor or of the mine-shafts, but after another hour's travel it faded quickly.

'This is grobi territory, lad. The skaven don't come down these ways,' Dammaz informed Grimli when he commented on this phenomenon.

As they continued their journey Grimli noticed even rougher, smaller tunnels branching off the workings of the dwarfs, and guessed them to be goblin tunnels, dug out after the hold fell. There was a shoddiness about the chips and cuts of the goblin holes that set them apart from the unadorned but neatly hewn walls of dwarf workmanship, even to Grimli's untrained eye. As he absorbed this knowledge, Dammaz led him down a side-tunnel into what was obviously once a chamber of some kind. It was wide, though not high, and seemed similar to the dorm-chambers of Karaz-a-Karak.

'This is where it happened,' Grimli said. It was a statement, not a question. He realised this was where Dammaz had been leading him.

'Aye, that it is, lad,' the Slayer confirmed with a nod that shook his bright crest from side to side. 'This is where Okrinok Skrundigor was ambushed. Here it was that Frammi and Gorgnir were slain by the grobi. How did you know?'

'I'm not sure as I know,' Grimli replied with a frown. 'I can feel what happened here, in my blood, I reckon. It's like it's written in the stone somehow.'

'Aye, the mountain remembers, you can be sure of that,' Dammaz agreed solemnly. 'You can rest here tonight. Tomorrow will be a hard day.'

'What happens tomorrow?' asked Grimli, unburdening himself of his shield and pack.

'Nothing comes to those who hurry, lad, you should know that,' Dammaz warned him with a stern but almost fatherly wag of his finger.

THAT NIGHT, GRIMLI'S dreams were troubled, and he tossed and turned beneath his blanket. In his mind he was there, at the betrayal so many centuries before. He could see Frammi and Gorgnir clearly, inspecting the bunks of the wide dormitory, protected by ten bodyguards. Gorgnir was wide of girth, even for a dwarf, and his beard was as black as coal and shone with a deep lustre. His dark eyes were intelligent and keen, but he was quick to laugh at some jest made by Frammi. The princess, to Grimli's sleeping eye at least, was beautiful; her blonde hair tied up in two tresses that flowed down her back to her knees. Her pallor was ruddy and healthy, her hips wide. Clad in a russet gown, a small circlet of gold holding her hair back, she was unmistakably the daughter of a High King.

In his dream-state, Grimli sighed. The lineage of those two would have been fine and strong, he thought glumly, had they but been given the chance to wed. At the thought, the deadly attack happened.

It seemed as if the goblins sprang from nowhere, rushing through the door with wicked cackles and grinning, yellowed teeth. Their pale green skin was tinged yellow in the lamplight, their robes and hoods crudely woven from dark material that seemed to absorb the light. The bodyguards reacted instantly, drawing their hammers and shields, forming a circle around the royal couple. The goblins crashed against the shieldwall like a wave against a cliff, and momentarily they were smashed back by the swings of the bodyguard's hammers, like the tide receding. But the press of goblins was too much and those at the front were forced forward into the determined dwarfs, crushed and battered mercilessly as they fought to get at the prince and princess. Soon they were climbing over their own dead, howling with glee as one then another and another of the bodyguard fell beneath the endless onslaught. The shield wall broke for a moment, but that was all that was needed. The goblins rushed the gap, pushing the breach wider with their weight of numbers.

This was it, the dark moment of the Skrundigor clan. It was Gorgnir who fell first, bellowing a curse on the grobi even as his axe lodged in one of their skulls and he was swarmed over by the small greenskins. Frammi wrenched the axe free and gutted three of the goblins before she too was overwhelmed; one of her tresses flew through the air as a sword blade slashed across her neck.

Almost as one the three remaining bodyguards howled with grief and rage, hurling themselves at the goblins with renewed ferocity. One in particular, a massive ruby inset into his hammer's head, smashed a bloody path into the grobi, every blow sweeping one of the tunnel-dwellers off its scampering feet. His helm was chased with swirling designs in bronze and gold and he had the faceplate drawn down, showing a fierce snarling visage of Grimnir in battle. The knives and short swords of the goblins rang harmlessly off his mail and plate armour with a relentless dull chiming, but they could not stop him and he burst clear through the door.

The other two bodyguards fell swiftly, and the goblins descended upon the dead like a pack of wild dogs, stripping them of every item of armour, weapon, jewellery and clothing. They bickered and fought with one another over the spoils, but soon the pillaging was complete and the goblins deserted the room in search of fresh prey. For what seemed an eternity, the looted bodies lay where they had been left, but eventually a low groan resounded across the room and one of the bodies sat up, blood streaming from a dozen wounds across his body. Groggily he stood up, leaning on one of the bunks, and shook his head, causing fresh blood to ooze from a gash across his forehead. He staggered for a moment and then seemed to steady.

'Skrundigorrrr!' his voice reverberated from the walls and floor in a low growl.

THE DREAM WAS still vivid when Grimli was woken by a chill draught, and he saw that the fire was all but dead embers. He added more sticks from the bundle strapped to his travelling pack and stoked the ashes until the fire caught once again. As it grew it size, its light fell upon the face of Dammaz who was sitting against the far wall, wide awake, his eyes staring intently at Grimli.

'Did you see it, lad?' he asked softly, his low whisper barely carrying across the room.

'I did,' Grimli replied, his voice as muted, his heart in his throat from what he had witnessed.

'So, lad, speak your mind, you look troubled,' Dammaz insisted.

'I saw them slain, and I saw Okrinok fight his way free instead of defending their bodies,' Grimli told the Slayer, turning his gaze from Dammaz to the heart of the fire. The deep red reminded Grimli of the ruby set upon Okrinok's hammer.

'Aye, that was a terrible mistake, you can be sure of that,' Dammaz grimaced as he spoke. The two fell into a sullen silence.

'There is no honour to be found here,' Grimli declared suddenly. 'The curse cannot be lifted from these enduring stones, not while mighty Karaz-a-Karak endures. I shall return there, swear the Slayer oath and come back to Karak Azgal to meet my death fighting in the caverns that witnessed my ancestor's treachery.'

'Is that so?' Dammaz asked quietly, his expression a mixture of surprise and admiration.

'It is só,' Grimli assured the Slayer.

'I told you not to be hasty, beardling,' scowled Dammaz. 'Stay with me one more day before you leave this place. You promised you would come with me, and I haven't shown you everything you need to see yet.'

'One more day then, as I promised,' Grimli agreed, picking up his pack.

THEY ENTERED THE goblin tunnels not far from the chamber where Grimli had slept, following the sloping corridor deeper and deeper beneath the World's Edge Mountains. They had perhaps travelled for half a day when they ran into their first goblins. There were no more than a handful, and the fight was bloody and quick, two of the grobi falling to Grimli's hammer, the other three carved apart by the baleful blade of Dammaz's axe.

'The goblins don't live down here much. They prefer to live in the better-crafted halls of Karak Azgal itself,' Dammaz told Grimli when he mentioned the lack of greenskins. 'But there are still plenty enough to kill,' the Slayer added with a fierce grin.

True enough, they had not travelled more than another half mile before they ran into a small crowd of greenskins moving up the tunnel in the opposite direction. The goblins shrieked their shrill war cries and charged, only to be met head-on by the vengeful dwarfs. In the confines of the goblin-mined cavern, the grobi's weight of numbers counted for little, and one-on-one they were no match for even Grimli. As he smashed apart the skull of the tenth goblin, the others turned and ran, disappearing into the darkness with the patter of bare feet. Grimli was all for going after them, but Dammaz laid a hand on his shoulder.

'Our way lies down a different path, but there will be more to fight soon enough,' he told Grimli. 'They will head up into Karak Azgal and fetch more of their kind, and perhaps lie in wait for us somewhere in one of the wider spaces where they can overwhelm us.'

'That's why we should catch them and stop them,' declared Grimli hotly.

'Even if we could run as fast as they, which we can't, lad, the grobi will lead us a merry chase up and down. They know these tunnels by every inch, and you do not,' Dammaz countered with a longing look in the direction the goblins had fled. 'Besides, if we go chasing willy-nilly after every grobi we meet, you'll never get to see what I have to show you.'

With that the Slayer turned away and continued down the passage. After a moment, Grimli followed behind, his shield and hammer ready.

GRIMLI WAS SURPRISED a little when the winding path Dammaz followed led them into a great cavern.

'I did not think the grobi could dig anything like this,' he said, perplexed.

'Grobi didn't dig this, you numbskull,' laughed Dammaz, pointing at the ceiling. Grimli followed the gesture and saw that long stalactites hung down from the cave's roof. The cavern had been formed naturally millennia ago when the Ancestor Gods had fashioned the mountains. Something caught the young dwarf's eye, and he looked futher into the hall-like cave. A massive mound, perhaps a great stalagmite as old as the world itself, rose from the centre of the cavern.

Grimli walked closer to the heap, and as he approached his eyes made out the shape of a small arm stuck out. And there was a tiny leg, just below it. Hurrying closer still, he suddenly stopped in his tracks. The mound was not rock at all, but built from the bodies of dozens, even scores of goblins, heaped upon one another a good ten yards above his head. Walking forward again, amazed at the sight, Grimli saw that each goblin bore at least one wound, crushed and mangled by what was obviously a heavy hammer blow. He looked over his shoulder at Dammaz, who was walking towards Grimli, axe carried easily in one hand.

'You recognise the handiwork, lad?' Dammaz asked as he drew level with Grimli and looked up at the monumental pile of greenskin corpses.

'Okrinok did this?' Grimli gaped at the Slayer, wondering that he could be even more astounded than he was before.

'Climb with me,' Dammaz commanded him, stepping up onto the battered skull of a goblin.

Grimli reached for a handhold and as his fingers closed around the shattered arm of a goblin, it felt as hard as rock beneath his touch. There was no give in the dead flesh at all and his skin prickled at the thought of the magic that obviously was the cause. Pulling himself up the macabre monument, Grimli could almost believe it had been fashioned from the stone, so unyielding were the bodies beneath his hands and feet. It was a laborious process, hauling himself up inch by inch, yard by yard for several minutes, following the glow of Dammaz's axe above him. Panting and sweating, he pulled himself to the top and stood there for a moment catching his breath.

As he recovered from his exertions, Grimli saw what was located at the very height of the mound. There stood Okrinok. He was unmistakable; his ruby-encrusted hammer was still in his grasp, lodged into the head of a goblin that was thrusting a spear through the dwarf's chest. The two had killed each other, and now stood together in death's embrace. Grimli approached the ancient dwarf slowly, almost reverentially. When he was stood an arm's length away, he reached out and laid a trembling hand upon his ancestor's shoulder. It was then that Grimli looked at Okrinok's face.

His helmet had been knocked off in the fight, and his long, shaggy hair hung free. His mouth was contorted into a bellow, his scowl more ferocious than any Grimli had seen before. Even in death Okrinok looked awesome. His beard was fully down to his knees, bound by many bronze and gold bands and beads, intricately braided in places. Turning his attention back to his ancestor's face, he noted the familiar ancestral features, some of which he had himself. But there was something else, something more than a vague recognition. Okrinok reminded him of someone in particular. For a moment Grimli thought it must be his own father, but with a shiver along his spine he realised it was someone a lot closer. Turning slowly, he looked at Dammaz, who was stood just to his right, leaning forward with his arms crossed atop his axe haft.

'O-Okrinok?' stuttered Grimli, letting his hammer drop from limp fingers as shock ran through him. He staggered for a moment before falling backwards, sitting down on the goblin mound with a thump.

'Aye, lad, it is,' Dammaz smiled warmly.

'B-but, how?' was all Grimli could ask. Pushing himself to his feet, he tottered over to stand in front of Okrinok. The Slayer proffered a gnarled hand, the short fingers splayed. Grimli hesitated for a moment, but Okrinok nodded reassuringly and he grasped the hand, wrist-to-wrist in warriors' greeting. At the touch of the Slayer, Grimli felt a surge of power flood through him, suffusing him from his toes to the tips of his hair.

GRIMLI FELT LIKE he had just woken up, and his senses were befuddled. As they cleared he realised he was once again in the mine chamber, witnessing the fight with the goblins. But this time it was different – he was somehow *inside* the fight, the goblins were attacking *him*! Panic fluttered in his heart for a moment before he realised that this was just a dream or vision too. He was seeing the battle through Okrinok's eyes. He saw Frammi and Gorgnir once more fall to the blades of the goblins and felt the surge of unparalleled shame and rage explode within his ancestor. He felt the burning strength of hatred fuelling every blow as Okrinok hurled himself at the goblins. There were no thoughts of safety, no desire to escape. All Grimli could feel was an incandescent need to crush the grobi, to slaughter each and every one of them for what they had done that day.

Okrinok bellowed with rage as he swung his hammer, no hint of fatigue in his powerful arms. One goblin was smashed clear from his feet and slammed against the wall. The backswing bludgeoned the head of a second; the third blow snapped the neck of yet another. And so Okrinok's advance continued, his hammer cutting a swathe of pulped and bloodied destruction through the goblins. It was with a shock that Okrinok realised he had no more foes to fight, and looking about him he found himself in an unfamiliar tunnel, scraped from the rock by goblin hands. He had a choice; he could return up the tunnel to Karak Azgal and face the shame of having failed in his sacred duty. Or he could keep going down, into the lair of the goblins, to slay those who had done this to him. His anger and loathing surged again as he remembered the knives plunging into

Gorgnir and he set off down the tunnel, heading deeper into the mountain.

Several times he ran into parties of goblins, and every time he threw himself at them with righteous fury, exacting vengeance with every blow of his hammer. Soon his wanderings took him into a gigantic cavern, the same one where he now stood again. Ahead of him the darkness was filled with glittering red eyes, the goblins mustered in their hundreds. He stood alone, his hammer in his hands, waiting for them. The goblins were bold at first, rushing him with spears and short swords, but when ten of their number lay dead at Okrinok's feet within the space of a dozen heartbeats, they became more cautious. But Okrinok was too clever to allow that and sprang at the grobi, plunging into the thick of his foes, his hammer rising and falling with near perfect strokes, every attack crushing the life from a murderous greenskin.

To Okrinok the battle seemed to rage for an eternity, until it seemed he'd done nothing but slaughter goblins since the day was born. The dead were beyond counting, and he stood upon a mound of his foes, caked head-to-foot in their blood. His helmet had been knocked loose by an arrow, and several others now pierced his stomach and back, but still he fought on. Then, from out of the bodies behind him rose a goblin. He heard a scrape of metal and turned, but too slowly, the goblin's spearshaft punching into him. With blood bubbling into his breath, Okrinok spat his final words of defiance and brought his hammer down onto his killer's head.

'I am a dwarf! My honour is my life! Without it I am nothing!' bellowed Okrinok, before death took him.

TEARS STREAMED DOWN Grimli's face as he looked at Okrinok, his expression grim.

'And so I swore in death, and in death I have fulfilled that oath,' Okrinok told Grimli. 'Many centuries have the Skrundigor been blamed for my act, and I have allowed it to happen. The shame for the deaths of Gorgnir and Frammi was real, and the High King was owed his curse. But no longer shall we be remembered as cowards and oathbreakers. The goblin king was so impressed that he ordered his shamans to draw great magic and create this monument to my last battle.

But in trapping my flesh they freed my soul. For many years my spirit wandered these tunnels and halls and brought death to any grobi I met, but I am weary and wish to die finally. Thus, I sought you out, last of the Skrundigor, who must be father to our new line, in honour and in life.'

'But how do I get the High King to lift the curse, to strike our name from the Dammaz Kron?' asked Grimli.

'If you can't bring the king under the mountain, lad, bring the mountain over the king, as we used to say,' Okrinok told him. He pointed to his preserved body. 'Take my hammer, take it to the High King and tell him what you have seen here. He will know, lad, for that hammer is famed and shall become more so when my tale is told.'

'I will do as you say,' swore Grimli solemnly. Turning, he took the haft of the weapon in both hands and pulled. Grimli's tired muscles protested but after heaving with all his strength, the dwarf managed to pull the hammer clear.

He turned to thank Okrinok, but the ghost was gone. Clambering awkwardly down the mound of bodies, Grimli's thoughts were clear. He would return to Karaz-a-Karak and present the hammer and his service to the current High King, to serve him as Okrinok once did. It was then up to the High King whether honour was restored or not. As he planted his feet onto the rock floor once more, with no small amount of relief, Grimli felt a change in the air. Turning, he saw the mound was being enveloped by a shimmering green glow. Before his eyes, the mound began to shudder, and saw flesh stripping from bones and the bones crumble to dust as the centuries finally did their work. Soon there was nothing left except a greenish-tinged haze.

Hefting Okrinok's hammer, Grimli turned to leave. Out in the darkness dozens of red eyes regarded him balefully. Grimli grinned viciously to himself. He strode towards the waiting goblins, his heart hammering in his chest, his advance quickening until he was running at full charge.

'For Frammi and Gorgnir!' he bellowed.

# A GENTLEMAN'S WAR
## by Neil Rutledge

THE SUN BEAT down relentlessly. Otto von Eisenkopf felt the back of his neck burning. He dare not shift the position in which he had secreted himself though, he thought, as his neck burnt even hotter – this time with shame as he remembered the ants' nest. His first action with this confounded crew and he had to try and conceal himself on an ants' nest! That huge fellow – Lutyens, or whatever his name was – he hadn't laughed, he hadn't made a single sound, in fact, adhering to thrice-cursed Captain Molders's silence order! The man may not have laughed aloud, but Otto had seen the mirth in his eyes all right. Bah! A pox on all of them!

By Sigmar, what was he doing lying here like a bandit, the rocks digging through his padded brigandine as the distant hoofbeats came closer? A mere brigandine! Where was his own armour? And his scalp itched enough to drive him insane. Only the gods knew what manner of lice were in the lining of the battered arming cap he'd been given. A steel arming cap! So much for the fine armet which his squire, Henryk, had polished until it shone. So much for the wonderful plumes, all the way from Araby, which his sister had

243

carefully dyed in the family colours. How proud of them he had been, even wearing them in his hat as he travelled up to join his father. Where was the glorious war he was promised?

Despite the faint sounds of the approaching enemy, Otto risked a slight movement, in quest of comfort alone of course, but a dislodged pebble clicked against another. He sensed the hidden eyes of Lutyens boring into him. By the Hammer, this wasn't what he had prepared for!

His mind drifted back to that journey of just two days ago. How different his mood had been then! He remembered the final stretch especially. They had travelled up and across open moor country, so very different from the fields and forests of his home. It had been like chancing upon a new land, bathed in sunshine, ringing with unfamiliar, haunting bird calls and the continual chatter of water over countless rocky stream beds. Water, to his mind, far sweeter and cooler than anything he had ever drunk at home. His heart had been as high and as bubbling as the larks that rose to sing as their horses had passed. He remembered that he had sung too, the old war ballads of the Empire. They had made Otto swell with pride, as he had thought he would soon be joining those illustrious ranks of legend. He had imagined himself charging head-to-head with the knightly orders.

So much for that! Here he was, baking on hot stones like a flat cake. Lurking, lurking with a tattered handful of mercenary pistoliers, fully half of them from outside the Empire. Even that fellow, Molders, the captain, had an accent which sounded more than half Bretonnian. How could his father trust such men? Trust them to reliably scout out which route the invading Bretonnian scoundrels would take?

Otto reflected that the Graf must be under terrible stress. His father had been made ill, perhaps, by the strain of having to defend their glorious homeland with only men such as these. Not a single knight! By Sigmar, what an insult! He resolved to himself to strive all the harder to not let his father down, to at least be a reliable pair of eyes and ears on this confounded mission. He was certainly confident he was more trustworthy than that scurvy Captain Molders. What manner of upstart was he to consider ambushing a Bretonnian noble like this? Lurking to trap a man whose code of honour would not permit him to flee even if outnumbered and who, if bested in fair combat, would certainly graciously submit to honourable capture and ransom.

Otto's anger began to rise. No, by Sigmar the Blessed, he would not permit this! It was his first combat and he was not going to enter it like a bandit. He would behave honourably, even if these low sell-swords would not. He could hear the hoof beats of the approaching Bretonnian party coming nearer. Abruptly he rose to his feet and crashed through the shrubs to stand on the path.

He stood straight and proud, sweeping the path with his eyes. The Bretonnian knight was just down the track, the scarlet of his horse's caparison dazzling in the sunlight. Riding beside him on a shaggy pony was a rough, leather-clad man with an eye patch, clutching a light crossbow, undoubtedly a local enlisted as a guide.

Otto raised his hand. 'Ho, sir knight,' he began. The Bretonnian reined in, his hatchet face looking startled. But it was the blur of movement to one side which caught Otto's eye. Just in time he ducked, and a crossbow bolt hissed past him. The guide, still holding the bow, had now swept out his sword with his free hand and was charging him. Otto struggled to draw his own blade. The knight was shouting something. Otto cursed and stepped smartly to one side, only narrowly avoiding the guide's murderous sword swipe. His own sword now in his hand, the young nobleman whirled to face the horseman who, rearing his mount, had turned with incredible speed to attack him again. His gaze locked by his enemy's one blazing eye, Otto desperately prepared to dodge again but suddenly the guide fell as Lutyens burst from the scrub and discharged a pistol into the side of his head.

Otto's mind reeled. The huge, rather slow pistolier had transformed into a raging colossus of action. He didn't seem to pause, even as he coolly dropped the knight's war-horse with his other pistol. Blonde hair streaming from under his burgonet, he charged to where the squires were riding up to protect their fallen master. He glanced back at Otto and shouted, 'Get at them, fool!'

Otto hesitated. He was staring aghast at his borrowed brigandine, splattered with blood from the slain guide. He looked up as a squire charged him. Gasping aloud, Otto just managed to roll behind the dead guide's horse. He barely parried a spear thrust from the Bretonnian and luckily managed to seize the weapon with his free hand. He stared up at the face of the squire: a grizzled, scarred man who hissed with exertion as he tried to wrest the weapon from the young noble's hand.

Otto stepped forward, trying to jab his sword at the Bretonnian's arm but he stumbled over the body of the dead guide, which was hanging, one foot trapped in the stirrups. Frantically, Otto tried to pull himself upright using his enemy's spear but he fell, twisting, amongst the horses' hooves. Through the stamping legs and dust, he stared into the scarred face as the squire grinned and stabbed down with his spear. Otto writhed but once more a pistol discharged close by and the Bretonnian, grin still fixed in place, toppled from his horse. His killer, a wiry pistolier in a dented helmet, paused just long enough to seize the horse's bridle and pull the beast away from the young noble, before running towards the main body of the Bretonnians. Otto, panting aloud, struggled to his feet and stumbled after him.

The knight, protected by a close knot of squires, was on his feet and ordering his men to the attack. Standing screened by his warriors, with one hand the Bretonnian attempted to beat the dust from his crimson surcoat, while with the other he held his sword aloft. 'They are only brigand dogs!' he yelled. 'Kill them!'

Charging forward, Otto almost screeched as he shouted with indignation, 'I am no brigand, but Otto von Eisenkopf of Barhaus! Defend yourself, insolent knight.'

Dimly, Otto was aware that there seemed to be very few pistoliers on the road or moving through the shrubs and boulders, but now his attention was fixed on the tight group of men immediately facing him. The squires hesitated, looking to their master for guidance. Slowly the knight gestured them aside and stepped forward. 'Very well,' the Bretonnian hissed, 'whatever honour you have, von Eisenkopf, prepare to test its mettle.'

The knight stood before him, looking almost warily at his young opponent. He held his sword – a fine, jewel-hilted affair – loosely by his side while his free hand toyed with a corner of his silk jupon. Otto sized his opponent up. The man was older and taller, very tall in fact, but sparsely built, with a thin face and hawk nose.

His reach would be long, Otto thought, but he himself had inherited his father's bull-like physique and he reckoned that, young though he was, he himself was perhaps the stronger. They were both shieldless but the Bretonnian was well armoured while Otto had only his brigandine. Otto smoothly raised his sword and took up his stance. He felt calmer now, on familiar ground. Just like the fencing hall, he thought to himself.

'A swordsman eh?' Was there surprise in the thin features of the Bretonnian's face, or even hesitancy? Then the knight seemed to compose himself and took up his own stance and immediately attacked. It was not the speed of the thrust that caught Otto off guard, but its clumsiness. He parried, almost, and, had he not been so startled, could have finished the fight there and then. The knight lunged again and this time Otto was ready. Smoothly parrying and riposting, driving the knight back so quickly that he tripped, falling backwards with a grunt.

'Rise, sir,' Otto said, stepping back graciously and preparing for another bout. The knight rose slowly, but when he bent to retrieve his sword he lifted it by the blade, not the hilt.

'I yield, von Eisenkopf. You have bested me.' The knight's words were drowned out in a sudden crashing of pistol and arquebus fire. Otto looked up. Molders must have sent men from further down the track up and over the outcrop to the north of the path. Now the pistoliers were firing down on the squires who were attacking their few, hard-pressed comrades around the track. Otto could hear the captain's voice booming, even through the gunfire. 'The horses, shoot the horses! Don't let them away, lads.'

The knight looked around too. 'Yield, my brave men!' he ordered. 'We are undone. Yield.'

The squires began dropping their weapons and, although somewhere further along the track there was still some shouting, the skirmish was over. Otto could see Molders standing on a boulder yelling, 'Round them up, you sluggards! Get moving!' He was shaking a wheel lock in the air in his strange staccato manner, the brandishes seeming to underline his words.

The Bretonnian knight turned back to Otto and bowed, 'Sir Guillame de Montvert. I am honoured to make your acquaintance.'

Otto smiled, somewhat surprised by the ease of his victory, 'And I yours, Sir Guillame.' Here at last was proper courtesy. Even in defeat, even as his men were being rounded up by the ragged pistoliers, this man could observe the proper formalities. The young nobleman continued, 'I should be delighted if you could dine with me tonight.'

The Bretonnian grinned. 'I seem to find myself with time to spare,' he shrugged modestly. 'I fear you find me inconvenienced, though. I regret my wardrobe is limited.'

'Fear not! Some arrangements will be made. Besides, my table is at present quite simple enough.'

At that moment Molders strode up. He moved with the typical briskness which had begun to irritate Otto so much. Molders was not a tall man and he seemed to Otto to compensate for his short stature with an exaggerated cockiness of movement, the jut of his chest only exceeded by the jaunt of his chin and bristling beard.

'You are our prisoner,' he addressed the knight sharply. Then turning to one of his men, 'Take him and tie him like the rest.'

'Indeed not!' Otto protested, 'This man is my prisoner and a knight of honour. He is to dine with me this evening.'

The captain gasped and stared. His pale blue eyes seemed to protrude from his face in an effort to out-reach the grizzled spade of a beard now thrust accusingly at Otto. The pistolier behind him snorted as he attempted to suppress a laugh. Molders, used only to being obeyed without question, stood silent, glaring in astonishment at the young man before him.

Otto dared continue, 'Furthermore, I have found your conduct this day most reprehensible. We have brought dishonour on the good name of the Emperor and the reputation of his troops.' He looked at the trooper standing behind Molders. 'You, man! Fetch my mount and obtain a horse for Sir Guillame, and be quick about it!'

The trooper, the wiry man who had saved Otto earlier in the skirmish, had been grinning in buck-toothed amusement but now his expression changed to one of discomfiture. He had lost his helm; now he pulled his somewhat greasy curls in perplexity as he glanced at Molders. The captain shrugged in rare indecision as Otto once more turned to him. 'We will ride ahead, captain. See to the rest of the prisoners and follow as fast as you can.'

The confused pistolier had returned with Otto's horse and another. 'Sir Guillame? Please?' Otto gestured to the second horse, smoothly vaulted into his own saddle and, with an imperious gesture, hurled the battered arming cap off his head and into the scrub. He turned to address Molders once more. The captain's face was the colour of pickled red cabbage. He was silently gesturing for Lutyens to mount and accompany Otto. Otto was about to protest but the captain looked up and his glare was so fierce that the young man held his tongue.

'Lutyens will see to your needs… young sir.' Molders's voice was clipped even more than usual and barely audible. Without a further word he turned his back and began issuing orders to his men.

'Well, Sir Guillame, shall we ride?' Otto said brightly, amused by what he took as Molders's pique at being reprimanded. 'We must ride hard if we are to be back at the forward camp by dusk.' The Bretonnian nodded and they set off briskly, Lutyens following behind.

At first they conversed lightly, exchanging details of their family, discussing the moor country and its prospects for falconry. Otto felt wholly at ease with the older Bretonnian but, his heart high once more, he was aware of his duties. Behind the bright chat, his mind was working furiously. Otto was far too good mannered to question the knight regarding military matters, but as the conversation went on, his prisoner, seemingly disarmed by his own good cheer, let slip a few clues. These clues pointed to what Otto already suspected; that Sir Guillame and his squires were scouting the route for the main Bretonnian attack. It was the obvious route, really! The one Otto would have taken, were he in their opponent the Duke de Boncenne's place. A far better route than the narrow, difficult southern pass or the long swing, deeper into the Empire to the north. A bold, direct approach across the moors and a sharp, honourable conflict to decide the issue.

'You are preoccupied, young sir.' Sir Guillame's voice broke into Otto's thoughts.

'Yes, yes, I am sorry. Please excuse my ill manners. It is no way to treat an honoured guest.'

'Perhaps you are missing a lady?' the Bretonnian asked smiling.

Otto blushed, 'I have been training hard, Sir Guillame, and hope for a commission in the Reiksguard.'

The Bretonnian laughed. 'Ah, you Imperials,' he chided mockingly, 'You are much too serious. A man must strive for honour, yes, but he can love too! What is life without a little romance?' Sir Guillame went on, expanding the other aspects of what he regarded as the highlights of a knightly life.

Otto nodded and occasionally added a polite word but his mind was elsewhere once more. The mention of the Reiksguard had reminded him of the opportunities which lay before him. His father would be well pleased. He had tempered the baseless actions of the pistoliers with honour, captured an important prisoner with due decorum and was now gaining valuable information. He could see the conflict unfolding. The Bretonnians would advance and be brought to battle on the moors. Otto himself would fight bravely and the whole affair would end in a most satisfactory manner. He was still vaguely worried about how reliable the pistoliers really were, but he was confident that his father would act quickly on his suspicions. Yes, all would be well. For the time being he set his concerns aside and determined to enjoy the ride, the scenery and the Bretonnian's company.

THEY ARRIVED BACK at the forward camp just as the dusk was deepening into night. Otto swelled with pride as they passed the pickets and he was able to declare himself and report he was returning with an honoured prisoner, Sir Guillame de Montvert. They made their way through the camp, Otto riding with head held high. He felt almost proprietorial as he looked around, eyes scanning the activity that was revealed only in fire-lit, flickering patches. Men huddled in their tent

groups, cooking, polishing weapons, binding arrow fletch-
ings. Troops engaged in the myriad small tasks necessary
when preparing for battle. Otto's spirits soared with the thrill
of it all. How he had waited for this, to serve with honour his
Emperor, land and family! His ears heard the camp sounds
almost as music. The subdued voices with the occasional
laugh or burst of song, the clink of a ladle against a cooking
pot, the heavier ringing from a distant field forge, the noises
from the tethered horses. Aye, horses. Horses, not knights'
chargers!

Otto's good spirits promptly vanished and he was suddenly
glad that they had arrived at sundown, so Sir Guillame could
not see the rag-tag composition of his father's advanced force.
He winced as he thought of it and remembered his own
shock at his first sight of the troops: scruffy woodsmen from
Stirland, ruffianly-looking local light horse and a large con-
tingent of mercenary hackbut men and pistoliers. He had
protested to his father that their forces were inadequate. The
memory of his father's response still made the blood flush
hot under his skin. His father, nobleman of the Empire and
respected general, had actually stated that pistoliers were
cheaper to field than knights and were a good deal more useful. Otto's very ears burned as he remembered his father's curt
words, 'This isn't a crusade against Araby, Otto! It's a border
squabble, provoked by the greed of that adventurer, de
Boncenne. He's using the usual territory problems as an
excuse to get his hands on the coal mines by Grunwasser. You
don't call out the Reiksguard to deal with bandits!'

Otto's worries for his father returned in a rush. How could
he think such of a duke, a pillar of Bretonnian chivalry? He
was obviously ill, worn out by the stress of attempting to
defend this difficult border with such paltry forces and, perhaps, was subtly misled by these unreliable mercenaries in
which he seemed to place such faith. Again, Otto resolved not
to let his father down. He, at least, was dependable and he
had the information that was so badly needed. But first he
had his chivalrous duties to attend to.

He guided Sir Guillame to his own tent where he found his
youthful squire busy polishing the buckles of his charger's
harness. They shone in the firelight but the sight, far from

pleasing Otto, only reminded him of how distasteful he found it to ride the rough-looking, if hardy, mount he had been given to accompany the pistoliers. Young Henryk rose immediately. Even in camp, his dapper form was immaculate in the red and white Eisenkopf colours. His face seemed to shine pristine in the firelight. 'Welcome home, sir! I see you have a guest.'

Otto's irritation showed in the brusqueness with which he ordered the squire to see to his distinguished prisoner. He ordered that the Bretonnian should have the use of his own tent, while his personal effects were to be transferred to the tent of his servant. He repented almost at once when he saw how courteous the good-natured Henryk was in addressing and attending to the Bretonnian and, to try and save the servant extra labour, looked for Lutyens to order him to see to the horses, but the mercenary was nowhere to be seen.

'Typical,' Otto muttered to himself. 'Uncouth, uncultured and unreliable!' He gave further instructions to Henryk, excused himself to Sir Guillame and went to wash and change, before presenting himself to his father.

Inside the cramped tent of his servant, Otto cleaned and arranged himself as best he could in the flickering lamp light. It was somewhat awkward but he was smiling to himself as he stepped outside to gain the headroom necessary to attach his plumes to his hat. He imagined receiving his father's congratulations on the capture of Sir Guillame. He pictured the Graf's serious face, as his beloved son explained the ill-dealings of the pistoliers and his suspicions of them. He saw in his mind's eye his father's pride and relief that he had such a son to count on. Still smiling, he checked briefly that his prisoner was comfortable, then made his way to his father's quarters.

The Graf's tent was in the very centre of the camp. It was large but made of plain leather, as tough and unpretentious as the man within. Otto straightened himself as he saw his father's standard hanging above the door, bloodied by the light of the great braziers in front of the tent, and his heart filled with pride as the two halberdiers on guard smartly saluted him and stepped aside to let him pass.

Immediately within was a large chamber, well lit with lanterns and furnished with a variety of folding wooden stools and tables. Otto smiled as Gunther, his father's veteran aide-de-camp, greeted him. It was hard to tell the scars from the lines of age on the old man's face but he still had a sprightly step as he moved to salute Otto.

'Greetings, sir,' the old soldier said warmly. 'You have captured an honourable prisoner, I believe.'

Otto found it hard not to grin like a schoolboy. 'I have won some very little honour,' he replied. 'I must report to my father.'

'The general is in conference,' Gunther told him. 'With Herr Lutyens, one of your comrades in the affray.'

'Comrade?' Otto clicked his tongue, his good humour dispelled. What was that oaf doing plaguing his father? Concocting some tale to cover the mercenaries' reprehensible behaviour, no doubt.

'Some warm wine, sir?' The aide was offering him a somewhat battered but gleaming pewter goblet, a gently steaming flask in his other hand.

'What?' Otto asked, preoccupied with what the dubious Lutyens might be telling his father. 'Ach, yes, why not?' he said grimly. Lutyens could have his crow but Otto would see his father got the true story! He settled himself irritably on a stool by the tapestries that curtained off his father's inner chamber and sipped at his wine. Gunther, ever the tactful servant, busied himself quietly at the far side of the chamber.

Otto could distinguish two voices on the far side of the tapestry – the deep drone of Lutyens and his father's terse speech. Habitually polite, the young noble was about to move to another stool out of earshot, when he again wondered what tale Lutyens might be spinning. He had best listen, he thought to himself. His father was obviously worn down by his onerous duties as warden and was already placing too much reliance on these brigands. He had better learn as much as he could if he was to help his father. Still sipping his wine, he surreptitiously leant a little closer to the tapestry.

'So they put up little fight?' the Graf was asking.

'Little enough, sir. They seemed of scant quality.'

Otto nearly choked on his wine. Scant quality! Who was this rustic to judge a knight of Bretonnia?

'And where is Captain Molders?'

'He is following with the main body, sir.'

'I expected a prompt report from him, Lutyens. Not advanced warning from you.'

'Young Master Eisenkopf was in haste to bring back the Bretonnian knight, sir.'

Otto coloured as he heard his father snort, 'Not that much haste, it seems! He hasn't reported yet! Your opinion, Lutyens: what of this Bretonnian party?'

'I'm not sure, sir, but they didn't seem up to much to me and Captain Molders reckoned they were odd too, sir. I believe he thought them some kind of ruse.'

Otto stood up rapidly. His father was listening to nonsense, or worse, treachery. Without waiting further, he brushed aside the hanging and strode into his father's quarters. Lutyens sat nearer, his huge bulk balanced precariously on a camp stool. Facing him across a folding table sat Otto's father, the Graf von Eisenkopf. The Graf was a powerful man but even he looked small compared to Lutyens. Perhaps it was this that seemed, to Otto's eyes, to lend him a shrunken air. To his anxious son, the Graf's broad, open face looked pale even in the warm lamp light. And was there more grey in that close cropped hair and beard?

'Father,' Otto began breathlessly, 'I have additional information regarding the Bretonnians' plans.'

Lutyens swung his ice-blue eyes towards him and his father looked up coolly, fixing Otto with the same stern gaze that had met his childhood misdemeanours.

'It must be important information, indeed, for you to have forgotten your normal courtesy,' the Graf observed, calmly.

Otto coloured but began again. 'This man…' He was about to berate the pistolier as a completely untrustworthy source of information but something in the gaze of his father made him change his mind. 'This man may not have all the facts. He has not spoken with our noble prisoner, Sir Guillame de Montvert.'

'I do not doubt it,' the Graf agreed. 'But he has made his report promptly, as a dutiful trooper should and I myself had hoped to speak with de Montvert, at least before too long.' His voice was soft but the rebuke was not lost on Otto. The young man knew better than to try to make excuses to his father, but inside he felt a burning sense of injustice. The general was still speaking, now to Lutyens. 'Thank you, trooper, for your report. You are dismissed for the present.'

The big pistolier rose and bowed somewhat awkwardly. 'Yes, sir.' He was usually slow of movement but Otto thought he detected reluctance in his measured step as he departed.

On pretence of straightening the curtain, Otto checked that Lutyens had indeed left. He turned and the Graf gestured to him. 'Sit down, my son. Congratulations on the capture of the prisoner. But I am surprised you have not brought him to me.'

'I... I thought it good manners to allow a man of his rank to prepare himself properly before presenting himself.'

'You are thoughtful but we are not at court, my son. We are defending our land. It is more important for me to get information quickly.'

'Sorry, father.'

'No matter. Make your report.'

Much of the fire and anger had been chastened out of Otto. He related his views to his father a great deal more quietly than he had imagined when riding back. He described the ambush, mentioning his distaste for such skulking tactics and telling how he had sprung forth and challenged the Bretonnian knight. He considered voicing his suspicions about the loyalty of Captain Molders, but the grim set of his father's jaw made him change his mind. He would keep his fears to himself for the present, and wait and see what actions were to be taken.

'So you sprung the ambush too soon.' His father's voice was steely.

'I acted as a gentleman, father.'

'I placed you under the orders of Captain Molders and expected you to obey him.'

Otto's resentment boiled over: 'Father! The man is a mercenary! He knows nothing of honour. Listen to his accent, he sounds more like a Bretonnian! You know the trouble these locals cause you. Brigands, as much a thorn for us as for their enemies. How can he be trusted?'

His father banged his fist on the table, silencing him. He was about to speak and then passed his hand wearily across his brow. Otto regarded him warily. He did look tired. These past months since he had been appointed warden must have been hard. Battling orcs or defending against beastmen in the east was arduous but at least you knew where you stood with an orc. Here the damned locals on both sides of the border were always feuding, raiding and seemingly caring little for Emperor or King.

'Father, I am here to serve you loyally.'

The Graf returned his earnest gaze. 'I know, Otto, but war isn't like the ballads or the parade ground. Molders is no knight but he is a veteran of this border squabbling and I'll stake my sword he is not false. I'm far from sure about just how chivalrous this opportunist the Duke de Boncenne is. What I am sure of is that the Emperor runs the South March on a tight purse and I have precious few forces to impede Boncenne. If he pushes up to the Grunwasser, he'll lodge himself like a halfling in a bakery and be twice as difficult to shift.'

Listening, Otto was a tumult of emotions: shame yet resentment at this chastisement, worry for his father and a tingling sense of excitement at being involved in such tense matters.

'I must have more information,' his father was continuing. 'Molders will report as soon as he arrives. Meanwhile bring me the knight and I will question him.'

'Yes, father. Will he be dining with us?'

'No he will not!'

Otto winced. 'I will fetch him at once.'

As Otto left, Molders was just coming into the tent. The pistolier captain pulled his shoulders back even further than normal and gave a strangled snort as he passed. The young noble glared at him before stiffly walking to his tent.

When he arrived, the Bretonnian was sitting by the fire, wrapped in Otto's second cloak and thanking Henryk who had just topped up his goblet. The knight looked up, 'Ah, greetings, Otto. I compliment you on your hospitality.' He gestured with his goblet.

'I fear I must interrupt your rest, Sir Guillame. My father…' Otto hesitated slightly, 'My father desires to speak to you. I am sure he will not detain you long. I will wait until you return and we can dine together. I shall escort you to the Graf at once.'

Otto's plans to dine were to be frustrated, however, and scarce three hours later he was in the saddle again.

OTTO PRIDED HIMSELF on his horsemanship and was indeed reckoned a natural in the saddle, but he had never encountered riding like this before. Throughout the scant hours of darkness that were left they pressed on like men possessed. There was no moon and Otto wondered how his horse could see to pick his way over the rough hillsides, never mind how Molders was guiding the troops. Dawn brought easier going as they reached the moorland plateau which marked the no-man's land on the south march between Bretonnia and the Empire, but there was no change in pace. The pistoliers dispersed themselves more widely but they did not even stop for breakfast, the men sipping from their flasks and eating on the move instead.

Otto was very weary but inside he was a conflicting mass of emotion. Pride that his father had seen fit to dispatch them to check his own theory and scout for a Bretonnian force coming over the moor. But there was anger at Molders's barely concealed contempt for what he saw as a wasted errand. The captain firmly believed that the main Bretonnian attack was coming by the southern route. The man was mad, or worse, an enemy agent. How could he doubt the honour of knights such as Sir Guillame? No! They would locate the Bretonnian force, his father would marshal his troops and battle would be joined on the moor.

It would be Otto's first battle. Not a large one admittedly, in fact more of a border skirmish over a couple of valleys and those wretched coal mines, but what mattered the size of the conflict when true honour was at stake? He had heard the pistoliers talk of the Duke of Boncenne as an upstart, keen to get his hands on the profits of those mines. How could they think so of a duke? They were the mercenaries! More likely the duke viewed the whole venture as a test of honour, an adventure to prove himself in his new post of march warden and quite right too! Any noble of courage and mettle would do similarly.

The day wore on. They had halted briefly but Molders was relentless, and by late afternoon they had picked up the cart road which ran from Dreiburg across the border. The pistoliers followed the road but were still well spread out in a long skirmish line. Otto looked to his right where Lutyens was riding, blonde hair streaming out behind him in the stiff breeze, his huge form dwarfing his small mount. It was worrying how the giant had always been somewhere near. Had Molders posted the big man to keep a special watch over him? Was the pistolier captain aware of Otto's suspicions? Anxiety twisted in his stomach. If the pistoliers proved to be traitors it would be very easy for them to kill him. He would stand no chance against so many. A cloud passed over the sun and the wild, open landscape of the moors seemed suddenly bleak. The craggy rock outcrops took on the guise of sinister watching heads, roughly haired with heather, peering at Otto. The incessant chatter of the chill streams, a babble which had once echoed Otto's bubbling spirits now seemed to mock him as they approached the rise to the scarp edge where the moor descended in a rocky jumble to the Bretonnian plains. Here Molders halted his men, and, leaving most with the horses, led a few forward on foot to look out over the land ahead.

The captain signalled that Otto should come too, and again the young man was irked to find himself chaperoned by the hulking Lutyens. Using the rough, boulder-strewn slope as an excuse, Otto tried to pick a route that led him away from his unwelcome shadow but wherever he moved Lutyens's slow footfall followed. Otto's heart beat faster, faster than the climb should have occasioned, as he wondered what lay at the scarp edge. Would this be the scene of his death at the hands of traitors? A supposed accident on the cliff edge? Apprehensively his hand rested on his sword hilt but he felt powerless. He hung back when, approaching the skyline, the pistoliers dropped and crawled towards the edge. Lutyens stopped beside him. Ahead, Molders was cautiously peering through the gap between two rocks. He reached down to a pouch at his belt and pulled out a small brass tube. A spyglass, an item of expense and rarity, looted doubtless! The captain scrutinised the land ahead.

There seemed to be a ripple of expectation amongst the pistoliers. Several glanced back. Their faces showed interest, expectation. Were they Molders's most trusted henchmen, here to witness Otto's murder? The captain turned impatiently and even behind that spade of a beard, Otto could clearly detect a wolfish grin. He gestured imperiously for Otto to come forward. The young noble moved forward, tensed for action. There was a touch on his shoulder and he whirled, sword half-drawn before his arms were caught in Lutyens's iron grip.

'Get down, by Sigmar! You will reveal us!' the giant hissed.

Shaking, bewildered, Otto crawled to where Molders beckoned with his spyglass. There was a glint in the captain's eye as he gestured to Otto to look ahead. Heart pounding and trying to watch the pistolier out of the corner of his eye, Otto glanced around the boulder in front of him.

He gasped at what he saw and his fears vanished in a rush of vindicated pride. Some distance from the bottom of the slope a long line of horsemen was trotting towards them, the sun glinting off their helmets and spear points. Squires screened the advance of the main force which was arranged along the road behind. He had been right! He glanced over to where Molders was lying but the captain did not look round. Molders was scrutinising the slowly advancing Bretonnians. Otto looked at them too. The main force was quite a distance away and some dust was rising but Otto could see a collection of bright banners floating above the head of the procession and beneath them a splash of colour he took to be the caparisons of the knights' chargers. Behind marched a column of infantry, a mixture of archers and men-at-arms most probably.

Molders just kept staring through the spyglass and the outriders were nearly at the bottom of the slope before he made any move, silently gesturing to Meyer, his lieutenant, to take the glass. Otto smiled to himself. Most probably the captain was sour at being proved wrong. Meyer looked for some minutes before lowering the instrument, his thin lips pursed and dark brow creased with concern. He passed the glass to Lutyens with a soft oath, 'By Sigmar! A ruse.'

Molders grinned harshly at Otto before wriggling backwards with Meyer, gesturing to Lutyens to pass the glass to Otto. The young noble paused to admire the instrument. It was crafted exquisitely; dwarf-made, Otto thought. Lutyens was impatiently signing to him to hurry so he lifted it to his eye. It took him a second to focus it and when he did he let out an involuntary whistle, immediately cut short by a vicious jab from Lutyens. The image was miraculous, far superior to that given by his father's own prized telescope, one of the best the craftsmen of the Empire could produce. He could see every detail of the faces of the horsemen, now beginning to pick their way up the long slope, and he was surprised at what an unkempt crew they appeared. This was nothing to the shock he got when he trained the glass on the knights leading the column further back along the road. He picked out the Duke by his banner and horse trappings but through the Dwarfish instrument he could see that the figure on the charger was not the darkly handsome, moustached warrior he'd heard of. Indeed it was only a young stripling of a youth, gawky and pale. The rest of the procession was equally startling. There was the occasional warlike veteran but most seemed youths or old men and many of the spearmen seemed armed with farm implements, not weapons of war. Lutyens was tugging at his boot. His mind in turmoil, Otto squirmed back and then ran over to where Molders was issuing a furious stream of orders.

The captain was addressing Meyer. 'Make sure they see you. Act just as if you had contacted their real force. Don't get too close, so that they stay confident we haven't spotted their ruse. You'll not have trouble with their skirmishers if you keep back, they're only there to try to make sure we don't get close enough to spot their damned deception. The rest of us must get back to the main camp at once. Sigmar knows, this will be too close!'

THE RIDE OUT had set a hard pace; the ride back was punishing. They slowed to a walk only where the going was so rough as to demand it, otherwise it was a constant gallop. Otto, who had been disdainful of the pistoliers' wiry mounts, was forced to concede that even if the small horses looked rough, their endurance was exceptional. His mind was filled with the face of the youth that had been masquerading as the Duke – and under the Duke's own banner! What perfidy! He felt almost physically sick when he thought of the base nature of the trick. Even now the Bretonnian force must be advancing unhindered, probably by the southern route, as Molders had predicted, damn him! Otto shivered when he thought of the implications for the honour of the Empire and for his father. How wrong he had been! He looked ahead, to where Molders was riding, resolute but seemingly unperturbed. A blush of shame coloured the young noble's face as he remembered his judgement of the pistolier captain. By the Hammer, what were they to do?

The long summer dusk was just deepening into night proper when Molders barked a curt command and most of the pistoliers wheeled off towards the south. There were only six of them now, still pressing on towards his father. Some of Otto's old anxieties resurfaced. Where were the others going? Was he now riding with traitors who would turn on him to ensure the news of the Bretonnians' vile trick never reached his father? Once more his hand toyed with his sword hilt and he began to try and scrutinise his companions as best he could in the closeness of the night. Each seemed entirely oblivious of him, silent automatons ploughing through the gathering darkness. He was exhausted and his mind was whirling. Would they be in time? Again he felt nauseous. How could a man fight with honour in times like these? The jolting as the horse pushed steadily over the rough ground seemed to shake him to the bone. Each shock from the saddle emphasised the jarring of his thoughts: perfidy, treachery, failure, dishonour! By Sigmar, they had to be on time! Instinctively he tried to spur his mount faster but the horse tossed its head and whinnied in protest.

'Patience!' came Lutyens's slow voice out of the darkness from Otto's left. 'The horse won't rush the broken ground in the dark.'

'Sigmar!' Otto hissed bitterly, 'What kind of world is this, where even a horse can act more aptly than I can?'

The nightmare hours dragged on, the ground studded with rocks, the miles with self-recriminations and doubt as Otto desperately tried to picture where the Bretonnians might have reached and their possible plans. If they successfully pushed through the southern passes onto the flat lands along the

Grunwasser all would be lost! The Graf's ill-assorted force of light troops, even stiffened by his own household halberdiers, couldn't face Bretonnian chivalry on the plains. Chivalry! The word had bitter ring to it now. Would they be in time? Otto's thoughts whirled on. The pistoliers were supposed to be able to doze in the saddle. He couldn't have slept now for worry even if he could keep his seat. Where was the camp? How much further?

The challenge from their own picket lines came suddenly and Otto almost cried aloud with relief. They hastened to report to his father. 'Fresh horses and prepare yourselves to be away again at once,' Molders ordered before he dismounted and strode into the Graf's headquarters. Confused by a sense of mingled anxiety and shame, Otto thought of returning to his own tent, but instead he trotted after Molders.

The captain was sitting on a stool in the foyer talking hurriedly with Otto's father. The Graf paced in front of him while old Gunther served the pistolier a hasty meal of bread and cheese. Otto studied his father nervously. His shoulders were still squared and he stood straight but his face was drawn and his fists were clenched. Once Otto would have bristled with indignation that a mere mercenary captain should sit while his father stood, but now the young man just waited awkwardly, the sick feeling in his stomach stronger than ever.

His father heard him enter and turned. 'Sit, Otto,' he gestured to a stool by Molders, 'and eat quickly. Gunther, send word to Otto's manservant to prepare for his master to depart again quickly.' He resumed talking to Molders. 'So, an elaborate ruse! You were right to suspect them. We may just be able to stop them if we despatch a fast force at once. I have the troops ready. It all hinges on how far the Bretonnians have proceeded on the southern route.'

'If they have taken that route,' Molders said through a mouthful of bread, crumbs falling from his beard. A twinge of Otto's old resentment returned. Such familiarity from a mere captain! The Graf showed no resentment, however, and spoke, even respectfully, to the pistolier.

'No, they will have. You are right about that too, I am sure. Besides, the Magister of Dreiburg is well placed to intervene in the unlikely event they have swung north.' The Graf clenched his fists. 'It is a matter of timing. I'll send ahead yourself and your men, two hundred of the Stirlander archers, all of the hackbut men who have mounts, von Grunwald with his light guns and fifty local horse. The Stirlanders will have to manage on foot or double up on horses; they've done it before. You will attempt an ambush in the foothills. I have alerted Dreiburg and I will follow you with the remaining hackbut men and the halberdiers. We will take up a defensive position at Ravensridge, should you need to fall back. If you are caught on the plain, it could go very ill for you!'

'We must hope against that, my lord, but by my reckoning we have a good chance of getting there.' Molders looked at Otto sarcastically. 'The lads set a good pace when their lives and booty depend on it.' The captain took a swig of ale and, standing up, abrupt as ever, continued, 'Right, swilling ale doesn't prime pistols. We'll be off.' He stared pointedly at Otto again. 'Besides I can't afford to fail you, I haven't had my full pay yet!' He gave a strangled noise that might have been a laugh and went out.

'Sigmar go with you!' the Graf called after the pistolier. Otto felt himself flush at the memory of his mistakes as his father turned to him. There were traces of worry around the Graf's eyes but there was no reproach in his face as he said, 'You had best hurry and join them, my son. You will acquit yourself well, I am sure. My thoughts go with you.'

Otto stammered, 'I am… sorry, father.'

'Sorry?'

'Sorry for my misjudgement.'

'We all misjudge things, lad. You are here to learn. Now go.'

'Thank you.' Otto turned.

'Otto, one other thing. Sir Guillame has disappeared, and so has your best palfrey. I fear the two disappearances may be connected. Don't blame Henryk. It is I who should have ensured a stricter guard.'

This news stung Otto more than anything he had yet heard. 'But… but he was a knight, a man of honour!'

His father shrugged. 'You can't keep ward over the honour of others. Just keep your own intact, son – and your hide! Now go and serve your Emperor and your father.'

'Yes, sir.'

But Otto was perplexed as he left the tent. The man whom he had trusted, looked to as an example of chivalry, had coldly manipulated him. Duped him! As he made his way to join the pistoliers, he felt sick in his heart.

IT WAS ANOTHER tough ride and, in truth, Otto was weary to his very core as they trotted through the darkness. This time they had a road to follow, albeit a rough one, and Molders was driving his men hard. Otto rode at the front of the column in the same group as the captain. To his discomfiture, even through his tiredness, he noticed Lutyens was still his shadow. Now, though, the discomfort wasn't fear of treachery but bitterness that he could have been so wrong. Lutyens was his chaperone – not to cloak some dark plot, but instead to look after him, and he had needed him! The memory of Lutyens saving him in that first action returned with the sharpness of a spear thrust and he squirmed in his saddle. The whirling succession of tortured thoughts returned again: perfidy, treachery, failure, dishonour! Above all was the incessant question: *would they be in time?*

His head slumped to his chest, Otto ground his teeth and left control to his mount; the hill pony he thought, with another wave of bitterness, that could act more appropriately than he, Otto von Eisenkopf, noble of the Empire!

The night wore on, measured out by the drumming of hooves, and the pounding thoughts: perfidy, treachery, failure, dishonour! Would they be in time? Otto looked to his side and there, sure enough, was Lutyens. The giant's head lolled. By Sigmar! He was asleep in the saddle! Otto had an urge to hurl his dagger at him. How could he sleep? Otto's fingers clenched the reins until they hurt. Couldn't they make better speed? The old notion of a traitorous Molders deliberately delaying progress came back into his head. Angrily Otto forced it aside, knowing it to be wrong, but a shred of the notion persisted. The young noble cursed himself. By the Hammer, was he himself so shallow? Was he so base as to hope for the imagined treachery to be true just so as to have the gratification of salving his own pride? His world seemed to have crumbled; was he now crumbling too? The hooves, and his thoughts, drummed on.

By dawn they were climbing into the foothills but the light brought no relief to Otto. The sunrise hurt his tired eyes and as he looked back over his shoulder he took little comfort in what he saw. The dust-shrouded column wound after them, now slowed by the narrowed and steep road. The slower pace was bad enough but Otto wondered, with a twinge of what felt disturbingly like fear, what was going to happen when they did contact the Bretonnians? How could this rag-tag force defeat battle-hardened knights? Boncenne may have behaved like some base, fairground mountebank but he was an experienced general who had stood in the lists against the most martial of Bretonnian nobility.

Who could they set against this formidable warrior? Molders, compensating for his short stature with an aggressive swagger and that ridiculous beard? Von Grunwald, head of an ancient noble family but a crank obsessed with the pack horse-toted light guns he had designed? Himself, a young fool who had once hoped for a commission in the Reiksguard and was now riding only with mercenary pistoliers?

Daylight or not, the hooves, and the thoughts, drummed on: perfidy, treachery, failure, dishonour!

Suddenly there was a stir. One of the advance scouts came cantering back towards them. Otto tensed wondering if they had contacted the Bretonnians. Was all lost, their opponents already descending into the plains? The man rode up to Molders. He was breathless, his jerkin plastered with dust that had also stiffened his sweat-soaked hair into absurd tufts. Otto edged his mount closer to Molders to hear the scout's report. The man was gathering breath. Was his gap-toothed mouth a grimace of worry or a triumphant grin?

'Report man, for Sigmar's sake,' Otto muttered under his breath.

'The valley is clear, captain,' the man grinned. 'It's the perfect spot for an ambush. The track is quite broad, steep slope one side, more gentle hills the other, but it's only an illusion of openness. The river is swift and deep, a formidable barrier to fleeing troops. Armoured men would never get across it'

'Very good, trooper,' Molders replied. He turned and began quickly issuing orders, marshalling his troops.

The road became steeper, winding up the rocky, wooded hillside. The sun was shining strongly and the woods rang with birdsong but there was a tension in the air and Otto noted nervous movements all around him as even the seasoned pistoliers checked and rechecked their wargear.

At the top of the hill Molders gave more orders. 'Von Grunwald, his guns and the archers will block off here where the path climbs steeply to the hilltop. The hackbut men will hold the steepest craggy slopes, yonder in the valley centre. The pistoliers and the light horse will close off the rear and block the Bretonnians' retreat. They must keep especially well up slope bar some few, well hidden, to signal when the last of the enemy pass. It is our best plan; we must hope they don't scout properly in their haste.'

Von Grunwald and his guns began deploying to cover the road up out of the valley. Watching the old man working with his men unloading the guns Otto's anxieties returned. 'This is an Empire noble?' he mused, bewildered, as he stared at the short, wiry old man wearing only tattered hose, his face grimy and his head crowned with an amazing shock of white hair.

BEWILDERED HE MIGHT have been but Otto was still impressed by the speed with which the troops deployed, and at such quiet determination and discipline. Even if they were rough and ready, unpolished and mercenary by calling, they certainly seemed apt to their work. Indeed it seemed to him that he was the one out of place as he handed his mount to one of the local horsemen assigned to keep their horses safely out of sight down slope, away from the line of Bretonnian advance. All of his training had been to fight from the saddle and in the open and here he was facing his second action, once more on foot, and once more in hiding. Woodenly, Otto followed the other pistoliers down from the boulder-strewn crest.

They descended into the woods that overlooked the valley but stayed well up the slope, picking their way with some difficulty through the tangle. At one point Otto looked down through a narrow break in the trees; even with his inexperienced eye, he could see what a splendid site for an ambush it was. Lutyens, scrambling alongside him, was grinning from ear to ear and Otto was amazed to hear the normally taciturn pistolier whisper to him, 'They are finished! This will be butchery.'

'We can hold back armoured knights?' Otto panted.

'Here,' the giant replied, 'here we won't hold them, we'll destroy them!' He gave Otto a pat on the back which almost knocked him down the slope.

'But if they scout ahead?' Otto feared that the worry he felt might sound in his voice but Lutyens just grinned more broadly.

'When have Bretonnians ever scouted properly? They ride into battle as brazen as Marienburg harlots. Besides, they will feel they have no reason to. They think they have duped us. It takes more than some gilded duke to fool old Molders though!'

Otto was amazed at the affection in the big man's voice as he spoke of his captain. But he had little time for reflection as he scrambled up the steep slope, his hose tearing on the brambles, branches scoring his face. He was almost trembling with exhaustion before, quite some distance higher, they came on Molders directing his forces down the steep, wooded slope to their final hiding place. The captain was jammed, seemingly at ease, in against a tree trunk, beard thrust out, his arms a jerky windmill of action as he signed his men into position. Where did these men get their endurance?

'Get comfortable,' Lutyens advised him as they reached their allotted position. 'And watch out for the ants!' The memory conjured up by the jibe stung even more than the ants had. Otto found a likely spot, settled down and began the wait.

Hours dragged past. As Otto brushed a fly away from his face yet again, he was glad he had taken Lutyens's advice and found a comfortable spot. Nestled behind the roots of a fallen tree, he was well hidden and could shift his position easily and without danger but it was still sweltering and it seemed as if he had been stuck here for days, not just hours.

The waiting cast a gloom over him. The nausea he had felt back at his father's tent was back. He lay listless, staring up at the shifting patterns of sunlight streaming down through at the waving screen of leaves. It bewildered him and made the sick feeling worse. The whole world bewildered him now. He was dog-tired but as he carefully rolled over, turning his eyes from the light, he knew he couldn't sleep. What if this was a mistake too? Had the Bretonnians really taken this route? He thought of their trickery and it depressed him. He thought of Sir Guillame stealing his best horse and fleeing like a common soldier, and his gloom was mixed with shame and anger.

More hours seemed to pass. He stared at a beetle crawling along a tree root. It was all right for the beetle, it just crawled around and did, well, whatever beetles did. It could live its life as it ought. But what about him? How should he live his life? What had happened to the rules and codes he had learned and loved? How could he live with honour? Eventually, as the time crawled past, these feelings turned into self-pity, as Otto remembered his joyful anticipation of battle as he rode up to join his father. Five days ago, or five years? A vast gulf at any rate. Where were the fine plumed armet and shining plate he had imagined? No lance by his hand either, but a clumsy wheel lock pistol. Sigmar save him! It had come to this, lurking again. His second ambush! Two actions, both sprung from skulking. He almost let out a bitter laugh but choked it back just in time.

Otto saw Lutyens's head turn. The blonde giant was wedged in what seemed like a tortuous position, yet he hadn't moved once. Otto expected a reproachful glare over his choked laugh but Lutyens didn't even look at him. He was concentrating on something else. Otto listened, straining to hear above the noise of the river, and eventually caught, faint but unmistakable, the sound of horses' hooves and the jingle of harness. His tiredness vanished instantly; he started to peer around the roots of the tree but Lutyens shook his head. The young noble felt the tension in the pit of his stomach. His pulse raced. They waited.

Were the Bretonnians just an advance guard? Had they sent squires to scout the steep slope? The faint noises continued. The minutes passed. They waited.

Lutyens looked as if he was dozing, confound the man! The noise of the hoof beats got louder. Was this the main party? Still no noise of alarm. They waited.

Otto's hand strayed to his pistol and closed on the grip. The sound of the unseen Bretonnians' progress continued. Still they waited.

Suddenly it came: the notes of a Stirland hunting horn drowned almost immediately by crashing blasts. Von Grunwald's falconets, Otto assumed. Lutyens was on his feet and skidding down the slope. Otto rose but almost tripped over his own stiff legs. Cursing, he plunged after the pistolier. The gorge now echoed with shouting men and neighing horses. On the right there was a continuous cracking as the hackbut men rained fire down on the unfortunate Bretonnians.

Otto was dimly conscious of other men charging downhill but through the tangle of trees and boulders he could see little. He tripped again, rolled and scrambled up. The noise all seemed to be ahead of him now. He skidded on towards the shouting and clash of fighting but was brought up on the edge of a crag far too high to jump. Down through the greenery he could catch glimpses of combat. Cursing again, he tried to make his way around the top of the crag.

There was a great crashing sound and a blood-stained figure appeared, struggling up through the trees. Otto stared into the wide eyes of a young Bretonnian squire. The squire fumbled with his bow. Otto raised his wheel lock and pulled the trigger. Nothing! Blast it! He hadn't cocked the weapon. The squire had an arrow nocked as Otto, yelling with frustration, hurled the pistol at him. The heavy weapon hit the youth full in the face and with a cry he staggered back. Otto, sword drawn now, lunged after him but the squire had tripped on a rock. The man clutched vainly at the branches, and screaming, fell over the crag. Otto bent to retrieve his pistol. His hands shook slightly as he wound back the lock.

*Sigmar!* What kind of war was this?

WHEN OTTO FINALLY burst out of the thick undergrowth at the edge of the road he could scarcely believe his eyes. A heaving mass of mounted men had been hemmed in against the river by the Empire forces. Molders's men were scrambling over a mounting wall of dead horses and men to get at the Bretonnians, who seemed scarcely to be putting up a fight at all. Some of the pistoliers were lifting spears from their dead enemies, that they might better goad the seething whirl of panic-stricken men and horses towards the torrent gushing behind them. Otto, horror struck, just stood and stared, his head ringing with the shrieks of the dying men and horses, the reports of pistols and the strident cries of the pistoliers and their local allies. This butchery could not be battle! How could a man of honour fight like this?

Further up the path, the situation was different. The hackbut men were well protected by the crags that lined the road at that point and could fire down on their opponents almost with impunity. This very protection, however, meant that they could not press the Bretonnians so closely, and amongst the milling crowd a more purposeful wedge of cavalry was being formed. A leader of authority was gathering his most experienced knights and rallying them to attempt a break out back along the road. In the confined space and press of men there was scant room to use their lances, never mind charge, but with determination born of hardened experience and desperation they fought their way along the road. Otto could see the line of Empire troops buckle. Shaken into action, he rushed to aid them.

'Sigmar and the Empire!' he yelled, entering the fray.

Almost at once he was in trouble. Knocked backwards by a blow from a lance shaft swung like a club, he narrowly escaped the flailing hooves of a knight's horse. The pistolier next to him was not so lucky and a hoof glanced off his burgonet bringing him to his knees. Seemingly frozen, Otto realised the felled pistolier was Captain Molders. With what seemed like unearthly slowness, Otto watched the knight raise the brass-bound lance haft. He recognised the arms on the surcoat as those of the Duke of Boncenne, himself. A wheel lock flashed; with amazement, Otto realised that it was he himself who had fired. The shot missed the Duke but felled his mount. The world sped up once more as Otto, consumed with rage, charged his foe.

The Duke's horsemanship was superb and he was out of his stirrups and saddle and leaping to his feet even before his dead mount had crashed to earth. He flung the broken lance at the still reeling Molders, knocking him flat. Then he swept out his sword and leapt at Otto.

'Base cur!' the young Empire noble cried as he aimed a vicious thrust at the man's head. 'Are you warrior or charlatan to resort to such trickery?'

The Duke was a skilled and powerful warrior, and he blocked Otto's thrust with ease, riposted and knocked the young noble back. Otto just kept his footing and the Duke, following up his own thrust, slipped in turn. He regained his balance but had to step back and for a moment the two opponents stared at one another. The Duke's face was as blank as the plates of his armour, his hard, dark features hardened yet further by the steel frame of his helm. The thin moustache and thinner lips seemed graven on his visage and, along with the stiff guard the Bretonnian had adopted, gave Otto the momentary but disconcerting impression that he was facing some form of animated, metallic statue.

'Base cur!' Otto repeated. The Duke made no reply but suddenly lunged forward in a lightning attack. Otto did well to turn or dodge the flurry of blows but was unable under this relentless storm to press his own attack. The young noble burnt with righteous indignation but, even through his fury, he realised the danger of this awesome warrior and the need for calm and concentration. The noise and confusion of the rest of the battle had faded, leaving Otto facing his enemy in a private miniature world as wide only as the stretch of their blades. Otto regained his rhythm but against the power and longer reach of the taller Bretonnian was able only to keep up a stout defence.

As he parried blow after blow, the young noble, lighter armoured though he was, began to be conscious of his waning strength as the strain of the past days caught up with him. The Duke seemed to sense it, too, and pressed his attack even more relentlessly. Thrust followed thrust and Otto was driven back, away from the main action. Using every shred of his skill, Otto turned the attacks and desperately strove to find an opening for his own blade. He was breathing heavily and realised he could not long maintain his defence. Pushed back, step by step, he strove to maintain his concentration on the Bretonnian's lightning blade. Focused on his opponent he failed to see the dip behind him and suddenly pitched backwards, landing winded, his sword clattering away across the pebbles. He stared helplessly up as the Duke, face still impassive, stepped over him, changing his grip in readiness to drive his blade down.

There was a gasp of pain but it was the Duke who cried out as a giant, gauntleted fist smashed into the side of his head from behind. The Bretonnian crashed over and frantically scrabbled for his sword as he stared up at Lutyens, who had pulled a wheel lock from his sash and levelled it at the knight. The shot cracked but flew wide as Otto struggled up and knocked the pistolier's arm aside.

'No, Lutyens, I will finish this... to my code,' the young man panted. Pointing to the fallen Bretonnian with his recovered blade, he put what strength he had into his voice and commanded, 'Rise and defend yourself, de Boncenne!'

The Duke lifted his own sword and rose. He face was still blank but, as he resumed his attack, his thrusts seemed to have lost some of their power. Whether it was due to Lutyens's blow or shock from his young opponent's actions, he was definitely less resolute in his offence.

Otto, despite panting with near exhaustion, realised he had a chance. Desperately he gathered his strength and smashed a thrust aside far harder than he had done before. Feinting quickly, he stepped back a pace and, wielding his sword in two hands, swung it around in a great circle, and hewed the head from his enemy with one blow. His face splashed with hot blood, he barely registered his victory. He recovered his swing and raised his sword for another blow, before swaying and collapsing, saved only from toppling over the lifeless body of his enemy by the strong arms of Lutyens.

The huge pistolier dragged Otto to the shelter of some large boulders and prepared to defend him. With the death of the Duke, however, what little fight there had been in the Bretonnians was gone. Some few of the determined knot of men which the Duke had rallied had broken through and spurred back down the road. Some others, lightly equipped squires, had somehow swam across the river and were fleeing away over the hill to the other side, but very few. It had been, as Lutyens had predicted, butchery.

Otto gradually came to his senses. He was propped against a boulder and looking out on a river where a raft of drowned men and horses had jammed against jutting rocks. Struggling to recall what had happened he turned to the bank and saw hackbut men laughing, already stripping the dead.

He looked himself up and down. He was drenched with blood and wondered vaguely if was it his own. He felt a sudden rush of weakness and leant back against the warm stone, staring down at his bloodied sword.

Gradually, Otto remembered his struggle with the Duke and looked to where the crumpled body of his foe lay. So this was victory. So much for honour!

Dazed, he struggled to stand up, leaning heavily on his sword. He remembered Molders and Lutyens and wondered what had happened to them.

He found them sitting by the river, Lutyens bathing his captain's badly bruised head with his soaking neckerchief. Molders looked pale and rather dazed but otherwise fine; at any rate, his chin was still thrust firmly forward. Lutyens looked up, grinning again; action obviously improved his spirits. Addressing Otto, the big pistolier said, 'You look more stunned than the captain and your head is intact!'

Otto slumped onto a rock, shrugged and gestured weakly around him with his sword. 'I didn't expect this,' he mumbled.

Molders met his eyes and suddenly, in spite of his pop-eyes and spade beard, he seemed less ridiculous to Otto. The captain said softly, 'My first battle wasn't what I expected either.'

'I have been so wrong,' the young noble went on. 'So many mistakes!' He sat down facing Molders. 'You have done the Empire a great service, Captain Molders. And you, Lutyens, you've now saved my life twice and I have never even thanked you. How dishonourable!'

'Dishonourable?' Molders asked. 'There is more honour in a man admitting his errors and facing them, than in his battling a hundred foes. I owe you my life and the Graf will be proud of you. No, sir; your honour is intact.'

'Yes,' agreed Lutyens, stepping over and thumping Otto on the back, making him wince. 'You fought by your code, remember?'

The blond giant paused and looked Otto in the eyes. 'I think you will always fight by your code,' he stated seriously.

Then stepping back, he added with a guffaw, 'But in spite of that, we'll make a soldier of you yet!'

# THE ULTIMATE RITUAL
## by Neil Jones & William King

PROFESSOR GERHARDT KLEINHOFFER, Lector in Magical Arts at the University of Nuln, looked down at the pentagram and the triple-ringed circle his younger companion had just drawn in chalk upon the floor.

'Lothar,' he said nervously, 'surely this is blasphemy?'

Across the chamber, Lothar von Diehl ran bony fingers through his dark beard and paused to give the appearance of reflective thought before replying.

'Herr professor, you were the one who taught me that it is those who seek to hold back the advancement of knowledge who are blasphemous. You and I are men of science. It is our *duty* to perform this experiment.'

Kleinhoffer adjusted his pince-nez glasses and glanced at the leather-bound volume which rested on the lectern standing beside the two men.

'De Courcy's book is an important piece of scholarship, no doubt of that. But Lothar, don't you think that it wanders too close to the forbidden lore of Chaos… towards the end?' He shivered. 'His final chapter is almost the ranting of a madman. Drunk on the wine of stars, false heavens, false hells, all of that stuff.'

Von Diehl glanced at his tutor, fighting down his mounting impatience. It had been Kleinhoffer himself who, years ago, had discovered *The Book of Changes*, written in Classical Old Worlder by the long-dead Bretonnian poet and mystic, Giles de Courcy. Kleinhoffer had spent the rest of his life translating it, worrying away at the cryptic symbolism until he was sure he had decoded it correctly. By then, he had become the foremost authority on magic at the ancient University of Nuln – and Lothar von Diehl, the single person in whom Kleinhoffer had confided, was his most gifted student.

'True,' von Diehl said, striving to keep his voice calm and reasonable, 'but that should not deter us. As you yourself have said, all magic is based, ultimately, on Chaos. The only way to tell if de Courcy was right is to perform this ultimate ritual. And if it works, then it will lead us to the most profound understanding of universe.'

'My boy, I am as committed to the project as you are but… but…' Kleinhoffer's voice trailed off.

Von Diehl stared at the old man's pale, sweating face. 'Herr professor, I thought you understood when I suggested this experiment. The ritual is not something that I can attempt without your help.'

The old man nodded shakily. 'Of course, of course. It's just that… Lothar, my boy, are you sure it's *safe*?'

'Absolutely, professor.'

Kleinhoffer swallowed and once more glanced around the secret chamber in the basement of von Diehl's residence. Finally, he came to a decision.

'Very well, Lothar,' he said with reluctance. 'I know how important this is to you.'

Von Diehl allowed himself a brief sigh of satisfaction. 'Thank you, sir. Now, please, if you will take up your position.'

Von Diehl lifted the rune-encrusted wand which he had carved from a beastman's thighbone and advanced towards the lectern. He lit the braziers and threw handfuls of cloying incense to fizz on them. As the echoes died away he began the chant.

'*Amak te aresci Tzeentch! Venii loci aresci Tzeentch! Amak te aresci Tzeentch!*'

Von Diehl's chant rumbled on, seeming to gain resonance from the echoes and the constant repetition. The fumes from the braziers billowed around him and seemed to expand his perception. It was almost as if he could see the edges of the world starting to ripple at the corners of his vision.

He continued to chant, visualising in his mind the form of the Tzeentchian steed he was attempting to summon, filling in the details, compelling it to take more concrete form. While doing so, he moved the tip of the wand through a complex pattern, pointing it at every angle of the pentacle in turn.

The effects of the narcotic incense, the constant chanting and visualisation distorted his sense of the flow of time. The ritual seemed to be going on for hours. He felt himself to be a vessel for transcendent energies. Finally, somewhere off at the edge of infinity, he sensed a hungry presence. He reached out with the power of his soul and touched it. The being sensed him and began to move closer, painfully slowly, seeking sustenance.

As if far off in the distance, he heard Kleinhoffer moan. The air was filled with the burnt tin smell of ozone. Von Diehl opened his eyes. The room was lit by a strange blue glow from the lines of the pentacle and circle. Sparks flickered in the air and his hair was standing on end.

*'Venii aresci Tzeentch! Venii! Venii!'* he yelled and fell silent.

There was a rush of air, a sense of presence and suddenly it was there before them: the steed of Tzeentch.

It took the form of a flat disc of sleek, silvery-blue flesh. The edges of the disc were rimmed with small, sardonic eyes. It flickered about within the pentagram as if testing the boundaries of its cage. After a while it seemed to realise it was trapped and ceased to struggle, simply hovering in mid-air.

*What do you wish from me, mortals?* asked a voice within von Diehl's head.

'We seek knowledge,' von Diehl answered certainly. 'We wish to travel across the Sea of Souls and converse with He Who Knows All Secrets.'

*Others have requested this in the past. To their regret. The minds of mortals are fragile things.*

'Nonetheless, we wish to go. Once we are safely returned here you will be released from this compulsion.'

*Very well. Advance, human, and meet your fate!*

With no hint of trepidation von Diehl walked down the corridor of chalk which connected the circle to the pentagram. He stepped over the side of the magical sigil and put one foot on the creature of light. Surprisingly it supported his weight. He felt a strange tingling pass through his foot and up his body.

*I will take both of you,* the voice said in von Diehl's head. *Both of you or neither.*

Von Diehl turned. Kleinhoffer had not moved. His lined face seemed to float amid the darkness, lit from below by the glow from the pentagram.

'Herr professor,' von Diehl called urgently, 'you must join me. Quickly now!'

Kleinhoffer licked his lips. A sheen of sweat had formed on his forehead. 'Lothar, I can't! I just can't!'

Anger pulsed through von Diehl. 'The book is explicit. We must be two – or else the steed can refuse to transport us, can break the binding spell. You knew. You agreed!'

'I know, but – Lothar, forgive me, I'm old. Old and afraid.'

'But Gerhard, you've worked for this all your life. Ultimate knowledge. Transcendence.'

The old scholar shuddered.

'Join me,' von Diehl commanded. 'Join me, join me, join me!'

Kleinhoffer sighed, and then, almost as if hypnotised, he shuffled down the chalk corridor and took his place aboard the steed beside von Diehl.

*Two,* the daemon said. *Two in search of knowledge. Now we go!*

There was a screaming rush of air, and the sound of a thunderclap.

VON DIEHL LOOKED down and found they were far above the city of Nuln itself. He could see the University quarter with its aged, many-spired buildings. His gaze wandered to the docks and the dark curve of the River Reik as it snaked northwards. Although he was hundreds of feet above the tallest tower of the Temple of Verena he felt no fear. Standing on the back of the Chaos-steed was like standing on solid earth.

The daemon-thing began to accelerate but there was no sense of motion or of the wind tearing at his clothing. He stood at a point of absolute calm. Only when he looked down at the Great Forest rushing past did von Diehl get a sense of their terrific speed.

In a few moments he saw an open glade where beastmen danced around a great bonfire and a two-headed black-armoured figure looked on. He saw strange monsters moving in the depths where no man had ever penetrated. Their steed hurtled like a meteor until the ground was simply a blur. They gained height until they were above the clouds. It was like skimming over a misty white sea whose surface was illuminated by the twin moons.

Excitement flooded through von Diehl's veins as they flashed along. He felt like a god. It seemed to him that no one could ever have travelled so fast before. The energy of the daemon passed up through his legs, filling him with a tremendous sense of well-being. Perhaps it was the steed's power which protected them from the cold air, he thought. Through a break in the clouds he saw that they were passing over a bleak steppeland only occasionally blotched by the lights of cities. Surely they could not have reached Kislev already?

Soon after, he felt no such doubts. They were moving across snow-covered tundra towards a bleak, stony land. The sky to the north was illuminated by a dancing aurora of dark-coloured lights. They had entered the Chaos Wastes.

Below he could see great troupes of warriors fighting. Champions in the blood-red armour of Khorne fought with dancing lascivious daemonettes. Enormous slobbering monsters pursued fleeing beastmen. The land itself writhed as if tortured. Lakes of blood washed across great deserts of ash. Castles carved from mountains erupted from forests of flesh-trees. Islands broke off from the earth and floated into the sky.

It was a horrific and awesome sight. Beside him, he heard Kleinhoffer call out in fear, but he cared not.

They flew straight towards the aurora, picking up speed as they went. They passed over a flight of dragons that seemed frozen in place so slowly did they move compared to the steed of Tzeentch.

Now von Diehl could make out a vast dark hole in the sky. It was as if the firmament were a painting and someone had torn a square from the canvas to reveal another picture beneath. He peered into a realm of flowing colours and pulsing lights, an area where the natural laws which governed the physical universe no longer applied. Von Diehl pointed the bone wand towards the Chaos Gate and the steed surged forward in response. They crossed the threshold into a new and darker universe.

'Lothar,' Kleinhoffer murmured, his voice full of awe. 'I believe that this must be–'

'Yes,' von Diehl replied distantly, 'we have entered the Sea of Souls.'

For a moment their steed paused on the threshold between the two worlds and von Diehl stared into what was the final and strangest realm of Chaos.

Off in the farthest distance, further away than the stars, he saw the things that he decided must be the Powers. They were vast eddies and whirlpools of luminescence, bigger than galaxies. Their twists and flows illuminated the Sea of Souls. Was that mighty red and black agglomeration Khorne, wondered von Diehl? He noted how its spiral arms of bloody light seemed to tangle with long pastel streamers of lilac and green and mauve. Could that be Slaanesh? It was like watching two nests of vipers fighting.

Then he made out a third pulsating mass that was clearly greater than the many lesser ones in this vast realm. It writhed and pulsed obscenely, and something about this one made the hair on the nape of his neck bristle. From his instinctive reaction he knew that this one had to be Nurgle.

Yet another form came into view. It was the most complex and convoluted of the gigantic structures of energy and he knew it to be Tzeentch, his ultimate goal.

These were clearly the Powers, the Four Great Ones and the many lesser. And this was the true realm of Chaos.

Beside him, Kleinhoffer clutched at his sleeve in panic. 'Lothar, what is happening?'

Von Diehl understood the old man's confusion. His own brain was reeling under this sudden influx of sensation. 'Our human minds are adjusting to the Sea of Souls,' he said happily.

He realised that they were not seeing the whole of this twisted realm. Their human minds were not capable of it. Instead, they were simply imposing their own ideas of scale and form and function on a place where these did not apply. It was a staggering thought.

Much closer than the Great Powers were tiny points of light that von Diehl somehow knew were the souls of mortals. They glittered like stars. Cutting a swathe through them, like a shark through a shoal of fish, von Diehl could see a long streamlined creature, all sucker mouths and questing antennae, a soul-shark. It devoured the small panicky shapes as they swam towards their distant, unseen destinations.

Again he felt Kleinhoffer's hand on his sleeve. 'Lothar,' the old man cried in a frightened voice. 'Lothar, look down!'

Beneath their feet, their daemon-steed had changed shape, so it now resembled the soul-shark. It, too, feasted upon the glittering souls as it swept ever on.

Von Diehl was not surprised. The beast was dangerous. He did not doubt that it would devour the essence of both of them if it could. Very softly, he chanted the words of a spell he had prepared. A thin line of radiance streamed from his bone wand, a pink-hued light that was indescribably richer here in the Sea of Souls. As the light touched the steed it opened up a delicate channel between their steed and himself.

As the creature fed it passed the merest trickle of that energy to him through the channel his spell had created. The energy flowed through von Diehl's veins like liquid ecstasy. He breathed deeply and sucked the pure essence of magic into his lungs. It was a totally exhilarating experience.

'It cannot harm us,' he reminded the terrified old man. 'Not as long as it is compelled by the binding spell.'

But Kleinhoffer only stared down with a look of utmost horror on his face, as if the steed were already dining upon his lower limbs.

The daemon-thing surged forward once more. Von Diehl felt that whatever awesome velocity it had achieved in the mortal world was nothing compared to what it was doing here. It seemed as if the creature was capable of traversing the universe.

As they raced along they passed other great rents in the fabric of the sea. Sometimes what von Diehl saw through them beggared his imagination. Worlds laid waste by war, hells presided over by false gods and heavens of endless serenity.

Suddenly he sensed a change of mood in their steed. He looked back and understood why. They were being pursued. Other creatures chased them, creatures not controlled by any binding spell. More soul-sharks. They could devour their flesh and their souls.

Kleinhoffer followed his gaze and cried out in alarm.

The soul-sharks came closer, their great jaws gaping. They were fast, faster than their own steed, not hindered as it was by two human riders.

Von Diehl raised the wand of bone and prodded the daemon with it. 'Save us,' he commanded the thing. 'Save us or you will never be free!'

A wordless cry of mingled rage and despair echoed inside von Diehl's skull. The daemon-steed suddenly veered and plunged through one of the gates.

Reality rippled like the surface of a pond. They hurtled over a desolate plain on which great pyramidal cities sat. As von Diehl watched, great beams of force flickered between the pyramids. Some were absorbed by huge, thrumming black screens of energy, but one city was reduced to slag in an instant. Their mount swept into an evasive pattern to dodge the webs of force-beams. Several came too close for comfort but none hit them. Von Diehl watched one of their pursuers get caught in the cross-fire and wink out of existence. The others came on.

Their supernatural steed raced through another gate above the greatest of pyramids. There was a sense of space stretching. Now they were above a hell of sulphur pits and dancing flames. Toad-like daemons pitch-forked the souls of some strange amphibian race into the volcanic fires. Von Diehl wondered whether this was real or the dream of one of the Old Powers. Perhaps it was a real hell of a real race brought into being by the imaginations of an alien people stirring the Realm of Chaos.

Their steed dived into one volcanic pit. Beside him, Kleinhoffer screamed uncontrollably, surely convinced that

The Ultimate Ritual 283

the creature had betrayed them and that they were going to die. He covered his eyes with his hands.

Von Diehl felt only exhilaration.

Once more though they hurtled through a gate. Fewer of the pursuing daemons followed.

They were in the blackness of space, hurtling through a void darker than night over a small world that had been re-shaped into a city. They raced by bubble domes from which creatures much like elves stared out. The workmanship of the buildings within the domes was as refined and delicate as spider-webs. They dipped and swooped into a great corridor holding another gate. Once more they vanished.

Von Diehl had no idea how long the chase lasted. They passed through vaults where rebellious daemons plotted against the Powers; frozen hells where immobile souls begged for freedom; leafy Arcadias where golden people made love and dreadful things watched from the bushes.

They swooped across worlds where great war-machines, shaped like men eighty feet high, fought with weapons that could level cities. They blazed along corridors in doomed hulks that had drifted for a thousand years in the spaces between worlds and where sleeping monsters waited in icy coffins for new prey. They zoomed across the surface of suns where creatures of plasma drifted in strange mating dances.

But eventually their twists and turns through the labyrinth of space-time threw off the last of their pursuers, and they returned once more to the Sea of Souls.

THEIR STEED RACED along the threads of the vast disturbance in the sea that was Tzeentch, picking their way along great arteries of energy until they came to the very heart of it all. They swept past great winged creatures which gave von Diehl knowing smiles. He felt as if the daemons were looking into his very soul and probing his innermost secrets. He did not care. He was exalted. He knew they were nearing the end of the quest and that soon they would both have what they had come for. Kleinhoffer was exhausted, his face bloodless. But the exhilaration of the chase and sharing their daemon-steed's energy had only buoyed von Diehl up.

They approached a mighty sphere of pulsing light. Colours danced and shifted on its surface like oil glistening on the surface of water.

They drifted closer and slid into, then through the wall. Within was a huge being, larger than a castle. In form it was similar to a man although its head was horned. It possessed great beauty but the shifting lights of the sphere reflected dazzlingly off its no-coloured skin and the brilliance caused von Diehl to look away.

*Welcome, mortals, to the House of the Lord of Change!*

The voice spoke within the travellers' heads. It was calm, polite and reasonable, but there was an under-current of malicious amusement.

Von Diehl peered back at the great figure, looking up into glittering gem-like eyes. He thought that those eyes could take in the entire universe at a glance. Before it he felt as insignificant as a flea.

'Thank you, lord,' he said gravely. He nudged Gerhardt Kleinhoffer with his free hand. The old man mumbled a greeting of his own.

*Why have you come here?* boomed the voice. *Why have you disturbed my servants who have other more important tasks to perform?*

'We have come,' von Diehl said, 'seeking knowledge, lord.' He gestured at his companion.

'Yes,' Kleinhoffer stammered after a moment, a dazed expression on his face. 'That's it. That's why we're here. Knowledge.'

*Knowledge. For what purpose do you seek it? To change yourself or your world?*

Von Diehl turned and waited for his companion to speak. The old man's gaze went back and forth between his student and the gigantic being. His mouth opened and closed several times but no words emerged. Still von Diehl said nothing.

'Neither,' Kleinhoffer blurted at last.

Lothar von Diehl smiled and turned back to face the Power. 'Both,' he said.

Gerhardt Kleinhoffer blinked, and then finally appeared to realise what von Diehl had said. He jerked around to face von

Diehl. His face was ashen. 'Lothar, what are you saying? Have you forgotten the ritual?'

*So then, mortal,* the gigantic being boomed, addressing only Gerhardt Kleinhoffer now. *Why then do you crave knowledge?*

'I– I–' Kleinhoffer's eyes bulged. He put his hands to his head, clearly wilting under the gaze of this enormous entity. 'Lothar, for pity's sake, help me!'

Von Diehl raised both hands. 'Lord, he seeks knowledge – for its own sake.'

*That is unfortunate.* The creature smiled malevolently. *Still, what does he wish to know?*

Again Gerhardt Kleinhoffer's mouth opened and shut and again no words emerged.

Smiling, von Diehl said, 'Everything.'

*Suitably ambitious. So shall it be.*

Lord Tzeentch reached out and touched Kleinhoffer. The old man went rigid.

At the same moment, von Diehl again murmured the words of the spell which had linked him to the steed as it had fed. Leaning forward, he pressed the tip of the bone wand to Kleinhoffer's temple. Knowledge was flowing into his companion, filling him. And Lothar von Diehl intended to witness it – from a safe distance.

A vast ocean of information cascaded into Kleinhoffer's brain. Von Diehl glimpsed the birth of the universe and the Sea of Souls, the creation of stars and planets, the rise of races, the structure of molecules. He saw the universe burst into a great flood of change and understood the nature of the power that drove it relentlessly onwards. He saw that the universe was never still but constantly altering itself. He knew instantly that he could never know everything because there were always new things coming into being.

Kleinhoffer's face contorted as the flow of knowledge continued inexorably. His mind was drowning in a flood of information, far too much knowledge to cope with. It had stretched his mind to the breaking point and beyond. As if from a great distance, von Diehl sensed the man's personality erode then finally collapse as he descended into screaming madness. And still the torrent of knowledge did not stop.

Slowly, still clutching feebly at von Diehl's tunic, the old man sank down to von Diehl's feet.

Enough, thought von Diehl, sensing his own mind begin to strain. Chanting the words of his spell, he drew back the wand, breaking the contact with the old man.

*Lothar von Diehl.*

He looked out at the vast unknowable being that was, or represented, Tzeentch.

*Your companion's wish has been granted.*

'Yes, lord,' von Diehl replied, glancing down at the huddled figure at his feet. He smiled. 'And I offer you thanks – on his behalf.'

A rumbling sound issued from the creature before him that perhaps was laughter on a cosmic scale.

*And you, Lothar von Diehl. You have also been granted the gift of knowledge – knowledge that you may take back with you into the mundane world you came from.*

'Accept my gratitude for that gift also, lord.'

*Of course, for that gift, too, there is a price.*

'I understand, lord, and one I am quite prepared to pay.'

*You will be bound to my service for eternity.*

Von Diehl bowed his head. Tzeentch the Great Mutator. Tzeentch the Changer of the Ways.

'Willingly,' he said.

Tzeentch, his chosen Power of Chaos.

*You will serve me in your world. You know what it is that I wish, that I thrive upon.*

'I know.'


ONCE MORE THERE was a flickering in the air and the smell of ozone. The steed reappeared in the tiny cellar chamber, a glowing disc of light within the pentagram. This time it bore two riders, one standing, the other slumped at his feet.

Lothar von Diehl stepped down from the daemon-steed. The secret chamber was just as he had left it. The Book of Changes still rested on the lectern, open to the page upon which Giles de Courcy had inscribed the secret of the ultimate ritual, the secret von Diehl had felt it wise to share only partially with his tutor.

In his mind, the memory of the ocean of knowledge still glittered. He had glimpsed at least some of what was to be. Change was coming to the Old World. Elves returning from their long exile in the west, eager for trade, disrupting the nations of men. The Empire itself about to totter as, tempted by that elven trade, its wealthiest province sought to secede from its rule. And a hint, a deep darkness growing in the north. The ancient paths. A shroud removed, to be replaced by the bloodied fog of conflict.

A truly moment for magic to take its place upon the battlefield, to become a weapon of war for the first time in recorded human history.

Von Diehl laughed aloud. The battle magic spells were in his mind now, knowledge Lord Tzeentch had granted to him. He would have a considerable part to play in the events that were to come.

*Change.*

This was what Tzeentch, the Great Mutator desired – what any true servant of Tzeentch craved more than life itself. And outside this chamber was an entire world, crying out for change. Eager to begin his master's work, von Diehl strode for the door.

Behind him, sprawled across the pentagram, Gerhardt Kleinhoffer raised a thin hand. Pure madness gleamed in his eyes.

'Seas of lost souls,' he mumbled as the door closed on his departing pupil. 'False heavens, false hells. All is change and the dreams of dark gods.'

# LET BATTLE COMMENCE!

NOW YOU can fight your way through the savage lands of the Empire and beyond with WARHAMMER, Games Workshop's game of fantasy battles. In a world of conflict, mighty armies clash to decide the fate of war-torn realms. In Warhammer, you and your opponents are the fearless commanders of these armies. The fate of your kingdoms rests on your shoulders as you control regiments of miniature soldiers, to do battle with terrifying monsters and fearless heroes.

*To find out more about Warhammer, along with Games Workshop's whole range of exciting fantasy and science fiction games and miniatures, just call our specialist Trolls on the following numbers:*

## IN THE UK: 0115-91 40 000

## IN THE US: 1-800-394-GAME

*or look us up online at:*

## www.games-workshop.com